Innocent Foxes

A novel

D0111937

Also by Torey Hayden

Innocent Foxes

A novel

HARPER

HARPER

An imprint of HarperCollins*Publishers*
77–85 Fulham Palace Road,
Hammersmith, London W6 8JB

www.harpercollins.co.uk

First published by HarperCollins*Publishers* 2011

1 3 5 7 9 10 8 6 4 2

© Torey Hayden 2011

Torey Hayden asserts the moral right to be
identified as the author of this work

A catalogue record of this book is
available from the British Library

ISBN 978-0-00-734093-4

Printed and bound in Great Britain by
Clays Ltd, St Ives plc

Chapter One

Three days after Jamie Lee died, Dixie almost got run down by a movie star. It was a deep, warm-as-breath August evening and Dixie was walking down Seventh Street on her way back from getting a loaf of bread and a jar of mayonnaise at the Kwik-Way. She'd just crossed over at the corner by the United Methodist Church when the pick-up truck appeared, careering wildly down the middle of the road. Abruptly it swerved, mounted the kerb and came straight at her. Dixie screamed and ran for safety up the steps of the church. Brakes squealed and then there was a slithery hiss of rubber on grass before the final jarring crunch as the truck came to rest against a brick pillar at the base of the steps.

Three men were crammed into the cab of the pick-up and they all roared with laughter. In fact, they seemed to be laughing so hard that at first they found it hard to get the doors open. When the driver finally emerged, Dixie recognized him immediately. Spencer Scott.

'You almost *killed* me!' she shrieked, and burst into tears.

The door opened on the passenger side and the others spilled out. They were all canyon folk. They were all drunk too and seemed to find the idea of running her over hilarious.

Dixie couldn't stop crying long enough to speak. It was their laughter that did it. That, and Jamie Lee and everything. She'd been coping pretty well over this last week, but this was just the last straw.

'You aren't hurt, are you?' Spencer Scott managed to ask, when he'd finally caught his breath from laughing.

'You near enough scared the life out of me, that's what,' Dixie sobbed.

He rooted in the pocket of his jeans and produced a red bandana handkerchief, the kind that tourists buy because they think it looks Western. He offered it to her.

What was she supposed to do with that? She was hardly going to get snot on a movie star's handkerchief.

'It's clean,' he said with an edge of annoyance.

Well, of course it was clean. Did he think she'd assume he would carry a dirty handkerchief? Oh dear Jesus, why did she have to be bawling in front of Spencer Scott, of all people?

Beyond him, the other two men were checking for damage to the pick-up. One climbed into the driver's seat, backed it up a little, got out again and examined the dented grille.

Spencer Scott smiled. 'I'm sorry we frightened you. No hard feelings?'

For the first time Dixie dared to lift her head enough to look at him properly. He was only an arm's length away and she could see everything about him. He looked better in person than on the screen, if that was possible. Older and wrinklier, but Dixie liked that. His California-perfect features looked more manly when a bit of living showed. The only surprise was that he was so short. She'd heard that about him from other folks who'd been up close to him, but she still hadn't expected she'd be taller.

'Come on, Spence,' one of the men called. 'It's OK. Nothing's happened.'

He turned to go.

'Hey!' Dixie cried. 'Something did too happen! You nearly hit me! And look at what you done to that pillar. You're drunk. You shouldn't be in a car. You can't just drive off. We need to call the police.'

Spencer Scott smiled disarmingly, his handsome face focusing only on her. 'We don't need the police,' he said chummily. 'This isn't anything really.'

'It is to *me*! And it will be to the United Methodist Church too. They don't got money to spend fixing what some drunk driver does,' Dixie replied.

His eyes were just as blue as in the pictures and they twinkled when he smiled. 'The police have more important matters to worry about. We don't want to keep them from solving real crimes, do we?'

'But you almost *killed* me! You could've, you know. If you'd been coming any faster ...'

Still the smile, still the twinkly blue eyes that had looked at all those beautiful Hollywood actresses and were now looking only at her. 'But you're all right, aren't you?' he said. His voice had the warm certainty of a Jedi knight using the Force. 'You aren't hurt.' Then without warning, he clasped Dixie's hand and kissed it. 'And you *will* forgive me for frightening you, yes?'

Without even intending to, Dixie nodded.

'And I'll let you keep the handkerchief.'

When Dixie got home with the groceries, she didn't say anything about Spencer Scott to Billy. He was watching TV and the last thing he'd want was to be interrupted by talk about the canyon folk. Instead, Dixie put the groceries in the kitchen and then went upstairs to finish packing away Jamie Lee's stuff.

It was amazing the number of things a baby could acquire in just nine months. Sitting on the edge of the bed, Dixie folded up each T-shirt and little pair of overalls before laying them carefully into the cardboard box. She paused over the tiny grey jogging shoes. It had been silly to buy them for a baby too young to walk and they'd cost way too much for something just for show, but Dixie had loved to see Jamie Lee wearing them. She brought them up to her face, cupping them in her hands, hoping to find Jamie's scent lingering, but she smelled only rubber, glue and canvas. Kissing them tenderly, she laid them in the box with the other things.

Mama had told her to get rid of it all. She'd said to pick one or two things to remember Jamie Lee by and then send the rest of it to the Rescue Mission. Dixie didn't want to do that. Giving Jamie Lee's stuff away so soon would make her feel like she was trying to get rid of Jamie Lee's memory as well. Besides, what other mother would want to dress her little boy in a dead baby's clothes?

Billy wandered up the stairs and into the bedroom. Pulling off his boots, he stretched out on his side of the bed. 'You shouldn't be up here, Dix, if all it's going to do is make you cry.'

'I got to cry sometime, Billy. He was my little baby.'

'Yeah, but he was going to die anyway, wasn't he? You always knew that.'

'We're all going to die anyway, Billy, but that doesn't make it hurt any less when it happens.' Pulling the tissue box off the bedside table, Dixie took one out to wipe her eyes.

'Come here,' Billy said and reached out his arms. 'You need cuddling.'

Dixie lay down beside him. 'Know what really breaks my heart?' she said.

'What's that?'

'That we can't afford to get him a proper coffin.'

'The one he's got looks good, Dix.'

'I remember seeing this picture once in *National Geographic*. There was a baby girl laid out in this white wooden coffin. It was so pretty. She looked like a sweet little angel lying there. Not dead at all. She had her head on this satin pillow and ribbons in her hair. That's what I wish we had for Jamie Lee.'

'Jamie Lee wouldn't want no ribbons in his hair, Dix.'

Dixie sighed. 'I didn't mean that part. I meant the white wood coffin. I want Jamie Lee to look nice. Like a little angel. Pure-like, you know?'

Billy let go of her and turned over on his back. Putting his hands behind his head, he fixed his gaze on the sloping ceiling over the bed and didn't say anything more.

Dixie glanced over. 'You heard anything on that railroad job yet?'

Billy just kept staring at the ceiling. 'Actually I'm thinking I won't go down there,' he said at last. 'They're taking on men at the sawmill and I was thinking tomorrow I'll go check that out instead.'

'I don't like thinking of you working around all them dangerous saws. And railroad work's more steady-like. It'll pay more over the long run.'

Billy didn't answer.

Dixie sat back up. There was a little knitted duck that Leola had made for Jamie Lee over on the bedside table. Reaching out, Dixie picked it up. She'd intended to put it in the box with Jamie Lee's clothes, but putting it away had made her feel too sad. Holding it in her lap, she stared at it.

'The thing is,' Billy said, 'I only need work till I get enough money for horses, Dix. Once I got those horses, I can start up my guide business. So, the way I reckon it, if I can get on at the sawmill and work a couple of months, I'll have enough for a small string of horses by Fall. That's when all the hunters come, so it'll be a great time to start up.'

'Where you intending to keep horses, Billy?'

'Well, at the start I'll be on the trail with them mostly, won't I? Won't need to keep them anywhere too permanent. They're going to be able to feed themselves wherever I stake out camp. I'm reckoning on running week-long trips when the hunters come in. Maybe even two-week trips, like Bob Mackie does, only I'm planning on taking the hunters way into the Crowheart Wilderness. I know that area so good. Like the back of my hand. And no one else around here takes hunters there.'

'That's because it *is* a wilderness area, Billy. The government put lots of restrictions on what hunting you can do, once it got declared a proper wilderness.'

'That's a *big* piece of land, Dixie. Nobody's ever going to be watching all of it.'

'Billy?' she said incredulously. 'Don't get silly ideas. You can't go advertising to take people hunting somewhere it's illegal to hunt and you won't get no business if you don't advertise for what you're doing.'

'Don't you think I know that? Besides,' he said and tapped the side of his nose, 'Billy knows his ways.' Then he grinned. 'And know what else I plan to do? Come summer and all those fucking tourists? I'm going to take me and my horses down by Simpson's Bridge and just ride along where they can see me from the highway. Then when they're driving through, the tourists'll be saying, "Look, Mom! A real cowboy!" and they'll stop and want to take pictures and I'll charge 'em. And I'll offer to give 'em day trips – you know, taking Mom, Dad and kids out, so they think they're getting to be cowboys too. They'll do it on impulse. People always spend money better on impulse. I can take them up to the old mines. Or over to Beul-erville, so they can see a real by-golly ghost town. Easy bucks, man. The tourists are always willing to pay so much just to do ordinary stuff. So, the only time I'm going to need to pasture the horses is in winter and we'll be rolling in money by then.'

'We ain't never going to be rolling in money, Billy, so don't kid yourself.'

'Yeah, but this time it's going to work out. This guide business will be it for us, Dix. You know how good I am with horses. And you just tell me who knows the Crowheart better than me?'

'I just wish we had enough for Jamie Lee to have a white coffin.'

'There's thousands of bucks waiting to be cut loose from all them city cowboys. No kidding. You can't believe the things some people pay serious money to do.'

'But we need the coffin right now, not in the Fall. Not next year. Not after the guide business takes off.'

'He's got a coffin, Dixie.'

'He's got a blue plastic box.'

'It's not plastic. It's fibreglass.'

'They're burying my baby in a blue plastic box.' The tears started again. 'You should have taken that railroad job, Billy. Leastways long enough to get Jamie Lee decently buried. I mean, he was near enough your own son. You're the only daddy he knew.'

'I would have, Dix. You know how much I always wanted to do right by Jamie Lee. But I'm no good at that kind of work. I need to be my own boss. Got too much cowboy in me. Can't you understand how great this guide business is going to be? Won't be nobody to worry about except me and the horses, and I love horses, man. Me and the horses and all those city dudes, waiting to get their pockets picked. I'll make you enough money to roll in. I promise.'

'That's what you said the other times too, Billy. Fact is, we need money now, not some far-off time that might never come. You should have took the railroad job.'

An injured silence followed. At last Billy sat up and reached for his boots. He pulled them on. Then he hunched forward enough to peer out of the small, gable-end window.

Dixie sighed. The knitted duck was still sitting in her lap, so she lifted it up and pressed it to her cheek. 'Know what? I almost got killed tonight,' she said softly.

Billy didn't reply.

'Did you hear me?' she asked, turning. 'And you know who almost done it? Spencer Scott. Him and two other guys from up the canyon. They were drunk as skunks. Weaving all over the place in their pick-up. I got up on the steps of the United Methodist Church just in the nick of time. Came this close to hitting me.' Dixie measured out the distance with her hands.

'I wish the canyon folk would all just go the fuck back to California,' Billy replied. 'I get so fed up with them around here. They think owning the land is the same as belonging here.'

'Spencer Scott's really handsome, Billy. Handsomer even than in the movies. He gave me his handkerchief.'

'I hope you told him you got hurt.'

'I didn't get hurt. I mean, thank the good Lord Jesus for those steps in front of the United Methodist Church, because that's what saved me. All that happened was that the truck knocked that brick pillar skew-hawed that's at the bottom of the steps.'

'Why didn't you tell Spencer Scott how hurt you were?'

'Because, like I just said, Billy, the pick-up didn't touch me. I was scared so bad, I practically wet myself, but that's all.'

'Should have said you were hurt anyway. Then we could have sued him. Maybe we can still do it. For, like, "mental distress". Folks get millions for that.'

'Don't be stupid, Billy.'

'Didn't you say they were drunk? So they were in the wrong, not you. And being drunk, they won't remember straight. Think of it. That's a really good idea. We could nail them. Dix.'

'But it wouldn't be right, Billy. I'm just fine.'

He shook his head wearily. 'Yeah, well, what ain't right, Dix, is that he's got more money than he can count and for what? For being a grown-up man playing make believe. Here's all us hard-working folk, just scraping by, and he gets millions for *pretending* to be what we got no choice about being and don't get paid for. There's no fairness in that at all. So it was you being stupid, Dixie, not me. You should have told him you was hurt. Then you could have got your white coffin and I could have got my horses. In fact, the way I see it, we'd be doing the right thing. Because he could easily kill somebody, driving drunk like that. Slap a big old lawsuit on him and even Spencer Scott would think twice the next time he wants to get behind the wheel.'

'He kissed me,' Dixie said softly as she set the knitted duck into the box with the rest of Jamie Lee's things. 'Spencer Scott kissed my hand.'

'Yeah, well, it would have been far better if he'd kissed your bank account.'

Chapter Two

The town of Abundance had had its heyday just as Montana approached statehood. The rich silver lode, first struck in 1876, was showing its worth by the 1880s. All three of the big mines – the Eldorado, the Inverurie and the Kipper Twee – were producing steadily and the Lion Mountain mine was just getting underway. Nearly 25,000 people lived in Abundance in those days. There were six banks, five hotels and 22 saloons. The Majestic Theatre on Main Street attracted shows all the way from Chicago, and the Masonic Hall was an architectural showpiece, its high false front and dramatic second-storey balcony characterizing the extravagance of the times.

Then in 1892 the world silver market collapsed. The Inverurie, the oldest mine, the one upon which Abundance had been founded, faltered first. The Panic of 1893 followed, and legend had it that within twenty-four hours of the Kipper Twee's closure, 1,500 people had packed up and walked out of their houses, right out of their lives in Abundance and left forever. By 1898, only the Lion Mountain mine was still in operation and that was more for the gold and lead mingled in its lode than for silver. The population of Abundance dropped below 10,000. By 1905, even the Lion Mountain gave way and Abundance came to the brink of death.

Unlike the nearby towns of Cache Creek and Beulerville, Abundance survived. A branch line of the railroad, originally built to carry ore, proved a life-saving link with the outer world. Sawmills sprang up to process timber from the vast mountain forests, and there was enough low-lying land in the river valley to make ranching viable. Abundance clung to life by filling the boxcars with lumber and cattle once the ore was gone.

By the time Dixie was born, the population in Abundance had fallen below the 3,000 mark. Remnants of the glory days were still everywhere. The derelict Masonic Hall dominated Main Street. Empty false-fronted buildings with elegantly carved façades stood cheek-by-jowl with the plate-glass windows of the 1960s drugstore and the unassuming modernity of the Texaco station. Whole back streets were nothing more than rows of vacant, crumbling houses, their ornate gingerbread tracing broken, their doors and windows gone. 'Ghost houses', Dixie and her friends had called them, and used them as a quirky, otherworldly playground.

Then one year the Masonic Hall caught fire and burned down. Two years later what was left of the derelict Majestic Theatre was demolished to make way for a drive-in bank. One by one, the old buildings disappeared, leaving gaps along Main Street like lost teeth in an eight-year-old's smile.

The town kept on fading. The hardware store closed. Then the dime store. Then Jack's Redi-Mart. There were Walmarts to shop at now, and even though it took a ninety-minute drive to get to one, people liked them. They were so big and full of things that it felt wondrous going through the doors, and you could make a nice day of it, having your lunch at McDonald's, which was another experience denied Abundance. Truth was, nothing was abundant in Abundance anymore. That's what everyone liked to say. Nothing abundant about it, except for the view.

A view they did have. Cupped into an east-facing basin, Abundance was surrounded by startlingly enormous mountains which rose straight up out of the flat river valley with such abruptness that tourists often brought their cars to a dead stop right in the middle of Simpson's Bridge when they got their first full view of them.

For the people living there, however, the mountains were much more than just something pretty to look at. In offering up the gold and silver from their rocky depths, they had created Abundance, and they had destroyed Abundance just as easily when the promising veins paled into worthless rock. Even now they dominated the remnants of Abundance, bringing snow in August, chinooks in February and evening shadows at a time of day when the rest of the world was still having afternoon. Their craggy profiles, the smell of their pine forests, the taste of their snow on the wind were all as much a part of the folk born and raised in Abundance as the blood running in their veins.

To Dixie the mountains were as familiar as family. They were like family in other ways too: always there, reliable and friendly some days, dangerous on other days, but always, always there for you.

When she was growing up, Daddy used to say, 'Too bad you can't eat the scenery.' What he meant, of course, was that the jaw-dropping panorama was the only wealth anyone had around there. He was right. Even the folks considered rich in Abundance weren't rich by the outside world's standards. Everyone was just getting by. For Dixie, however, it had been enough. Unlike some of her friends at school, she'd never dreamed of escaping to bigger places like Billings or Missoula. Life in Abundance held all she'd ever wanted.

The mountains were what had attracted the canyon folk too. It started out innocently enough when this screenwriter guy bought a run-down summer cabin up on Rock Creek. Just the fact that he was a foreigner – or 'furriner' as Mama liked to call him, meaning that he came from outside Montana – was enough to make people's ears prick up, but the fact he was from Hollywood ... well, you might as well have said Captain Kirk had landed the *Enterprise* on Main Street. At the church picnic that summer, no one could talk of anything else.

Soon, though, folks got bored with it and went back to talking about hunting and fishing and cattle prices. While it was true that the screenwriter guy had bought the cabin, he was hardly ever there. When he was, he kept himself to himself. Not in an unfriendly way, but just in the way foreigners did, so that you got to know nothing about them. Spotting him was harder than spotting the mountain lion that occasionally wandered into folks' yards and ate up the dog's food and, if you weren't careful, the dog as well.

A couple of summers later, however, it started all over again, when word got around that the screenwriter guy had brought some movie stars to stay with him and they were going fishing on the river every day. Someone said they saw

Spencer Scott standing in waders right by Simpson's Bridge, and that's when everyone forgot about bluebirds and started using their binoculars for other things.

They liked Abundance, did the screenwriter guy and his friends. More of them came to visit and they started staying longer. They began coming into town, hanging out at the Stockman Bar or eating lunch at Ernie's Diner. They never ever talked to folks, just to each other, but that was OK. Most folks weren't so sure they wanted to talk to them anyway. The screenwriter's new movie had come to the showhouse over the winter. Everyone had gone, just to see what he'd been up to there in his cabin on Rock Creek, and everyone was disappointed. It was full of sex and gore and not at all the sort of thing decent, church-going folks went to see. There were a few, of course, who got starstruck. They tried to cosy up whenever they saw them and be friends, but that never happened. The canyon folk always brought their own friends with them.

More and more started staying. For a couple of years, there was a mini land rush as they bought up the dilapidated cabins that peppered the narrow mountain canyons. When those ran out, they started buying ranches along the river. You couldn't blame folk for selling up, because it was like they'd won the lottery. Never, ever in a million years could they have got that kind of money selling local. Everyone knew it was all bad land, even down by the river. Scrubby, dry and alkaline. It wasn't fit for anything except running cattle, and you needed five thousand acres at the very least to make a living doing that. But then canyon folk would turn up out of the blue, knock on your door and right there on your doorstep they would offer you more for fifty acres than the whole ranch was worth. If you had a good view of the mountains, you could name the most unbelievable amount you could think of, and like as not you'd get it.

Tom O'Grady, the real-estate agent, was the person to know in those days. He was good at sizing the canyon folk up, at knowing which piece of property would suit them, and then charming them into feeling they got the best of the deal when he sold it to them. Truth was, though, never for a moment did Tom forget that he was an Abundance man. He fleeced every one of them.

Almost as good as the money he got for people was the gossip he gleaned. Because Tom spent so much time with the canyon folk, he always knew what was going on with them and it was often juicy as a mango.

The canyon folk brought with them a lifestyle that people in Abundance had only ever read about in stories. They bought ranches just because they liked the scenery and not because they had to make a living from it. They bought up, tore down, threw out and built back up again without ever once using a local man. The bathroom tiles came from Italy; the oak in the cupboards came from Vermont; the man who made it into a kitchen came from Mexico. The canyon folk did all that and then only lived in the houses a few weeks in the summer. This made no sense to anyone local but you still felt in awe of it.

Dane Goodman was the first big-name movie star to move into the canyon and stay there on a fairly regular basis. He bought Grampa Cummings's ranch house up on Dry Creek and first thing he did was knock down the old porch on the west side and build a cedar deck. Then he installed a Jacuzzi hot tub and there was all sorts of gossip about naked starlets running through the woods. At the time, Dane Goodman was married to a well-known actress, but she only lasted four months before she went crazy and had to go back to California. So he took up with the screenwriter guy's wife, which was all right because the screenwriter guy had already taken up with one of the naked starlets. Then Dane Goodman went off to do a movie and fell in love with someone else and brought her up from California. Meanwhile, the screenwriter guy's wife moved in with Tim Mason. This shocked folk considerably, not only because Tim Mason was a local man but because everyone in town knew he was gay. There was no end of speculation about what Tim and the screenwriter guy's wife were getting up to amidst the white wine, cedar decks and hot tubs.

Spencer Scott was the next big name to make the Abundance area his home, and after him came that director guy, who had done all those anguished movies about poor people, and finally the Writer From Back East. They thought they were being cowboys, but they behaved like mountain men, letting their hair and beards grow, clomping down Main Street in raggedy jeans and boots and getting very publicly drunk. Mostly, however, they liked owning things: Hummers, vintage pick-ups and cattle from breeds nobody local had ever heard of. Most of all, however, they liked to own land. It had gone beyond the land-rush days by this point. The canyon folk and their hangers-on now owned most of the river valley, the canyons and even the mountains themselves.

As a consequence, the look of the canyons changed. Roads were cut through the virgin forest. A landing strip was bulldozed down along the river. There was a helipad beside the highway just beyond Simpson's Bridge. The novelty of having movie stars walking around had long since worn off for the residents of Abundance. Celebrity faces in the drugstore or the supermarket became an ordinary event. No one really noticed anymore. Not that the canyon folk were part of things now. They weren't. They still kept themselves to themselves, while the Abundance folk went on as usual. Almost nobody mixed.

This wasn't to say, however, that the canyon folk weren't good to Abundance. One year they decided the town ought to have a Fourth of July picnic, like the kind you read about in books, with sack races and watermelon-seed spitting contests. They set up a committee, got money for it and organized it as well. It was good fun. There was a parade and a pig roast and a huge fireworks display at the end. Another time, the canyon folk decided there ought to be a pretty white wrought-iron gazebo in the park so that a band could come and play on Sunday afternoons in the summer and they got that done. And they brought live theatre back to Abundance for the first time in ninety years with what was probably the most star-studded local dramatics group in all of the West.

It wasn't that the locals were ungrateful. These things were meant for everyone and the folk of Abundance really did enjoy themselves too. It was just that while a band playing in a gazebo on Sunday afternoon was nice, a new scanning machine for the hospital would have been nicer. This was the whole problem. The canyon folk only seemed interested in Abundance as a dreamy kind of place where they could do storybook stuff. When they got tired of the crappy internet connection or the bad coffee or having only two full-time doctors, they would fly away. For Abundance folk, however, Abundance was all there was.

On Tuesday evening when Dixie went to the funeral home to dress Jamie Lee, Main Street was alive with high-school kids 'turning the point', as they called the ritual of relentlessly driving around the two-block downtown area in their parents' cars. Entering the mortuary was like stepping into another dimension. The heavy oak doors closed behind Dixie, and there was a sudden vacuum of silence before her ears adjusted enough to hear the softly piped organ music. Her eyes took longer to leave behind the summer evening's brilliance for the mortuary's shadowy interior of burgundy carpets and heavy velvet drapes.

The funeral director came out of his office to lead her down a dimly lit corridor to a small room adjacent to the chapel. Right in the middle of the room was what looked to Dixie like one of those little folding tables you put your dinner on when you eat in front of the TV. On top of it was the tiny blue coffin. Jamie Lee lay inside, swathed in a white baby blanket.

'Is your husband coming?' the funeral director asked.

'He's not my husband,' Dixie replied softly as she bent to take the clothes out of the plastic carrier bag.

'I just wondered if I should leave the door unlocked. It's the kids, you know. They get up to mischief at this time of night.'

'It's not his little boy, you see.'

The funeral director looked at her.

'I mean, he's been good to Jamie Lee and all. Just like a proper daddy. He didn't even mind about Jamie Lee being the way he was. But it got kind of hard. 'Specially right here at the end. Know what I mean? But Billy tried to be good to Jamie Lee. Better than Jamie's real daddy. His real daddy never even seen him ...'

'It's all right. I understand,' the funeral director said gently.

'I just didn't want you to be thinking Billy isn't here because he doesn't care. It's that he's been working all day and he's real tired. He's just got a job out at the sawmill, running one of them strippers, and he comes home dog-tired from it.'

The funeral director nodded.

'He'll be coming tomorrow though,' Dixie added. 'He wouldn't dream of missing the funeral. He was real attached to Jamie Lee.'

After the funeral director left, Dixie went over to the coffin. Jamie Lee lay on his back, his head turned slightly to one side, his eyes closed. The way he looked that moment, you really would have thought he was just asleep. He didn't have that bluish colour of death about him. In fact, he looked better now than he had when he was alive. His poor little heart never could cope, so Jamie Lee had always looked a little blue. Now he was pink and rosy as any baby.

Dixie felt an almost overpowering urge to lift up his eyelids and see if his eyeballs were still there. She didn't know why this insistent thought had come to her but she forced it away before it spoiled the moment.

Very gently she reached into the coffin. When she picked Jamie up he felt ... odd, almost slippery; she hadn't expected this so when his head lolled lifelessly to the side, she nearly lost hold of him. And he was so cold. Not that she hadn't known in her head that he would be, but there's a big difference between what your head knows and what your heart expects.

In the corner of the room was a white rocking chair. When the funeral director had shown her into the room the first time, he'd explained how sometimes mamas and daddies liked to hold their babies one last time and that was what the rocking chair was for. Taking Jamie Lee over, Dixie sat down. 'I got you some nice new clothes.' She laid him on her lap and reached into the carrier bag. 'Look at what I bought you. Lookie here at these little jeans. See? Aren't they cute? And this little shirt. It's just like Billy's rodeo shirt. And see these, Jamie Lee? These sweet little baby cowboy boots Auntie Leola got you? You're going to look all snazzy when you meet Jesus.'

Tears came and she let them. It was safe here. No one to tell her not to get upset, to say how Jamie Lee had been going to die anyway, so it was better he didn't have to suffer any more. No one to tell her she shouldn't feel so bad, because with the kind of defects he had she should have been expecting it. No one here except the funeral man, and if he did this job every day, he had to be used to crying.

As she removed the babygrow, faintly stained with the funeral parlour make-up, Dixie thought how she had cried, too, when she'd found out she was pregnant. The last thing she'd wanted was Big Jim's child. The relationship was already over; in fact, if it hadn't been for Daddy making such a big deal out of saying 'I told you so', and how she only ever attracted trash, Dixie would have finished with Big Jim long before that. Then there she was, carrying his bastard baby. Sitting in the bathroom, with little splashes of pee still gleaming on the plastic pregnancy indicator, Dixie had stared at the thin blue line and cried so hard.

Mama, of course, had said there was no need to tell Daddy about it to begin with. You could fix things, she said, and men didn't even have to know. But Dixie couldn't do it. The baby was alive, and killing was killing. Maybe ordinary men wouldn't know what she'd done, but Jesus would know and that's what she told Mama.

Mama got angry when she'd said that. 'You been born again or something?' she said scornfully, 'because this family's not so churchified that we can give Jesus as an excuse for our own stupid behaviour. We accept ugly things need doing sometimes. That don't make them right and that don't mean we won't have to pay on Judgment Day, but they still need doing. And it ain't Jesus who'll do them. You, of all people, should know that.'

Dixie cried then because she knew what Mama was referring to, but she still stayed firm. As ashamed as Mama and Daddy said they were of her for having a baby when she had no man, Dixie refused to get an abortion.

She'd cried again the day Jamie Lee was born, as the doctor stood over her explaining what Down's syndrome was and how this meant Jamie Lee's heart wasn't made quite right and they might not be able to fix it. 'You just done nothing but make me cry, little man,' she whispered as she dressed his small, cold body.

Chapter Three

Spencer fiddled with the espresso maker, trying to get it to work. As always, it produced enough steam to power a locomotive, followed by a trickle of dark, murky liquid that looked like engine oil. He had been absolutely *assured* this was the best-quality machine around and yet it routinely turned out sludge that even Starbuck's wouldn't call espresso. 'Sidonie!' he shouted angrily and bashed the side of the machine in frustration.

When there was no answer, Spencer turned around. 'Where the fuck is she?'

The boy, who was sitting at the kitchen island, shrugged. 'How should I know?' Cereal fell out of his mouth when he spoke.

'What *are* you eating? You sound like a pig at the trough,' Spencer said and came over to pick up the box of cereal.

'Coco Pops.'

'How the fuck did you get hold of them?'

'The store,' the boy replied derisively. 'Sidonie bought them for me.'

'Yes, well, that was a waste of money then.' Spencer turned on the garbage disposal and emptied the contents of the cereal box into it.

'Hey! What did you do that for?'

'Because we don't eat crap here. And I can't imagine your mother lets you eat this junk either,' he said, crumpling up the empty container. 'She's still in her vegan phase, isn't she?'

'As far as I know, they don't kill anything to make Coco Pops,' the boy replied.

'Watch your mouth.'

The boy's eyes went wide with fake innocence. 'How am I going to do that?' he asked and tipped his head as if trying to look down at his mouth. 'Because my eyes are up here and my mouth is down here and I can't see it.'

'Cut it out.'

The kid leaped off his chair. 'OK. So where are the scissors?'

'You know what I mean.'

'You said, "Cut it out," so I'm just going to get the scissors.'

Angrily Spencer threw his espresso cup into the sink. There wasn't the satisfaction of its breaking. It just clattered noisily against the metal. Coffee splashed everywhere. 'Where the *hell* is Sidonie?' he shouted at no one in particular. 'Sidonie? *Sidonie!*'

The boy, his expression placid, watched Spencer storm across the kitchen.

'I'm going out on the deck. When Sidonie finally turns up, tell her that's where I am.'

The boy picked a bit of Coco Pops out of his teeth and flicked it off on the floor. He shrugged. 'Yeah, well, whatever.

Just don't yell at me. It's not my fault I'm here. I don't want it any more than you do.'

Spencer had only two children: Thomas and Louisa. They had been part of his 'Life Before' – that period of struggling early in adulthood when he was still nobody. He and Kathryn had been high-school sweethearts. Two kids in two years and a basement apartment followed, while he did Shakespeare in the Park and worked the night shift at the warehouse. His big break had come from the ignominious fact that he had been willing to play second fiddle to a ten-foot python in an experimental Off-Off-Broadway production. What that snake was getting up to with the scantily clad girl in the lead part proved so outrageously controversial that the play actually garnered an audience, although perhaps not for the reasons the playwright had intended. Spencer, seeing his chance, managed to successfully upstage both the girl and the snake.

Despite being so supportive during those lean years when Spencer was on the theatre circuit, Kathryn didn't enjoy success when it finally came. She had liked being married to an artist but she saw herself as intellectually above being a movie star's wife. Hers was an old Connecticut family and they didn't 'do Hollywood', as she put it, which was OK with Spencer, as by that point he was no longer doing Kathryn. He had, however, taken seriously his obligations to her and to the kids, so when the divorce came, he provided well for all three of them, even in the later years, long after he and the kids had drifted out of regular contact. He paid for their braces, their private schools, their summers at camp. He paid for Thomas's business degree at Harvard and

Louisa's long-drawn-out doctorate in ancient Persian culture, which seemed mainly to involve spending years in remote Arabian deserts peering into archaeological trenches; and he had done it all simply because they were his kids.

This boy wasn't. Spencer didn't care whose DNA the kid had. Phoebe had been just another of the countless good-looking girls who made it their life to follow fame. A groupie, elevated to a fuck-buddy, but nothing more. That was how the game was played, sex, drugs and fame being traded like so many casino chips. Nothing was meant for real. There was no relationship, no commitment and most definitely no baby.

She was wily, was Phoebe, and so much more of a player than Spencer had ever imagined at the time. He still found himself running those events back over in his mind, trying to figure out exactly what had happened, because he was no one's fool. He'd always been so very, very careful to avoid just this situation. Certainly there'd been a lot of times with too much to drink, too many drugs, but even so, he'd *always* been careful, always taken responsibility himself. But Phoebe was just so brilliant at fucking. That was her secret weapon. If you do it so much, so often and in so many different ways, sooner or later a condom will come along that can't cope. Either that or Phoebe had saved the spent condoms and done something kinky with a turkey baster. Spencer wouldn't put that past her either.

When he found out about the pregnancy, Spencer thought he'd handled it all very coolly. He hadn't got upset. He hadn't blamed her in any way. In fact, he'd smiled and caressed her solicitously while reassuring her that he'd pay for the abortion and all her care.

Phoebe wouldn't even consider it. No fooling that old fox. By the time Spencer had sent his lawyer around the next morning to help her see reason, she had already vanished into the mist.

The birth announcement arrived unceremoniously by email right along with the rest of the spam in Spencer's inbox. Phoebe had named the boy 'Tennesee', of all things. She wasn't even classy enough to spell it right.

Her lawyers' letters started arriving only a few days later. It made no difference that Spencer had never wanted the child, that he had done all he could to prevent the boy's conception and, indeed, his birth. The paternity test established Spencer was the father and that was it. The kid was the perfect blackmail tool. Whenever Phoebe wanted money, it was always 'for the boy' and the court always listened.

Worse was to follow, however, because motherhood didn't suit Phoebe all that well. She frequently needed to 'take a break', disappearing for days, sometimes weeks at a time. To her mind it made perfect sense that she could just foist the kid on to Spencer any time she got fed up with him, because, as she pointed out, he was Spencer's son too.

More lawyers followed and then more money, this time to hire a full-time, live-in nanny for the boy so that any time Phoebe felt the need to chant with the Indians in Colorado or beach comb in Baja, she could go. Even this, however, was not enough to free Spencer from the mess. In the latest turn of events, the new nanny had been found not to be Filipina after all but Mexican and illegal. Documents had been forged and God knows what else, and Phoebe hadn't paid attention to any of it right up to the point where immigration officers turned up on the doorstep to take the nanny away.

A perfunctory email was all the notice Phoebe gave Spencer that she had plans to be in the Virgin Islands, so the boy was coming to him until all this nanny business was resolved. The way she worded it, you would have thought Spencer had hand-picked this crap nanny and then personally sent the immigration service in to get her. Before he could get her even to answer her fucking phone, the kid was in Montana.

Spencer was furious. The ranch had always been his private retreat. He only ever brought Sidonie. That was the whole point of Montana: to get away from the agents, the entourage, the hangers-on, the hustlers, the sycophants. The ranch was Spencer's idyll. He hated Phoebe for tainting that, because he knew she'd done it on purpose. She lived to smear shit on anything he valued, and that's all the boy was to him: shit.

Spencer considered those matters as he sat in the pinewood rocker on the deck. Slowly, the primeval motion calmed him. His gaze wandered to the mountains.

The ranch was tucked into the lower foothills of Lion Mountain. When sitting on the deck, his view of the massive range was oblique rather than full on, the mountains on the left of his field of vision, each rising one behind the other, their pine-covered foothills eroding down into the broad river valley below. It was a startlingly beautiful view that never lost its intensity for him. Whenever he took the time to really see it, he was always astonished by it all over again, and he liked that. It helped keep things in perspective.

'Here.' Sidonie appeared with a cup of espresso, properly made. She was wearing only her bathrobe, her hair still wet from the shower. As she leaned down to hand him his coffee, the robe gapped to expose the moist roundness of her breasts. Spencer felt himself harden. He smiled and took the cup.

'Do you want a croissant or anything?' she asked.

'No, I'm OK.'

She was barefoot. The perfume of her shower gel was still clinging to her, the robe short enough to show almost all of her long, long legs. He wanted to fuck her there and then. Spencer considered it, considered how they'd do it. He envisioned laying the robe open on the deck to make languid love there in the cool Montana morning sunshine.

Reality snapped back like a rubber band as the boy slid open the screen door and came out on to the deck. 'Can I use your computer?' he asked.

'No,' Spencer replied irritably.

'Why not?'

'Because I said so.'

'Why?'

'Because I *said* no. I don't want you messing up my stuff on it.'

The boy stood there. He was small for almost ten. Like his mother in that regard. Spencer had found Phoebe's petite stature a turn-on when they'd first met. He liked his women young and nubile and Phoebe's small size gave her a perkiness that had made her seem more youthful than she actually was. That small size wouldn't do the boy any favours though. Women always preferred tall men.

'Will you give me some money then?' the kid asked.

'What for?'

'A game for my PlayStation.'

'No,' Spencer replied.

'Why not?'

Spencer swung his arm out wide. 'See this?'

'Yeah.'

'It's called the out of doors.'

'Yeah, so?'

'So go explore it.'

The kid quirked his lip up on one side in a disdainful expression. 'And I want to do that because …?'

'Because it's there. Shit, Tennesee, what's the matter with you? When I was your age, all I had was the street to play in. I would have killed to have somewhere wonderful as this.'

'Good thing you didn't get it then, huh? Or you'd be in prison now.'

Exasperated, Spencer rolled his eyes.

'Can I go look around the stores in town then?'

'When we drove through Abundance yesterday, did you see that big shopping mall?' Spencer replied.

The boy's expression lit up with interest. 'No, I didn't.'

'Precisely.'

'What's that mean?'

'That Abundance has three thousand people living in it and it's ninety miles from any place bigger, so you're lucky to get milk and a newspaper. And that's why we come here, Tennesee. That's what we like about it. Otherwise we would stay in LA.'

'There's a DVD section at the back of the Pay'n Save. I could take him there,' Sidonie offered. 'Maybe they have games to rent.'

'Yeah!' the boy cried.

'Sidonie, stay out of this. He can fucking well entertain himself.' Spencer looked over at the boy. 'Go down to the barn. Guff can show you the horses.'

'I don't like horses. They stink.'

'I don't care. Go down anyway. Hang out with Guff a while.'

'Why?'

'Because he's a cowboy.'

'Yeah, so?'

'A genuine cowboy, Tennesee.'

'Yeah. *So?*'

'So that's cool. Cowboys are cool. He can teach you how to be a man.'

The look of contemptuous ennui on the boy's face did away with any need for an answer.

'What the fuck's wrong with you?' Spencer said. 'Normal kids would be grateful for all this.'

'What the fuck's wrong with you?' the boy replied. Then he turned and went back into the house.

Chapter Four

They buried Jamie Lee on Wednesday morning. It was a bright day, cooler than the previous ones, but very still. The sky was completely cloudless and the air so clear that it magnified the mountains, pulling them right up close to the small party at the graveside, as if they were family mourners.

Abundance had two cemeteries. The new one out on the edge of town looked like a park. In fact, it was a lot prettier than the real park. An irrigation system pumped water up from the river so that its grass stayed green even in the hottest part of the summer and there were ornamental cherries planted all around the perimeter. Because of the rule about only having flat headstones, you would have never known it was a cemetery if you were just driving past it, except for all the vases of plastic flowers.

The old cemetery, in contrast, sprawled over a dusty, treeless hillside east of town. It was seldom used any more because the county stopped maintaining it once the new one was built. A rusty wrought-iron fence was all that separated it from the vast, wild hillside beyond.

There had never been any question in Dixie's mind about where to bury Jamie Lee. She had loved the old cemetery all her life, if 'love' was the kind of word you could use about such a place. Its location high up behind the town gave the most panoramic view you could find that included both the river basin that cupped Abundance and the enormous mountain range beyond. Throughout her growing-up years, Dixie had regularly made the three-mile uphill trek from home to the cemetery. She'd spent many hours wandering in the crowded solitude, reading the tombstones and speculating on the lives of the people beneath them. In one place six young children from a single family had died of diphtheria in the spring of 1901. The six slabs of stone marking their graves were amateurishly hewn, the names etched crudely on the stone by hand. Dixie visualized a heart-broken father struggling with chisel and hammer himself because he was unable to afford so many tombstones made by a stonemason. In a different part of the cemetery, a child of four named Laura Mae lay beneath a most exquisite white marble lamb. When Dixie was young, she would stroke its nose, cool even on the hottest day, and make chains of clover to hang around its neck. At the far back of the cemetery where the earliest residents of Abundance had been laid to rest, there used to be an old wooden tombstone inscribed 'Charles Turner, aged 23. Hanged Nov. 1889' and nothing more.

Daddy had asked her once why she spent so much time in a place full of dead people she'd never known, only Daddy being Daddy he'd said 'worm-eaten corpses' instead of the word 'people'. She hadn't replied. It was impossible to explain the sense of peace she felt there with the mountains gathered in close, cradling the open hillside, and the locusts and meadowlarks embroidering the stillness. And there was something deeper yet about the place that Dixie never could find words for, something about those worms and bugs and seeking roots of grass being the real gods of resurrection, turning death back into life. She found a sense of rightness in the cemetery, a feeling that maybe there wasn't really anything wrong with death and dying, that it was just another part of living, not so very different. Even on this sad, sad day now, with Jamie Lee, the place brought comfort to her. If she had to leave him anywhere, Dixie was glad it would be here.

Only the immediate family came to the funeral. And Billy, of course, who was wearing that awful black polyester suit with the decorative red stitching that Dixie abhorred. He looked like a cheap Elvis Presley impersonator in it, but it was his only black suit – his only suit, period, if truth be known – and, as he was always pointing out, it still had a lot of wear left in it.

Dixie's sister Leola came, but Earl Ray didn't, so Dixie knew what Mama had been saying about Leola's marriage was probably true. And Daddy came, Mama doggedly pushing his wheelchair up the grassy slope to the graveside. Dixie was surprised to see him. What with the way things were between them, she wouldn't have thought much about it if he'd decided to stay home. Most likely Mama made him come. That was the big problem with being in a wheelchair. You were at the mercy of other folk. Even Daddy was.

The graveside service was very short. The small fibreglass coffin was lowered into the ground and the preacher bent to pick up a handful of soil. As he cast it into the open grave, an unexpected breeze played across the hillside, dispersing most of the dirt over the yellow prairie grass. *Ashes to ashes, dust to dust.* Dixie watched the blowing soil as it drifted away. A locust buzzed by and landed with an audible thunk on the lid of the coffin. The air was heavy with the scent of sagebrush. The mountains shimmered in the heat.

Since it was just family at the funeral, Mama made the meal for afterwards so that there wouldn't be the expense of taking folks to the diner. There was cold fried chicken and potato salad, a relish tray with green onions, carrots, celery and some of those little sweet pickles Dixie liked so well. Even though she hadn't been able to come, Aunt Ethel sent over a big batch of her special home-made rolls.

They ate outside in the shade of the house because the August heat had really set in by the time everyone got back from the cemetery. Dixie enjoyed meal. She'd expected to feel too sad, but it wasn't like that at all. Everyone ended up relaxed and laughing. Even Daddy smiled, so that it felt almost like their family picnics in the old days, back before he'd had his accident.

Billy stepped back into his jeans, fastened them and did up his belt, clamping shut the big silver and copper buckle he'd won at the Abundance rodeo for staying on 'the red-eyed roan' till the buzzer sounded. Then he sat down on the edge of the bed to pull on his boots.

'The funeral was good,' Dixie said. 'I think it went well.'

Billy nodded.

The heat in the small upstairs bedroom was absolutely suffocating, even with both gable-end windows pushed wide open to catch the slightest whiff of a late-afternoon breeze.

Taking one of Billy's folded handkerchiefs from the top of the dresser, Dixie wiped the sweat from her face. 'I thought the service was nice, didn't you?'

'Yeah.'

'I liked the bit where the preacher was saying how Jamie Lee was perfect in Jesus' eyes, and all innocent, you know, and Jesus was going to welcome him with open arms.'

Billy was still sitting on his side of the bed. The suit was lying rumpled on the floor and he just stared at it, not making any move to put it away.

'I reckon that's true, don't you?' Dixie said. 'I reckon Jesus don't care one whit that Jamie Lee had Down's. He just sees how perfect Jamie Lee really was.'

Billy didn't answer.

'Anyway, I liked for the preacher to say that.'

'It cost almost a thousand dollars for him to say that,' Billy replied morosely.

Dixie looked over. Billy had his forearms on his knees and his head hanging down so that all she could see was his rumpled hair. 'You worrying about the money?' she asked.

Billy didn't answer.

This wasn't the right time to be pointing out how much better it would have been if he'd taken the railroad job. Work at the sawmill would only last through August, and even if he saved every single penny he earned from it, Billy still wasn't going to have enough money for more than a couple of horses by the end of it, even without Jamie Lee's funeral to pay for. But at least it was a proper job and he wasn't off cowboying.

Dixie reached a hand over to comfort him. 'I already paid two hundred dollars towards it. And that man from the funeral home, he's real nice. I told him you got steady work now, so he said we could give him the rest of the money in payments as long as we got it all paid off by the end of September. If I put the groceries on the credit card, we'll be able to do that.'

Billy sighed.

Getting up, Dixie came around to his side of the bed. She sat down beside him and put her arms around him. 'Don't worry, Billy. We'll manage.'

Chapter Five

Billy was late. The shift at the sawmill ended at six thirty and now it was almost a quarter of eight. Dixie took the casserole out of the oven and set it on top of the stove. Billy hadn't said anything about being late home but you couldn't always trust him to remember those kinds of things. More than likely he was making up the time he'd taken for Jamie Lee's funeral. It never went down right to start a new job and then have time off right away.

Or maybe they were running a late shift. It being the middle of the summer, the daylight would last another hour. Like as not, Dixie reckoned, they'd be running the sawmill double time.

When eight thirty came, Dixie put the casserole in the refrigerator. She opened a second can of Coke and took a packet of potato chips with her to watch TV. She toyed with the idea of going over to Mama's but decided against it. It was almost nine and too late to turn up without an explanation. Dixie didn't want to admit she didn't know where Billy was.

It was hard not to think about Jamie Lee at times like this. Nothing on TV could fill up her mind enough to push Jamie Lee out. It was the weight of him she missed most, as if her arms had a kind of memory of their own. She picked up a pillow and cuddled it against her but it wasn't heavy enough. And it wasn't alive. That's what her arms yearned for: weight with life in it.

A quarter of ten and Dixie knew it couldn't be a late shift keeping Billy out. Odds were, he was carousing. Usually he came home first and at least offered to take her with him, but maybe there had been something to celebrate at work and the boys had gone straight out.

She phoned Leola. Dixie didn't say anything about Billy being missing. They got to talking about Earl Ray and what a piece of shit he was and that took Dixie's mind off things at hand.

At half past midnight she flipped the TV off because she was sick of watching. She was sick of drinking Cokes too, and, most of all, sick of cuddling a lifeless pillow.

What if Billy had run off? That's what Jamie Lee's real daddy had done. One day he was there, lying in bed next to Dixie like a great big lump, next day he was gone. Big Jim. That's what people always called him. Bigger than Billy, that's for sure. Billy had a cowboy's build: small, wiry and loosely strung together at the joints. Big Jim was *big*. All except for his heart, that is, and that was shrivelled up like a prune. But what if Billy had done the same? What if he just got fed up with all the hassle and took off? Tears came to Dixie's eyes. What was the matter with her anyway? Why couldn't she ever find a good man?

At 2. 20 a.m. the screen door banged.

'Where the *hell* have you been?' Dixie cried.

Billy brushed past her.

'Do you know what time it is? You scared me half to death, being gone so late.' She grabbed his arm.

'Let go of me. I need a piss.'

Dixie followed him into the bathroom. 'You been drinking all this time? Jeez, Billy, it's almost two thirty in the morning. Who were you with?'

'You sound like your goddamned mother, Dixie, with all your fucking questions.'

'I was *worried*, for Pete's sake. Why didn't you call me? I was practically ready to phone the police.'

Billy pushed past her in the bathroom doorway and headed upstairs.

'So where were you?' she asked, following him.

Furiously Billy turned around. 'For Christ's sake, Dixie, would you shut the fuck up?' He gave her a little shove. Not hard. Not enough to push her down the stairs like last time, but she stumbled and had to grapple quickly for the handrail to catch herself. Billy went on upstairs.

Dixie hurried after him. 'Who *were* you with? Why ain't you telling me?' She couldn't keep from crying. 'What's her name? Because if there's somebody else, Billy, I want you to tell me now.'

'It ain't no one,' he said and fell on to the bed. He fumbled with the buttons of his shirt.

'Don't go humiliating me in front of everybody.'

'Dixie, would you shut the fuck up? I wasn't out with no woman. It was just the boys.'

'What boys?'

'The *boys*. The usual.'

'*What* boys?'

'I said, shut the fuck *up* with your nagging.' And he hit her.

Dixie ducked to miss his fist but he wasn't as drunk as she'd thought, because his aim wasn't off any. The blow landed hard against the right side of her face just where the cheekbone meets the bottom of the ear. Clutching at the pain, Dixie crumpled.

'I *wasn't* out with no woman,' Billy said, his voice gentler, 'because that's what you're still thinking, isn't it?'

Still doubled over, Dixie continued to clutch the side of her face.

Billy knelt down in front of her. 'Did you hear me, Dix? That's the truth. Ain't no woman in my life but you.' His voice was apologetic, the way it always was after he'd hurt her. 'Why did you make me hit you? I'm sorry. But come on now. Everything's OK.'

Dixie struggled to stop the tears.

Billy rose up. 'If you got to know the truth, I was out with Roy and Mike.'

'Roy and Mike?' Dixie asked, perplexed. 'I thought they were working up Indian Creek. On Baker's ranch.'

'Yeah.'

'So what were you doing out with them?' she asked, still cupping her hand tenderly over her cheek.

Stripped down to his underpants, Billy rolled into bed and pulled the sheet up. 'We'll talk in the morning. I'm dog-tired now.'

Dixie sat down on the edge of the bed. Reaching for a tissue, she blew her nose as best she could and sat a few minutes, waiting for the pain to settle down. Then she looked over. Billy was acting like he was already asleep but she could tell by his breathing that he wasn't.

'What *were* you doing out with Roy and Mike?' she asked quietly.

'If you got to know,' he said without bothering to open his eyes, 'me and them were working together.'

'At the sawmill?'

'Fuck the stupid sawmill, Dixie,' Billy said and looked over wearily. 'Standing there in that hell-hot building, running that fucking stripper. Having that asshole supervisor coming around every two minutes like I'm a fucking kid. Fuck it all to hell.'

'So what you're saying is you haven't been working at the sawmill, even though you were telling me you were?'

He didn't reply.

'Instead, you been out at the ranch all this time? Doing what?'

'Branding.'

'*Branding?* That's going to last like, what? A week?'

Suddenly she realized what was going on. 'Ah, OK, I get it. That's why you were boozing tonight, huh? *Today* was your last day.'

'It's a good deal, Dix. 'Cause if I get in with the foreman, I reckon he'll get Baker to rent me some pasture there next year for my horses, once the guide business takes off.'

Dixie's vision blurred with renewed tears. 'It might be a good deal if you had some horses, but you don't, Billy. Cowboying's never a good deal, and you know it.'

'Oh shit, don't cry again.'

'What am I going to tell that funeral man? Where am I going to get his money by the end of September?'

'What about you going back on the checkout at Pay'n Save? You don't got Jamie now. Hanging around here by yourself all day isn't going to help you feel better, Dixie. And Jesus, they want someone. I was just in there the other night and the line was a mile long.'

Dixie bent forward and covered her face with her hands.

'Don't be so gloomy all the time,' Billy said in a cheery voice and patted her back. 'We'll get through. We always do.'

Dixie couldn't sleep. She lay in the dark and listened to Billy's soft, drunken snoring. Her cheek hurt something terrible and she knew she was going to end up with a black eye. Mama would see straightaway that Billy had hit her, no matter what explanation Dixie came up with. Better just to stay away from Mama until it went down. That was easier than explaining Billy.

Tears again. Dixie swallowed to keep them down. She wasn't crying so much about having to keep making excuses for the things Billy did or even about the money. Mostly it was just that she hurt. She was sick of hurting. Sick of pain, whether it was because of Billy or because of Jamie Lee, or just because life was such a bitch.

Chapter Six

In the morning when she looked in the mirror, things were worse even than Dixie had feared. Her eye was nearly swollen shut and what little eyeball showed was bloody red.

Stupid Billy.

Dixie leaned down and got her make-up case out from under the sink. What was the story going to be this time? She ran into a door? God, people were going to think she had the most dangerous doors in Montana, she'd used that one so many times. Fell over? Over what? None of Jamie Lee's toys were lying around now to blame. Maybe she should say she'd decided to become one of those girl boxers like they had on the cable channel.

That thought made her smile and, for just a moment, she became aware of herself, looking at herself in the mirror, and it reminded her of long ago. She had been little then, five maybe or six, and she'd been left home alone with Daddy. Mama and Leola had gone to church. She couldn't remember now why she hadn't gone too, and of course,

Daddy never went. He didn't believe in that kind of stuff. Said if there was really someone like God up in heaven, how come He'd created such a mess of a world?

On that morning she'd been playing by the steps that went down to the outside cellar when Daddy told her she was being a nuisance and to stop playing there. When she didn't stop fast enough, he'd pushed her. It hadn't been a hard push. She knew he hadn't meant for her to fall down the steps, but she'd lost her footing and fallen anyway. What Dixie remembered most about the incident was that she hadn't cried at all and she'd felt very proud of herself for that, even though she'd scraped the side of her face. Later she'd gone inside and pulled a chair into the bathroom in order to be able to see what her face looked like in the mirror over the sink. That image came to her now, that vision of herself as a little girl, examining her face in the mirror for injuries. Not much had changed.

Billy left the house before lunchtime. He didn't say where he was going and Dixie knew better than to ask. Probably off to hang out with Roy and drink up whatever little bit of money was left from the branding.

Dixie went to a lot of trouble to make her eye look decent. Then she ironed her white blouse, the one with the nice, crisp collar and the bit of edging along the button placket, and put on her black skirt. She decided the black kitten pumps she'd borrowed off Leola looked better than sandals, even though it really was too hot for anything you couldn't wear bare-legged.

Mr Roberts was in his office in the back of the Pay'n Save when Dixie arrived. He said hi and looked really pleased to see her. 'Sorry to hear about Jamie Lee,' he said. 'That's just a crying shame.' Then he asked if she'd like a glass of iced tea.

'I was sort of hoping I could get back on,' Dixie said. 'It's too quiet at home now. And I could do with the work.'

'I wish I had an opening,' Mr Roberts replied.

'You were always saying how much folks were missing me at the checkout.'

'Yes, that's so true. Make sure we have your details, so that next time we're hiring …'

'Thing is … well, I don't mean to sound begging, but things are kind of tight right now. What with Jamie Lee's bills and all,' Dixie said. 'It's real important I find some work.' She was trying to keep the pleading tone out of her voice. 'I'd be willing to do anything. Even part time.'

'Yes, I'm really sorry we don't have anything for you,' Mr Roberts said. 'I wish I could help.'

Dixie managed not to cry while she was in the Pay'n Save, but by the time she got out on to the street, the worry just grabbed her. It didn't matter if she was crying in the street. No one was out walking around in the heat of an August afternoon anyway, and if they were, they would have just thought it was sweat because she had a lot of that pouring down off her face too, washing away the carefully applied make-up from her black eye.

She should have gone home so that she could change out of her good clothes before she sweated all over them, but Dixie couldn't face returning to the empty house. Instead, she went down along the street to the railroad crossing and headed for Leola's house.

'Lordy, look at you!' Leola cried on opening the door. 'Aren't you a mess? Come on in.' She had Carrie Dee on her hip. Little Kenny was peeking around her leg, his lips bright blue from the popsicle he held in his other hand.

Leola didn't ask what happened with the eye. She and Billy didn't get on, so she was already inclined to think the worst of him. She did, however, wonder why Dixie was all dressed up. 'Come sit down in front of the fan,' she said. 'You want a popsicle? That'd help. Kenny, go get Aunt Dixie one of those like you got, OK?'

It was a relief to talk to Leola. They were only eighteen months apart and Dixie was the elder, but truth was Leola was the one born with an old head. She'd always known how to keep life sorted. Even Earl Ray's cheating seemed to roll off Leola. As long as he brought his paycheck home, she said, she couldn't be bothered chucking him out.

So Leola listened. She didn't say much. Talking wasn't Leola's way. She just listened carefully and nodded when Dixie came to the part about Billy and his stupid schemes. She nodded again when Dixie said how he couldn't ever keep a proper job and she was just about fed up with that. Then Leola reached over on the counter and pulled off a deck of playing cards.

'You want me to do you a reading?'

Dixie nodded.

Leola shuffled the cards. She closed her eyes partway and weaved back and forth just a tiny bit as she did it, which always made it feel eerie to Dixie, because Leola was so ordinary otherwise. She wasn't like one of those fake fortune-tellers at the fair, the kind who dressed up like gypsies and used spooky-looking cards with skeletons and hanged men on them. Leola just used common old playing cards and never did her readings for money, never did them for anyone else except friends and family. But she could lay those cards out and what they told her, well, it was a gift. No doubt about that.

Mama hated Leola's cards. She said it was a gift all right. Satan's gift. She was always coming over and reading the Bible at Leola, saying, 'Leola, it's right here in Deuteronomy, "Let no one be found among you who … practises divination or sorcery, interprets omens, engages in witchcraft, casts spells or is a medium or spiritist."' And Leola would say, 'Yes, Mama,' and let it roll off her. She always went to church on Sundays and took communion and prayed for her soul like everyone else, but she just couldn't keep playing cards from speaking the future to her.

'OK, we got to form the question in our minds,' Leola said.

'Me and Billy. Needing money bad,' Dixie replied.

'Well, put your mind on that a minute then, so it's real clear. Then take your seven cards.' She fanned the deck out face down in front of Dixie.

Carefully Dixie selected the cards and handed them back to Leola.

One by one, Leola laid the seven cards out in front of her in a V shape that she called the Horseshoe of Fate.

First came the eight of spades, then the five of spades, the five of diamonds, the joker. 'Well, he's not supposed to be there,' Leola said as she laid him in the fourth position – the point of the V. 'I thought all the jokers were out of this pack. You got a surprise in store. That's what he means, turning up like that. And he's your fourth card. Your "challenges" card. That's what's going to challenge you. Something you completely don't expect.'

She continued laying out the three remaining cards. Nine of spades, two of clubs, six of spades. Leola leaned forward and studied them.

'Way too many spades,' Dixie said. 'That's not good. Danger and misfortune. And two fives. Disappointment.'

'You want to do your own reading?' Leola asked.

'No.'

'Then let me get on with it.'

Silence then as Leola lingered several moments over the cards.

'Well, yeah,' she said at last, 'I can't say they're good cards. You're right. Too many spades.'

'Does this mean we aren't going to get the money we need?'

Leola raised a hand to shush Dixie. 'The eight of spades right here – this first position, it's your past. Talking about what kind of history's influencing your question. And eight of spades, well, it says you're in a situation you ought to get out of, Dix, but you aren't willing to leave it. I'm thinking that's Billy.' Leola looked up. 'Don't you?'

Dixie said nothing.

'This five of spades, it tells me you're going to change your opinion. You're going to come to your senses. I'm thinking you might get that money, but it's going to come at a cost in other ways. There's going to be rivalry, jealousy. That's what an eight and a five of spades together talks about. So you're in some kind of mess with Billy and you're going to have to struggle with him. And see, the five of diamonds says that too. That your money worries are going to be a right struggle for you. There's two fives here. Disappointments. Then that's when the joker shows up. It's the joker here that worries me. That card is your challenges card and it's the wild card. You've got something coming up that you just totally don't expect.' Leola paused. 'I'm feeling that … what you think now is the situation – money – well, that isn't really going to be what you end up focused on.'

Skipping over two, Leola tapped the final card, a six of spades. 'That card's actually good, though, where it's at. Whatever's happening to you, even with this here unexpected challenge, you're going to come out of it all right. Keep that in mind, whatever comes up. Because this here last card is telling me that your troubles will pass at the end. I'm thinking there's going to be a journey involved. Six of spades always means movement. Can't tell if it's a real journey or just journeying through life. You're going to need this to succeed …' She pointed to the two of clubs. 'That's an intuition card. Being here in the sixth place, that tells me that intuition is what's going to help you most in dealing with the joker, so don't forget that. Don't rely on what others – what Billy – tells you. Two of clubs says to rely on your own instincts.'

Leola drew in a long breath. Sliding her finger back to the fifth card, the nine of spades, she tapped it softly. 'This nine coming after the joker. Talks of losses; that's not good news. You're going to have worries about what to do with this unexpected challenge. I wish I could say better to you, but the truth is, Dix, you've got a real struggle ahead. Lots of disappointment and opposition in these cards. You're going to have to fight hard to get here …' she said and touched the six of spades again, 'to get to where your sorrows pass.'

Dixie sighed. 'I didn't actually need cards to tell me that.'

Chapter Seven

Opening the side door, Spencer let himself into the barn. In the moments that it took for his eyes to adjust from dazzling sunshine to the daylight darkness inside the building, he stood quietly, deep breathing to release tension, the way his yoga instructor taught him, in order to draw in the peace he sensed in the warm, complex scent of horses and molasses-coated feed mingled with straw, wood and the ever-present pine-and-sagebrush tang of the mountains.

Beyond came the quiet rustling of the animal in his stall. Spencer approached. The horse lifted his head.

'Hey, Ranger. How you doing?' Spencer held his hand out flat to show the mint candies.

The horse's ears twitched forward. Crossing the stall, he reached out and delicately picked the mints from Spencer's palm.

The door at the other end of the barn slid open and Guff entered. 'Morning, Mr Scott. I was just coming to saddle him for you.'

No screenwriter could have invented Guff. He didn't look like a cowboy, more like a casting reject for a mall Santa Claus. Not that he was fat exactly, but a fair bit of extra weight hung over Guff's belt. Short and bald except for white tufts near his ears, all he was missing in the Santa Claus department was a white beard. That, and decent skin. He had some condition, probably from the sun, that left his complexion a scaly assortment of sunset colours. None of this slowed Guff down any, however, as despite being seventy-two, and looking every day of it, he could spring up onto the back of a horse with a graceful agility that Spencer's personal trainer and two hours a day at the gym had yet to give him.

Horses were what it was all about for Guff. He wasn't a horse whisperer exactly. Even Spencer knew that horse whispering was probably just a romantic idea invented for the movies. What Guff had was a grittier, more obsessive connection with the animal that meant he really couldn't think, talk or even live with anything else but horses. In fact, that was how Spencer had acquired him. He had come with Red Ranger.

This had seemed hysterically funny to Spencer at the time – that a man should belong to a horse and be sold right along with it, because that's pretty much how it happened. In LA, he had often told this story as entertainment to illustrate what a curious world Montana was. But then Ranger wasn't just any horse. He was the first quarter horse to take all three top cutting prizes and achieve National Cutting Horse Association Champion on his first year out, and Guff was his trainer, his rider, his carer and everything else to Ranger except his owner.

When Spencer had first decided he wanted to buy a horse, horses were just horses to him. He had never heard of 'cutters' – horses that were able to 'cut' a single cow out of a herd of cattle – nor the highly competitive world cutters belonged to. The first time one of the locals had taken him to a cutting championship, it was as if Spencer had happened across a secret society, what with the elaborate rules, the special clothes, the almost holy devotion to the horses. Spencer couldn't quite get into it, but he had always appreciated quality and he liked owning the best. At $65,000 Red Ranger was just that. Guff had been a bonus. He was insanely devoted to the horse and he instinctively knew what he should be doing to keep both the animal and Spencer happy. He knew, for example, to 'run Ranger off' in the mornings, as he called it. Spencer wasn't an experienced horseman. He'd hardly ever been on a horse before buying the ranch, and he didn't have the time to acquire such skills. Guff understood this. He knew Ranger was 'too fresh' at the start of the day for Spencer to control, so he always took the horse out first thing so that if Spencer felt like riding later on, Ranger would be quiet enough. Spencer never had to tell him what to do. Nor did Spencer have to tell him to stay down in the barns and not come up to the house asking for coffee or expecting to be a part of what was going on there, like some of the other local help had. When Spencer stayed at the ranch, Guff always kept to himself, except when horses were needed, and even then he was good about not talking or making too much eye contact with Spencer or his friends, which was important. The whole point of getting away from LA was to not be stared at. Spencer liked that Guff just knew all this stuff naturally.

Spencer stroked the horse's neck, ruffling up under the mane.

'We been out along the ridge,' Guff said as he pulled the saddle blanket from where it had been draped over the side of the stall. He lofted it up on to the horse's back. 'Up over the top and down that draw where all the aspen are, all the way down to that slough at the bottom, Ranger and me, we seen a moose and her calf this morning. It's pretty new.'

'I'd like to see that,' Spencer replied. He walked with Guff as he led Ranger out into the corral. 'And listen, if you see the boy … I'm *trying* to get him outside. He ought to be enjoying this place, not stuck inside with a bunch of computer games. If you see him, could you spend some time with him?'

When Spencer returned to the house after his ride, the kid was in the screening room. Laid out flat in one of the loungers, he was watching an ancient Vin Diesel movie. The volume was turned so high that Spencer had identified the film before he'd even entered the house.

When Spencer grabbed the control for the metal blinds and pressed it, allowing blindingly brilliant sunshine to stream in, the kid screeched like a vampire.

'It's eleven o'clock in the morning, for God's sake.'

'Fuck off.'

'I don't want you sitting around indoors every day, all day. Go outside.' Spencer turned off the television.

'Fuck *off*!' the kid cried and leaped from the lounger. Clutching the remote so that Spencer couldn't take it, he went over and turned the TV back on.

Not wanting the little bastard to wreck the mellowness of his morning ride, Spencer gave in. If he wanted to rot his brain, so be it.

Spencer turned and nearly ran into Sidonie in the doorway, her arms clutched around a small stack of scripts.

'As soon as I've put these away, I'm going in the kitchen to make some cookies,' she said to the boy. 'Do you want to help me?'

'Leave him alone,' Spencer said. 'He's being a little fucker.'

'He's bored, Spence. We can't leave him doing nothing all the time.'

'Sidonie, there's a whole world of things out there for him to do, if he'd just get off his fat little ass and go do them. Don't pander to him.'

'But it can't be very nice here. There aren't any other kids around. He doesn't know anybody. And I don't mind doing things with him.'

'You *guys*. I'm right here. Why do you stand there talking like I can't hear you?' the boy said.

'Tennesee, would you like to come make some cookies with me?'

'"Tennesee, would you like to come make some cookies with me?"' the boy mimicked back sarcastically.

'See?' Spencer replied. 'What's the point of being nice to him? He's got his mother's genes.'

Sidonie could never deal with conflict. No matter how much you pointed out the contrary, the world was all bunnies and rainbows to her, so she kept on with the Care Bear routine. 'I'm making three-kinds-of-ginger cookies. My grandma's special recipe. I'll show you how to make really cool gingerbread men out of them. Come on. It might be fun.'

'Quit acting like you think you're my mom.'

'I don't think I'm your mom,' Sidonie said. 'I'm just saying it might be fun to do.'

'Why would I want to do anything with you? You think you're so cool, but really you're nothing but my dad's latest fuck,' the boy replied and flipped her the finger.

'Hey!' Spencer said sharply. 'I'm not having you talk to her like that.'

'You mean I'm not allowed to tell the truth?' the kid said, widening his eyes in fake innocence.

Spencer came back into the room. 'Apologize.'

The boy sprawled nonchalantly over the lounger like a basking lizard.

'I said, apologize.'

No response.

Spencer crossed over and pushed the lounger sharply into the upright position, knocking the boy forward. 'Go to your room then. Right now.'

The boy held out his hand. 'You gonna give me the money for a ticket? Because my room's in LA.'

'Get your ass out of that chair. *Now.*'

The boy just sat.

Spencer grabbed hold of the kid's T-shirt and yanked him up to his feet. 'You fucking well do what I say.'

For all the stage-fighting Spencer had done in his career, this was the first time he'd had to fight with someone for real, and a fight it turned out to be. The boy refused to do anything he was told and Spencer had had enough. He would not take no. There was no alternative to physically forcing him into obeying.

When he grabbed Tennesee, Spencer had assumed all the time he had to devote to the gym in order to keep his six-pack would give him the advantage over a fat nine-year-old, but the kid had insane strength and no concept of fair fighting. He gripped on to door jambs, slid on rugs, squirmed, snarled and screamed. God almighty, did he scream; '*I hate you! I hate you! I hate you!*' the whole time, at the decibel level of a death-metal concert. I hate you too, Spencer was thinking, but he hated Phoebe even more for managing to ruin Montana by sending the kid up. She needed serious paying back for this.

At last Spencer managed to get the kid down the hall and into his room. Slamming the door shut, he held the handle to keep it closed.

'I'm not staying in here!' the kid shouted.

'Indeed, you are,' Spencer shouted back. He could hear the kid trashing the room. 'And you're going to fucking pay for everything you break.'

'I HATE you!' the kid howled through the door. 'I won't stay here. I'm going to run away from here and never come back.'

'Good!' Spencer said, still hanging on to the doorknob.

'I will! I'm not just saying it.'

'Good. You do that then. See how much it bothers me.'

Chapter Eight

It was just after five thirty when Dixie got home. Billy wasn't there. She had no idea where he was or what he was doing. Truth was, she didn't really care. The previous night's casserole was still in the fridge. That would have to be good enough, if Billy wanted something to eat. Popping open a can of beer, Dixie turned the TV on and flopped down on the sofa.

About eight in the evening the backdoor banged and there was Billy with a bag of groceries and the biggest, stupidest grin across his face. He plopped the bag down on the kitchen table.

'You look in there,' he said gleefully, 'and you're going to find two of the best T-bone steaks they had at the store!'

'What's going on?' Dixie asked suspiciously. 'We can't afford hamburger, much less T-bones.'

'This here's our celebrating meal.'

'Celebrating what? Being in the poorhouse?'

'What would you say if I tell you that me and you are going to be millionaires pretty soon?'

'I'd say go put your head under that faucet, 'cause clearly the heat's done in what little brain you got.'

He grinned good-naturedly. 'Nope. Just your Billy's taking care of things for you. We won't have to worry about that money for the funeral any more. You cook us them steaks and then after dinner, I'll show you.'

'Show me what?'

'Show you how we're gonna be millionaires.'

'What fool thing you done now, Billy?'

'You fix us them steaks first and then I'll show you.'

Dixie turned uneasily away and took the frying pan out from under the stove. 'I'm not going to be able to enjoy the steak if I'm worrying the whole time. I know you, Billy. So tell me what you done. Sold something? What? It wasn't the truck, was it?' She felt alarm at the thought. 'Oh gosh, please tell me it's not the truck.'

'Truck's right out in the garage. How would I have gotten home, silly, if I'd sold the truck?'

A long moment's silence followed as Dixie stood, frying pan in hand, and stared him down.

Billy's goofy smile started to slip. 'Why do you always got to ruin things with your worrying, Dix? Why can't you just be happy for once? Has that always got to be too much to ask of you?'

'Billy, tell me what you've done.'

He eyed her.

She eyed him back.

'Here's me, trying to give you a good surprise,' he muttered.

'I'll cook the steaks. I promise,' Dixie said. 'But first just tell me what's going on.'

A dramatic sigh and then he relented. 'OK, well, come out to the garage then, because I got it in the toolbox.'

Curious, Dixie followed him.

The garage door had been put down, which was maybe only the third time it had been lowered since they'd moved into the house. It took Billy a moment of fumbling to find the light switch, then he had to get out the little stepladder so that Dixie could climb up into the flatbed of the pick-up from the side, because with the garage door closed, there wasn't enough room to let down the tailgate. Just behind the cab was a built-in toolbox where Billy usually stored his gear, but the gear was lying out all over the open flatbed. Once they were both up in the back, Billy unlocked the toolbox and lifted the lid. Inside was a little boy, maybe seven or eight, bound up with duct tape, a dirty rag tied over his eyes.

Dixie yelped with shock.

Billy grinned. 'Know who that is? It's Spencer Scott's son.'

Chapter Nine

Spencer spent most of the afternoon shut in his study, doing things on the internet. Just after six, he switched the computer off and that was the first time he noticed how quiet the house was. None of the usual squealing tyres, gunfire or explosions.

Coming through the French doors into the hallway, Spencer went to the door of the screening room and looked in. Nothing there but the boy's mess. Dirty plates, a Coke can on its side, countless open DVD cases. This annoyed Spencer. He liked things orderly. Everything in its place and all that. Here was one more important reason the kid shouldn't be in Montana. He messed up everything he touched. Spencer felt just about as much annoyance with Sidonie, however, because she knew how much clutter upset him.

Sidonie's official title was 'personal assistant'. PA. A good title, that, Spencer thought, because it covered everything. *Including* making sure the place was tidy. Sidonie *knew* how he felt about things like this. That's why she had the frigging job. So where was she? Why hadn't she done it?

Crossly, Spencer stomped down the hall and through the kitchen to the small room at the back of the house which Sidonie used as an office. She was in there, sitting behind the desk piled high with scripts. She looked up.

Sidonie was wearing her glasses, those black-rimmed ones that made her look like a school teacher. Her long blonde hair was bound up so casually that more tousled strands had escaped than were held in. She wore a plain black tank top with no bra and the shortest of short-shorts, showing off tanned legs as long as the Missouri River. It was her bare feet, however, that turned Spencer on. He loved clean, youthful feet. He loved it too when she dressed like that, all fresh and natural, but with just the slightest hint of streetwalker.

Indeed, this intuitive sexiness was what got Sidonie here at all. When Spencer had first met her, she was just another of the flawlessly beautiful girls who worked on movie sets while waiting to get famous. He was down in Mexico at the time filming *Intimations*, and Sidonie was assistant to the assistant make-up artist or something equally insignificant. She was drop-dead gorgeous, but then they all were, their plastic-surgery-and-orthodontics perfection so commonplace that Spencer seldom registered girls' actual faces. He wouldn't have been aware of Sidonie either, except that whenever she leaned over to wipe the make-up from his face, he noticed perspiration on her skin. It was never wet or runny, just a dewiness, as if someone had misted her, and it was always pristine. Unwiped, unsmeared, untouched. Mixed in with the usual young woman's scent of shower gel and shampoo, this faint musky smell always gave him the sense that she was up for it. Spencer would get hard just sitting there in the make-up chair.

And she *was* up for it. Sidonie not only bathed him in her sexy smell as she worked, but she let him touch her. Just enough for him to know she liked it. Just enough to make him slip her the key to his trailer.

Not that Spencer didn't slip most of the girls his key at one point or another. That was the culture of the movie set, all these luscious ripe things trading the currency of desire to buy their dreams. Sidonie could have been just one more faceless fuck, except that she proved to be that little bit more aware than the other girls. She didn't just fuck. She observed. She paid attention. So afterwards, she would bring him coffee. That's what impressed him. A good lay and then she got him coffee without his asking for it. And she remembered what kind of coffee he liked and exactly how he liked it.

He hadn't expected it to turn into anything more. He wasn't doing relationships these days. After the fiasco with Phoebe, Spencer had got the snip, so he knew for certain that would never be an issue again. Even so, Phoebe had left him paranoid. You just couldn't trust people.

Plus, Sidonie wasn't all sunshine and flowers. When he'd first met her, she had a coke habit that must have kept half of Columbia in riches and a boyfriend named Raoul next to whom a junkyard dog would look civilized. And she was stupid. Spencer had found that was generally true of all really beautiful girls. God obviously couldn't give any one person everything. So, if you got the to-die-for bone structure and lips like swollen labia, you also got the brain that thought Shakespeare was the name of a porn star. Sidonie's saving grace was that she knew she was stupid, so she didn't try to bullshit about having Harvard degrees; and she'd already learned that the best way to hide stupidity was to keep your trap closed. After his experiences with Kathryn and Phoebe, Spencer was more than happy to trade intelligence in a woman for one who knew when to shut up.

He got so used to being with Sidonie in Mexico that when he came back to LA, he missed her. At first he thought it was just not having the routine he was used to, but when he woke in the night, it was her scent he longed for. He couldn't stop himself wondering where she was, or worrying who else might be having her.

It took a bit of work to track her down. By the time he found her, Sidonie was in Croatia, working on Matt Damon's set. Jealousy influenced Spencer's decision to fly her back first class, although he never told her that.

Still, it was just a job he was offering her. Spencer was very clear about that right from the beginning, because he didn't want Sidonie to have any misconception. A *job*, not a relationship. Personal assistant. Very personal, yes, but she was still simply an employee. With perks. So, yes to travelling with him. Yes to staying in his house. Yes to sex. No to the red carpet. No to eating out in restaurants with him. No to being seen anywhere in public that the media might interpret as a date. Spencer had his lawyer draw up a contract spelling it all out so that Sidonie would always know exactly where she stood.

Sidonie took it all in her stride. They'd been together two years now, and if she'd wanted something different from her life, it never showed. Spencer admired her for this. While Sidonie might not be book smart, she was canny. Most of the beautiful girls who came to Hollywood ended up typists or druggies or working on the street. Sidonie had about her a natural shrewdness. She recognized a good deal when it came along.

'Where's the kid at?' Spencer asked.

Sidonie had been reading through scripts Spencer's agent had sent over to see if any of them were worth Spencer's consideration, and she was completely barricaded in by the stacks. Bleary-eyed, she sat back in her chair, stretched to ease tight muscles and pushed the glasses up on her head. 'I don't know,' she said. 'I've been in here since before three.'

'He's left a mess in the screening room,' Spencer said. 'Clean it up. It looks like a pigsty.'

She rose.

Could it be that the boy had actually taken his advice and gone outside? Spencer went into the kitchen and then out on to the deck. The barn wasn't visible from the house because of the pine trees, but he gazed in that direction anyway.

It was a hot day. The mountains blocked the sun by that late point in the afternoon, leaving the deck in a warm, only-just-comfortable shade. The heavy scent of the pines wafted over Spencer as he stood. Focusing his mind in the way he'd learned to do from his meditation teacher, Spencer let the trees fill his senses. First the smell, then the sound of them. They were very still because of the heat, so he listened for the sound of birds and pine squirrels instead. He turned his attention back to the scent, trying to draw it in enough to get a taste of it, and the taste was there. Only very, very slightly but he could indeed sense the pines, pitchy and acrid, on his tongue.

He should meditate. Right then and there on the deck. It would be such a good place and Spencer kept meaning to establish a meditation practice. Meditation was so good for you, doing all those things like making you compassionate and lowering your blood pressure. If only it wasn't so *boring* …

He lowered himself into a lotus position. His teacher in LA had complimented him on his flexibility and it was true. At forty-eight he could still do a full lotus perfectly. Spencer spent several minutes getting settled. Into the lotus. Out of the lotus. Back into the lotus. It was quite hard to imagine sitting for half an hour in such a position. All right for people who were malnourished anyway and would be lucky to see forty-five, but not so great for someone needing his joints to last eighty years. Spencer settled for just crossing his legs. Forefingers to thumbs, he rested his hands on his knees and exhaled deeply three times to release tension. Then he started into following his breathing in and out. Perfection, Spencer was thinking. Sitting here on the deck in the warm shade, the scent and sounds of the Montana mountains wafting over him. What could be more peaceful than this?

'Have you found him yet?' Sidonie asked when Spencer came back into the kitchen.

For just a split second Spencer wondered who 'he' was. Pleased with himself for having managed to spend a good twenty minutes properly meditating, Spencer had forgotten about the boy.

'Maybe he's with Guff,' Sidonie said. 'Could you ring the bell? I've already started dinner. By the time he gets here and washes up, we'll be ready to eat.'

A wrought-iron triangle of the sort used on chuck wagons in the old West hung off the edge of the deck. Spencer took down the iron striker and clanged the triangle noisily. It was a rewarding activity. Like banging pot lids together when you were a child. He clanged it again. It was an effective means of communication too. You could hear it halfway across the valley.

For several moments Spencer waited on the deck to see the boy come up the path from the barn. When no one appeared, he clanged the triangle a third time, then he went back into the house. Sidonie was taking chicken kebabs out from the broiler. She spooned a sticky orange Chinese-influenced sauce over them.

The boy still didn't show up.

'Let's eat,' Spencer said. 'It's going to get cold otherwise.'

Sidonie's brow furrowed. 'Don't you think we should see where he is first?'

'You really shouldn't do that, Sidonie,' Spencer replied and gestured at her face. 'Frown like that. You're what? Twenty-six?'

'Twenty-five.'

'You're already getting lines on your forehead from doing that and you're young. You want to stop. It's just a mannerism.'

'About Tennesee ...'

'Botox would sort it out. Dr Margolis. I've really liked what he's done for me. Right up here, see? Just a little Botox right here' – Spencer pointed alongside his eye – 'and it's completely removed any hint of crows' feet. Make an appointment next time we're in LA.'

Sidonie looked at him.

Spencer looked back.

'About Tennesee?' she said. 'Don't you think we should find him before we eat?'

'No,' Spencer said with finality and sat down at the table. 'He knows how to tell time. It'll serve him right, because he's just doing it to be annoying. Besides, it won't hurt the little porker to miss a meal anyhow.'

By seven o'clock Spencer was irritated. He knew what was going on. Under his laconic exterior, Guff was a marshmallow, particularly when it came to stray animals. How many damned cats did he have living down there with him now? The boy would have shown up with his sob story: *Oh poor me, having to be here where I don't want to, having nothing to do*, and Guff would have gone all gooey and grandpa-ish.

'Go down to the bunkhouse and tell Guff we can't have this,' he said to Sidonie. 'If the kid thinks he can move in down there, he's got another think coming.'

Half an hour later, Sidonie was back. 'Guff says he hasn't seen Tennesee at all today,' she said, still slightly out of breath from the climb up the path from the barn.

A small, frozen moment followed when, caught off guard by that information, Spencer had no idea what to think next. 'Fuck him,' he finally said with weary irritation. 'He's hiding.'

When he went in to search the boy's bedroom, Spencer found the note. *I'm going back to LA. Don't come after me becose you can't make me come back. I hate it here. I hate you. Good by.*

'Oh fuck,' Spencer muttered and stormed out into the hall. 'Look at this.'

Sidonie came over.

'He's fucking run away,' Spencer said. 'The goddamned little turd has fucking picked up and fucking taken off. Just like his motherfucking cunt of a mother would do.'

Spencer wanted to scream with frustration. Here he was in the only place in the whole world where he could have any peace and all he wanted was to be left alone to enjoy the mountains. Was that asking too much of life? Phoebe obviously thought it was. *Why* had she had to send her fucking little bastard here? Why was she so hell-bent on destroying him? He wadded up the damned note and threw it to the floor.

'I think we better call the police,' Sidonie said.

'Shit, *no*.'

She frowned again, as if she wanted to wreck her looks on purpose by doing that all the time. 'Come on. We have to, Spence.'

'The police *here*?' he said crossly. 'Think for two seconds with that pea-sized brain of yours, would you? What kind of police are we going to find in Abundance, Montana, for god's sake? Some fucking little two-bit country copper who doesn't know his gun from his asshole.'

'Yes, but—?'

'If the little turd wants to run away, fucking let him. I don't want him here anyway.'

'Spencer, we can't do that. He's only nine.'

'Yeah, nine going on thirty-nine. And it would fucking well serve Phoebe right to have him turn up on her doorstep, that's what. See how she likes it.'

'Phoebe's in the Virgin Islands, Spencer.'

'Yeah, well, what the fuck do I care?'

'*Spencer.*'

'What the fuck *do* I care, Sidonie? He can stay with the maid when he gets to LA. I never asked that kid to come up here. I never wanted anything to do with him. I don't care what the courts say. He's *not* my responsibility. Even *he* knows that, because he doesn't want to be here any more than I want him.'

Sidonie furrowed her brow more deeply.

'*Stop* doing that with your damned forehead, Sidonie! You look like fucking Mr Toad. I've told you to stop a hundred times now, so stop it. Or you can just go yourself. If you don't respect how I do things, you can get out of here too.'

She clapped a hand over her forehead, as if to smooth it out physically. Tears filled her eyes.

'Oh *shit*,' Spencer said. He sighed. 'Sidonie, listen, calm down. Now listen. We can't get the police involved. The press will find out. God, it would be a nightmare. It would totally destroy this place. The paparazzi would stake it out from here on to forever. We simply can't do that.'

'He's only nine, Spencer. We can't just let him disappear either.'

'Be sensible, Sidonie. He's probably not even off the property. Think about it. How would he leave, even if he wanted to? There's almost two miles of private road. Then you come to River Road and no one drives on that except the local ranchers. It's five more miles before you get to the old highway, and that *is* the old highway. Again, almost no traffic. Then another seven miles before you get to the main highway and five more after that to Abundance. So he'd have to walk almost twenty miles to get to any kind of civilization. He's not going to manage that. Not as fat as he is. And he's not stupid enough to try. He's a smart boy, Sidonie. He's playing us. He'll be hiding somewhere around here, just trying to get the fuck back at me. And I'm not falling for it.

I'm not going to play his fucking little game. If we wait long enough, he will come out.'

'What about coyotes or something?' Sidonie said.

'Don't be blonde. He's not a chihuahua.'

Sidonie kept on with the sad eyes.

'OK, look, here's what I'll do. I'll call Jamieson,' Spencer said. Jamieson was his primary bodyguard in LA, a big burly black dude who looked as if he could bite the balls off a bull. 'In the morning I'll call the security agency and ask them to send a couple more guys with Jamieson. They can do everything the police do and much more quietly.'

'In the morning?' Sidonie asked dubiously.

'Yes, in the morning,' Spencer said decisively and lifted a bottle of Casa Nueva Meritage from the wine rack. 'Now leave me alone.'

Chapter Ten

They always say in stories how folks go speechless with shock. Up to that point it had been just a tired old cliché in Dixie's mind, but really, until it's happened to you, you just never realize what a paralysing experience shock is. Standing in the flatbed of the truck, Dixie stared at the bound-up child, and it was as if the duct tape had fixed her too into motionless silence.

Billy was like a Labrador puppy, bouncing and grinning and waiting for her to get happy. 'That there's our ticket to heaven,' he said.

'To hell, more likely,' she replied when she finally found her voice. 'And jail most certainly. Oh Billy.' Dixie covered her face with one hand and turned away. 'I can't believe this. Dear Jesus, dear, dear Jesus, please make this just a real bad dream.'

'Let me explain my plan.'

'*Plan*? Billy, do you know what you just *done*? This isn't playing. This isn't some game. Do you *understand*?'

Irritably, Billy slammed the toolbox lid down. 'For fuck's sake, Dixie. There's no pleasing you, is there? First you're moaning on and on about me taking the job out at Baker's ranch. And I heard you. So then I go trying hard as I can to set things right, to get Jamie Lee's funeral paid for and get us a decent life, and you're still not happy. Nothing I do is ever good enough for you.' He hopped over the side of the truck and headed back in the house.

'No! Billy, *no*.' Dixie ran after him into the kitchen. 'We can't just leave that kid there, shut up in your toolbox. It's too hot!'

'That's how come I put the truck in the garage, stupid.'

'Billy, the garage is even worse than outdoors. It's like ninety degrees in there and it's all closed up. He'll die.'

'Oh, for Christ's sake. I'll go roll the window down, if that'll make you happier.'

'He's not *in* the cab. He's in the toolbox and you've got tape over his mouth.'

'Would you stop screaming? You want all the neighbours to hear? If you want to get us in trouble, that's the way to do it.' Taking a beer from the fridge, he opened the tab and drained it in loud, thirsty gulps.

'What if that boy's thirsty?' Dixie said in a quieter voice.

Billy crumpled the beer can with one hand and lofted it at her. Dixie didn't flinch when the can bounced off her shoulder and clattered to the linoleum.

'If I knew you were going to act this way, I wouldn't have bothered,' he said sulkily. 'I only did this for you.'

'I certainly didn't ask you to go do something like this, so don't blame me.'

'Well, it's *your* fault. You and all your harping about money all the time. You want me to pay for some goddamned funeral for some fucking bastard who isn't even my kid, and then you think you got the right to tell me how to do it. I'm a cowboy, Dixie. I was a cowboy before you met me; I was a cowboy when you met me, and I'm still a cowboy; so you shouldn't keep thinking I ought to be something different. You should know I need to be my own man.'

'Let him go, Billy. Right now.'

'You had me right up against the wall with all your belly-aching about not having enough for that funeral.'

Lowering her head, Dixie pressed her hands over her ears, then her eyes. 'Please, Billy. I don't care about any of that any more. I don't care if you go cowboying forever. I don't care if we never get the funeral paid off and that funeral man makes me go bankrupt. Just please let that boy go. Now. *Please.*' She pinched the bridge of her nose.

'Oh Jesus. Now you're going to cry again. Jesus H. Christ, Dixie. This whole thing is your fault.'

'I'm *not* crying! I'm just trying to figure out how the heck to get us out of this. You don't got the sense God gave a goose, Billy. You don't even know what you just done. You've *kidnapped* this kid. Oh dear Jesus. You've kidnapped *Spencer Scott's son!*'

'It's not kidnapping. Not really kidnapping,' Billy said and his tone became more conciliatory. His face brightened with the hint of a smile. 'I'm *protecting* him, if you want to know the truth. Because know where I found him? Walking all alone along River Road. That's dangerous there, because there ain't nowhere to walk without being on the road itself. And know what he was trying to do? Hitch a ride. No kidding. To California! He's just a little bugger and there he was with his thumb out. So, see, I'm actually doing Spencer

Scott a big favour here, because some pervert could easily have come along and took his kid.'

'Keeping him safe by putting duct tape around him and throwing him in your toolbox is going to make folks think *you're* the pervert, Billy.'

'I didn't start out putting duct tape on him. First, I was just picking him up to take him somewhere safe, because he's too little to be out wandering around and I reckoned his folks would be worried. I didn't know he was Spencer Scott's son until he told me. The way it all happened, I reckon God sort of planned this for me.'

'I can tell you right now it certainly wasn't God who got into your head in that moment.'

'No, listen to me. Here's how I got it figured. You and me can pack up a few things and say we're going camping. Like we do every summer anyway. No one will think anything of it. We'll go up on Crowheart for a few days till news gets around that he's missing. Then we'll bring him back safe and explain how we found him and were protecting him. We'll ask for just a little money. For taking care of him.'

'*That* makes it kidnapping, Billy.'

'No, it doesn't. Because we didn't set out to do it. Kidnapping means that you planned it all and you *meant* to do it and you're holding the kid for ransom. We're just caring for him and keeping him safe. It's only fair we get paid for doing that.'

'And what happens when this kid tells people you tied him up with duct tape and shut him up in your toolbox? Because folks aren't going to interpret that as "caring for him".'

'I'll say sorry to him once we're up in the mountains. I'll explain to him how important it was for me to keep him safe from what could have happened to him. That's true, Dix. I mean, Jesus, all them perverts you hear about doing horrible, disgusting things with little kids. Even murdering them. A pervert could easily have been the one to find him walking along all by himself like that, and then where would he be? We're doing a *good* thing here. And then just asking a little money for our trouble.'

Dixie shook her head wearily. 'Billy, if your brain was in a bird's head, it'd fly backwards.'

Dixie cooked the steaks, because there wasn't going to be any way of keeping Billy from that steak dinner, but she couldn't get her mind off the boy. Every ten minutes or so, she went out and lifted the lid of the toolbox and poked him to make sure he was still alive. Because of the tape over his mouth, he couldn't make much noise, so in the end she decided it was safe to leave the toolbox lid up and the door into the house open in an effort to keep the garage ventilated, but still she worried about him.

Billy demolished his steak with gusto and knocked back a second beer. 'You're not going to waste all that, are you?' he asked, pointing at Dixie's plate of untouched food.

'Go ahead.'

Eagerly he pulled the plate over and gobbled down the second steak.

Billy was like a kid let out of school for all his excitement in getting the camping stuff up from the basement. Probably all he was thinking about was what a great excuse to spend time in the mountains this was. They hadn't been up at all this summer because Jamie Lee had needed so much doctoring at the end, and Billy was really missing the wilderness. Probably he wasn't thinking about the boy at all.

Dixie, on the other hand, could think of nothing else. Again and again she went out to check on him.

'Billy?'

He was removing his .22 from the gun cabinet. 'Hmm?'

'He's pooped his pants.'

Using one of Jamie Lee's old muslin diapers, Billy lovingly wiped the gun down. He didn't reply.

'Should I bring him in the house?' Dixie asked.

'What for?'

'Well, to clean him up …'

'Nah, leave him be. He'll be all right.'

'You haven't been out to smell the garage.'

'Well, he's going to crap, isn't he? We can't take him out every time he needs to go. Put some newspapers under him and I can just hose the toolbox out when we're done.'

Crossing over to the gun cabinet where Billy was standing, Dixie snatched the gun cloth out of his hand. 'Billy, listen to me. He's a little boy, not some animal. We can't leave him lying in his own poop.'

'We're only talking about till we get into the mountains. It won't hurt him for that long.'

'Billy!'

'Jesus, Dix, would you give me that cloth back so that I can finish?'

She clutched the cloth more tightly.

'Well, fuck,' he said in frustration. 'Do what you want then.'

* * *

Dixie raised the lid of the toolbox. The heat and confinement had made the smell so overpowering that she had to step back a moment to keep from retching. When she finally found the courage to touch the boy, he jerked away from her and strained against the duct-tape binding before going still again.

'I'm not going to hurt you.' She laid a tentative hand on his head. 'You've done a stinky in your pants, so I'm going to take you inside and clean you up.'

There was no response, no movement, nothing. Scared he might have passed out, Dixie leaned over him. 'Can you hear me all right?' she asked.

The boy burst back to life. Startled, she jerked back.

The duct tape and car rag over his face made it hard to tell what age he was, curled up in the toolbox like that. Dixie tried to get her arms under him. He was pudgy. Not obese. More what Mama would call 'solidly built', but it was a struggle to lift him. Dixie finally managed to clear the rim of the toolbox.

As soon as she did, the boy began to writhe. Dixie did her best to keep hold of him, but he was too big and, because of the poop, too slippery. He fell with a thud on to the metal flatbed of the truck.

Dixie clamped a hand over her mouth to keep herself from yelping. The boy started to make a snorting-in-and-out noise through the tape.

'Listen, don't fight me, OK?' she said and knelt down beside him. 'I'm not going to hurt you. I'm just going to take you in and clean you up. OK?'

She'd thought at first that the noise was the boy trying to cry, but Dixie realized then it was a bull snort, full of rage.

When she went to pick him up again, he exploded at her touch, kicking out as viciously as his bound legs would let him.

Dixie darted into the house. 'Billy? Billy, you got to come help me,' she cried.

Groaning with annoyance, Billy followed her. 'Fuck, Dixie. Why couldn't you leave well enough alone?'

Dixie climbed into the back of the truck. Billy hopped in with one easy motion. 'Hey, kid. Stop it,' he said.

At the sound of Billy's voice, the boy struggled even more fiercely against the duct-tape bindings. Billy kicked him. Hard. Then again. Then a third time.

'*Don't*. You're going to kill him!'

Without so much as a second's hesitation, Billy turned and grabbed the front of Dixie's blouse. He pulled her right up close to his face. 'You shut up. It's all your fault that we're in this mess to start with, so if you don't want to feel my boot next, you shut your trap. I mean it, Dixie. I'm pissed off. I won't take no more fucking around. You understand?'

Dixie nodded meekly.

Billy let go of her. Kneeling, he bent down close to the boy's head. 'So, you want to fight me some more, kid?'

The boy whimpered.

'Good thinking.' Then he picked the boy up by the waistband of his shorts, carried him inside and dumped him unceremoniously on the bathroom floor. Without saying anything to Dixie, he went back out into the living room.

Dixie softly shut the bathroom door. The boy, lying in an ungainly heap on the floor, made squeaky little noises through the tape, like the mewing of a newborn kitten.

Tentatively Dixie touched his head. His hair was an uninteresting birdy-coloured brown, a bit wavy and flowing down over his shoulders like girls' hair. Boys around Abundance would have laughed so hard at long hair like that. Dixie felt pity for him. She hated it when parents didn't notice things that made their kids look weird to other kids, when they just left them to get on with being teased or left out. Gently she tried to smooth his hair back and soothe his crying but it wasn't really possible because of all the binding.

The boy kept making creepy noises. His nose was congested from the crying and so there were all sorts of gurgles and strangulated sounds that worried Dixie.

'Listen, I'm going to take that tape off your mouth, because I don't think that's good for you at all. But you got to be nice, OK? You got to not yell or anything, because if you do, my man's going to come back and beat the crap out of you again. You understand?' She carefully peeled back the tape. In the process the car rag came off his face as well, giving her a first proper look at him, but there was no time to think about that, because the boy was coughing and gagging. Dixie thumped his back to help knock the breath back into him. The second he managed to draw a decent breath, he screamed blue murder.

Billy flung the bathroom door open. 'What the *hell* are you doing in here?' he shouted. The boy stopped screaming immediately, but it was too late. Billy hauled off and kicked him so hard that he slid right across the floor and up against the bathtub. He howled.

Grabbing the car cloth, Billy whipped it around his wrist to make a gag out of it. Terrified the boy sucked in his pain and the small room fell into a sudden, jarring silence. Billy knelt and tied the cloth firmly around the boy's mouth.

'What the fuck were you thinking taking the tape off his mouth? And that off his eyes?' Billy asked. 'He's seen us now. He can identify us.'

'I was worried he was going to smother.'

'Yeah, well, if anything goes the fuck wrong here, it wasn't me who let him see stuff. And *you*,' Billy said, looking at the boy, 'if you want to stay alive, you behave yourself, understand? Because there's a gun out there in the other room and my finger here is just itching to use it on a little shit like you.' He twitched his trigger finger menacingly at the boy. Then he turned and stalked out, slamming the door behind him.

The boy was crying through his gag again, snot and tears making the whole of his face wet.

'I'm sorry Billy done that to you,' Dixie said, kneeling beside the boy. 'He's not really a bad man, but it's important you do as he says, 'cause he can hurt when he wants to.'

Taking her nail scissors out of her make-up case, she started to cut through the tape binding the boy's legs. The boy jerked away when the metal touched his skin.

'We got to get you cleaned up. You don't want to stay all poopy like this. So hold still. I don't want to cut you.'

Dixie paused a moment to figure how to do things. She sure didn't want the boy saying she'd been touching his privates, but then how else did you clean up a mess like this?

'You understand why I'm doing this?' she said, as she began to ease his shorts off. 'You're all poopy and it'll make you sore. My own little boy, if you left him even the shortest time without changing a dirty diaper when it was hot like this, he always got the worst rash and it just made him miserable. We don't want that happening to you, do we? So I'm going to clean you up, but that's all I'm doing. Nothing more.'

Dixie grimaced as she finally got his underpants off. Straight into the garbage with those. She ran the sink full of warm water and got out a washcloth. 'You done just like cows do, you know that? When cows get scared, the poop just runs right out of them.'

The boy lay tearfully on the bathroom floor. He didn't struggle any more. Indeed, the fight seemed to have gone right out of him.

'I'm sorry you been treated like this,' Dixie said softly. 'I really am.'

Carefully she washed him. His pecker was absolutely tiny. He'd been circumcised and, honestly, what was left wasn't much bigger than a sticky-out belly button. Even at nine months Jamie Lee had had more of a pecker on him. It occurred to Dixie to wonder about Spencer Scott. Wouldn't that be funny? All those movie-star looks and nothing but a two-inch prick?

Dixie rose and took a hand towel from the cupboard. She folded it into a diaper. 'Now, this ain't because you're a baby or anything,' she said gently. 'It's just that we might not be getting you to the bathroom when you need it. If I can, I'll get Billy to stop at the supermarket and we'll get some of those big-boy diapers because they won't be so messy, but this will have to do for now.'

She cut the legs off an old pair of Billy's pyjama bottoms and pulled them up over the makeshift diaper. Then came the duct tape to bind his legs back together again. Large purple bruises were forming where Billy had kicked him. Dixie tried not to think too much about it. No point dwelling on what you couldn't change. Leaning forward, she caressed the boy's head. 'I'm sorry this has been hard on you. But don't be scared. Long as you're a good boy, you'll be back with your daddy soon enough.'

Chapter Eleven

Billy had the camping gear already packed into the pick-up when Dixie finished cleaning the boy. Grabbing the kid like he was a bag of dog food, Billy carried him out to the garage and thumped him into the toolbox; then he returned to the house, popped open a beer and sat down in front of the TV.

'What're you doing?' Dixie asked.

'I want to watch the baseball first.' He was settling back into the lounger like it was just an ordinary night. 'Get me another beer, would you? Because this is definitely chugging weather.'

How could Billy be like this? He had just packed some kidnapped kid into the truck in a hell-hot garage, and he was going to sit around drinking beer and watching base-ball? Holy Jesus. All Dixie could think about was phoning Leola and telling her that however stupid she'd said Billy was in the past, Dixie forgave her, because she was right.

'Maybe not a good idea to drink too much when you're going to have to be driving later,' she ventured.

Billy looked over. 'Have a beer yourself, because listen, you got to just relax. OK? I have everything under control.'

That was what worried Dixie so much.

'You want something to stay busy with?' he asked. 'Then call up your mama. Tell her you and me are going to have some time off camping.'

'Billy, I can't talk to Mama. She'll know I'm lying straightaway.'

'It ain't lying, Dix, to say you're going camping, because that's exactly what we're going to do. And your mama ain't going to ask you if you're going with Spencer Scott's son. So there's no lying to do. Just go phone her. Otherwise, she'll worry where you're at.'

Sighing, Dixie left him to his beer and TV. She went out to the garage and opened the lid on the toolbox to let the air circulate better. It was still stiflingly hot in there, even if she left the kitchen door open. Finally she went and got the fan from the bedroom and set it up so that it blew into the toolbox.

Her hands shook. It had been hard to get the fan to balance on the side of the truck in a position that reached the inside of the toolbox. The boy lay motionless throughout. Only his eyes followed her.

The way Billy reasoned, what he was doing made sense. He was like Daddy in that respect, only ever seeing his own version of the world. Mama always said you just had to love men. You couldn't expect to understand what they were thinking, because men thought differently. It was a woman's job to love them anyway, no matter what. And that's what Mama did. She always stood by Daddy. She'd say, 'Daddy's only upset because of you.' Or, 'He doesn't mean what he does to hurt. You just got to understand him.' That was Mama's credo. *You just got to understand him.* Which, of course, was the complete opposite to what she said about how you couldn't expect to understand men. This inconsistency never seemed to bother her.

'Just a camping trip, Mama. Billy and me, we decided to get away for a few days. Maybe longer, I don't know … depends …

'No, *not* depending on Billy ever keeping a job,' Dixie said in frustration. 'Depending how good the mountains are at healing, Mama. Ain't everything about Billy not being able to keep a job. It's me this time. *I* need the mountains. Folks are expecting me to get over Jamie Lee too quick. Just doesn't happen like that, Mama. He was my little baby.

'No,' Dixie said. 'He didn't take the sawmill job. Been branding instead. Up at Baker's ranch and they finished already. So he's got the time free to go camping.

'Yeah, I know. I wish he'd taken the sawmill job too. Yeah, Mama, I know cowboying's no kind of living, but Billy's got his own mind. Yeah. Yeah. I wish he was different too, but that's how God made him.

'I know this isn't much notice, Mama. I'm sorry you feel I'm not talking to you as much as I should. Yes, I know you would have made us potato salad. I *do* love your potato salad. I do, Mama. I wasn't trying to imply I don't want things from you. I'm not meaning to sound ungrateful for the things you do.

'No, camping was Billy's idea, but he was thinking of me. It's a good idea, Mama. I need to be up there. I really, really do. I just need to get my head straight after Jamie Lee. So Billy's thinking of me. He's thinking of me real good.

'Just up in the mountains. We haven't decided where yet. Maybe up by that little lake we found last summer near the tree line. We caught a good mess of fish up there. And it was pretty.

'No. No … No, I understand. Things never do turn out like you think.'

They didn't leave until after ten thirty, mostly because that's when Billy's baseball game finished on TV. Dixie was numb by then. She'd paced continuously between the house and the garage, checking on the boy. He'd gone very quiet since Billy had put him back into the toolbox. At first he'd look at her when she peered in, going all cow-eyed each time she leaned close, but after a while he lay inert. Worried that even with the fan he was getting too hot, Dixie began putting a cool cloth on his forehead.

Finally Billy was ready. He turned off the TV, locked the front door, locked the door between the kitchen and the garage, closed the toolbox lid and opened the garage door. Silently Dixie got into the trunk and backed it out so he could shut the garage door again. Then she slid over into the passenger's seat. Neither of them said a word.

It was dark by then, but still hot. Dixie rolled down the car window. The air was soft, almost silky in the way it slid over her skin. Human smells still hung heavily over the town: car fumes, the railroad yard, the feed silo, lingering smoke from the sawmill. These would slowly disperse during the dark hours. By dawn there would be nothing but the primeval scent of rocks and pine.

Billy turned down on to Clark Street, which bypassed the main part of town and ran instead through the oldest part of

Abundance. There was almost nothing left of the old town these days, just overgrown tangles of grass creating indistinct lumps from the foundations. One or two ghostly shells remained of what had once been fancy houses with porches and intricate gingerbread decoration. Dixie looked at them through the darkness. There were no streetlights down in this part of town and no moon was in the sky. Their outlines were still easily discernible, in that clear-but-shadowy way that dreams are when you first wake up.

The street petered out into a gravel road heading for the river and the Old Bridge. Its proper name was Cavett's Bridge after the man who owned the Lion Mountain mine. Built of wood and steel, it had been a marvel of engineering in 1907 when it became the first proper bridge to span the river directly from the town and make the nearby mountains accessible to wagons and eventually cars. Cavett's Bridge had remained the only crossing until Simpson's Bridge was built during the Great Depression as part of the government's effort to get people back to work. Eventually Simpson's Bridge had been bypassed too when the new highway was built. These days, ordinary steel-and-concrete bridges went back and forth over the river with such ease that most folks had forgotten how formidable the water used to be.

The Old Bridge had been declared unsafe way back in the 1980s and ought to have been taken down, except that the historical society in Helena got the idea of preserving it. All this meant was that they put a sign up saying the bridge could only take one car at a time and you had to use it at your own risk. If Dixie had had her way, she never would take that risk. The Old Bridge made a horrible clatter when-ever you drove over it, as if all its wooden planks were coming apart that instant, and you could feel them individually moving right through the floor of the car. She didn't dare to drive over it herself, because she could never keep from squeezing her eyes shut in anticipation of being pitched into the wild water below. Billy, however, never used any other bridge, if he could help it. It was the fastest way up into the mountains and he knew all the back roads from there by heart and that was all that mattered to him.

Once the river was behind them, the road went sharply uphill for a mile or so until it hit a higher, flatter area that led into the foothills of Crowheart. In ancient times, the mountain had been a volcano and there were still slides of lava rock visible on some of the hills. Juniper grew well in these conditions and cattle didn't seem to eat them, so they were dotted generously over the landscape. Amidst them, almost indistinguishable in the dark, were mine tailings, piled up here and there like oversized gopher hills.

'Where we going?' Dixie asked softly into the darkness.

'I was thinking Aspen Gulch up behind the old Inverurie mine,' Billy replied.

'That's not very far. Don't you think it would be safer further up?'

'Nah. See, you're still thinking we done something wrong here, Dixie, and that's what you don't understand. The difference between kidnapping and what we're doing is that folks that kidnap somebody, they got to hide out. They got something to be scared of, because they don't want to get caught.'

'Billy, *we* don't want to get caught.'

'We aren't going to get caught. We got nothing to get caught for, because we're not kidnapping nobody. Aspen

Gulch is good because I can still get radio reception from there. I mean, all we're waiting for is them to announce a reward. So we don't have to hide, because nobody is looking for us.'

Bracing her elbow on the open window of the car, Dixie covered her eyes with her hand and slowly shook her head. 'Leola sure was right about that joker showing up.'

'Huh?'

'My sister. She done a reading for me. I'm just saying she sure did read me right.'

'Did she see a million dollars in those cards?'

'Not quite.'

Chapter Twelve

Between the embrace of the deeply cushioned leather viewing seats and its capacity for total darkness, Spencer's home-screening room was like a return to the womb. He trusted its comfort, the yet-unseen film the Academy had sent, and the bottle of wine to take him away from what was going on beyond the door.

The wine, however, let him down. Gem-red and heavy with the overtones of blackcurrant, a whiff of cinnamon and – what? – cherry? – it did not bring the relief Spencer had anticipated. What came instead were memories of mellow afternoons with friends, spent meandering through the vineyards of Napa Valley, and the languid, genial evenings that followed in Calistoga when they would sit out on the hotel patio, sampling their day's finds. Depression settled over Spencer at the unavoidable truth that he was here, sitting in the dark, miserable and alone, and not there, having a good time.

That fucking little bastard. It was his fucking fault for causing this fucking mess. And then fucking Phoebe would get involved. There was going to be no way Spencer could avoid contacting Phoebe or, worse, having her come to Montana, if the boy didn't turn up.

The longing to be in Calistoga, to smell the faint scent of the hot springs and enjoy the carefree conviviality of his friends, came over Spencer with such strength that he was almost in tears. *Why me? Why does all this crap always have to happen to me?* Spencer hated the boy bitterly in that moment for all that he'd destroyed.

One bottle of wine hadn't been enough, but the time the second was almost gone, Spencer felt relaxed. Or at least plastered enough not to care any longer. Sidonie was sound asleep by the time he fell into bed beside her.

His tranquillity didn't last. Spencer woke just two hours later, his mouth feeling as if it had been carpeted. As he went into the bathroom to get some water, the whole mess roared back into his head. *The fucking boy was gone.* Spencer stared bleakly at his rumpled image in the mirror. The boy didn't stare back at him, because there was absolutely nothing about him that had ever looked the least bit like Spencer. He had Phoebe's coarse brown hair, Phoebe's piggy little eyes. And he was a lard ass.

He's probably not even my kid.

The DNA test had said otherwise, of course. Spencer lifted a second glass of water to his lips, staring at his image as he drank. *Maybe it was wrong. Maybe Phoebe bribed somebody.*

Was it possible for a man to feel absolutely nothing for his own child? This was the question that wouldn't let Spencer go, because the truth was, he did feel absolutely nothing for that boy. If he was brutally honest with himself, if he looked right into the depth of his soul, his first reaction to the news that the boy couldn't be found had been 'Thank God, he's gone.'

That wasn't a psychopathic thought, was it? A normal man could feel that way, couldn't he? Spencer wasn't proud to be thinking like that, because only a crap father would be relieved that his kid had disappeared, but there were extenuating circumstances, weren't there? It wasn't as if Spencer had ever wanted this kid. Plus, Phoebe was such a total bitch, and anyone could see that. So while maybe somewhere out there there was some saint who might feel bad because a kid he hated was gone, a normal man would be pretty damned relieved, wouldn't he?

When Spencer next turned his head to look at the bedside clock, it was 4.13 a.m. He toyed with the idea of taking a sleeping pill, but the way his mind was galloping along, he'd need two to get any benefit and then he'd end up sleeping into the afternoon.

Slipping out of the bed, he went into the dressing room and exchanged his pyjama bottoms for jeans. He pulled on a T-shirt and stepped into his boots. Grabbing the denim jacket hanging in the back porch, he let himself silently out of the back door and headed for the barn.

There was no moon. Spencer had no idea whether the moon had set or whether it was even the time of month to have a moon. He'd never really understood how people could keep track of stuff like that. Guff was always watching the stars and would tell you the date by which constellations were rising over which mountains. Such knowledge seemed quaint to Spencer. Romantic, yes, but without much of a point to it when someone had invented calendars. And Google.

An owl flapped out of the trees in front of the barn as Spencer traversed the last few yards to the building and he threw his arms up to shoo it away, in case it was flying at him. Sliding open the big door just enough to slip in, he entered warm, impenetrable gloom and flipped the light switch on. There came sudden shifting of weight in the stalls as startled horses rose to their feet.

Shit. What was this? A forty-watt bulb or something? In the daytime there was always enough light coming through the skylights. Spencer had never noticed there was only one dim bulb to illuminate the entire barn. When he arrived at Red Ranger's stall, it was still largely in shadow.

'Hey, boy,' he whispered and let himself in with the horse.

The animal moved nervously.

'It's just me, boy. Hey?' Spencer reached his hand out slowly to take hold of the halter. 'Just me.' He ran his other hand down along the horse's flanks.

Ranger allowed Spencer to stroke him, to push the coarse hair of his forelock back, to fondle his jaw, his ears, his delicate nose, soft as a kitten's toes.

'Hey, boy. How you doing?'

The horse nosed him.

'Think I got mints in that pocket? Nope. I came out without anything this time. You just got me.'

Spencer was tempted to try saddling Ranger. How primeval would that be, to ride a horse into the mountains at this time of day? He'd done so once before, when he was starring in the movie *Eldorado McCann*. The whole crew and cast had been out then, standing in the chilly morning darkness, waiting for just that right moment of dawning light that the director insisted on. Spencer had no trouble now pulling himself back into the mind of the laconic lawman, driven to the point of obsession by his need to see justice done. Arm slung over Ranger's neck, Spencer pressed his cheek against the warm hair and relived the character for a few moments. Then he just clung to the horse.

'Shit, you're lucky to be a stupid animal,' he whispered. Stepping back from the horse, he leaned against the door of the stall. 'You haven't got a clue where any of your children are, do you? And you don't give a fuck. And no one cares that you don't.'

The horse turned away.

'I don't know where my kids are either,' Spencer said. 'Not any of them, to be honest.'

Thomas worked on Wall Street. Spencer did know that. And he knew that at one point Thomas had been living in SoHo, but that was right when he'd started out at the stock exchange. He'd moved since then. They always exchanged birthday and Christmas cards, but Spencer's staff handled that kind of thing, so he didn't remember the last time he'd seen Thomas's address. Was he even still in Manhattan? Was he married yet? No. Surely Spencer would know if that had happened. Did Thomas have a girlfriend? He fingered back through his memories trying to recall the last time the two of them had talked. Occasionally Spencer would phone Thomas to ask about stocks, because Thomas was damned good at what he did and Spencer respected that about him, but for a very long time there had been nothing more to the relationship than that.

And Louisa? God alone knew where she might be. Syria? Jordan? Iran? Last time Spencer had seen a photograph, she was wearing a hijab and showing a couple of grotty potsherds off to the camera as if they were Oscars. Kathryn had assured him Louisa hadn't converted or anything like that, just that wearing the hijab made working in Islamic countries easier. But who knew? Anyone who was happy to sit all day in the dirt, not caring that she looked like crap, or that after seven years of higher education she earned hardly more than a manual labourer, had probably long ago fried her brains in the Arabian sun.

Did he care? Spencer stared through the gloom at the horse, who stared charily back at him. Did he care that he had no relationship with either Thomas or Louisa? Did he feel he was missing something? Was there any lingering, unfulfilled attachment to a boy and girl who carried his genes but with whom he had had hardly any contact since before they went to school?

No. Not really.

Was this wrong? Was this fucked-up thinking? Or was all that stuff about blood and family just romantic bullshit?

Spencer was well informed about romantic bullshit. He made his living at it. The *Eldorado* set came back to mind. None of them standing around that morning had cared about the mountain sunrise. It was fucking freezing, and they were all trying to keep warm by clutching paper cups of foul-tasting coffee while waiting for what the director simply referred to as 'the right working conditions'. The exquisite splendour created as the sunlight cut across the horizon would be what the audience saw, but it was mostly the work of lenses and filters and photo-editing software. Add some swelling music in the background, fade in on the lawman's handsome, determined face and for a moment the audience would experience the world as safe and beautiful. All these cheesy dreams about good guys winning, comrades sticking together and love that never ended up in divorce court: that's what sold movies. That was how Hollywood made money. That he could see through such blatant manipulation, Spencer had always taken as proof his thinking was sane.

As he pondered, leaning motionless against the stall door, the horse relaxed. No longer concerned about the unexpected intrusion, Ranger ambled over to the trough and snuffled around it in case he'd missed anything tasty. Finding it still empty, he moved on to the hayrack and began to pull hay down. Lifting his tail, he farted noisily.

Chapter Thirteen

'Well, I don't know what's going on,' Billy said petulantly. He clicked the car radio off and got out of the front seat. 'I don't know why they don't say nothing on the news.'

Sitting on the ground, her back slumped against the tyre of the truck, Dixie unwrapped a cereal bar.

'What's the matter with you?' he asked and poked her thigh with the toe of his cowboy boot.

'I'm tired.' Even when the rest of her was near asleep, Dixie's ears had remained alert the whole night, listening into the owl-embroidered gloom for the sound of engines or voices. Now exhaustion lay down over her like tar.

'I would have thought there'd be *something* on the news by now,' Billy said in a tone that made it sound as if it was her fault. He reached over to take the cereal bar.

'No, this ain't yours. Get your own,' Dixie said, jerking it away.

When Billy went off to find something to eat, Dixie stood up. Going around to the back of the truck, she climbed up into the flatbed. 'You hungry?' she said to the bound boy lying in the opened toolbox. 'I broke this all up in little pieces. I'm going to take your gag off and then put them in your mouth. You got to chomp down good now, understand? Because it's real chewy and you don't want to choke. Then I'm going to give you a drink.'

Lunchtime came and Billy was still sitting in the front seat, glued to the radio. The day had grown very hot and with the heat had come the locusts. They whirred over the open grass in much greater numbers than had been up at the cemetery. They dropped on to the seats and into the toolbox and everywhere. Dixie didn't really mind locusts the way Leola did, but they got annoying after awhile because there were so many, and tiredness was making her short-tempered.

The entrance to the old Inverurie mine was visible on the opposite hillside. Dixie studied it through the heat shimmer. Inside the mine it would be cooler, Dixie thought, and for a moment she contemplated suggesting to Billy that they try to get up there. Then she thought better of it. Too much of a foxhole. Nothing seemed worse to her than the idea of being chased to ground and trapped.

'We got to go higher up,' she said finally. 'We're too close to town. It keeps me jumpy. And it's just too hot here. It's going to spoil our food. And cook that boy.'

'What I think is that we should go back down to town,' Billy replied, 'and find out what people are talking about. They got to be saying something about this by now.'

'Billy, don't be nuts. What if someone saw us? And what would we do with him if we were in town? He couldn't stay in the toolbox in this heat. He can't stay in the toolbox here.

We got to go higher up where it's cool and get him out or we won't have no boy to worry about,' Dixie replied.

'Fuck!' Billy said and banged the dashboard in frustration.

Crowheart was crisscrossed with dozens of old roads built by miners or loggers, but since the area had been declared a wilderness and development was no longer allowed, most of the roads had fallen into disuse and become little more than deer tracks. This didn't stop Billy any. The only thing that he hadn't ever exaggerated was how well he knew the back country. His grandpa had been a Crow and that's where he said he got it from, his ability to find his way around in the wilderness. It just came naturally to Billy. So within half an hour, they were bumping along on an old disused logging road.

Eventually Billy pulled the truck over. 'This is a good place. Down over the side of that there slope there's a creek, so we got water, and we don't need nothing else.'

Dixie liked the spot. The sound of a vehicle engine would be audible long before it reached them. Even voices would carry far into the deep silence of the forest. Nonetheless, she insisted they set up camp down beyond the first embankment of undergrowth where they weren't visible from the road and it would be easier to get away into the trees if someone did happen along. Billy muttered under his breath at the inconvenience of having to lug everything through the brush, but he did it.

Together, they set up the tent. Billy strung the food up high in the trees to discourage curious bears, while Dixie collected wood for the campfire. Then Billy stowed the rest of the equipment inside the tent, forming a small barricade with it. Behind it, he lay down the pile of newspapers and old rags they'd brought along. Lifting the boy out of the truck, he carried him down and put him in the tent.

'God, that kid's a ton of lard,' Billy gasped and sank down on a log near the tent. 'If we run out of food, we could eat him.'

Dixie frowned and put a finger to her lips to shush Billy. Then she went back to arranging rocks on the ground to form a campfire pit.

'I'm going to go down the mountain again for a while,' Billy said. 'I can't get no radio reception up here. I might even go back into town to nose around a bit, if there's still nothing on the news.'

'What if Mama or Leola sees you? They think we're camping.'

'I'll just tell them we forgot something. Don't you worry about me.' He winked at her.

'And what exactly are me and him supposed to do till you come back?' she asked tartly.

'You'll be OK. Even if someone came along, they wouldn't go down over the bank and inside the tent, would they? Even if they did, the way I built stuff up in there, they wouldn't see him.'

'Well, that reassures me a whole lot, Billy, you talking about someone coming around here. I don't want to be left up here all alone with no car.'

'Ninety-nine per cent of your problems come from your mind working overtime, Dix. I was just saying *if* someone did. But fact is, no one will. There's two million acres of wilderness here. Who's going to find this place?'

'And if they do?' she asked.

'Then tell them that your man's just gone in the bushes to take a crap and he'll be back up any minute.'

'I'm going to have to tell them you got diarrhoea, Billy, 'cause it'll take you at least two hours to get down the mountain and back up again.'

'Well, you better get used to it, because I can't hang around up here, can I? I need to be where I can follow what's going on or we won't get over this.' Heading back up to the truck, he opened the passenger side door and lifted the rifle off the gun rack on the back window of the cab. 'Here,' he said, returning to her.

'I ain't taking that.'

'Just in case.'

'No "just in case", Billy. What we done is bad enough already. I'm not going to go shooting people as well. If someone comes along looking for this kid and finds him here with me, I'm not going to stop them taking him.'

'You need something up here, Dix. Maybe not for the sheriff or anybody, but just in case. What if someone *did* come by? You're right to be worried about that, so we got to be prepared. You're a good-looking woman, Dix. Can't trust folks these days. Done up on drugs or something and they don't even think about what they're doing. See a woman on her own and who knows what's going to happen?'

'Jeez, you know how to make me feel real safe, Billy.'

'Or it don't have to be a person. Up here, more likely it's going to be a grizzly coming out of the trees. Or a mountain lion. There's plenty of mountain lions around and they're what's dangerous, 'cause they sneak around. Remember that one that chased me and Roy last year? That wasn't too far from here, and you don't got a car to climb into like we did. So take the rifle.'

With a sigh, Dixie reached out for the gun.

He leaned over and kissed her. 'I won't be gone too long.' Then he headed back up the bank.

As she watched him, Dixie ran her fingers along the barrel of the gun. The metal was as smooth and cool to the touch as a garter snake's skin. Billy started the truck and turned it around, churning up an unexpectedly large cloud of dust. It hung in the air between the trees. Long after the engine noise had disappeared, Dixie remained standing there, watching the dust drift unhurriedly upwards through the shafts of sunlight piercing the green darkness of the forest.

The tent was stuffy and alive with deerflies. Peering over the barricade that Billy had constructed to hide the boy, Dixie found him lying in a crumpled heap, his bare legs a mass of insect bites.

'I got some calamine lotion in the first-aid kit,' she said gently.

He didn't respond to Dixie's voice.

Worried, she pulled aside the things Billy had stacked up and knelt to touch the boy. 'Are you OK? It's awful hot in here. Did Billy give you a drink before he left?'

The boy squirmed and made a noise.

'I know I probably shouldn't be doing this, but you know what? I'm going to take this here gag out of your mouth. We can't keep putting this on you and I reckon if you want to holler, you can just go ahead up here. We're so far from anywhere there's nobody to hear you except me and the bears, and you can decide for yourself if you think bears would be better company.'

Although she had expected the boy to cry out once the gag was removed, Dixie was unprepared for just how ear-splitting he would be. The moment the gag was off, he shrieked like a cat with its tail in a rat trap. Leaping back in surprise, Dixie knocked the centre pole of the tent, causing the whole works to shudder. All his energy didn't go on screaming, however, because almost immediately the boy began to strain fiercely against his bindings.

'Whoa! Whoa! Don't get too excited now!' Dixie tried to grab hold of his legs.

'Lemme go, you fucking bitch!' he yelled and flopped wildly about on the ground like an oversized trout. The rag Billy had retied over his face came off, revealing his rage.

Dixie squeaked in alarm. She had been expecting he'd be grateful for her kindness. A little fretful maybe, what with all the upset and insect bites, but not fury. Fury, however, it most definitely was. Even though he was still all trussed up, the kid had nothing but killing on his mind. Endlessly screaming, 'You fucking bitch! You motherfucker bastard bitch!' he started to writhe towards Dixie. It was like having some kind of nightmare walrus after her.

The boy battered against Billy's barricade of camping equipment and managed to knock it over. Things went everywhere. When Dixie dashed to shore up the tent pole after he bumped against it, he flopped towards the doorway and within seconds was outside. Amidst the litter of moss and pine needles on the forest floor, the boy continued to struggle ferociously against his bindings, rolling steadily down the gentle slope away from the camp as he did so.

'Stop it!' Dixie shrieked. 'Stop it right now!'

The boy was so enraged he was literally foaming at the mouth. Over and over he rolled.

'I'm going to kick you!' Dixie cried, running after him. 'Just like my man did last night. I *will*.' She was still several feet away from him, so she couldn't actually kick him, even if she'd wanted to, but she knew she was going to have to stop him somehow, because what if he rolled into the creek? Worse, what if he broke the duct-tape bindings? Knowing Billy, it was just cheap Walmart duct tape, that kind called 'duck tape' because people didn't know you were actually supposed to be fixing ducts with it, and it wasn't made properly strong.

Dixie tried to grab hold of the boy's legs. It took three tries before she was able to get a good grip without being kicked. 'Now *stop* it!' she cried. 'If you don't settle down, I'm gonna take you back up to that hot old tent with all those flies and tie you up so you can't ever move. And I can. I've roped wilder calves in my day than you.'

'You goddamned fucking bitch, let me go!' the boy screamed.

Much as she wanted to carry out her threat, there was no way Dixie could move him on her own, when he was struggling that much. The best she could manage was to hang on to his feet and wait for him to wear himself out, and that took quite a lot of doing. He writhed and wriggled and fought. But God bless Walmart duck tape, because it held.

Finally the boy gave in and lay panting in the dirt. His lips were covered with pine needles, moss and other debris. His face was bloodied from scraping along the forest floor.

Dixie glanced up the small slope to where the tent was. He was a fat kid; he probably weighed not much less than she did. She wasn't sure she could drag him back uphill, but she needed to secure him. All she could think to do was to go get the rope from Billy's gear and tie him up here. That meant having to let go of him in order to get the rope, but Dixie didn't see any other way.

Tired as he must have been, the boy had still managed to squirm off into the underbrush twenty yards or so before she got back.

'You don't give up, do you?' Dixie grabbed his feet and pulled him back out of the bushes. She looped the rope around the trunk of a nearby pine and lashed his feet tightly to the base of the tree.

'Let me the fuck go! Fuck you! Fuck you!' the boy shouted the whole time she worked. 'You fucking bitch, let me go!'

'You sure do know how to talk dirty. My daddy would have washed my mouth right out, if I'd talked like that at your age.'

He spat at her. 'Fuck you, cunt.'

'Jeez,' Dixie muttered. 'I'm beginning to think we might have done your folks a favour, taking you.'

Dixie had intended to put lotion on the boy's insect bites, but he wasn't going to let her near him, and truth was, she was in no mood to try. For half an hour or more he thrashed around, screaming the most ugly hate words she'd ever heard come out of a little kid. Then he started to cry in an angry, frustrated way that didn't make you feel any sympathy for him at all. At long last, he fell silent.

Dixie sat on a log and watched him. She didn't want to hate him. He was, after all, just a little boy and it wasn't his fault he was in this situation. The way he acted, however, sure didn't help things any. Didn't help either that he was kind of ugly. He wasn't piggy fat, but he was too fleshy and it gave him folds where folds shouldn't be on a kid, and his skin had that dull, washed-out colour people get when they don't go outdoors enough. He looked hardly anything like Spencer Scott. There was no gallant cleft chin, no flashing blue eyes. Just a pudgy freckled nose and a tangle of much-too-long brown hair.

Dixie lit a campfire in the fire pit and dumped a can of chilli into a pot. The problem with cooking over a newly started fire was that the heat was uneven – too hot in some places, too cool in others. By the time she got the chilli heated, most of it was stuck to the bottom of the pan, but you could still eat it.

'Hey, kid, you want some food?' she asked, once she'd finished. 'I got chilli up here.'

'Fuck off.'

'Aren't you hungry?'

'Fuck the fuck off.'

Dixie scraped the remaining chilli into a big enamel cup and carried it down to where the boy was. 'Sure you don't want some?' she asked, holding the spoon out. He couldn't reach it. She was checking first to see if he was going to be nasty.

Dixie knew he had to be hungry, because all he'd had since they'd taken him was the cereal bar. 'I want to give you food,' she said. 'I ain't a bad person. I know you're suffering here. But I'm going to have to feed you, because I sure ain't going to untie your hands.' She knelt down beside him. 'Here. Open your mouth.'

The boy tasted the chilli cautiously at first, and then greedily sucked it off the spoon.

'Yeah, there now, you *are* hungry, aren't you? Tastes good, huh?'

As she spooned the chilli in, she smiled at the boy. He was a much more enthusiastic eater than Jamie Lee had ever been, and it was nice to have someone to take care of again. 'You and me, we can get on just fine, can't we? This is much better than fighting, huh?'

The boy said something.

'What's that?'

He burbled again, so Dixie leaned closer. 'I can't hear what you're saying 'cause you're talking through your food.'

Forcefully, he spat, spraying her face with half-chewed beans. 'I said, fuck you, cunt!'

'I was *trying* to be nice to you,' Dixie replied and pitched the remaining chilli into his face. 'But there. You can just eat it that way, if that's what you want.'

Chapter Fourteen

Against the rich, natural hum of the forest, Dixie could just make out a dissonant rasping. She paused, listening intently. A vehicle engine. Still distant, but discernibly an engine. Fear crawled up the back of her neck.

It's just Billy. Don't be stupid. Only Billy.

Going into the tent, Dixie found the cloth they'd used as a gag. She slipped down over the slope to where the boy lay, still lashed to the tree by his feet. 'I'm going to have to put this back on you, little man. Sorry.'

The boy wasn't having it. He shrieked at her and writhed fiercely away from Dixie's grasp.

'Listen, kid, I don't want to whip you, but I will,' she said and grabbed him forcefully. Her hands were shaking. 'Come on now. It's for your own good. That's Billy coming and he'll do far worse to you if he finds you don't got this on. Remember what he done to you last night? He'll do it again and just as bad. So quit fighting me.'

When he wouldn't stop struggling, she grabbed the boy more roughly and thumped the side of his head. This stopped him long enough for Dixie to tie the gag.

Frantically she bolted back up to the tent. As annoyed as she'd been earlier with the kid for rolling down the slope like that to where he was almost in the creek, Dixie was grateful now because it put him out of sight of the camp, and the rushing water disguised his angry grunting noises. None of this was visible from the track. You had to come over the first embankment to see the tent, and then down the slope beyond the tent to see the boy. Dixie hoped desperately no one would want to do that.

The vehicle groaned on the last bit of incline. Panic started to overtake Dixie, because she could tell by now it wasn't Billy's truck. Grabbing the rifle, she went up to the track.

A forest ranger came into view, his Jeep moving slowly over the rough road.

Dixie put on a big smile and waved. 'Hiya!' she called and headed over to the vehicle before he could get out.

The ranger leaned through his open window. 'You camping here?'

Dixie nodded. 'My man's just down that away a bit, fishing. I got our permit to be camping in the wilderness. And both our fishing licences. You want to see them?'

'No, that's OK,' the ranger said. 'But I am here about that campfire. They spotted the smoke from the lookout tower, so I thought, Oh shucks, we got a forest fire starting up here.'

Dixie gave a broad, reassuring smile. 'Oh well, that's a big relief for you then, huh? Because I'm here, taking good care of it. We made a proper pit for it and would never leave it burning without tending it. We're just up from town. We know these mountains real good, and how careful you got to be with fire.'

'If you're local, then you also know that no fires of any kind are allowed outside the designated campgrounds at this time of year,' the ranger said none too good-naturedly.

'Yes, sir,' Dixie said and looked extra-special sheepish, hoping that catching them at having a campfire would keep the ranger distracted from noticing anything else. 'We thought as we know these mountains so well we might get by with it, because we were being real careful. Just made it for cooking our fish. But I'm sorry we done it. We did know it was wrong. You want me to put it out right now?'

'Can you put it out safely? Or you want me to do it for you?'

'No, sir. The creek's just down over the hill where my man's fishing and we got a bucket and a shovel along. Right over there. See? I'll put the fire out now.'

'How long you intending to stay here?'

'We just came up for the fishing. Still good fishing this high up. Too hot down below.' Wiping pretend sweat off her brow to show how hot it was in the valley, Dixie smiled as appealingly as she could.

'So how long you staying?'

'Just tonight, sir. We'll be home again tomorrow. My man's got to go to work.'

The ranger paused a moment longer, surveying the camp-site, but he never got out of the car. Dixie kept forgetting to breathe, so when she did, it got caught in the back of her throat, as if maybe she was going to be sick.

'OK,' he said at last. 'Just see you put the fire out.'

'Yes, sir. I definitely will.'

The ranger didn't turn around and go back. Instead, he carried on up the track and Dixie knew he would have to come back by at some later point. She busied herself getting the fire put right out so that it didn't give off even the smallest wisp of smoke. The panicky feeling lingered on, making her hands shake and her stomach sick.

The ranger must have gone a long ways up, because by the time he passed by again, evening gloom was starting to settle into the undergrowth. Dixie smiled and waved enthusiastically at him, hoping to distract him from looking too closely for someone else there with her. The ranger smiled and waved back, but he didn't slow down. Only when he was finally out of sight did Dixie at last manage to take a deep breath.

She lit the lantern, but without the fire, there was no way to keep the biting insects away. She slathered on insect repellent and retreated into the tent, where she sat with her knees drawn up and her cardigan pulled tight. The boy needed tending to. He couldn't be left outside where it would get cold and God alone knew what animals would walk by. At the moment, however, Dixie couldn't bear even to think about him.

Billy didn't return until well after dark.

'Where the hell you been?' Dixie snapped.

'What's the matter with you? Shit, are you on your period or something? What are you crying for now?' he asked.

'*Nothing*,' she replied angrily. 'Nothing 'cept I'm sitting here by myself in the dark and freezing to death and being bit to death by bugs. We can't have a fire 'cause you thought being in the wilderness was such good thinking, but they don't allow no fires. And I can't go to bed, because you took such a nasty little boy, and he got out of the tent and tried to get away; so he's down over there by the creek, and I had to leave him there so nobody could see him.' She started to cry again.

'*Shit*,' said Billy in astonishment.

'And *you* been drinking. I can smell it on you. You been off having a good time and left me alone with all this mess.'

Billy opened his arms. 'Hey, come here. Let me give you a squeeze.' Drawing Dixie into a bear hug, he kissed her on the top of the head. 'There. That make you feel a little better?' he asked, holding her tight.

She nodded tearfully.

'Now, come on. Your man'll sort things out for you. And I'll start by getting that little bastard back up here.'

Lantern held high, Billy slid down the slope to where the boy was tied to the tree. He inspected the area the boy had hollowed out of the soil with all his thrashing about.

'You been messing around, kid?' It wasn't really a question. 'You been giving her a hard time? Is that how come you're laying out here in the dirt and not in the tent like you should be?'

In the lantern light, the boy's eyes were as black as a trapped cat's.

'You ain't a very fast learner, are you, kid?' Billy said. Without pausing, he pulled back and kicked the boy ferociously in the ribs. 'This one is for not doing what she says. Got that? And this one,' he said and kicked the boy again, 'is for not staying where I put you. So, are you getting the message here? You do what I say; you do what she says. And nothing else. You don't do fuck-all thinking for yourself. Got that?'

Sobbing, the boy nodded frantically.

Billy kicked him a third time so hard it moved him across the dirt.

'Billy, he's got it,' Dixie cried. 'See? He's nodding. He's got it. You got it, don't you, boy? You're going to be good from now on, huh? Don't kick him anymore, Billy. *Don't*. You'll hurt him.'

Billy leaned down close to the boy's head. "'Cause you're kind of a stupid little boy, I'm going to take the trouble to explain something real careful to you. Want me to do that?'

Dixie could tell the child didn't know whether to say he did or he didn't want that. Tears rolled down over the side of his face, washing little paths through the debris stuck to his skin.

'What I'm going to explain is this,' Billy said and lowered his voice menacingly. 'We're way up here in the mountains. Ain't nobody around except her and me and you. Know what that means? Means I can kill you, kid.' His words were as soft as if he were whispering a lullaby. 'You make yourself too much trouble … Clear up here, well, anything could happen to a little boy, couldn't it? And nobody would ever, ever, *ever* find out.'

'Well, I don't give a shit what they say about not making fires,' Billy muttered. 'That's the fucking government for you. Sticking their fucking nose into everything. I been in these mountains all my life. I know how to take care of a goddamned campfire and I don't need them telling me what to do. The government wants to run everything. Wants to wipe your ass for you. Well, I don't give a shit. If I want a fire, I'll fucking well have a fire. It's a free country.'

He tossed kindling into the pit and put a match to it. 'And you'll damned well cook me a meal. I haven't eaten since lunch.'

'You been drinking your supper,' Dixie said. 'Where you been all this time?'

'The Horseshoe. I was waiting around to see the news on TV, because there hasn't been a single word about that kid yet.'

'Wow? Really?' Dixie said in astonishment.

'That's why I've been so fucking long. Shit. Nobody's saying *anything*.'

The fire blazed up. Dixie set up the little cooking grate and balanced the frying pan on it. She opened the beans. The fire wasn't really hot enough yet to warm them unless she set the can right in the middle of the blazing logs. Twisting the little key, she opened the can of Spam, sliced it and laid it in the frying pan. 'So what do you think's going on?' she asked.

'Dunno. I can't figure it.'

They sat in silence for several minutes as Dixie tended the food.

'Here,' she said finally. Lifting the meat up with a spatula, she let the grease drip back into the frying pan before putting it on the tin plate. She handed it to Billy. 'Help yourself to the beans there. They're probably not hot, but they're good enough.'

Dixie hadn't eaten herself since the episode with the chilli. Worry had taken away her appetite to the point where she hadn't even noticed how long it had been and, truth was, she still didn't feel hungry now. Billy had no such problems. He tucked into his food enthusiastically. Polishing off the last of the beans, he then finished up the rest of the Spam. When that was gone, he got up to find a slice of bread, wiped the grease out of the frying pan and ate that. 'Mmm-mm!' he declared. Leaning back, he patted his stomach. 'You know what they say. Hunger's always the best sauce.'

'I don't want you to think I'm nagging you,' Dixie said, looking across the fire at him, 'but we got to talk about all this. What are we going to do?'

Billy straightened back up. 'If you don't want to nag, then that's easy, Dix. Keep your mouth shut. Because I'm *thinking*. I *am* thinking. What do you suppose I been doing all day long?'

'Yeah, I realize that, Billy. But the longer we keep this boy, the worse it is. We aren't going to be able to go much longer saying we just accidentally got hold of him and been saving him from perverts, because they're going to want to know where he's been. Plus, nobody's going to believe we been protecting him when he's covered head to toe with your bruises.'

'Can't help that, Dix. He's a little bastard.'

'Well, yeah, I know. Tell me about it. That's half the problem. He's *horrible*, Billy. I'm not kidding you. He's the nastiest little kid I've ever come across. His parents might pay better money to be rid of him than get him back. But you can't keep whaling on him like that ... and jeez, what was that garbage about "I'm going to kill you"?'

'Just scaring him, Dix.'

'That isn't a nice kind of scaring.'

'I wouldn't ever do it. You know that.'

'You *sounded* like you might do it. Even to me. And the thing is, we can't have you messing around like that, Billy, because what about when we let him go? If we're treating him nice, that's one thing. But if he goes back and says, "They said they were going to kill me," well, that's something else again. I'm just getting really worried about how this will turn out.'

'It'll be OK.'

'No, I don't think it will,' Dixie said. 'What I'm trying to say to you is that I think this needs to stop. Pretty much right now.'

'I only done this to make things good for you, Dix.'

'Yeah, I know it. But I don't want it this way. There's too much at stake here, Billy.'

'Think what we could have,' he replied. 'Just think about it a minute.'

'The only thing I'm thinking about is keeping what I already got. I don't got these big dreams you do. Ordinary stuff's good enough for me. That's what's been on my mind all day today, how I don't need to live like a movie star to be happy. I don't need diamond rings or fancy clothes or a big house. Yeah, I've had some hard times, and this here lately sure has been one of them, but everyone has hard times, Billy. Being with you and my family, belonging to this beautiful place, they're simple things, but they're enough for me, and I'm starting to get scared I might lose even that, if this goes wrong.'

'It ain't going to go wrong, Dix.'

Silence came then. Dixie leaned forward to spread the burning logs out so that they wouldn't smoke too much.

'It's not like I'm doing all this without thinking about it,' Billy said in a softer, more peace-making tone. 'All day, that's what I been doing. Not just drinking, like you think. I been trying to figure out how to make this work.'

He paused.

'At first I was thinking I could just drop the kid off, you know? That I could drive up that road where Spencer Scott lives and give the kid back, and he'd, like, give me a reward because he was so grateful. But from what you're saying, who knows if they'll be grateful he's been returned?'

'I think we should just let him go,' Dixie said.

'You kidding? After all this trouble? No way. I want money for him.'

Dixie shook her head. 'This isn't right, Billy. So let's just stop it here. Let's just take him down the mountain, leave him off somewhere safe and go home. We'll manage somehow for money. Even with the funeral man. I mean, he's not going to dig Jamie Lee up, is he? So, if we haven't got the money by the end of September, he'll just have to wait.'

'No.'

'*Yes*, Billy. It's bad enough what we already done, but we can still get out of it at this point.'

'*No*.' His voice was petulant. 'I want that money. Maybe what you got is good enough for you, but I want my chance.' Billy rose and went over to get another log for the fire. 'I want a good life.'

'We got a good life, Billy.'

'No, we don't. We got a shithouse life compared to them up there in the canyon.'

'We got a different life than them, that's all. It's still a good life.'

Billy flung the log on the fire and sat down again. Silence, irritated and injured at the same time, drew out between them.

The burning wood popped loudly. Dozens of orange sparks darted fleetingly up through the pine smoke like frightened fairies. Dixie watched them, thinking how beautiful they were and knowing how easily even one could destroy a forest.

'You know what Roy was telling me, when we were branding?' Billy said at last, his voice quiet.

Dixie shook her head.

'You know Guff Maguire? Who works up at Spencer Scott's ranch? He was telling Roy about that cutting horse Scott bought. Scott paid sixty-five thousand dollars for it. One horse. *Sixty-five thousand*, Dix. I could buy horses, set up my guide business, hire another wrangler, pay for pasturing and still have money for a new truck from sixty-five thousand. But you know what's worse than that? Guff was saying that Spencer Scott doesn't know anything about cutting horses at all. He doesn't do any cutting. He doesn't even send Guff to the championships with the horse. Guff says Spencer Scott can hardly ride. He just bought it because he can. So every morning Guff has to ride the horse off so that Scott can then take it out like a trail pony.

'That's the way they are, Dix, those folks. They buy stuff they got no use for, just to own it. That's so false, man, and they don't even know they're being false. And here's me. If I had a great cutter, I could make a real living off him. I could do all the championships and rodeos and show him off. I could make him do handstands, if I wanted, because I'm a *cowboy*. I'm not just pretending in some movie. I'm that guy, for real. But instead, Spencer Scott's got a sixty-five-grand horse he can't ride. And me, I can't even afford to buy that horse's shit. That's plain unfair, Dixie. So I don't see anything wrong with what I'm doing. All I want is a fair chance in life, nothing more.'

Chapter Fifteen

When Spencer returned to the house from the barn, Sidonie was at the kitchen table. Clad in the over-sized terrycloth spa robe Spencer had received as swag for appearing on that afternoon talk show hosted by the ex-model with the meth problem, she was sitting with her knees drawn up, arms wrapped around them, like a little girl.

'What are you doing up?' he asked. 'It isn't even five thirty yet.'

'He isn't back.'

'Make some coffee, would you?'

Sidonie pulled her knees closer.

Spencer regarded her. As a natural blonde, she was some-one who needed make-up. Without mascara and eyebrow pencil, she reminded him of a pickled pig foetus. Not a good look.

'I'm too worried to sleep,' she said.

'Jamieson will be here by ten. He'll know how to handle everything. Make some coffee, would you?'

'We need to call the police, Spencer,' she said.

'Don't be blonde. It's five fucking thirty.'

'He's nine. He's been gone overnight. We don't know where he is.'

'And … you're telling me this *why*, exactly? Because you don't think I've noticed this for myself?' Spencer fixed her with a stare. 'Make some coffee. That's what you're here for.' He took off his jacket and hung it over the back of the chair.

'Spencer?' she said. Her tone was soft, tentative.

'What?'

'Sometimes it can't just be about you.'

He scowled. 'What do you mean by saying that?'

'I know you don't want to call the police because of the press and all that, but …'

'But *what*?' Spencer said scornfully as he opened the cupboard to get out mugs. 'I *know* he's nine, Sidonie. I *know* he's been gone all night. I don't need someone with the IQ of a pheasant to point out the fucking obvious. It's *under control*. I said Jamieson will take care of it and he will. No one asked for the blonde's opinion on anything.'

She continued to sit there, her expression hurt.

'Shit. All I want is a frigging cup of coffee. For *God's sake*, Sidonie. It's fuck o'clock in the morning and I haven't had any coffee. Is it too much to ask you to do your job?' He slammed the cupboard door shut.

Still she stayed on the fucking chair and defied him.

Furious, Spencer stormed out of the house.

Going back down to the barn, he lifted Red Ranger's bridle from the hook. The horse turned in anticipation.

'You want food? Do you think that's why I'm here? I got bad news for you, buddy. Some days are tough shit. Come on. Get this in your mouth.' Spencer shoved the bit in and looped the top of the bridle over the horse's ears.

'Can I help you, Mr Scott?' Guff appeared in the doorway of the barn.

'Well, I want to fucking ride him, don't I? And he isn't ready.'

'This is earlier than usual, sir,' Guff said in a quiet, matter-of-fact voice. He came down the aisle between the stalls and let himself in with Spencer and the horse. A bucket of feed in one hand, Guff pushed the enthusiastic horse out of the way and poured the contents into the trough. Then he tugged the still-unfastened bridle off Ranger's head to let the horse eat.

Spencer wanted to scream at him but he didn't. Guff was a strange mix. He was an old-fashioned, Roy Rogers kind of cowboy, all about decency, loyalty and going to church on Sunday. Yet, beneath Guff's politeness, Spencer often detected an aura of ... what? ... resentment? Disdain? Disapproval? It was very subtle; so restrained, in fact, that Spencer often wondered if he was simply projecting his own insecurities on to the reserve so typical of the natives here. Most of the time, however, he was quite sure it wasn't his imagination and it annoyed the hell out of him. Not because Spencer expected to be surrounded by sycophants. He could man up to criticism with the best of them. No, it was because who the fuck did a nobody like Guff think he was to judge?

It was the same now. The casual way Guff had come into the stall with the oats and pulled off the bridle Spencer had struggled to put on communicated clearly that he was putting the horse's needs first and didn't give a damn that Spencer was upset.

'The whole point of my keeping you on here, Guff, is so you can have this fucking horse ready to ride,' Spencer said irritably.

'Yes, sir,' Guff replied. 'As soon as he is done eating, I'll ride him off for you. He'll be ready by ten o'clock.'

'Ten o'clock is when I normally come out, Guff. I want to ride now.'

'Yes, sir. As soon as he's done eating, I'll ride him off for you. Or would you rather I saddled up one of the others now?'

Guff's tone was calm and entirely respectful. Was he taking the piss? Spencer was pretty sure that's what was happening, but there was just no way to prove it. Perturbed, Spencer watched the old cowboy fuss over the horse and wished it didn't matter so much to him.

Back in the house Sidonie was pouring coffee beans into the espresso machine. There were still-hot croissants on a baking tray on top of the stove. Spencer took one and broke it open.

'What the fuck are these?' he asked. 'Out of a can from the refrigerator cabinet?'

'They taste all right,' Sidonie replied. 'And there's home-made huckleberry jam on the table. They were selling it from a table in front of the supermarket. United Methodist Church bake sale. So, it's local.' Then her voice was drowned out by the espresso maker going to work on the beans.

'Shit, we might as well be eating breakfast at the Pittsburgh Steelworks with all the racket that thing makes. And these are *not* croissants, Sidonie.'

'I'm sorry. It's the best I could do for something fresh,' she said and put his coffee down on the table in front of him.

'Yeah, well, it's not good enough. What's the matter with this place? It's not like I'm asking for beluga caviar or something. What makes it so hard to find a fucking decent croissant?'

Sidonie didn't reply.

'I'm going to go back to LA.'

'When?' she asked.

'Today. There's no point in being here. Jamieson can do everything. I might as well take advantage of the plane being here.'

Sidonie's expression grew faintly anxious. 'Don't you think maybe you should stay here too?'

'No, I don't think I should stay here too,' he mimicked. 'If I thought I should stay here, I would stay here, wouldn't I? *Duh.*'

Sidonie's expression grew more vulnerable and she stopped asking the fucking questions.

'I want to get out of here,' he said in a low, measured voice. 'It's not like I'd be looking for the kid myself. Once Jamieson's here, he'll handle everything and he'll do it discreetly and sensibly. So I might as well be where at the very least I can get a decent croissant, because what you are giving me is pig shit.' He threw the plate at the sink, croissant untouched.

At ten o'clock when Jamieson arrived, Spencer and Ranger were at the top of the ridge. Returning sweaty and horsey-smelling, Spencer found the kitchen transformed into a command centre. Maps, mobile phones and iPads lay scattered across the kitchen table while Jamieson and his posse demolished a box of jam doughnuts they'd picked up at the local bakery as they came through town.

Spencer had anticipated handing the whole mess over and that would be the end of it. The boy would be located, sorted out, sent back to the housekeeper or whoever the hell would have him, and the horrible cost of paying for all this would be worth it, because Phoebe would learn her lesson. No more fucking him about when he was in Montana, because look what happens.

From the moment Spencer walked into the kitchen, however, everything went wrong. He was weary from the ride. He needed a shower. He needed more coffee. And quite frankly, he needed the coke Jamieson had better have brought along. He didn't need Jamieson sitting there like a turd, waiting to be told what to do. Wasn't it obvious? *Find the boy.* Yet Jamieson just sat, cramming another doughnut into his mouth, shedding crumbs all down the front of his shirt as he did so. Spencer was fucking exhausted. Didn't they know that? Shit, he had hardly slept at all. He felt like absolute crap and yet no one took his needs into account at all.

And Jamieson's idea of handling the situation was insane. The first thing he said he was going to do was call in the local police. Then he wanted to call up one of the Billings TV stations and have Spencer do an interview. '*Shit*,' Spencer shrieked in frustration. 'What about the word "discreet" does no one around here understand?'

By lunchtime, they were openly arguing. Jamieson wasn't even pretending to listen to Spencer by that point. He kept saying their priority was to find the boy and the only way they could ensure that was to notify the authorities and get everybody looking for him. This was common sense, Jamieson said. Spencer pointed out *yet again* that if he'd wanted to do it that way, he would have fucking well got the police up there himself instead of paying an outrageous sum for Jamieson to fly up from LA to act like a dickhead.

Jamieson wasn't easily put down. Why the fuck *had* Spencer flown him up, if Spencer didn't want him to do the job? How the hell was he expected to work, if Spencer kept tying his hands? Didn't he *want* the kid back?

That's when Spencer fired him. Told him to get the fuck out of there and back to LA, and if Jamieson thought he was going to work again for Spencer or anybody else Spencer knew, if he thought his agency was still going to manage Spencer's security needs after this debacle, then he had another fucking thought coming.

Slamming doors loudly behind him, Spencer retreated to his study. The stress had given him a terrible headache. Probably a fucking migraine. He closed the blinds against the radiant Montana afternoon and sank morosely into the chair beside the desk.

The room was overly warm because it faced west, got too much sun in the afternoon and needed the air-conditioning vents fully open to be comfortable. However, they were always half-closed whenever Spencer went in because Sidonie couldn't cope with the early-morning chill of the mountains, yet she never remembered to come back later and reopen the vents. He just sat with the heat, too stressed, too overwhelmed to get up and adjust them.

Beyond the closed door of the study came the sounds of rooms being vacated, of cars starting up, of leaving. Jamieson had taken him at his word. Spencer hadn't really meant for that to happen. He had just wanted Jamieson to understand the necessity of doing things Spencer's way. That *was* why

Spencer had hired him, after all. Now everything was going to be fucking complicated in LA as well as here, because Spencer would have to find another security agency. Putting his hand over his eyes, he lowered his head. It really did hurt.

Eventually the sun sank below the glowering hulk of Lion Mountain. Spencer's study fell into late-afternoon shadow made dismal by the closed blinds.

Sidonie opened the door without knocking. Wordlessly, she crossed the room, and when she reached him, still sitting in the desk chair, she put her arms around him and endeavoured to comfort him.

Spencer resisted. 'Go away,' he said.

'Why don't you come out now?' she said softly.

He didn't reply.

'They're gone. It's just you and me.'

'What the fuck am I going to do about this mess now?' he said wearily.

'We'll figure something out. It'll be OK.'

'Wow, thanks,' he muttered sarcastically.

'Don't be like this.' She kept her arms around him.

Upset and still in pain, Spencer remained unyielding.

'You're a good man, Spencer,' she said very quietly.

'Oh? And who do you think you are? Sigmund Freud?'

'No, just somebody who loves you,' she replied softly.

'You love Spencer Scott,' he said. 'Not me.'

'I love you in spite of Spencer Scott.'

'Fuck off, Sidonie.'

Chapter Sixteen

A ll Spencer wanted was to sink into the soft oblivion of
sleep. He fully understood how Michael Jackson had
ended up as he had. People had been so judgemental of him,
but fuck them for being so lucky as to have a mind that
would turn off at night.

Insomnia had plagued Spencer for as long as he could
remember. Over the years he'd used everything he could get
his hands on to buy a few hours of unconsciousness, and he'd
never regretted anything he'd tried. Unconsciousness was
the only thing that soothed the unrestrained, inarticulate
emptiness of night.

OxyContin would take the edge off the ghastly day, but it
was going to require wine to put him out properly. Spencer
didn't bother with the pretence of a good bottle. From the
wine rack he took a Tempranillo of uncertain pedigree and
opened it. Someone had brought it along as a house gift, so
there wasn't a second bottle of the same; in fact, there wasn't
even another Spanish wine in the rack. Spencer grabbed a
bottle of Bordeaux he'd bought cheaply at the airport. By the

time he got to it, he wouldn't care about grapes, regions or even what it tasted like.

The drug helped the wine work better that it had worked on its own the night before. Spencer had no memory whatsoever of going to bed, although he must have, since that's where he woke up. Rolling over, he hit the light on the clock to see the time: 3.28 a.m. Then the lingering effects of intoxication pulled him under again.

The dream, when it came, started out as one of those peculiarly real ones which are as mundane as waking life. Spencer was in his study, going over scripts, and the one that had caught his attention was set in Montana. It was about a washed-up cowboy, and Spencer felt upset that Sidonie had passed it on to him to read. What was she trying to imply? That he was washed up himself? He was more irritated, however, by the way the scriptwriter had portrayed Montana. The story was full of gang warfare, shootings and other kind of crap that happened in LA. Clearly he knew nothing about Montana and was just cashing in on it as a panoramic setting.

Spencer wanted to complain to Sidonie about the script, but he couldn't find her. A frustration sequence followed where Spencer made repeated efforts to locate Sidonie and was thwarted every time.

In the way of dreams, suddenly he was in LA, talking to Michael, his agent. Spencer tried to explain that he needed to find Sidonie, but all Michael would talk about was the film script. It was a remake of *The Electric Horseman*, Michael explained, and the producer really wanted Spencer to take the lead role. Spencer asked who would be playing the Jane Fonda part and Michael replied, 'Phoebe.' He told how the producer had said the frisson on camera between the two of them would make the movie, and then Michael went on to say how this would be such a crucial career move for Spencer, because 'to be honest now, Spencer, your star is on the wane'. Phoebe, on the other hand, was hot. Everyone wanted Phoebe these days.

Then Spencer was back in his study, sitting in his desk chair, the script in front of him, and a sense of doom pressing down on him like a hand from above. Starring opposite Phoebe was a horrific enough idea, but worse was the sense of displacement. When had Phoebe become hot property? When had she even managed to break into acting? The sense of everything he thought he knew being out of control overwhelmed him.

That was the point Sidonie opened the door to the study. The dream had wandered away from his initial search for her, but seeing her flooded Spencer with profound relief. Sidonie crossed the room and, as had happened in the afternoon when he was awake, stood over him as he sat in the desk chair and pulled him into an embrace. This time, however, Spencer did not resist her. He allowed himself to relax into her arms. Sidonie pulled him close against her in what was almost a maternal hug. For one lucid moment, Spencer felt comfort. Not arousal. Not lust. Just plain, unadulterated consolation, and with it the recognition of a singular diamond-sparkle of happiness.

It was that solitary perfect moment which gave the dream its nightmarish power because the moment he allowed himself to feel that support, he looked at Sidonie and realized it wasn't Sidonie at all. Phoebe smiled her elfin, gap-toothed smile and kept her arms locked tight around him until the frantic hammering of his heart against his ribs forced him awake.

Relief at waking was diminished by the startlingly brilliant daylight reality of the dream, which kept the dark bedroom from gaining hold. Spencer groped across the bedclothes to feel Sidonie beside him and reassure himself he was awake. She murmured groggily and reached a sleepy hand out to touch his face.

He turned his head to look at her. The metal shutters were down and they made the room so dark that it was hard to discern even the shape of her. There still clung to Spencer a residual, atavistic fear that she might not be Sidonie, so he sat up, not so much to see her as to shake away the hangover-heavy remnants of sleep.

His thinking felt cumbersome and gluey, as if a rhinoceros with gum on its feet were lumbering through his brain. Obsessive thoughts of Phoebe still haunted him: *You can't control her. You can't predict what she is going to do. She messes with your life for the hell of it and you're powerless to stop her.* Spencer *knew* they were confused thoughts, knew they were just the aftermath of too much cheap wine, too many pills, but he was helpless to stop them.

As Spencer came fully awake, a more terrifying thought crawled out of his muddled brain. *Phoebe would come.* He sat bolt upright in the bed. This wasn't the stuff of dreams. Jamieson might well have already contacted Phoebe about the boy. He shouldn't have, but he was fucking out of control when he'd come up, what with his insistence on calling in the authorities and all sorts of other stuff Spencer had specifically told him shouldn't be done.

The inevitability of Phoebe coming to Montana caused horror to sluice over Spencer like sleet on a November day. He shivered. Oh God. Oh *shit*. Panic dispersed the last vestiges of the peace bought by wine and drugs.

The darkness was exacerbating his anxiety. Spencer knew there was no way he was going to go back to sleep, so the best idea was just to get up.

Beyond the shuttered darkness of the bedroom, dawn was well advanced. He dressed, brushed his teeth and went downstairs to the kitchen.

Spencer didn't even try the espresso maker. Out came the crappy coffeemaker from Walmart and the God-knows-how-old bag of ground coffee from the fridge. It stank of staleness. Once made, Spencer ended up pouring the whole pot down the drain. He felt half sick from the hangover and didn't actually want coffee anyway.

Only the mountain air, pre-dawn cool and pungent with the resinous scent of pines and the faint, dusky undertones of sagebrush, was soothing. Standing on the deck, arms wrapped around himself against the chill, Spencer gazed at the still-shadowy immensity of the mountains. He felt brain-dead.

Chapter Seventeen

'Come on, you,' Spencer said to the horse and lifted up the bridle. 'It's time you and I got to know each other as men. Here. Open your mouth.' He slipped the bit in and fastened Ranger's bridle.

He was less certain about putting on the saddle, but he'd often seen it done, both with Guff and on film sets. So Spencer lofted the horse blanket on to Ranger's back and, with a grunt, the saddle. Laboriously, he tightened the cinch.

He led Ranger out into the corral and closed the barn door. The sun had crested the hills on the opposite side of the valley. It came first as an orangeish glow against a peach-coloured horizon, visible rays shooting up through the haze to give it the momentary look of a child's drawing. Within moments, however, the full orb had cleared the hill and the crisp mountain air turned golden. Spencer did one last check of the saddle, then opened the corral gate, mounted the horse and headed out.

Ranger was eager to move. In the best of times, Spencer had to work at staying in control, but the amount of leverage he needed on the reins just to get out of the barn area was ridiculous. Irritation overrode his fuzzy-headed numbness as he tried to restrain the animal. Spencer jerked angrily on the reins. He wasn't going to be bullied by a fucking horse. Ranger danced to the side, but another sharp jerk brought him back.

Following his usual morning route, Spencer rode the horse up out of the gully where the ranch buildings were and along the aspen-embroidered edge of the forest. Ranger took the distance at a crisp trot. Spencer couldn't hold him to a slower pace, but this was an acceptable détente. The only problem was that consequently they covered the usual distance much more quickly and soon arrived at the point where the trail divided. Spencer normally took the lower one that circled back to the ranch.

He wasn't ready to return to the ranch. They'd sprinted over the route in half the time and while the exertion needed to manage the horse was hardly relaxing, such effort did keep Spencer from thinking. He needed it to last longer than this. There was also a more mundane reason for not return-ing yet. Even on the days when Guff had taken the horse out first, Spencer still found it difficult to keep Ranger from 'getting his head' once they had passed this halfway mark and breaking into a gallop to race home. It would be impos-sible to control him today, not only because he hadn't been ridden off, but also because he hadn't had his breakfast, and while he still didn't know a great deal about horses, Spencer had come to realize they behaved as if they had clocks in their stomachs.

Instead of veering onto the lower trail as usual, Spencer turned the horse onto the upper trail and followed it into the forest. It had been a long time since he'd gone this far along the trails. He'd done quite a lot of riding the first year he'd bought the ranch and had always meant to keep it up but just never seemed to get around to it. As he recalled, however, this trail went up through the forest for two or three miles before coming out onto a broad, open ridge high above the valley that gave a vast overview not only of the basin but of the mountain ranges to the south.

Spencer could remember that ride and the unexpectedness of coming out of the forest to be greeted by the immense panorama, row after row of mountain peaks extending into the distance. It had been late in the afternoon and the haze had taken on a yellow glow so that each range was a slightly more delicate shade of gold than the one in front until they dissolved into the haze itself. The place had a sacredness to it. It had left him wordless at the time, and feeling slightly overawed, which perhaps was why he had never gone back. Some things don't stand up to memory, and so are best not experienced twice.

Today, however, was different. He was not interested in the holiness of it but in its infinity. When he reached the ridge, he would just keep riding. Over this mountain range. Over the next. Over the one after that.

Spencer imagined escaping this way. He would just ride off into the sunset, like they did in the movies, and leave everybody else to solve all the problems. Just keep going. Ride for days. Make this fucking horse earn his keep. End up in Wyoming or Idaho or whatever was on the far side of these mountain ranges and then just keep going from there. Grow a beard. Dye his hair. Live a life where no one recognized him, no one wanted anything out of him, no one bothered him. He would become Ranger's new Guff.

Chapter Eighteen

The noise of the pick-up engine starting up woke Dixie, but by the time she'd struggled out of the sleeping bag, all that was left of Billy was a cloud of dust.

Billy had moved the boy before he left. The kid was back down over the slope again, his feet lashed to the tree. Dixie started when she first caught sight of him, because he looked dead. He lay with his face pushed into a mound of star moss, his long, messy hair splayed around him. Sliding quickly down the bank, she poked him with her foot. To her relief, he moved.

She knelt down to be closer to his eye level. 'We got off to a bad start yesterday, so let's start over. OK? To begin with, you're going to be a whole lot more comfortable without this, and I actually do care if you are comfortable or not, even though I know you don't think so.' She pulled the duct tape off his mouth. 'And next thing is: what's your name? Because know what? You and me already spent all this time together and I still don't know who you are.' She smiled at him.

'Fuck off.'

'That's a funny name,' she said, still grinning.

'The fuck if I'm going to tell you.'

'Oh. OK. Suit yourself,' she replied. ''Cause it's nothing off me if you want to keep on being a nasty little snot. Except that you might want to think on this: I got the food. See here? I was bringing you down a cereal bar.' She held it up. 'But you might find I'm much more likely to give it to you if you're nice to me.'

'The fuck I want to be nice to you. That man really hurt me.'

'Yeah, I know. And I'm sorry about that.' The bruises from Billy's kicking had grown dark purple and spread out around the edges of the boy's T-shirt. Dixie very much hoped Billy hadn't broken any of the boy's ribs. He'd done that once to her and the ache had been awful. She leaned forward to lift his shirt.

'Don't touch me!' he snapped.

'I just want to take a look, 'cause maybe I got something in the first-aid kit that would make you feel better,' she said.

The boy, who never seemed to know a kind act when he met one, spat when Dixie tried to touch him and screamed, 'Fuck you, bitch!' So she got up and left without giving him the cereal bar.

Dixie felt filthy. She hadn't even changed her underwear since leaving Abundance. Returning to the tent, she took out a towel and soap and walked downstream along the small creek until she came to a place deep enough to have a good wash.

She knew she ought to wash the boy too. His long hair was a matt of spewed chilli beans and debris from the forest floor, and he was still wearing the makeshift diaper she'd put on him the night they left. It had long since become sodden with urine, accumulating a coating of dirt and pine needles as he'd moved around and now the flies were all over it. She considered the matter, trying to figure out how she could get him down to the water without letting him loose. Just the thought of it tired her out.

After bathing, Dixie climbed back up the slope to the main campsite and sat down on a fallen log to comb the tangles out of her wet hair. She could see the boy from there but wasn't close enough that he could cuss at her. He lay trussed up like a pork roast, his nose pressed into the moss as if he were sniffing it.

Languidly Dixie combed her hair, noticing, as she did so, the scent of lichen that covered the log where she was sitting. She tried to tease out how it fitted into the complex tapestry of smells in the late-morning forest. They were different from earlier. At this altitude, the mornings were cold even in August and when you first woke up, the scent of the forest was crisp and invigorating; but as the day wore on, it grew heavy and just a little hard to breathe in, like a church lady's perfume.

I bet Jesus smells like this, Dixie thought. Like the mountains. It was beautiful but at the same time almost too big to take in, so she'd always ended up feeling a little sad underneath the joy. Jesus and the mountains had always seemed very much the same to Dixie.

'Lady?' the boy called.

Dixie looked down over the slope.

'Come here,' he said.

She rose and came down. 'What you want?'

'I've got to poop.'

'That's really tough, because I'm not untying you,' Dixie said.

'I don't want to go in my pants. Come on. You got to help me.'

'You've been a little monster. So I can't trust you. I can't untie you.'

'I'll be good. I promise. I just don't want to do it in my pants. My butt hurts already.'

'I'm *not* stupid.'

He made a whiny noise. 'Come on,' he pleaded. 'Please?'

Dixie regarded him. These were the things you never got told about when you read stories of kidnappings in the newspaper or saw some thriller on TV. Not these everyday matters of putting food in and getting it out the other end. You knew people had to be doing them, of course, but how they coped with the monotonous regularity of them was never mentioned.

'I'll take your diaper off but that's all.'

'*No.* I'm going to have to lie on it, if I can't move.'

'I'm sorry, but, like I said, I ain't going to untie you.'

'Please? *Please?* I won't do anything. I promise. Please? My butt hurts so much from wearing this towel thing. *Please* don't make me poop in it.'

Dixie felt terrible. What if this was Jamie Lee, left in a dirty diaper for two days? She would have been just heart-broken if she found out someone had treated Jamie Lee so bad, and yet here she was, doing it to some other mother's boy.

'OK, look, here's what I'm going to do. I'll untie you from the tree but I'm not going to take the tape off your arms or your legs. I'll just hold you up enough that you can go. Then you won't be laying in it.'

Saying it and doing it were two very different things. He was a heavy kid and having his limbs taped together didn't help at all. Dixie finally managed to get him propped up over a small log but she had to hold him in place because he couldn't balance with his ankles taped together.

'I don't want you looking at me,' the boy said.

'I seen little boys' peckers before. I had a little boy of my own.'

'I can't do it with you looking.'

'Listen, it was me who cleaned the poop off you the other night. What's going to come out this time ain't no different. And it ain't no different than what comes out of anybody else's behind. So just get on with it.'

'I can't do it like this.' He started to cry.

Dixie's resolve began to waver because the boy looked just pitiful, what with his bruises, his chilli-encrusted hair and his grubby, tear-stained cheeks.

'OK, I'll tell you what I'm going to do. I'm going to take the tape off your legs. OK? I'm not going to let go of your arms, but I won't have to hold you in place, so I can look the other way. But I'm trusting you to behave now, understand?'

The boy nodded fervently.

Taking out her pocket knife, Dixie cut through the duct tape restraining the boy's legs.

The second the tape loosened and the boy's ankles were free, he jerked away. Pulling his feet under him, he was up and off, his little bare bottom flickering through the undergrowth.

'Oh my God!' Dixie cried in astonishment. 'Come back here!'

The boy didn't stop. He was much more agile than she'd ever dreamed a fat kid could be, especially as he still had his hands taped behind his back. He quickly disappeared from sight, crashing away into the forest.

Dixie bounded up the bank to the campsite and grabbed the .22 out of the tent before taking after him.

He didn't get far. Only about fifty yards into the deeper part of the forest, the undergrowth had snared him. He was struggling fiercely to break free when Dixie located him.

'Stop!' she shouted.

He managed to break the branch that had caught him and took off again, plunging deeper into the trees.

'Stop! I'll shoot. I mean it, kid. *Stop.*'

The boy looked back at her and when he did, Dixie raised the rifle to her shoulder and aimed.

Without his hands free, turning had overbalanced him. He fell sideways into the brush, rolled a few feet down the slope and struggled unsuccessfully to rise.

'You stay right where you're at, kid. I mean it. You stay laying right there or I'll use this. I *mean* it.' Dixie kept the gun aimed as she approached him.

The little devil had fear in his eyes but not enough to stop him. He was on his feet again and off.

Dixie pulled the trigger. The crack of the rifle tore through the forest, the sound ricocheting around the mountainside as if guns were firing from every side. The boy screamed and fell.

'Get up,' Dixie shouted. 'I didn't hit you.'

He lay motionless.

'I *didn't* hit you, you little dickens. If I'd wanted to hit you, believe me, you'd be laying there dead. But you ain't, so I didn't. So get your damned butt up.' She poked the gun barrel into the underbrush.

The boy struggled to his feet.

'Now come out of the bushes. *Now.*'

Ashen-faced, the child hobbled back towards her.

'You stupid boy. You stupid, *stupid* boy,' Dixie shouted angrily as he approached. She pushed the mouth of the rifle against his chest. 'Where do you think you are? Disneyland? You think this here's all full of bunnies and Bambis? Or maybe you think you're on one of your daddy's fake movie sets where you can make believe you're tough, because nothing ain't ever going really happen to you except pretend bad stuff? You think that?'

His eyes still terror-round, the boy gave a small shake of his head.

'Because I'm going to tell you something right now, and you pay attention to me. Yeah? This here place is real. You ain't in control here. So you got to respect it, because it don't care pig shit about you. You go running off and get lost up here and you'll be dead by nightfall. Bear, mountain lion, wolf – I can guarantee one of them, if not all three, is sitting right this minute where it can see us and is just watching for you to be stupid. That's how they get their dinner, waiting for things to be stupid. And if none of them makes a meal of you, then the cold will have you. I'm not joking. You got to be respectful up here, if you want to stay alive. Understand that?'

He nodded.

'And you got to be respectful of me too,' she said and jabbed him again with the barrel of the gun. 'Bears and such ain't your only danger. Billy, if he'd been holding this here rifle, you'd be laying dead now, because Billy's got no patience. He shoots first and thinks later. So count your lucky stars it was me. But if you're this stupid again, I'll shoot you myself. I promise. You got that?'

Again the boy nodded.

'And one more thing. Just in case you might be thinking I didn't hit you because I don't know how … See that sticky-out bit on the side of that trunk over there? Watch it.' Dixie deftly aimed the rifle and fired. The bole went flying off. 'Just make sure next time that ain't your head.'

Back in camp, Dixie taped the boy's legs together again and lashed him once more to the tree. She had to work carefully, because her hands were trembling so badly that nothing went the way she wanted. When at last he was secure, she climbed back up the slope to the campsite. Exhausted, she lay down on her sleeping bag in the tent.

Dixie was still shaking from the fright at what had just happened. The boy really wouldn't have had much of a chance, half-naked and half-bound. Mountain lions were the biggest danger. This part of Montana was just crawling with them and they were so sneaky. She remembered a forest ranger once saying that at any given moment in the wilderness, folks were never more than two hundred feet away from a mountain lion, yet most people would go their entire lives never seeing one. Like cats, mountain lions knew how to stay hidden when stalking their prey. They lurked in the underbrush, watching, waiting, ready to pounce if anything good came along. They especially liked catching kids, because kids were small and squeaky.

Dixie could still remember how one of her neighbours had been out on a Sunday walk with her family one balmy summer's afternoon when her six-year-old grandson had lagged a little way behind to pick wild strawberries. Before anyone knew what was happening, a mountain lion had popped right out of nowhere and grabbed him. The grown-ups managed to rescue him by running at the lion and screaming, but the boy had a bad bite on his shoulder and he never could use his right arm again properly.

Thinking about mountain lions eating up Spencer Scott's son was scary enough, but that wasn't the only thing to leave her shaky. What was really scary was realizing just how easy it had been to aim that rifle at him. In her mind's eye Dixie kept seeing the boy's naked little butt disappearing into the undergrowth and feeling all her anger with him, all her frustration with Billy and with the situation itself swelling up inside her head to where pulling that trigger would have been such a relief. Lying motionless in the fly-ridden heat of the tent, Dixie felt sick to her stomach to know that about herself.

Chapter Nineteen

W hy not just keep riding? Spencer thought. It wasn't as if he had any frigging family that cared about him. The only person who would really miss him was Michael, his agent, and that was simply because without his cut from Spencer's work, Michael would never pay off the hideous mortgage on that vulgar mansion in Bel Air.

In some detail Spencer fantasized his escape. Not the rather tricky part about how he actually would get from up there in the forest back down to civilization, but rather what would happen once he and Ranger had reached Idaho or wherever his new life was going to take place. Mostly Spencer was thinking about how he could get his money without anyone tracing it, especially considering he had taken nothing with him on this ride – no bank cards, no identity, nothing. He enjoyed the thoughts. They were challenging without the burden of needing to be executed, and they took his mind well away from the problems back at the house.

They took his mind well away from the ride itself, as well, because when the horse baulked unexpectedly and Spencer was abruptly brought back to what he was doing, he realized he had no idea how long they'd been travelling along the trail through the forest. Half an hour? An hour?

He paused, pulling Ranger to a full stop. Turning around in the saddle, Spencer looked back down the way they'd come. He was quite sure this was the right trail, that it would meet up with a logging road soon and then come out on the ridge, but it was surprising how, once you got into the forest, there seemed to be so many different trails. They weren't prominent, none of them were, not even the one he was on, but they were definitely trails. Who all went on them? It was private land. He owned everything. All the way around Lion Mountain to where it joined up with the wilderness area.

He turned back in the saddle. The trail ahead kept climbing. They'd been going uphill ever since leaving the familiar route back to the ranch, and how far was that? A couple miles? Four? Five? How long *had* he been riding? Spencer looked upward, trying to discern where the sun was, but the canopy of trees was too dense.

'Come on, you,' he said to the horse and flicked the reins. 'We've come this far, we might as well keep going.'

There was no logging road. Spencer was quite certain they should have come to it by that point, but if anything, the forest seemed closer and more impenetrable. When he saw a wider trail going off to the left, he decided to take it because it looked less steep. Bringing Ranger to a stop, he studied the junction carefully in order to recognize it if he came back this way, then he headed onto the other trail.

It was indeed wider than the path Spencer had originally followed, but he was unsure this meant humans were using it. What else was up here? Moose? Did they make trails? Elk? Yes, more likely elk. They were herd animals, weren't they?

Absorbed in these thoughts, Spencer didn't notice any change in Ranger's behaviour until the horse abruptly reared back. Lifting both his front hoofs off the ground, he swivelled his hips like a double-jointed belly dancer and came down sideways to the direction he'd been going. Spencer scrambled for a hold on the pommel of the saddle to keep from falling off. If he hadn't already tied the reins together in the way Guff so hated him to do, he would have lost them completely. As it was, they dropped loose onto the horse's neck.

The source of Ranger's fright sauntered out onto the path in the form of an enormous, golden-shouldered grizzly bear. While it was clearly aware of them, it also appeared unconcerned that they were there and continued to amble indifferently towards them. This proved too much for Red Ranger. The reins already loose on his shoulders, he easily got his head. Veering to the left of the bear, he took off at a flat-out gallop. The track that had seemed gentler to begin with suddenly turned steep. Ranger clambered frantically upward. The forest parted and there was a ridge, although not the one Spencer had been looking for. Before he could get his bearings, Ranger plunged back into the forest and kept going. Spencer didn't dare try to rein the horse in. He was too worried that taking even one hand off the saddle horn would lose him his purchase and he'd fall. All he could do was hold on for dear life.

When the saddle started to slide, it happened in that eerie slow-motion manner that defines disasters, where every second is so drawn out that you remember it exactly. From the first movement, Spencer panicked, because he knew he was going to fall. *Fuck you, Guff, for not being there to fix the frigging saddle right! You know I can't do it myself. Fuck you for not riding off Ranger's extra energy! Fuck you for letting him be such a dangerous horse!* He frantically grabbed up the reins and pulled as hard as he could to stop the horse. *Fuck you, Ranger! You know what this tugging means. You know exactly how to behave. Don't do this to me!*

Crash! Both Spencer and the horse went down together in the rough underbrush. Almost without pause, the horse found his feet again. The loose saddle momentarily snared him on a nearby bush and he reared back in fright, stumbling, crashing once more to the ground. Then he was up and off again. Within seconds he had disappeared through the trees. The whole incident from first slip of the saddle to being alone in the forest had lasted perhaps only three minutes.

Spencer lay entangled in the underbrush for several moments, too overwhelmed with shock and adrenalin to move. What was hurt? That was his first question and he tentatively moved his limbs to find out. Not much. The bushes that made up most of the forest floor in that area had cushioned his fall. He had scrapes and scratches but nothing else. Spencer stood and brushed himself off.

Now what?

He looked around. It was fucking forest everywhere, one tree looking pretty much like every other. He saw nothing that would tell him where he was.

Spencer replayed the events leading up to the grizzly bear encounter. The original trail had been steep. The one he had turned off onto traversed a slight slope but the horse had then started galloping upwards. There was the open bit. Then back into the forest. By the time the saddle came off there was no trail at all. When Ranger had disappeared, he'd gone straight through the underbrush.

Spencer looked up through the trees, down through the trees, and over at the horse-made path through the underbrush. Which way?

Shit. *Shit!* This wasn't fair. This fucking wasn't fair! Why did all the crap in life always have to happen to him? Spencer kicked out angrily at a knee-high bush in his way. A small brown butterfly fluttered up into a shaft of sunlight piercing through the trees. Spencer smacked it dead.

This wasn't doing any good. He needed to be sensible. He would meditate. That would calm his mind, so that when the frigging horse finally returned, he wouldn't be so wound up that he'd scream at it and frighten it away again. That was a good plan. Spencer prised off his cowboy boots and sat down in a lotus position in the forest litter.

Too much adrenalin was coursing through his system for him to be able to close his eyes, so for five or ten minutes Spencer just sat, quietly watching the shifting patterns of dappled sunlight on the leaves of the undergrowth. His anger ebbed away, but his mind continued to wash restlessly back and forth over the events of the morning.

The horse didn't reappear. Time passed – a half an hour, an hour – no way of knowing. And no horse. Not even the sound of the horse moving nearby. Nothing but birds and flies.

Spencer hadn't expected this. Once Ranger got over his fright at encountering the bear, Spencer just assumed he would return. Wasn't this what horses did? Loyal friends who stood over the fallen soldier on the battlefield for days and all that?

Fucking horse. Why did everything in Spencer's life have to be such a disappointment? Sighing, Spencer pulled his boots back on, stood up and brushed his jeans off.

But now what? He wasn't a fucking mountain man. No skills at reading spoor. No talent for killing small fuzzy animals. Plus, he was sore. The fall had hurt.

Spencer stood a little longer, considering and hoping beyond hope the horse would turn up. He inspected the scrapes and scratches acquired in the fall one more time and then did a few warm-up stretches to loosen his muscles.

The first task was to get out of the deep undergrowth and the most sensible way of doing that, Spencer reckoned, was to follow back along the broken branches and squashed bushes where the horse had crashed through.

This was easy to do at first, so easy, in fact, that Spencer wasn't particularly concerned. He felt confident of being able to follow the damage the frightened horse had caused back to the trail, back to where he would recognize where he was.

What a tale this would make. The grizzly bear, the runaway horse, the spectacular fall and now the daring escape from the mountains. For quite some while Spencer entertained himself by creating the vivid story he would tell friends when he was back home in LA. He minutely pictured the scene – where he'd be, whom he'd be with, which bottles of wine would be washing it down – *and it was all true!* Everyone else had fucking publicists make up their stories.

Spencer liked this image of himself. This would be a good story to share with the media when he was next on a promotional junket. Distracted by these thoughts, Spencer enjoyed the walk. It was still easy to pick his way through the trees, following more or less where the horse had galloped through.

At one point, Spencer stopped to peer up at the sky because he had no idea what time it was. The tall trees blocked the view. He hadn't come to any path or trail or even a break in the forest, which surprised him. How far could the horse have galloped after sighting the grizzly bear?

Grizzly bear. Hmm. There was something else to think about. He knew you were supposed to wear bells on your rucksack to let them know you were there. But why the hell would you want to tell a bear that? Besides, he didn't have any bells. Better sing. '*We are the champions! We are the champions! We are the champions of the world!*' he belted out, throwing a little air guitar in.

It was at least an hour's steady walking before Spencer finally found a discernible trail. Nothing about it, however, looked familiar. Or perhaps, better put, everything looked familiar. Every fucking tree looked just like the one next to it. He didn't know whether to go left or right. For several minutes he tried to orientate himself, mentally reversing the gallop on the horse. In the end, he chose to go right for no better reason than that the trail appeared to be a bit easier to follow in that direction.

Thirst was beginning to get the better of him. As he crossed a tiny stream, he paused. Could he risk drinking the water? Spencer's stomach lurched at the very thought. Deer peed in water, or so he'd heard, and that made it full of

Giardia. Spencer recalled one of his friends catching giardia-sis from drinking from the fountains in Rome and he'd had such foul-smelling farts they wouldn't let him back on the plane to go home. He decided it would have to be a larger, faster-running stream than this one before he'd try.

Hunger also made itself known. Spencer had felt too hungover to eat before leaving the house. Normally he welcomed the gaunt, empty feeling as proof he was keeping his body lean and attractive, but now it left him shaky and very slightly anxious.

The trail deteriorated. For some time it had been going level across the side of the slope and had provided easy, if somewhat irregular walking; now, however, it appeared to go uphill through a fall of moss-covered stones, but maybe not. Was that the trail? Spencer paused and gazed around at his surroundings.

Fucking hell. Everything looks like everything else. It was past a joke now. He didn't want to see another fucking pine tree or lump of moss. He was thirsty, hungry, sore and scraped. There was no 'We Are the Champions' about it.

The sound of water was audible over the ambient noise of the forest around him. Water would go downhill, Spencer thought, so it might make more sense to follow that. He crashed off through the underbrush in the direction of the sound.

The stream was smaller than Spencer had expected from the noise. He couldn't quite jump across it, but almost. Unable to resist his thirst any longer, he knelt and drank from his cupped hands. There was just the tiniest little gag, because he hadn't quite successful at keeping the image of peeing deer from his mind. Then he reminded himself that this was just the way Daniel Boone would have done it. Spencer had almost got the Daniel Boone part in that biopic. Yes, his agent had insisted on a rather spectacular price, but he would have earned that back for them. And look what happened when they went with the Dutch guy. *Dutch?* To play Daniel Boone? No wonder the movie failed.

Following the stream downhill led Spencer at long last into a small clearing in the trees. It wasn't large enough to be a meadow, just an open area, but big enough that Spencer could finally see the sky.

He looked up. A mountain rose above the forest on the left. A mountain rose above the forest straight ahead. Lower aspects of the same mountain rose above the forest on his right. Only behind him did there appear to be no mountain, but that was the direction he had been coming downhill from. Bewildered, Spencer turned in a slow circle, trying to get his bearings. He didn't recognize any of the slopes as Lion Mountain. He couldn't even discern if they were all part of the same mountain or two different peaks.

Fuck.

A bitter hour followed. Spencer was lost. He'd been in fucking denial these last few hours, acting as if he was out for a stroll, as if he had everything in control. Follow the trail. Go downhill. *Fucking hell.* He was lost. He had been lost since falling from the horse. He'd been fucking lost all along and just pretending he wasn't.

Anger then. Anger at the boy, who was at fault for all of this. At Phoebe for having the boy. At Sidonie for not being awake to comfort him. At Guff for not being there to put the saddle on properly. At the forest for being bewildering when all he had ever asked of it was refuge and calm. He kicked at a clump of wild lupins, shattering the purple heads and sending the small spear-like leaves flying. He growled. He screamed. He screamed again, not only because he hoped it might catch someone's attention, but because it helped relieve the pent-up tension. Not even an echo came back to him.

Then despair. He *was* lost. Utterly alone in a wilderness the size of a small country with no food, no water, no knife, no matches, nothing.

Chapter Twenty

Billy got back so late that he didn't get up the next morning until half past ten. When he at last emerged from the tent, he stretched his arms way up over his head in a luxuriously slow, almost dopey manner, like a yoga teacher on weed. Then he started to scratch. Standing in a shaft of golden-white sunlight midst the pines, almost as if he was taking a shower, he started by scratching over his head, then his face, his arms, his chest and finally his balls.

'You got coffee?' he asked when he came over.

Dixie shook her head. Sitting cross-legged on the forest floor, she was playing solitaire with a set of cards, laying them out in front of her on the carpet of pine needles. 'We can't be making campfires, Billy. Not just because the ranger says we can't, but also because this time of year folks are going to always be on the lookout for forest fires, so any time smoke goes up, someone will come to investigate.'

'Yeah, well, I fixed that, because I brought the gas ring with me. It's in the back of the truck. But I didn't unpack it, because I been thinking.'

'About what?'

'We need to move on. We're too close to town.'

Dixie's heart sank. 'I was more hoping that you'd been thinking about how to fix this so we can go home.'

'That'll happen, but just not now. I want to take us up into the high country. I've figured out a good place. We'll get more freedom up there.'

Billy had brought sensible stuff up with him this time, like the little gas cooking ring and much more food. Setting up the gas ring on the tailgate of the pick-up, Dixie made coffee and a breakfast of tuna-melt sandwiches. Billy unwrapped a cereal bar and took it down to the boy. From the truck Dixie couldn't see what was going on between them, and that was probably just as well.

After breakfast they set about taking down the campsite. Billy whistled cheerfully as he loaded the truck, packing the boy up right along with the rest. Once everything was to his liking, he told Dixie to climb into the cab and off they went.

Billy drove confidently through the upward maze of old logging roads and rutted mining tracks. When these petered out, he still kept going a while longer along a trail that didn't look as if it had been used by much more than deer.

'Driving here is going to leave tracks someone might notice, Billy,' Dixie commented, seeing the deep grass. Not that it would likely matter much when it wasn't hunting season. The wilderness covered almost two million acres and there were only three rangers to cover it. Fishermen wouldn't bother coming this high up. Except for hunters in the Fall, very few people ever bothered to venture beyond the designated campgrounds.

Billy nodded. 'Yeah, I know. Which is why we're going to stop here,' he said and brought the pick-up to a juddery halt in the trees. 'We'll walk the rest of the way.'

Dixie looked over questioningly. 'You're kidding, yeah?'

'Nope. I'm taking you somewhere really special. Leave the tent, because we ain't going to need it. Just the sleeping bags, the food and cooking gear.'

'What about the boy?'

'He can walk too. It'll do him good.'

'You're going to have to take the tape off his legs,' she said hesitantly. She hadn't dared to mention the boy's near escape the day before.

'Well, *duh*,' Billy said and smacked the back of her head playfully. 'Of course I'm going to have to take the tape off. Don't worry so much about everything. He won't go anywhere he shouldn't.' Then he took his handgun in its holster out of the glove box and strapped it on.

'Yeah, well, this is exactly why I'm worried.'

Billy did seem to have it thought through, because he strung the three of them together with rope like mountain climbers, the boy in between himself and Dixie, plus he kept the boy's hands taped behind him and put the tape back over his mouth. If this wasn't enough, Billy not only had his handgun, which he kept playing with menacingly, he also carried the .22 slung over his shoulder.

The kid had bigger problems than Billy's antics, however. About half a mile into the walk, Dixie noticed his face turning red. He began to stagger and then he went pale as death. When green bile started coming out of his nose like snot, Dixie rushed to rip the tape off. The boy came around soon enough once he'd thrown up. Probably it was just the altitude. The fact he was fat and had a hard time keeping up with Billy's pace wasn't helping any either. They ended up having to go very slowly, the boy grunting and puffing and puking between them.

The pines tailed off into aspen and then, all of a sudden, a large, surprisingly flat clearing opened in front of them. The entire meadow was knee deep in the most astonishingly blue flowers. Some kind of gentian, probably, because those were the only flowers Dixie knew to have that deep, almost unnatural colour, a polyester blue the same as you found on old ladies' blouses in Walmart. There were so many of them that it was as if the sky had fallen into the grass and every so often there were daisies, great big enormous ones almost the size of a saucer, gleaming among the blue flowers like stars. Dixie gasped at the sight.

'Yeah, see, didn't I tell you it was going to be something special?' Billy said with a grin. 'And see over there?' He pointed. 'There's our hotel.'

Scanning the perimeter of the clearing, Dixie spotted ancient logs and a half-collapsed sod roof tucked in amid the ghostly white trunks of aspens on the far left-hand side. 'That?' she murmured.

'It's better inside than it looks. Me and Roy, we've stayed up here lots of times when we were bear hunting.'

'How long ago was that? Crowheart's been a wilderness area for what? Three years now? Five? They ain't been allowing bear hunting up here for a very long time.'

'Yeah, well, that's all the better for us then, huh, because nobody's going to be bothering us.'

Dixie knew by the log-and-sod construction that the cabin was most likely a relic of the area's early mining days.

Probably it had been some prospector's home while he'd scoured the nearby creeks for gold, and it looked as if it had been just about that long since someone had lived there. It was nothing more than a ruin. Two roughly constructed rooms stood under a roof that had probably never been much higher than a man could reach. The logs of the back wall had long since slid apart, dropping the roof in the second room at a sharp slant to where the sod and the ground behind had grown into one. There was a door that looked as if someone had made it later. It was gaping open, but Dixie could see that it shut well enough to keep the outside out. That, however, was just about as civilized as it got.

'This is a cave,' Dixie muttered.

'No, it's not. It's a nice little cabin.'

'Very long ago it might have been nice.'

'OK, yeah, so it's a bit old, but if you look at it careful, you can tell someone long ago took a lot of trouble with this,' Billy retorted.

'OK, so it's a man-made cave.'

There was still evidence of former occupants. In the front room there was a rotting wooden table and two chairs, although one didn't have its back any longer. There was a shelf on the side wall that still had an empty, rusting coffee can sitting on it. In the back room, there were two pages of an Abundance newspaper jammed into a crack between the logs. It was dated September 25, 1985. In the interim there had been plenty of animal occupants, birds mostly, judging from the droppings everywhere, but an elk had sheltered fairly recently near the doorway, leaving mountains of pellets to step over, and wood rats had taken advantage of the fallen back wall to nest in the logs.

Billy was stupid with delight. 'We can put the kid in there,' he said, indicating the back room, 'then you and me can have some privacy in here.' He winked saucily.

Sodden depression was settling over Dixie. 'This is all a big game to you, isn't it? What's next? You got in mind to bring your horses up? You imagining us being some kind of frontier family, Billy? Me and the boy living here while you go out hunting to bag us a moose or something? Because that's how you're talking, but let's get it clear right now. That's not what this is all about.'

'Well, fuck, I *know* that, Dixie,' he said irritably. 'Jesus, I'm just trying to cheer you up. What's the matter with you? Because here I am, trying to do something nice for you and this is how you act. Shit. I don't know why I bother sometimes.'

She dropped her shoulders in a gesture of desolation. 'I know you mean well, it's just … it'll take *ages* to go back down to town from here. It was taking ages already when we were at that other place. But this … we'll need half an hour just to get to the truck.'

He leaned over and kissed her. 'All you do in that little head is worry. You leave it to your man.'

Billy must have realized just how close to the end of her rope Dixie was, because he stayed on his best behaviour the rest of the day. Cleaning out the bird crap and fixing the table and chairs so they were a little sturdier, he did what he could to make the cabin habitable. Later, he showed her where a tiny little creek was flowing through the aspens at the back of the cabin. He even boiled up some coffee for her. After all that, Dixie felt bad about complaining, so she made him a hearty dinner of corned beef hash and fried eggs.

In the evening they sat together in the doorway of the cabin. 'You got to admit now, this is a pretty place,' Billy said softly and put his arm around her shoulder. 'Pretty as my woman.' He smiled at Dixie.

It *was* beautiful. The slanting rays of sunset lingered over the meadow, gilding everything lightly with a luminous, not quite transparent gold. The air, already growing cool, was so fragrant with pine and aspen and meadow flowers that it would catch for a brief moment in the back of Dixie's throat each time she breathed in, a sweet sharpness that she could taste as well as smell.

'You know, I never realized before how miserable you can get,' Billy said. His voice was gentle. 'You're like your daddy in that way, Dix, and it ain't an appealing characteristic. You'd find life better if you just took things lighter.'

The way he was saying it, Dixie knew he meant it to be a comfort to her, that he was just showing how he cared. He couldn't help it that even his loving came off as criticism.

'Life's a bitch,' he said softly. 'Not much we can do about it. But if we think about it all the time, we'd end up doing nothing but crying. Me, I think it's better just to sit here and look at that beautiful sunset and let that be enough.'

Dixie sighed. 'Maybe you're right.'

Billy cuddled her a little more. He had such a nice smell about him, a manly smell of dust and sweat, but clean sweat. Not the kind that had gone stinky. And he had strong arms. Billy was a skinny guy. He didn't have any bulgy macho-man muscles, but his were strong, sinewy arms that threw calves and worked horses, and when they hugged, Dixie could forget just about everything.

They made love on the moss beneath the aspen. It was the first time since Jamie'd got really sick in April that Dixie enjoyed it. She hadn't been in the mood before. Too much worry in the beginning and then too tired, and then somehow it had just seemed disrespectful to Jamie Lee to be wanting to do something like that when he was dying. She wasn't altogether in the mood yet, but Billy was being so tender with her that for a short time he managed to shrink the world right down to just the two of them. Dixie lost herself in his slow kisses and the feel of his taut, warm skin to the point where nothing else mattered except how her body felt.

It didn't last. Almost as soon as Billy had spent himself and rolled back onto the grass, Dixie started worrying that it wasn't a good time of month for them to have done that. Dixie had never gone back on the Pill after Jamie Lee, because she was afraid of what it might do to her milk, and Billy never could remember to carry condoms.

How awful it would be to get pregnant now. What was going to come out of this mess? What if the sheriff caught them with the boy and sent them to jail? The night sky above her blurred as Dixie thought about how awful it would be to have a baby in prison. What kind of way was that to start your life? And maybe they wouldn't even let her keep it. That was the worst thing Dixie could imagine, feeling love like she'd felt for Jamie Lee and then losing that baby too. She couldn't even think on it without tears.

Next to her, Billy was smiling. 'Jesus, this is the life, isn't it?' he murmured. 'Up in the mountains. Laying out under the stars with my woman. All this.' He gestured drowsily at the trees. 'Just the way to live.'

'That wasn't exactly where my mind was,' Dixie said and turned away from him.

Chapter Twenty-One

Desperate to get out of the dense forest, Spencer kept walking. Common sense told him that however lost he might be on the mountain, whatever direction was downhill had to be the right way to go. If he travelled downhill far enough, sooner or later it would have to lead out of the trees.

There was no longer any path. Spencer wasn't quite sure how he'd lost the trail he had originally started out on, because it had been quite plain in the beginning, but soon there was only underbrush and fallen debris from the trees. Spencer continued, going wherever the walking was easiest while keeping his downward angle. During the first few hours, he assumed that the conifers would give way any time to the broken terrain of juniper and sagebrush covering the foothills, and so he kept looking up for a glimpse of open countryside through the distant trees. As time passed, however, he assumed less and hoped more and kept his head down, his eyes on the undergrowth to avoid being tripped up on the rough ground.

As evening fell, there was still no sign of a break in the forest. Spencer kept moving, but less confidently, as the underbrush closed in around him. In the end, he took shelter in the lee of a fallen tree, curling up as best he could against the cold. He didn't sleep so much as pass out from exhaustion.

The next morning Spencer woke cold, stiff and very hungry. Dawn was just lifting the darkness from the tops of the trees, the sky going a fainter, starless colour against the still-black pines. With no watch to tell him the time, he had no idea how long he'd slept, but it had been deep and dreamless.

He was sore. The fall from the horse hurt now. Not badly. Spencer knew no real damage had been done, but there was a noticeable ache, the kind that would be much soothed by time in the Jacuzzi and Sidonie's pampering, and he felt dispirited to find himself damp, cold and lost in the fucking forest.

And hungry. Jesus, he was hungry. It had gone beyond the empowering feeling he'd had the day before, knowing he was in control of his calories; it had gone beyond the mild high he always got when fasting. Now it was just pain that, if he wasn't careful, sucked everything else into it.

Spencer was also aware of being very sober. He not only felt wide awake, but his head felt oddly, almost startlingly clear. Not that Spencer considered his use of alcohol and drugs, legal or otherwise, in any way excessive, but there weren't too many mornings when he woke up without one of them in his system. For several moments, Spencer explored the new sensation. He wasn't sure he was impressed.

Sitting on the fallen log that had sheltered him overnight, Spencer looked around. The forest was unbroken. Just endless conifers stretching out in all directions. Beneath the trees was a tangle of plants fighting for the light and an obstacle course of fallen trees, broken branches and boulders.

The sun was fully up. Spencer could tell by the level of light, but he couldn't discern where it was. Either the mountains were blocking it or the trees were simply too dense. Even if he could see the sun and knew that, as it was morning, that way was east, how would that help him? Where was the ranch, direction-wise?

Spencer endeavoured to translate what he knew about the location of the ranch from survey maps to the reality of trees and mountains. The ranch was east of the river. The river valley pointed south. The ranch was on the northwest side of Lion Mountain. Spencer turned his body, holding his hands out, left and right, to orient himself to east and west. OK, so if the trail he had taken from the ranch went parallel to both the river and Lion Mountain, was that south?

Shit. *Shit*. In a world of sat-navs and chauffeurs, who knew stuff like this?

Spencer sighed in frustration and rubbed his face. In doing so, he became aware of the faint stubble of a beard. People were going to see it was grey if he had to go too long without a razor.

He set off again. There wasn't much of an incline, which made it hard to discern the best way to continue moving downhill, but Spencer picked up a fairly well-worn path after about half an hour's walking and started to follow it. By now he realized that it was most likely made by animals and not a proper trail, but it was easier going.

The path terminated beside a large, fast-running stream. He was over his squeamishness. Water was water and if deer had pissed in it, so be it. He paused to rest, to wash and to drink his fill, because the water took his mind temporarily off his aching stomach.

How long could a person go without food?

No. No point thinking about that. He found a place he could cross the water and, once on the other side, he kept walking.

The helicopter went directly overhead. It was afternoon by that point, hot shafts of sunlight spearing through the trees and bringing to life all the flying insects that that rested during the cooler hours. Hearing the helicopter approach, Spencer had stopped where he was, stripped off his shirt and waved it over his head in hopes of making himself more visible amidst the thick cover of trees. The helicopter's shadow briefly wiped across his face and then was gone. Screaming in frustration at the lattice of branches above him, Spencer knew he hadn't been seen.

All through the afternoon the sound of the helicopter taunted him. It never came as near again, but he could hear the sound undulating – closer, further, closer and then further again – as it searched the mountainside. Desperate to find enough open space to be seen, Spencer crashed frantically through the forest, looking for even the smallest clearing.

Shadows lengthened. The noise of the helicopter grew fainter and at last it disappeared, leaving Spencer with only the sleepy chirping of mountain birds as they settled for the night. What had started in the morning as a clear-headed, thought-through plan to find his way out of the forest on his own ended in sodden despair as Spencer realized how much of the day he had spent chasing after the sound of the helicopter, and how it had led him in directions he really hadn't been able to pay proper attention to as he ran after it. Now, as night fell once again, he had no idea where he was in relation to where he had been in the morning, but worse, there was no 'downhill' here. He had worked his way into a pocket and whichever direction he chose to go, he was soon confronted with the need to go uphill.

Depression settled over him. Weak and exhausted, he lay down and for the first time allowed in the thought that he could die here.

Chapter Twenty-Two

Billy was like a horse with blinkers on. He saw straight ahead and nothing to either side. The next morning, as he sat down to eat his breakfast, the first thing he said was: 'How much do you reckon this reward is going to be? I been laying there thinking about it before I got up. Trying to figure out what we can expect.'

'It's been four days and nobody's even mentioned a reward yet. Nobody's mentioned anything, period,' Dixie replied. 'Don't you think that's kind of odd?'

'It'd be a million, don't you think?'

'It's not going to be a million, Billy.'

'Five hundred thousand? Come on. Give me a figure. What do you think?'

'Ten thousand, if you were lucky.'

'Ten *thousand*? For Christ's sake, Spencer Scott would pay more than that to get his kid back. He's filthy rich.'

'Yeah, if it was a kidnap. But this isn't kidnapping. And we got to keep it that way, Billy. Don't even *think* about going out and making this worse than it is. Most you can expect and still stay out of jail is a reward for information. Like maybe where to find the boy. That's the kind of thing we got to concentrate on.'

Billy paused and considered while he spooned pork and beans onto his eggs. 'Well, I suppose we could manage that. I guess. Roy says Ben Nicholson might be able to put me on to some cheap horses. I bet I could set up for five thousand. How much do you need? You got to pay off the funeral guy. What else?'

'Billy, we don't have this money yet, so let's not spend it.'

'If it's a reward, do we got to pay taxes on it?' he asked.

'Billy, I haven't a clue.'

'Maybe when they offer the reward, we could ask them for, maybe, like another five thousand on top. Just in case there's taxes.'

After breakfast, Billy got ready to leave. Dixie begged him not to go. Mostly she didn't want to be left by herself with that horrible little boy, but also because it seemed like the best idea was just to hole up for a while and wait things out. Whatever was happening with Spencer Scott, he'd have to go public sooner or later. Then they could reappear with the boy and say they found him wandering, which was a kind of truth. In the meantime, however, they needed to be patient. The only problem, of course, was that Billy had zip in the patience department.

Dixie could see other problems too. If Billy went back down to town, he'd end up with Roy at the Horseshoe. The drinking was bad enough, pouring away what little bit of cash they had left to them, but Dixie was more worried that he would let slip to Roy what was going on. Billy never was very good about keeping his mouth shut, even when he wasn't drinking. Especially if it was about one of his schemes, because they were all 98 per cent talk anyway.

That was bad enough, but worse was the possibility that Billy would run into someone like Leola's husband, Earl Ray. He went to the Horseshoe quite a lot, and while Earl Ray and Leola weren't exactly on speaking terms at the moment, it could still cause real trouble if he mentioned seeing Billy. Leola would think straightaway how peculiar it was that Billy was hanging around the Horseshoe while Dixie was up camping by herself.

Dixie pondered the matter. This was what was so awful about this kind of thing. You couldn't just leave it at one bad deed. It kept multiplying. She hated lying to Leola, because Leola was the one person who'd always be loyal, but she would have to lie if Leola found out. Dixie considered how she could explain the situation. Maybe she could say that Billy and she'd had a bad fight and he'd gone off and left her at the campsite. Given Earl Ray's behaviour, Leola would understand that well enough, except it depended on no one asking Billy his side of it. God forbid Billy should have to think on his feet.

After Billy left to go back down the mountain to town, Dixie spent time straightening up the front room of the dilapidated cabin. She tried to make the rickety shelf a little sturdier so that she could put the cans of food on it. Afterwards, she changed her clothes and gathered together what was dirty. Finally she went into the little back room where the boy was.

'I'm going out to the creek to do washing and I'm going to take you with me. We need to get you washed too, 'cause you're a stinking mess.'

Dixie had been debating how to do this. She didn't want to take the gun, because she would have to lay it down to wash either the boy or the clothes. The best idea seemed to be to cut his feet loose but keep his hands bound, the way they had done when moving him the previous day, but instead of tying the rope around his waist, to tie it around his neck and use it to control him, like a dog's leash.

She made him sit down right in the water. The creek wasn't very big, never wider than a man could jump across and shallow in the flat area beneath the trees. It only came up to the boy's belly button when he sat down. He gave a muffled squeal through the tape and struggled to his feet.

'Yeah, it's cold. But you got to sit in it, 'cause you're getting horrible sore down there,' Dixie said and grabbed hold of his hair to push him back down. 'But know what? I can take this off.' Leaning over, she carefully peeled the tape off his mouth.

The kid screamed bloody murder.

'Yell all you want here. Only the bears to hear you.'

'It's *freezing*!'

'Yeah, I know. But you got no choice. You need to get washed. So sit down.' She pushed him back into the water.

'Get your hands the fuck off me! I'll sit down myself!'

Tying the rope to an overhead aspen branch, Dixie turned to put the washing into the water. 'It's a good thing you ain't my little boy,' she muttered. 'Because if my little boy had a mouth like you got, his butt would be so red he could beacon planes in at the airport with it.'

'Yeah, well, if you were my mother, I'd kill myself.'

Dixie decided to wash the clothes first so that the boy could soak in the water in hopes that would help his sores, but he refused to stay in. Dixie worried about him accidentally strangling himself with the rope around his neck, so she didn't try tying it in a way that would force him to remain in the water. Instead, she just gave up the fight. If he didn't want his butt to feel better, that was his choice. So she ignored him when he wouldn't sit down and got on with the washing.

This irked the boy. Not content with just getting out of the water, he soon managed to work himself along the bank until he was next to her. Arching his back, he started to pee. The stream of urine splashed over the shirt Dixie was scrubbing.

'You think you're making me mad, don't you?' Dixie said quietly. She didn't look over. 'But you're not.'

The boy pushed the pee out so hard he farted.

'Instead, you know what? You're helping me. Pee makes clothes nice and white.'

'Does not.'

'In Roman times they used to want folks to come pee in their laundry. The buildings were made special just so people walking by on the street could stop and pee down into the laundry where they were washing clothes.'

'They did not,' the kid said grumpily. 'You're just making that up.'

'No, it's true. Look it up sometime. So thanks for doing that, for being helpful without being asked. That was real sweet of you. And see? See how nice and sparkly clean this shirt is now?' She held it up.

The boy spat at her.

Washing him was an ordeal. Even with the rope around his neck and his hands bound behind his back, Dixie had to wrestle him back into the water and then struggle every moment to keep him there.

'Stop fighting. You got throw-up on you and you don't want that, do you? And you got *beans* in your hair. You look like a great big sicky taco.' She grinned at him as she sluiced water over his head with a tin cup and then rubbed the bar of soap through his hair.

The boy squealed and squirmed. 'Stop it! Fuck you, leave me alone!'

Dixie dumped more water over him. 'You think this is bad. It's going to get worse in a moment, because I need to wash your behind.'

'Don't you dare touch me there! That's child abuse and I'm going to tell!'

'Leaving you sitting in your own mess till your butt falls off is worse child abuse. Now, come here. Quit fighting.'

'Fucking leave me *alone*!'

It was just one big battle. Dixie was utterly exhausted by the time she had the kid clean. 'If you could be nice for two seconds, it'd go a lot better for you,' she said, 'but you make everything so much work.'

'Fuck off.'

'Yeah, well, that's exactly what I'm going to do,' she said, flopping him down into the damp grass on the bank of the creek. She rewrapped the duct tape tightly around his hands and legs. 'I'm fed up looking at you. You can just lay here like a plucked chicken for now.'

'The fuck I care,' he said and glared at her. 'Just piss off.'

So she did. Taking the wet clothes, Dixie went around to the front of the cabin and laid them out over the flowers in the clearing so they could dry. Then she went into the cabin and made herself a sandwich.

The afternoon wore on. That was one of the worst parts of this, the endless hanging around without much to do. Dixie dug into her rucksack to find her deck of cards. At least with the cabin, dilapidated as it was, there was a table. She lay out the cards to play solitaire. Staring at her in the first column was the nine of spades. *This nine coming after the joker. Talks of losses … You're going to have worries about what to do with this unexpected challenge*, Leola had said when doing her card-reading. Dixie touched the black symbols with her fingertips. She didn't understand how cards could tell you the future but if ever there was a joker in the form of an 'unexpected challenge' it was that boy, and sure enough he'd been nothing but worry and loss.

With no warning whatsoever, tears filled Dixie's eyes. She missed Leola so much. She missed sitting in Leola's kitchen, drinking coffee with her and talking. She missed the snap and smack of the cards as Leola laid them out, even the fug of Leola's cigarettes, although Dixie normally did nothing but complain about how bad they made her clothes stink. Most of all, however, Dixie missed the ordinariness of it all. That's what made her cry, realizing how precious ordinary was. Realizing how easy it was to take everything you loved for granted, no matter how dearly you loved it. Realizing how quickly it could all be gone.

Chapter Twenty-Three

A subtle rustling through the underbrush woke Spencer to pre-dawn darkness. The fear was immediate, sending the sound of his heart into his ears and the skin at the back of his neck crawling.

A bear? In his hunger-weakened state, Spencer knew he couldn't outrun it. Could you outrun bears anyway? He thought he remembered reading something somewhere about them being unexpectedly fast when they wanted to be. Would he be able to escape up a tree? Could he play dead? Lie very, very still and trust the bear would just pass him by? Or would it smell him out? Did they have good noses? Shit, why had he never bothered to pay attention to stuff like this? What value did knowing who were the players in the industry or being able to discern which estate the Merlot came from, if you ended up a bear's breakfast?

The bushes parted not more than ten feet from where Spencer lay, rigid with fear, but it wasn't a bear. An elk stepped out, a huge bull elk with a heavy rack of antlers.

One, two, three, four, five, six, seven … Spencer endeavoured to count the points.

It turned its head and looked at him. Even though he had made no movements whatsoever beyond breathing, the animal knew he was there. Through the pre-dawn gloom, it regarded him for several moments, then it turned and moved on, disappearing into the undergrowth.

Once it was apparent he was in no danger, Spencer briefly entertained the wild idea of springing up to kill the beast and eat it. The next idea was more rational – to follow it. While there was no reason to think the elk would lead him out of the mountains, it might well lead him to an open area. Elk grazed, didn't they?

Rising quickly from where he'd slept, Spencer trotted after the animal.

It realized immediately what was happening, and while at first it did not run, it picked up pace, moving effortlessly through the heavy brush. Spencer struggled to keep up. Within five minutes or so, the elk vanished, leaving Spencer stumbling clumsily along through the bushes. He halted.

Now what?

Spencer listened into the forest. It occurred to him as he did so that over the last couple of days, his entire world had shrunk to this dense, dark landscape. Little else except staying alive had crossed his mind in any substantive way for what … two days? Three, was it? Not the boy, not Sidonie, not his property, not his possessions, not his work. Every moment had been focused on the here and now of survival.

The 'here and now'. The irony was that Spencer's meditation teacher was always banging on about that, about how, if people could only stay present to the here and now, they would be able to let go of all the neurotic thought patterns that were holding them back. Yeah, well, he'd discovered a great way to master that one.

Somewhere mid-morning, the sound of rushing water became audible. Spencer chased the noise until he came to a fairly good-sized, very fast-running stream. He rested a while beside it, drank deeply of it to pacify his hunger and then started to follow it downhill.

After about an hour or so, he arrived at a small clearing. It was perhaps only twenty or thirty feet across, but so relieved was he to be in the open after two days of continuous trees that he threw himself down, spread-eagle, in the sparse, raggy grass. Staring up at a sky gone pale in the midday heat, he listened for helicopters. The only drone he heard was of bees busy in the lupins that grew sporadically across the small open space.

As he lay, Spencer's gaze wandered over the terrain looming above the treetops. To his left, a mountain rose up. To his right, a mountain rose up. Straight ahead a mountain rose up.

Recognition dawned abruptly. He had been here before. That first day, not long after he had fallen off Ranger, Spencer had come into this clearing. He recollected seeing the mountains rising up in all the wrong places then too. On the move almost continuously since and here he was, right back where he had started.

Despair washed over him. And then sleep.

* * *

Spencer dreamt vividly of being home in LA, of the airy, open mansion with its Mexican-inspired faux adobe arches and cool terracotta tile floors. He dreamt of food and wine and lying by the pool. When he awoke, hot and slightly sunburned, the dream clung to him in a pleasant manner, leaving him feeling refreshed and even, perhaps, relaxed.

Sitting up, Spencer remained still for several minutes to let the dream melt away naturally. He looked around the small clearing without really seeing it. Then he looked up and listened for any sounds of rescue – a helicopter, a plane, anything. He thought he might be detecting the far-off sounds of an engine but they were too faint to discern for certain. He rose to his feet. 'Hallooooo! Hallooooo!' he called, just in case.

There was no point moving on from the clearing. He'd only use up energy he could now ill afford to waste and for what? To go in circles again?

Spencer had always found the reality programme *Survivor* compulsive viewing, fascinated in particular by how the selfish gene always won through. He'd also noticed that there was a correlation between kindness and the ability to manipulate others. *Survivor* was brilliant at revealing that at the end of the day, it was always every man for himself.

He had not, however, ever viewed *Survivor* as a template for actual survival. Picking back through his memory of the show, he tried to recall what the competitors had done first when they were stranded. How did they build a shelter out of nothing? Find food?

It helped to think of this horrible situation as a reality programme. Here he was, a contestant. It was just another acting job. Spencer could hear the narrator explaining his decisions as the fly-on-the-wall camera followed him.

Spencer Scott makes the decision to stay in the clearing. This is a wise move. He has remembered he is more likely to be rescued if he stays in one place.

Spencer starts building a shelter from fallen branches. Proving he's not just another pretty face, he shows amazing tenacity in this hostile environment despite having been brought up in New York City. He's doing far better than the younger contestants on the other side of the mountain ...

Making a small shelter in the lee of a fallen tree kept Spencer well occupied for a couple of hours. The fly-on-the-wall *Survivor* narrative faded to be replaced by the possibility this was one of those candid camera programmes. Maybe he was being punked. Maybe Ashton Kutcher and the camera crew would jump out from behind a tree at any time. Truth was, Spencer had longed to be one of Kutcher's victims. It was a younger, hipper crowd in Hollywood who were involved in that sort of thing and it brought with it a certain cachet of street credibility Spencer coveted very much. He knew it would never happen, because he moved in such different circles, but he wanted it anyway, and it was easy to imagine what a brilliant punk this situation would be.

Building the shelter had been a useful way to pass the time, but Spencer's main concern was food. His body had adapted quite well to his diet of water. The frantic, gnawing hunger had been replaced by something subtler, although ever-present, that gave him a heavy, lactic-acid-build-up-type tiredness in his muscles and made him fall into such deep, unconscious sleep that it felt rather too much like a practice run for death.

Spencer knew nothing about the plants in the forest. He had seen berries growing on some of the bushes in the undergrowth, but most were clearly not ripe and those that were ... were they edible? How would you know? Having seen *Into the Wild* not once but twice, he was more worried about a hideous death from poisoning than the slow, sleepy drain of starvation.

But what about fish?

Spencer Scott investigates the stream. It's too small and fast for ordinary fishing, but Spencer knows there are trout in all these mountain streams. Look! He's seen the minnows! How will he catch them?

How *would* he catch them? Lying motionless on his stomach, Spencer watched as several minnows gathered in the quieter water of the downstream side of a large rock.

In the end, Spencer managed to fashion a makeshift net out of his shirt by knotting the sleeves closed and using a sock to tie the collar end together enough to be able to scoop with it. This, of course, didn't mean the fish were impressed. It took several tries with considerable waits in between for the water and the fish to calm down before Spencer finally hit upon a successful way to chase the minnows in the right direction and scoop them up in the shirt.

Seven. He caught seven. Bringing the makeshift net far enough up onto the bank that he knew the fish couldn't get back in the water if they flipped out of it, Spencer carefully opened it. The water had magnified their size. They were all minute, maybe only three inches long. Minnows in the true sense of the word.

Spencer looked at them, flopping helplessly on the wet, stained material of what had once been a favourite custom-made shirt. Now what? He had no means of gutting them. No means of cooking them. They were only a bite each anyway.

Oh well. He picked up the first one. *It's sashimi tonight.*

Chapter Twenty-Four

S hadows lengthened. Dixie knew she was going to have to go and get the boy, who was still on the bank by the creek, but she delayed as long as possible, hoping Billy would return and do it for her. She hated being trapped alone with him. He was spoiling the mountains for her, making her detest being up here in the wilderness that she had always loved so much.

What would happen if she just cut the boy's bindings and then turned her back? The longing to be rid of him had been quietly building for most of the afternoon, but Dixie had tried not to notice it. Now as night drew in and loneliness grew, she couldn't fight it off any longer.

If she just let him go, would that be the end of this mess? She turned the thought over in her mind, teasing it like a tongue does a loose tooth. In her mind's eye Dixie could see the boy melting into the forest as he had the other day when he'd got loose, only this time around she wouldn't chase him. He'd just disappear among the trees and that would be the end of it. No one would ever know what had happened to him. She and Billy could go back to Abundance, back to everything like normal, and pick up as they'd left off. What had happened to Spencer Scott's son would become the stuff of campfire stories or conspiracy theorists or maybe turn into one of those famous mysteries like with Amelia Earhart.

The boy, still bound hand and foot, had curled up best he could in the deep grass beside the creek to keep warm. In the gloom of twilight his body gleamed like a little white slug.

Dixie knelt beside him. 'I'm going to cut the tape on your legs so that you can walk back to the cabin by yourself,' she said.

He was shivering badly, his teeth chattering. She'd left him out there way too long. She hadn't meant to. Not really. She'd just needed some time away from him.

Inside the cabin, Dixie threw one of the sleeping bags around the boy's shoulders. Too bad there wasn't a fire, because his little body was quaking something terrible. She sat him on one of the chairs in the front room and pulled Billy's hooded sweatshirt down over him, making him look like Kenny from *South Park*. He wasn't saying anything, which worried Dixie. His eyes were as blank as a fish's.

'I'm going to make you some soup,' she said. 'That's what you need. Some hot food in you, and I bet you're hungry because you didn't have no lunch. I got chicken noodle here,' she went on as she turned on the little gas ring. 'That used to be my favourite when I was your age. You like chicken noodle?'

'Never had it,' he replied softly.

'Never had it? Never had chicken noodle soup? You're joking me, aren't you?'

He shook his head.

'Well, it's good,' she said and brought the hot soup over in a mug. 'You want me to dip some bread in it for you?'

His brow creased.

'Never had that either? What your folks been feeding you? Because it don't look like you missed many meals.' She broke up a slice of white bread and dropped it into the soup. 'Try it this way. It makes it more substantial.'

He didn't fuss as she began to feed it to him.

'It's real hot now. Be careful eating it.' She blew on the soaked bread, then paused before spooning it into his mouth. 'You're not going to spit this back at me now, are you?' Dixie said, only half joking.

Very slightly the boy shook his head.

He was so hungry that it was like putting food down a Labrador's gullet. Whomp! and it disappeared off the spoon. He took everything she gave him.

'There. That's better, isn't it? You're getting warmer now.' She smiled at him.

While she still thought he was an ugly kid with his too-long hair and his pudgy piggy cheeks, Dixie noticed he had nice eyes. They weren't the searing blue that had made Spencer Scott famous, but they had the same long lashes and, when he got older, Dixie could imagine girls would think they were sexy.

'Know what? I still don't even know your name,' she said.

'Tennesee.'

'Huh?'

'That's my name. Tennesee.'

'You're joking me, right?'

'No.'

Dixie sat back and grinned. 'That's not a person's name. It's the name of a state.'

'Phoebe liked it.'

'Who's Phoebe?' Dixie asked.

'My mother.'

'Why do you call her Phoebe?'

'Because that's her name, stupid,' he replied and Dixie knew the soup had done its job, because he was starting to feel good enough to be nasty again.

'Yeah, I guessed that. But why don't you call her "Mom" if that's who she is?'

'Because she doesn't like to be called "Mom". She likes to be called Phoebe.'

'How come she gave you a state name?'

'Because she had a spiritual awakening there once. So that made Tennessee meaningful to her, and she wanted to give me a meaningful name.'

'What's a "spiritual awakening"? Did she find Jesus or something?'

The boy pulled his shoulders up in a shrug. 'I don't know really.'

'Wow. In that case, guess I'm real lucky my mama didn't call me Squaw Gulch, because that's where our preacher always does his baptizing.'

For a long while after the boy had gone to sleep in the back room, Dixie lay awake in the darkness, listening. Cupped into the curve of Crowheart's peak the way they were, she reckoned she ought to be able to hear Billy's truck on the mountainside from a long ways off. She listened intently for it through the faint scritchings and scudderings of small animals around the logs of the cabin, through the almost silent whooshing of owls passing outside. No engine could be heard.

Dixie fell into a doze, and then woke with a start at the sound of Billy approaching the cabin. Jumping up from her sleeping bag, she opened the door wide to welcome him in, only to startle back. It wasn't Billy. A cow moose ambled out into the clearing, followed shortly by her gangly calf. Their coats silvery with starlight, they stood a moment midst the closed flowers and stared at her, then they moved on.

Without Billy there, Dixie couldn't sleep. The night was alive with small sounds, the sort that normally didn't even register when he was snoring softly beside her, but now they were impossible to ignore. Dixie brought the .22 in against her like a lover and pressed her cheek to its cold, smooth barrel. The tangy scent of steel and spent gunpowder filled her nose.

While the gun was a comfort against the noises of the night, it did nothing to quell other anxious thoughts that loomed every time Dixie grew still. Mostly they were about how to get out of this mess without losing everything, without going to jail. Coming up with a way to pay the funeral man for Jamie Lee's funeral now seemed like such an itty-bitty problem in comparison. Even coping with Jamie Lee's health problems and his dying, while terrible, had at least been something Dixie knew she would manage because she had folks around her to take care of her while she was doing it, and Jesus was there to take care of Jamie Lee. But this? How did you cope with this? Dixie couldn't see any way out of this mess other than letting the boy go and hoping that something catastrophic would happen to him before he could tell on them. And what kind of horrible person hoped for that?

Chapter Twenty-Five

The boy had gone to sleep wearing Billy's sweatshirt and jog pants because he was still cold. His wrists and ankles were both bound and somewhere during the night he had got himself in a tangle with the too-big sweatshirt. Consequently, he was lying face down in the dirt when Dixie came into him in the morning. She pulled him around and up into a sitting position. 'Jeez, look at you. You got bird poop all over. You could be one of them clowns, you know, with the white faces.'

'It's not funny,' the boy said crossly.

'No, I know it's not funny. I'm not laughing at you, not really. I'm just remarking.' Dixie rocked back on her heels. 'Know what I decided during the night?' she said as she grabbed the sweatshirt and pulled it off over his head. 'That it's bad enough we're up here and all this is going on without keeping you trussed up like a shot deer. So I'm going to take all this tape off your arms and legs.'

'I could run away now,' the boy said in an emphatic tone.

'Yeah, I know. And the bears could eat you too. Who knows?'

'I *could*.'

'Yeah, I *know*. But I been thinking about it and I decided this isn't good like this. You get to decide how stupid you're going to be.'

Taking out her pocket knife, Dixie cut through the tape. 'There. That's better, isn't it? Now, put the clothes back on proper, because it's still cold out.'

Sitting on the floor of the cabin, the boy rubbed his chafed wrists and ankles. He said nothing more.

In the other room Dixie took her knife and eased up the disc of congealed grease on the bottom of the frying pan and picked out bits of debris that had fallen into it from the ancient roof. Then she lit the gas ring and put the frying pan on the small flame.

The boy wandered out.

'You want a fried egg?'

The boy curled his lip in distaste. 'Yuck.'

'You don't like fried eggs?'

'I've never had one, but I don't like eggs. They look like shit.'

Dixie cracked two into the pan.

'How come you eat so many eggs?' the boy asked.

'They got lots of nourishment in them for what they cost.'

'Phoebe says they're bad for you. She only buys egg substitute. She says yolks are, like, poison, because they're totally full of cholesterol.'

'Yeah, but egg substitute is just made-up food. Why would I want to eat something out of a factory when there's real food to eat?'

The boy shrugged indifferently.

'Do you guys eat fancy food all the time?' Dixie asked. 'Because you don't seem to have eaten any ordinary food. What do you have? Lobster and caviar and stuff?'

'Hardly. I eat pizza and hamburgers mostly. Normal stuff like that. And pasta. I like Italian food. And Mexican food. María-José – she was my nanny for a while – she could make really, really good things like tamales,' he said and gave a slight quirk of his lips that just might have been a smile.

Dixie grinned at him. 'Well, what do you know,' she said. 'You *are* able to get some other look on your face besides "nasty little sucker".'

He ate the egg. He made a big deal of it, screwing up his face as if he were having to suck on baboon testicles or something, but the egg disappeared in a few bites and Dixie saw him looking out of the corner of his eye at the frying pan, in case there might be more.

After breakfast, Dixie took her playing cards outside. On the edge of the clearing about thirty feet from the cabin was the trunk of a very large fallen tree. The bark was gone from it, as were all but a few stubs of branches. What was left had turned a pale grey in colour, meaning that it had fallen many years before. The top side provided a sizable smooth, flat area. Sitting down on the narrower end, Dixie laid her cards out on the log for a game of solitaire.

The boy wandered over. 'How come you're always playing cards?' he asked.

'It passes the time.'

'It looks boring to me.'

'Good thing you're not playing then, huh?'

He climbed up on the log, straddling it and watching her. Several moments passed with just the quick snap of the cards breaking the silence.

'Why did you untie me?' he asked at last.

'Don't you think it's better this way?' Dixie answered without looking up.

'Yeah.'

'Well, then that's reason enough, isn't it?'

There was a long pause.

'What if I run away now?' he asked.

'Yeah? Thinking about it?'

'You said you'd shoot me if I did it again.'

'Yeah, I did.'

'Would you?' he asked.

Dixie was holding the jack of hearts and she paused to see where she could place it. 'Planning to take that chance?' she asked, still not looking at him.

'No …' The boy hesitated. 'It's just … I want this to be over.'

'Well, see there? We're batting on the same team then, because that's all I want too … Billy told me you were running away that night he picked you up,' Dixie said as she started a new game. 'That true?'

'Yes.'

'How come?'

'It sucks so much being at my dad's.'

'How come?'

'Because I hate it.'

'How come?' Dixie asked.

The boy shrugged. 'Because LA is way better.'

'I bet you got lots of nice things to do at your dad's. Somebody told he's got a room just for watching movies in and the screen is almost as big as the one at the showhouse.'

The boy shrugged again. 'So? Everybody's got that in LA.'

'I never been to LA. Never been anywhere really except Montana. Went to Idaho once following Billy and the rodeo, but I can't be doing with all that travelling.'

'I don't mind it.'

'So that's where you were taking off for that night Billy got you? You planning to go all the way to LA?'

He brought his shoulders almost up to his ears before dropping them wearily. 'I don't know. I guess.'

'What do you mean, you guess? You were running away but you didn't know where you were going?' Dixie asked. 'No wonder Billy caught you.'

'I *knew* where I was going,' the boy replied in an injured tone. 'Away from my dad's.'

'That's not "going". "Going" means "going *to*",' Dixie said.

'Doesn't have to. "Going" can mean "going from" as well.'

'It doesn't.'

'It does.'

Dixie went back to her cards.

'I'm right,' the boy said. 'You're stupid, if you think you're right. I know a lot more than you do.'

'I wouldn't think so,' Dixie said casually, keeping most of her attention on the cards. 'I'm a lot older than you.'

'I'm a genius.'

'Good for you.'

'I am. I've got an IQ of 152. I belong to Mensa.'

'Like I said, good for you.'

'You probably don't even know what Mensa is.'

Dixie laid down the two of hearts.

'Nobody in Abundance is smart. My dad says everybody is so inbred in Abundance that their shoe size is bigger than their IQ.'

Dixie played out her ace.

'He says the people in Abundance can't tell their brains from their assholes.'

'They can tell enough to know when to wash their kids' mouths out with soap when it's needed,' Dixie replied, 'which is something your father doesn't seem to have figured out yet.'

The boy fell silent. He stayed, however, continuing to sit astride the large log and watch Dixie play endless games of solitaire. The sun grew hot. The meadow became vibrant with the sound of insects, the air blowsy with the perfume of wildflowers.

'What I was planning was to go back to our house in Santa Monica,' the boy said after a long silence. 'Nobody's there. Puni had to go back to the Philippines because her visa wasn't any good. But I was thinking maybe I could get the security guys who patrol our neighbourhood to let me in.'

'Where's your mom?' Dixie asked.

'Phoebe, you mean?' He shrugged. 'I don't know. I think maybe she's in Acapulco.'

'Couldn't you just phone her up and say you wanted to go with her?'

'No way. She's got a new boyfriend. She wants to be alone with him. She'd get so pissed off with me if I did that.'

'Yeah, but she wouldn't want you to be unhappy either.'

'Phoebe says it's tough if I don't want to go to my dad's. She says it's only fair she has some free time too and it's his obligation to have me. She says it's not her fault he's a bastard and hates me.'

'I'm sure he doesn't hate you,' Dixie replied.

'He does,' said the boy matter-of-factly. 'But I don't care, because I hate him just as much.'

'I'm sure it's not hate, not really,' Dixie said. 'Sometimes dads fight with their kids and it feels like hate. I know, because my dad fights with me too. But down underneath I know he loves me. It's just hard for him to show it.'

'My dad just says how he never wanted another child and it was Phoebe's fault she got pregnant, not his, so he shouldn't have to have me around.'

'He *says* that to you?' Dixie asked.

'He says it to Sidonie when I'm standing right there.'

'Who's Sidonie?'

'His girlfriend, the one that's living with him now. He tells her he never wanted any more kids because it cost too much to educate Kathryn's kids.'

'Who's Kathryn?'

'His ex-wife. He's always saying that Phoebe got pregnant just to get her name in the gossip columns and further her career, and he'd never marry someone like that. But Kathryn says he won't get married because he doesn't want to pay more alimony.'

'Wow,' Dixie muttered, 'you got one complicated life.'

'Yeah, I know.'

'And I'm sorry folks are talking like that in front of you. Those aren't the kind of things kids should be hearing.'

'Do you have any kids?' the boy asked.

'I did. I had a little boy. His name was Jamie Lee.'

'What happened to him?'

'He died,' Dixie said. 'He had Down's syndrome. That meant his heart wasn't made quite right. The doctors tried to fix it, but they couldn't.'

'I knew a kid with Down's syndrome once. He was at my school,' the boy replied. 'The teachers told us how he was special and we had to be nice to him, but actually he was just a retard. Was your little boy a retard?'

Dixie looked up at him. She thought she heard something else in his voice, a little undercurrent of meanness perhaps, and it put her on her guard.

'He was perfect in my eyes,' she replied.

Chapter Twenty-Six

'Hallooooo? Hallooooo!' Spencer shouted at sun-up from the middle of the clearing.

The sharp morning air carried the sound better. He could hear a faint echo of his voice off the surrounding hills, so he called again. And again. And again.

'Hello?' came the distant answer.

'*Here!* Over here! This way!'

It took about ten minutes of calling back and forth with the distant voice for him to locate Spencer; then came a loud, welcoming crash through the undergrowth and Guff appeared astride the small buckskin mare Spencer had bought for Sidonie.

'Holy shit, Guff. *Where* have you been? Where the fuck has *everyone* been? I've had no food, no water!'

The old cowboy dismounted.

'What the fuck took you so long?' Spencer asked. 'Do you know what I've been through?'

Guff looked him straight in the eye. 'It ain't my fault you're out here, Mr Scott, so don't go yelling at me. What the hell were you thinking of, taking Ranger out like that, when he hadn't been ridden off?'

Having assumed Guff would be as relieved to find him as he was to be found, Spencer rocked back in astonishment at the reprimand. 'Why are you pissed off? I'm the one who got thrown on the ground. And I'm the one who's been stuck out here all this time, for fuck's sake.'

'You shouldn't ought've treated Ranger that way,' Guff said brusquely.

'I didn't mistreat him in any way. He's my fucking horse and I just took him out for a ride.'

'You don't got the experience to ride him, Mr Scott. So you shouldn't ought've ever been taking him out when he's fresh. He came home lame and all covered in sores where that saddle rubbed. Anything could have happened to him.'

'Anything could have happened to *me*. Did you stop to think of that?'

The old man wasn't backing down. He jabbed an accusing finger at Spencer's chest. 'This ain't about you, Mr Scott. It's about him and about the fact you got a brain Ranger don't have, so you got to always be looking out for him too. He ain't a sports car. You don't get on him just 'cause you want to feel something big between your legs. If you can't ride him, you *don't* ride him. God gave you that brain in your head so you can tell what's sensible to do.'

Spencer was speechless. The old boy had never strung more than about three sentences together in the entire time Spencer had known him, and now he came out with this? What the fuck? Had he been lying in wait all this time for an opportunity to catch Spencer when he was vulnerable? *Who the fuck do you think you're messing with?*

'I have been out here with no food, no water, no way to get back. Shit, Guff, that horse threw me off in front of a fucking great grizzly bear. I could easily have been killed, and you're upset about the *horse*?'

'I'm saying, Mr Scott,' Guff repeated in slow, emphatic words, 'that this ain't about what's happened to *you*. You got yourself in this pickle because you let a horse do the thinking and you got to understand that. If you're going to sit on his back, that horse needs you looking out for him. Not 'cause you own him. Not 'cause he cost you a lot of money, but because he trusts you. A man shows he's a man by how he lives up to the trust of those who's innocent.'

With that, Guff turned away, lifted the stirrup of his saddle up and checked the cinch. He ran his hand along the horse's legs the way a man does with a car when he's checking the paint for chips. Then he walked the horse down to the small stream and let it drink its fill. He waited patiently for it to crop the leaves off a nearby bush and have a massive piss.

Spencer seethed silently. At Guff's mercy out in this Godforsaken wilderness, he knew there was no point antagonizing the old cowboy further, but if Guff thought he was going to get away with this kind of insolence, he was badly mistaken. *You're on your way out, old boy. I'll show you who owns Ranger.*

Guff brought the horse into the small clearing again, put his foot into the stirrup and was back in the saddle. He lifted the reins and turned the horse's head.

'Hold on a minute!' Spencer cried sharply. 'Where are you going?'

'I ain't taking you on this mare, Mr Scott. She's too small. She can't carry two. Not over this land.'

'You can't just *leave* me here!'

'I know where you're at now. As long as you got the sense to stay right here, it'll take me only an hour or so to go back and get another horse.'

'You *can't* leave. I'm starving. I haven't eaten. I'm covered in fly bites. Look at me! You can't leave me here!'

Twisting in the saddle, Guff tugged open his saddlebag and pulled out a handful of protein bars. 'Here.' He tossed them to Spencer. There were four of them and Spencer hadn't anticipated that Guff would toss them at him. He caught one but the others tumbled into the dirt.

Being expected to grovel for food tossed to him as if he were a beggar was a push too far for Spencer. Furiously he shot his hand out and grabbed the left-hand rein at the horse's neck. 'No!' he shouted. The horse danced sideways in alarm, but Spencer held on. 'Take me with you. *Now*. Your fucking horse can manage that much, Guff. At least take me as far as one of the roads so that I know where I am. So I know you can fucking find me again.'

Guff appeared unruffled. 'Trust me, I can "fucking find" you here.' He held his hand out. 'Give me the rein, Mr Scott,' he said.

'No. Take me with you.'

'The mare can't carry two. She's a small horse, sir, and this is rough country. She just physically can't do it. Give me the rein, please.'

Spencer refused to let go.

Guff adjusted himself in the saddle to reach for the rein, but as he did so, his body made a quirky movement, like a lop-sided little jerk. For a split second, he cocked his head almost as if he were listening for something, and then, in one fluid movement, he melted off the horse, sliding down the side opposite to Spencer, his nearside boot clipping Spencer's chin as he did so.

Startled, Spencer took a moment to register what had happened. Guff had fallen to the ground on the other side of the horse and it seemed as bewildered as Spencer was. Concerned that the animal would step on Guff, Spencer used the rein he held to back it up. Then he flapped his hands to get it to move away.

'Guff?' He knelt down and shook the old man's shoulder. Guff remained motionless.

Spencer felt for a pulse. Guff was alive, his heart beating quite soundly. Why had he suddenly lost consciousness? 'Guff?' Spencer shook him more roughly. 'Come on now, don't do this to me. Guff, wake up.'

The old guy never stirred.

Shit. What was that saying? 'Just when you think it can't get worse, it gets worse.' Because this was definitely worse. Before was bad. This was worse.

'Guff? Guff, come on. You don't want to do this.' Squatting down beside the old cowboy again, Spencer loosened his collar for want of something better to do. 'Guff?' He patted the cowboy's cheeks firmly. 'You so don't want to do this. Not here. Not with me. Fuck, don't you know what an idiot I am with practical stuff? You're always thinking it. So don't trust me to know what to do now. Come on. Open your eyes.'

Shit.

Rocking back on his heels, Spencer glanced around at the underbrush, the trees, the munching horse. Helplessness engorged his body, pushing upward and outward from his stomach until he tasted bile. His limbs felt swollen. His head hurt. *What to do?* Spencer screamed in wordless frustration, startling the stupid horse.

Rising, he paced away from Guff's motionless body, paced back. 'You fucked up big time here, Guff. I can't help you, buddy. I don't know what to do.'

He looked at the horse.

'Hey, you.' He took a step towards it. 'You got to help me get out of this.' The horse stepped back. 'Come here.' Spencer held his hand out flat as if he had something to offer the horse.

Not fooled, the horse regarded him warily.

It was a pretty animal, a pale buttermilk in colour with faint dapples on its flanks and the sort of long, elegantly rippled black mane and tail that horses had in fairytale books. That was the reason Spencer had bought it for Sidonie, because, like her, it was beautiful to look at. He'd even told Sidonie that in an affectionate moment.

Longing for Sidonie twanged abruptly through Spencer. She'd know what to do. Even now. Even here. She was hardly more than a kid and yet she was always so amazing when it came to dealing with the unexpected. She wouldn't be daunted. She'd just get on with it, and he wanted that so much. Someone to hand all this over to, because he couldn't cope.

Again, Spencer reached out for the horse. What had Sidonie called it? Starbright? Starlight? Something very girlie. Except that the horse had never learned its name, because Sidonie never went near it. Two years or whatever and she still made excuses for not riding. Spencer knew the reason behind it. She was afraid of horses. But she wouldn't admit it. Fear was a weakness that annoyed him, and the fact Sidonie wouldn't come clean about it annoyed him even more.

'Come here, you. You've had it easy all this time, eating my oats and never having to do anything for it. Here's your chance to make it up to me.'

Inch by inch Spencer approached it. It was browsing nonchalantly amid the scraggly underbrush, but it wasn't off its guard. With each step he took, it stepped back just enough to stay out of his reach.

'Look. I've got something for you.' He picked up a handful of grass.

The horse ignored him.

Taking one of the protein bars out of his pocket, Spencer unwrapped it and broke it in half. Eating one half himself, he held the other half out in the flat of his hand. 'Hey, look at this. You want this?'

The horse raised its head, nostrils flaring to take in the scent of what he held.

'Now you're curious, huh? Come on, stupid. Come see what it is.'

Continuing to offer the protein bar, Spencer edged towards the animal. He got within about eighteen inches of the horse's head but then it stepped back again.

Frustrated, Spencer pocketed the broken protein bar and just stood, waiting for the horse to start browsing again. When it finally lowered its head to take a bite off a nearby bush, he lunged to grab the bridle. The horse, however, was faster. It started back abruptly, turned and rapidly retreated in among the trees, stopping only when it was apparent Spencer wasn't following.

'Shit, horse, give me a break, would you?'

Nonchalantly, the horse sauntered off.

'Shit. Shit! *Shit!*'

Returning to where Guff lay, Spencer knelt and felt the old man's chest. There was a definite heartbeat.

'What the hell am I supposed to do?' he asked the comatose man. He loosened Guff's collar more, unbuttoning the chambray shirt to reveal an undershirt tinged with the same lived-in grime that covered Guff all over. God alone knew if he washed. He didn't smell. Well, no. Truth was, he did smell, but Spencer had never minded it. It wasn't an offensive odour, just a Guff smell or a cowboy smell. Maybe it was the way all Montanans smelled if you shut them up in an airless room.

Spencer stared at the motionless body. A stroke? That was the only explanation he could think of. What were you supposed to do when someone had a stroke? How did you handle them? All Spencer knew for sure was that Guff needed more help that he could give – a doctor, a hospital, *something* – and how the hell was he going to accomplish that? Panic rose as bile into his throat again.

The hours passed. Hearing the drone of a helicopter engine two or three times, Spencer waited anxiously in the small open space to flag it down, but it never passed overhead. The horse didn't run off but neither would it allow him to get hold of it. Guff's condition remained unchanged.

An overwhelming cycle of emotions set in. First came panic, then came rage, but as the hours wore away, it became desperation and depression by turns. Then Spencer would try once again to catch the horse or signal for help and fail, sliding back into fear and impotent fury again.

The sun was soon high overhead. Concerned about leaving Guff lying in August heat, Spencer struggled to lift him up and move him into the shade of the trees. There, however, the air was vibrant with flies, many of which bit, leaving large itchy welts, and he found it impossible to keep the old man free of them. Angry and anxious, Spencer was reduced to shrieking at the flies, but even that brought no relief, neither from their relentless presence nor his unhappiness.

Shadows lengthened. The air began to cool. Spencer strained to hear if there were any engine sounds anywhere, any sign of rescue. Nothing met his ears except the rush of water, the sleepy twitter of birds and the incessant but almost silent movement of the trees.

Darkness started from the ground up, filling in around the stones and underbrush while daylight still arched wanly above the trees. Spencer felt Guff's pulse again. Still there, although perhaps a little more reedy than before. Spencer wasn't sure. He spent several minutes pressing different fingers to Guff's wrist, then his neck, and finally slipped his hand under the cloth of Guff's shirt to feel his heart.

Guff was so fucking intimidating. He seemed the embodiment of traditional sensibilities where duty and decency mattered above all else, an approach to the world that Spencer embraced in movies where things always worked out, but he had never quite identified with it in real life. This morning had been the first time Guff had openly argued, but it only confirmed what Spencer had already suspected: that Guff despised Spencer, evidenced by the way the old man would glance at Ranger, as if the horse were in on some great secret, or colour otherwise accommodating words with a slightly mocking tone. It annoyed Spencer whenever he detected it, because who the fuck was Guff to judge him? Guff had nothing in the world but a horse he didn't own. He was nobody. Nonetheless, it upset Spencer when Guff treated him this way, and this annoyed him even more, because why did it matter what an old cowboy thought? Spencer had become inured to disapproval from everyone else. You had to. Criticism was the gristle that ran throughout the meat of celebrity and if you choked over it, you'd soon be dead.

Spencer sat. There was an air of expectancy in his sitting, as if he were waiting. But for what? Desolation flooded over him as he asked that question of himself, because here was his rescuer, lying flat on his back on the ground.

'How could you do this to me?' he asked of the comatose man. Reaching out again, he gave Guff a sharp shake. 'Come on, now. Enough of this. I'm done. I'm ready to go home. Come on. Wake *up.*'

Guff remained motionless.

Moments passed.

What can I do? The helplessness was crucifying. Screaming, crying, lashing out at the stones and brush – none of it brought relief. Not even vomiting. Spencer was skilled at vomiting on demand. You had to be, if you wanted to be taken seriously as an actor, because these days it was the screenwriter's act of choice for expressing extreme emotion. But, as Spencer discovered, it didn't really relieve anything.

As shadows passed from gloom to darkness, Spencer didn't know what else to do except try to sleep. It was too difficult to move Guff to the makeshift shelter by the fallen log, so Spencer cleared away the stones, the small pine twigs and cones and other debris around Guff and lay down beside him. Above the treetops, it was still not quite fully dark. Lying on his back, looking up through the pines, Spencer could see birds wheeling in the dimming sky. They were very high, just specks, and he had no idea what kind they were. When he focused his hearing on them, he could detect faint, piercing cries. At least he thought he could.

As his attention drifted from the birds, he became aware of his tense muscles and began, one by one, to relax them the way his meditation teacher had taught. Could you meditate like this? Flat on your back on the forest floor, chilly, hungry and worried sick? Spencer spent a few minutes gently feeling around in his mind the way one feels around on skin for bruises to see what hurt. His attention drifted again before he got far.

Turning his head, he looked at Guff beside him and watched the faint rise and fall of the old man's chest. On impulse, he moved closer and pressed his face against the soft chambray of Guff's shirt. There again was that Guff-smell, that Montana mixture of sweat, sagebrush and horses. A masculine smell. The kind of scent you wanted your dad to have, because it spoke of caring about more important things than how a body smelled.

'I don't remember my father,' Spencer said aloud. 'I don't even have a picture of him. The closest I come is from this time he took a photograph of me when I was a toddler. I was sitting on one of those little rocking horses for babies – you know, the kind with a chair seat – and it was in front of our picture window. It was dark outside. So when the flashbulb went off, it caught his image in the plate glass behind me. That's all I have to remember him by: a photograph of a reflection.

'James Oliver Duck. That was his name.' Spencer laughed self-deprecatingly. 'You could make yourself five hundred bucks off the *National Enquirer* straightaway selling that one, Guff.'

The old man remained inert.

'He was already married. Quite a prominent man. In banking, whereas my mother was a labourer's daughter. And a schoolgirl. For real, Guff. I'm not kidding. She was still six months short of graduation when he got her up the duff. Today we'd call him a paedophile.

'But I can tell you this, Guff, it would never have been just James's fault … Jim. Do you suppose he was called Jim? By his friends? Strange, isn't it, to think I don't even know that about my own father.

'Anyway, as I was saying … my mother always had a weakness for men with money. And she was such a manipulator. She was beautiful. She used beauty like currency. She was very good at parlaying what she had into what she wanted.

'But what upset it caused in my family. My mother's parents weren't rich, but they were good, upright people. They had scruples. So they weren't about to put up with the shame of an unwed mother, because that's how it was in those days. Not like now. If you had a bastard in those days … Her family wouldn't stand for it. So, a quickie divorce here. A quickie marriage there. Then out popped Spencer Arthur Duck.' He grinned at over at Guff. 'Even my initials are sad.

'So I *did* have a dad. It's not like I didn't. It's just I never knew him. Their marriage lasted only about eighteen months. I was just a toddler in that photograph. He was gone before I was old enough to have any memory of him.'

Spencer paused. 'Wow. How did you get me talking like that?' He looked over at Guff, motionless beside him, and grinned again. 'What can I say? You're a good listener.'

Chapter Twenty-Seven

Billy came back very late that night. Dixie was already asleep, but roused at the sound of him stumbling through the doorway. He knocked something off the table in the dark and then tripped over the unlit lantern beside her sleeping bag. Next came the sound of her sleeping bag being unzipped and a familiar weight on her body.

'Billy, I'm sleeping,' she whispered.

'Not now you ain't,' he replied.

'You're not going to be able to manage anything anyway, Billy, you're that drunk. Jeez, smell you. How did you even manage to get here from the truck?'

He paid no attention. Dixie felt him fumbling to unbutton his jeans and then there he was, hard and hot against her.

'Billy, not now.'

He wouldn't take no for an answer. Putting his hand firmly over her mouth, he carried on. It didn't matter much because it didn't last long. He came before he was even inside her. The semen spurted across her thigh and then ran, hot and sticky, down into her sleeping bag. Spent, Billy collapsed on top of her.

In the morning, he was still there; his head nuzzled down like a snoozing pup's into the folds of her bedding. He had managed to pull his own sleeping bag over them sometime in the night, but he'd never got inside it.

Dixie regarded him as he slept. In spite of his stupid schemes and everything, she did love him. He never meant to be so much trouble. Billy just didn't know any different. Leola kept telling her she should dump him, but who was Leola to talk? Everyone always went on about what a good catch Leola had made in Earl Ray, but the truth was, he was a turd. The things Leola had told Dixie about him, like how he kept trying to toughen Carrie Dee up by grabbing her by her baby-grow and tossing her up in the air, but then if she cried in fright, he smacked her. Or what he did to Leola's kitten when it peed on the couch. Billy could be mean at times, but he never did it on purpose, like Earl Ray did. And he never took with other women, like Earl Ray did, thinking he was a stallion. Leaning forward, Dixie kissed Billy's tousled hair. Then carefully she extricated herself from her sleeping bag.

The boy was sitting cross-legged on the floor in the other room when she opened the door. 'Still here, huh?' Dixie said, only half-jokingly.

'I didn't think you were ever going to get up,' the boy replied in an annoyed tone. 'I'm hungry.'

'Sh-sh-sh.' She put her finger to her lips. 'You don't want to wake Billy up. Come through. We'll go outside.'

It must have been about eight or nine, because the sun was well up. Dixie went to the large fallen log on the edge of the clearing where she'd played solitaire the day before. In trying to get out of the cabin quietly, all she'd been able to grab was a can of Spam. Carefully, she peeled back the wrapping and put the key in. 'This will have to do you for now,' she said as she opened it. Taking out her pocket knife, she sliced thin layers off the top of the loaf.

'Don't you have any cereal bars left?'

'I don't want to wake Billy by digging around for them. He had a lot to drink last night. No kidding, he'll be in a bad mood if he gets woken up and we don't want that.'

'I won't eat *that*,' the boy said scathingly. 'It even smells like puke to me.'

Dixie shrugged. 'Suit yourself.' She popped the slices into her own mouth before pushing the top back on the can and setting it in the shade.

The boy frowned. 'I want *something*.'

Dixie smiled. 'I reckon we all want something, Joker.'

'My name isn't "Joker".'

'All right, Oregon, then.'

'It's not Oregon either.'

'Oregon, California, Utah, whatever.'

'It's *Tennesee*.'

'Like I said, whatever. But I'm not calling you that.'

'You have to. It's my name.'

'Tennessee ain't the name of a person, Joker. It's the name of a place. And I'm not going to call you the name of a place. It's disrespectful. Like you're not even human.'

'So you think it's better to call me after, like, some insane criminal in a comic book? Because that's who the Joker is.'

'I don't know anything about comic books. I'm talking about the joker in my pack of cards here, 'cause that's who you are. The wild card I didn't know was going to show up.'

'I won't answer you if you call me that.'

'That's your choice,' Dixie replied, got up and left him standing beside the fallen log.

Dixie had always found running water soothing. When she was little, she had loved lying prone on the big cotton-wood branch that hung out over the river. The other kids used to make fun of her, thinking she was lying down like that because she was too scared to stand up and jump off into the water as they did, but it was never about swim-ming for Dixie. She loved the hypnotic lure of the water moving beneath her. It didn't make her dizzy as it did Leola, didn't make her want to jump in. It just washed her mind clean.

The little creek behind the cabin was broad and shallow and looked to be hardly moving at all, but after she had finished washing herself, Dixie lay down on the grass and spent a several moments staring into it. The tiny pebbles on the bottom were the same dappled greeny-brown as Jamie Lee's eyes.

Dixie tried to calculate what day it was. Had Jamie Lee's funeral been only last week? It seemed so long ago. Tears filled Dixie's eyes, blurring the opulent growth around her. She had to remind herself that Jamie was with Jesus now and all his suffering was over.

It was easy to picture him hand in hand with Jesus. A whole beautiful image came into her mind whenever Dixie thought about it. They would be walking through a field as pretty with flowers as this clearing was. More beautiful, even, because they were heavenly flowers. Jamie Lee wasn't a baby anymore. In fact, he didn't really look much like Jamie Lee any more, but like the sweet little boy in the leaflet about Down's syndrome that the doctor had given her. He looked so happy and so did Jesus.

Dixie sobbed. No matter how pleased she knew she ought to be for Jamie Lee, she couldn't help longing to have just one more minute of him here on earth. She knew they'd meet again in Jesus. Whenever she thought about dying now, she knew Jamie Lee and Jesus would be there to meet her, but that thought wasn't always a help because it made her want to die right away.

'I ate some of that Spam crap.'

Dixie jumped. She hadn't heard the boy approach. Embarrassed that he'd seen her crying, she lowered her head. 'Don't it occur to you that if someone's off by themselves, they might just want to stay that way a while?' she muttered.

'It tasted like puke, just like I said it would,' the boy muttered back.

'So why you bothering to tell me about it?'

'Because you were trying to get me to eat it.'

'I wasn't trying to get you to eat it. I said, do what you want.'

'So, I'm just telling you. I ate your pukey food.'

Dixie heard the insolence in his voice and hated him for it. Leaping to her feet to chase him off, she screamed, 'I don't *care*. Do what you want, you understand? Eat the food; don't eat the food. Stay here; run away. Who cares? Not me. Don't you get that? I don't care anything about you. So, just leave me alone.'

The boy's eyes dilated. He didn't move. He didn't say anything. But it was as if someone were letting the air slowly out of a balloon, because his features, his shoulders, his cocky little head deflated little by little and his eyes filled with tears. 'OK, I got it,' he murmured, then he turned and walked away.

'I didn't mean to make you feel bad,' Dixie said.

'I don't feel bad,' the boy replied sullenly. 'Why would you think I felt bad? Why would I fucking care about what you say?' He was hunched up against the shady outer wall of the cabin, knees drawn up, arms wrapped around them.

'I am glad you ate the Spam. You'll feel better with food in you.'

'Fuck you.'

'Look, I am sorry. I shouldn't have said what I did, because it isn't true,' Dixie said. 'You just caught me off guard. I was kind of praying. See, I didn't go to church this week, so I was feeling the need to talk to Jesus.'

'Just piss off, would you?'

When Billy finally got up, he had a sore head. Crossly, he rummaged through the first-aid kit for Alka-Seltzer.

'You want coffee?' Dixie asked.

'What I need's some hair of the dog,' he muttered.

'I wish you wouldn't drink so much. It don't do you any good. I wish you'd just stay here.'

'And do what, exactly?' Billy dropped the tablets into a mug of water. 'How the hell we going to get this sorted out if I just stay here?'

Then suddenly he saw the boy standing outside the door.

'What the *fuck* is he doing there?' Billy shrieked. 'How come he's out walking around? You! *You!* Get the fuck in here!'

Startled, the boy did as he was told.

'Billy, hold on. It's not his fault. I done it. I let him loose,' Dixie said. 'Him and me, we worked it out between us. Didn't we, Joker?' She looked pleadingly at the boy.

'Shit,' Billy said in a tone Dixie couldn't read. It could have been an exclamation of amazement that she could let the kid go and he was still there, but most likely it was just exasperation that so much was going wrong. He looked over at the boy. 'Come here, kid.'

Tentatively the boy took a step closer.

'How come your dad ain't looking for you?'

The boy didn't respond.

Billy bent down and picked up a chip of wood from the floor of the cabin. He lofted it at the boy. 'Hey, you, answer when I talk to you. How come your daddy ain't put out no reward for you yet?'

'He will,' the boy murmured softly.

'Yeah, well, I want to know why he hasn't done it. How come no one even acts like you're missing?'

Pulling his shoulders up into a shrug, the boy said, 'I don't know.'

Billy picked up another small piece of wood and threw it at him. Hitting the child's arm, it fell to the ground. 'That ain't a good enough answer. So why the fuck is nothing happening?'

A desolate expression crossed the boy's face and his shoulders sagged.

Billy reached down for a third bit of wood.

'Don't,' Dixie said and put her hand out.

'I'm not hurting him any. I'm just waiting for an answer.'

'Probably because they just think I ran away,' the boy said faintly.

'Yeah, OK, so why haven't they figured out yet that you haven't?'

'I don't *know*,' the boy said, tears thickening his voice.

Dismay crossed Billy's face. 'You little shithole. Fuck.' He glanced over at Dixie. '*Fuck*.' He pushed the boy roughly aside and stormed out of the cabin and off towards the tree.

Dixie rushed after him. 'Billy?' She grabbed his arm. 'Where you going? Don't leave already. Stay here.'

'Nobody's even *looking* for him.'

'Well, that's *good*,' Dixie said, her voice optimistic. 'Then we can get out of this.'

'Don't be stupid.'

'Billy, wait. Listen to me. I've been thinking it over. Let's just let him go.'

Billy jerked his arm free. 'Why the hell does everything in my life have to go wrong? Fucking shithole bastard kid!' He stomped off into the trees.

'No, wait. Couldn't we? If no one's looking for him yet, then nothing's gone wrong yet. Couldn't we just drive him down and let him off somewhere so he can get back by himself? You want out of it. I want out of it. He wants out of it. So let's finish this with nobody getting hurt. Please?'

Billy whirled around. 'It's your fucking fault we're in this mess. You've done one stupid thing after another, Dixie, starting with taking off that kid's blindfold back at the house. You think the little fucker won't tell people who we are, if we let him go?'

'He just wants to go home, Billy. I'm sure if we explain that he needs to keep quiet or else we can't let him go …'

'Dixie, don't be so stupid. He'll tell. Of course he'll tell. That would be the first thing he did, the minute he was away from us. The only way we're going to get out of this without looking over our shoulders the rest of our lives is if me and him pay a little visit to the ridge.'

'What do you mean by that?'

Billy gave a small jerk of his left shoulder to indicate the direction. 'The ridge above Six Mile Creek. It isn't that far from his daddy's ranch. Little fatty like him wouldn't be used to the forest. They'd think he just didn't know the ridge was there.'

'*Billy*. Don't scare me with that kind of talk.'

'I'm just saying …' And Billy turned and disappeared into the trees.

Chapter Twenty-Eight

The boy was once again sitting in the damp shade at the side of the cabin. Legs drawn up, he forlornly rested his cheek against his knees.

'Hey, don't feel bad. That was just Billy being Billy.'

He wiped tears from his eyes.

'You don't want to sit there. It's too damp. The skeeters will get you. Come out in the sunshine.'

The boy didn't respond.

Dixie held her hand out. 'Come on. Look. I got my cards. Do you know how to play gin rummy?'

'No. And I don't want to learn.'

'OK, that's fine. I'll show you a card trick instead.'

'I don't want to see your stupid tricks.'

'Bet you can't guess how I do it.'

'I don't care the fuck how you do it.'

Sitting down cross-legged in the grass opposite the boy, Dixie took out her pack of cards. Sorting through them, she picked the joker out. 'This here's the detective. And know what? He's smart, just like you. He can prove how smart he is by how good he is at catching criminals. Want to see him do it?'

The boy didn't say anything.

Dixie laid the joker face up. Then she counted out two piles of fifteen cards each. 'This pile is yours. This one's mine. Now, cut them. Cut yours into two piles. Any way you want.'

The boy didn't move, so Dixie reached over and divided his cards into two groups, then her own. 'OK, now, from these cards left, you pick out a card.'

The boy remained unresponsive.

Dixie pulled a card out randomly without looking at it herself. She held it up in front of him. 'That's the criminal. Memorize what he looks like. And I'm not going to look. Now, here. You take him. Lay him on top of one of my piles. Good. That's exactly right. And then lay the joker on top of one of your piles. Lay him face up, so we can see him doing his detective work. Good. Now I'm going to collect all four of our piles together.' Dixie gathered them into one stack and then started to deal them quickly out again into two. 'First the joker is going to detect which town the criminal is in. This pile is Abundance. What place shall we call that one?'

'LA?' said the boy.

'Yeah, good. LA. Now, let's let the joker figure out if the criminal is in Abundance or Los Angeles.' As she dealt the up-facing joker into one pile she pointed to it. 'Which is town is that?'

'Abundance,' the boy said.

'That's right. Clever joker. He has figured out the criminal is in Abundance, not Los Angeles.' She discarded the pile without the joker and started to deal the remaining cards out into two piles again. 'OK, now to find what street the criminal is on. This pile is Fifth Street and this pile is ... what?'

'Sixth Street.'

'Good. OK, what street does the joker think the criminal is on?'

'Sixth Street,' the boy said as the joker went into that pile.

'Clever detective. Now he's figured out what street the criminal is on. He's so smart. Probably in Mensa, don't you think? So let's find out which house on the street your criminal is in. The blue house or ... what colour shall the other house be?'

'Red,' the boy said.

Dixie dealt the remaining cards into two piles. 'And the joker says he's in ... which house is the joker in now?'

The boy pointed. 'The blue one.'

'Yup, the blue one. And now the joker is just about to catch the criminal. He knows the guilty party is in Abundance on Sixth Street in the blue house, but which room? The living room? Or the bedroom? Watch.' As Dixie dealt the final cards again, one pile contained only the joker and a card facing down. 'Ah ha! The joker's in the bedroom, so that's where your criminal is!' she said and flipped it over. 'That's him. The king of clubs. Yeah?'

The boy smiled in spite of himself. 'Cool. How did you do that?'

'It's easy. You want me to show you how?'

They spent a good hour or so in the shade of the cabin as Dixie taught the boy how to do the card trick and then a second trick and finally how to play gin rummy.

They moved out of the shade to sit on the large fallen log and continued playing. Dixie picked up bits of wood and showed the boy to how to bet on the game.

'You're enjoying this, aren't you?' she said at one point, because for the first time she saw him laughing.

'Yeah. This is fun. I've never played cards before, except for, like, dopey stuff like Go Fish.'

'Don't you play cards at home?' Dixie said in disbelief.

He shook his head. 'No. I don't think we even have any cards at my house. My dad plays poker, but he goes to Las Vegas to do it. Once I saw him playing celebrity poker, but I don't remember much about it because I only saw him on TV.'

'What kinds of things do you at home then?'

The boy shrugged. 'Mostly play with my game console.'

'I mean with your mom and ... do you have any brothers or sisters?'

'Not full ones,' the boy said. 'I got a half-brother and a half-sister on my dad's side and my mom was married when she was really young and the guy she was married to had some kids, and they'd be my step-sisters. Or -brothers or whatever they are. But I don't know any of them. I've never even met them.'

'Well, what about your mom? What does she play with you?'

He shrugged. 'Phoebe ... she's not really into games.'

'Wow. I can't imagine never playing cards,' Dixie said. 'We've played in my family for as long as I can remember. The neighbours from down the street sometimes come over too, so there's about five or six of us most of the time. My mama makes popcorn and we have Coke and play pinochle or canasta. Me and Leola, even though we're not living at home anymore, we still usually come over on Friday nights, because we have so much fun when everybody's there. Cards've always been right at the centre of our good times together.'

There was a long pause. Evening was coming. Along with the settling coolness, there was a shift in the sounds of the clearing. The din of buzzing insects subsided, leaving soft, susurrant noises.

The boy stared off across the meadow. Tears welled up in his eyes.

'What's wrong?' Dixie asked.

Without answering, the boy rose to his feet and walked off.

'Hey,' she said, 'hold on a minute,' and went after him, grabbing his shoulder. He jerked away and trotted in through the gaping door of the cabin.

Dixie found him huddled in the cave-like darkness of the tumbled logs at the back of the inner room.

'Don't just run away from me like that. What's wrong?'

Hiding his face in his folded arms, he sobbed.

Dixie sat down beside him. Gently she reached an arm out and laid it across the boy's shoulders. 'Feeling kind of overwhelmed? That's how I was feeling this morning. Remember? I was crying too. So I understand.'

He just wept.

'You've really been brave, Joker. You know that, don't you? I know how tough this has been on you. You been a real fighter. I bet your daddy would be proud of you.'

Still he cried.

'But now it's all got a bit much, hasn't it?' she said gently. 'I understand that too.'

He nodded.

'You want a hug?' She opened her arms.

The boy came willingly.

As she hugged the boy close against her, a strong sensation washed through Dixie's body. Her private parts throbbed. It wasn't a sexy feeling, but more like the feeling Jamie Lee had given her when he was breastfeeding: a deep-down feeling that had love and life and bodies all interconnected. Dixie held the boy close and rocked him in the twilight gloom of the tumbledown cabin.

When he had stopped crying, the boy remained unmoving in Dixie's arms. The air had grown humid and over-warm between them, but beyond the cabin door, high-altitude chill had descended and with it almost total darkness. A wood rat ventured out and crept noiselessly along one log.

'Look at him,' Dixie whispered.

She could feel the boy nod against her, but he didn't speak.

Silence spun out over several minutes. Somewhere far off a coyote howled. Or maybe it was a wolf.

'What's going to happen to me if my dad doesn't give you any money?' the boy asked in a small voice.

'I'm sure it will all work out.'

'But what if he doesn't?' The boy sucked in a deep breath. 'I mean, what if my dad doesn't want me back?'

'Well, of course he wants you back, Joker. Don't be silly. You're feeling bad right now, because it's been a rough day. Plus, things always seem scarier at night,' Dixie replied.

'But what if he didn't?'

'He will. You're his little boy. I bet your dad's worried sick about you right now. And I'm so sorry we're putting him through it.'

The boy began to cry again.

'You've had a hard day, sweetie.'

Dixie could feel him shaking his head. 'Uh-uh,' he murmured. 'Because I told my dad I was going to run away. And when I did, he said good. He said he would just let me do it because he didn't want me there.'

'Sounds to me more like he was mad,' Dixie replied. 'If you were being a little devil like you've been sometimes here with me, I can understand that your dad might end up saying angry things to you sometimes. Folks are that way with their kids, especially when they've been naughty. But that's just feelings talking, and lots of times, feelings talk nonsense.'

'No. My dad meant it,' the boy said. 'He always calls me "Phoebe's Revenge". He says he wanted her to get an abortion, but she had me just to get back at him.'

'Oh, honey,' Dixie said and smoothed back the boy's hair, 'I'm sorry to know he's saying that kind of stuff to you, but you got to understand people say all sorts of things that deep down they don't really mean.'

'Phoebe doesn't want me either. She was just about to get her break as an actress, but then she had me, and she says now she's box-office poison because she stood up to my dad. She says you should never have kids if you want to get on in life. Kids just drag you down.'

With her thumb, Dixie gently pushed away the tears on his face. 'Sometimes families are just crap, aren't they? Me and my daddy, we don't get along all that well either, so I understand. I've heard some awful things come out of his mouth.'

'Like what?' the boy asked.

'Like my daddy used to always think everything was my fault. Never had a reason. Just always blamed me. I can remember sitting at the dinner table once and my sister spilled her milk. Daddy said it was my fault because I filled her glass too full. I said I didn't fill it. Mama had. So, he says, well, if I hadn't been distracting Leola so much by talking, Leola would've paid better attention to what she was doing and wouldn't have knocked the glass over. Then he told me to go get a cloth and clean it up. I said why didn't Leola have to do it, since she was the one who knocked the milk over? That made my mama mad, because I was talking back and getting Daddy upset. She said just for once she wished we could have a nice, quiet meal and if it wasn't for me, Daddy would never get so upset.'

'How did you make your dad change?'

Dixie smiled at the boy through the darkness and caressed his hair, pushing it back again from his face. 'You don't want to take lessons from me on that, Joker. I don't think my way of going about it made things any better. What I'm really trying to tell you is that families can do some really nasty things to each other, but that doesn't mean they don't still love each other. Love's more complicated than that. Mostly when we hurt people we love, we don't even know why we're doing it. Or rather, I suppose we do, but we just don't know how to make ourselves behave better.'

Chapter Twenty-Nine

S pencer woke to utter darkness.

He had been dreaming about Angelina Jolie. He didn't know her in waking life. They didn't move in the same circles socially. He'd seen her, of course, at awards ceremonies or other industry events, and had been introduced a time or two, but that was as far as it went. In the dream, however, they were seated next to each other at a big dinner in a Vegas hotel and Angelina was very intimate with him. Indeed, she started to come on to him, touching him, stroking his cheek, smiling at him in a ripe, knowing way, even though they were still seated at the table with everyone else. It was so obvious she wanted him that the energy of it seemed to flow from her, from her eyes and her smile and her fingertips. They made arrangements to meet elsewhere for sex, but when Spencer endeavoured to reach the trysting place, the dream became one of frustration. Each attempt he made was thwarted by obsessive fans or paparazzi, cunning and persistent as jackals. The anxiety they caused Spencer was bad enough, but it was made so much worse because his lover was to be Angelina. If any of them succeeded in following him, he knew she would think he'd betrayed her to the press on purpose for the publicity. That wasn't how it was. This was love. Real love. Spencer would prove it to her, if he only got the chance.

At last he was successful in reaching the small boutique hotel, which, in the way of dreams, was now in the south of France instead of Las Vegas; and thus he found himself struggling to speak French to the man behind the front desk in order to get the room key. Sudden recognition crossed the man's face as he realized whom Spencer was meeting. Yes, yes, Angelina often stayed here. She lived nearby, the hotelier said, and he had in his eye the glint of a man with secret knowledge. Spencer realized this must often be a trysting place for her, that the man was seeing him as only one of many.

The French came easier to him as Spencer assured the man behind the desk that this time would be different. Angelina had shown such fascination in her attentions to him in Vegas that he was certain she would again. It wasn't just a fling. Angelina had chosen Spencer above all others.

'By the way,' he had asked the hotelier, 'do you know if Angelina is still living with Brad?'

'*Oui*,' the man said as if it were a casual, irrelevant question.

Then there Spencer was in the room, alone with Angelina. She greeted him passionately, all kisses and caresses, the desire surging from her again like a current, and Spencer knew he was right. He wasn't just a passing fancy. Out of all the men she could have had, she had chosen him specially to be a lover. Spencer, however, did not return her affection.

Instead, he tenderly lowered her arms and said no. No, they couldn't do this, because he knew she was still with Brad. He wouldn't make love to her when she was in a committed relationship. Angelina stared at him in disbelief, her disillusionment naked in her eyes.

Spencer woke at that point. It was a gentle, natural waking, not caused by his uncomfortable sleeping place or the nightlife of the forest, but the dream clung to him, its false reality in bright tatters that the alien darkness of the trees could not easily disperse. What a peculiar dream it had been too, Spencer thought as he lay. The intimate touches and nuanced glances had seemed so vivid and natural with someone whom in reality he did not know at all. More peculiar yet had been his behaviour, because should it happen in real life, should Angelina Jolie ever approach him and seem even the least bit willing to be as intimate as she'd been in the dream, Spencer knew he'd have her in a minute and Brad be damned. Slowly, however, the vibrant colours of the dream dissolved into the darkness. Spencer grew more awake to the forest and its noisy night-time silence.

It was very dark. Looking directly up, Spencer could see the sky luminous with starlight through the treetops, but there beneath the branches it was murky as Mordor. He couldn't make out much more than Guff's outline beside him.

'You OK, Guff?' Spencer's fingertips moved gently over the lined face and then down under the jaw, feeling for a pulse. 'Shit. You're freezing, aren't you?'

The underbrush around them provided some shelter from the mountain chill, and Spencer had been warm enough, curled up in the mossy litter; but Guff, unable to move, clearly wasn't. There was nothing available to cover him with, so Spencer pulled the old man against him in an effort to warm him with his body heat.

It was the sort of thing he could imagine himself doing in a movie. Spencer could visualize the scene as it might appear in a script. Some kind of survival movie and he was the hero, a guy with a name like Jack or Sam, saving the life of his companion with the warmth of his own body. Risking his own life …

For as long as the image lasted, warming Guff against the night chill was easy to do. Spencer's imagination compensated for the hard ground and the uncomfortable position. He was too tired to sustain it for long, however, and it didn't work if he forced it. The fantasy had to come upon him unawares to be powerful enough to take him away from nightmare reality.

An eerie keening began. The sound was far off in the mountains, echoing slightly, which made it all the more otherworldly. A coyote, most likely. Spencer was familiar enough with their noises. In the Hollywood Hills there was a surfeit of the horrid creatures, boldly feasting on lapdogs and kittens, arguing among themselves and fucking on people's lawns. Probably *just* a coyote, he reassured himself. Pulling Guff closer, he buried his face in the material of the old man's shirt and tried not to listen to the pale, mournful noise.

The boy came to him. Spencer felt as if he were quite ordinarily awake. His thinking, however, drifted in the uncontrolled way of dreams, eddying into vortexes of thought he couldn't break free from.

The boy hadn't entered his thoughts at all before this. Ever since Spencer had ridden out from the ranch on Ranger, there had been such a total absence of him anywhere in Spencer's mind that it felt as if the boy were nothing more than a character in a film – capable of commanding, over-powering, overwhelming everything when present, but then, once off-screen, ceasing to exist.

In what was not quite like a dream sequence, Spencer saw the boy at the bus station in Abundance, boarding a bus for Los Angeles. He was clutching a ticket in his hand and nothing else. No jacket. No bag. No food. No money. A nine-year-old boy, setting off to travel 1,500 miles alone. He would pass through all those seedy bus stations at God knows what hours, a prey to all the drunks, the druggies, the paedophiles. Alone.

Spencer pulled himself into full consciousness. *OK, that's a sad story, but it* is *a dream.* There was no bus station in Abundance. Nor any train station, nor any other form of public transport that could take the boy out of town. *It is just a dream.*

Spencer felt none of the usual relief at coming awake from a dream, however. If there was no way for the boy to escape and yet he was gone, then most likely he'd run off into the mountains. Spencer could still hear the desolate howling, deeper now, closer, and he realized it came not from coyotes but wolves. The boy was dead. Spencer knew that with certainty.

Again he pulled himself back into full consciousness. *That's just another dream.* The sound of the keening animal, whatever it was, had long since ceased.

Sitting up, Spencer tried to shake off the last terrifying remnants of sleep. Small, unseen things scurried into the underbrush as he moved. Mice? Rats? Who fucking knew? He was so strung out that he felt an impulse to cry. Honestly. He just wanted this all to be over.

Even awake, Spencer could not free himself of the boy. *Tennesee was only nine years old. How had he let him just walk out?*

What kind of father did that?

For several minutes, Spencer sat, staring into the endless darkness of what was becoming an endless night. The scuttering had stopped. He could hear nothing other than the rushing water of the nearby creek. White noise, Spencer thought. The kind of sound they fabricated at the spa to relax you. He listened carefully to it, trying to understand what about it might possibly be considered relaxing. All he felt was anxiety.

That had been Spencer's whole issue with therapy and meditation and all that crap. If science had shown mountain streams produced a relaxing sound and yet he wasn't relaxed by it, this had to be a failing of his, didn't it, and not a flaw of the water? His fault. And then it became his job to correct it, to work at becoming a different, better person. But it wasn't as if he were *choosing* to be this way. If it were genuinely a choice, who would choose anxiety? Who wouldn't choose to listen to the fucking water and feel relaxed? That was the whole point of drugs, wasn't it? That in taking them you could *choose* to be relaxed. You had control. Snort the line and your body did what you wanted it to. Listen to the water and all you heard was your own fucking heart going a million beats a minute. Who could control that?

Spencer lay down again. Discouraged, confused and exhausted, he pressed against Guff. The old cowboy was growing chilly again, so Spencer wrapped his arms around him and drew him in against his own body. 'Nobody would choose to feel like this, Guff,' he whispered. 'Nobody would choose to be me, if they knew how to be different.'

Silence then. Except for the water, of course.

Water had so many sounds hidden within the fast downward rush of the stream. A smooth sliding sound; a chatter; a murmur like voices in a distant room; a deep, regular thump like a beating heart.

'I was lying before,' Spencer said quietly.

He stared into the darkness, unable to see anything except Guff's outline, blurry in its nearness.

'Earlier. When I told you my father was James Oliver Duck … all that. Everything I said. It isn't true. Not a word of it. It's a story my publicist came up with.'

Spencer paused.

'No … that's not quite so. I told it to my publicist. It wasn't his idea. He just bought into it.'

He stopped.

Spencer could picture James Oliver Duck very clearly: reserved, stern – a bit dour even – balding with tufts of white hair at his ears. He was a bit overweight, not fat, but rather the weight of a man who appreciated good food and knew his wines. He was always dressed in a grey three-piece suit, and sat behind an oak desk in his panelled office at the bank. Occasionally Spencer had even imagined the way in which James had been seduced by the young schoolgirl. How had he met her? How had she shown interest? Had he made the first pass? It wasn't Spencer's mother in those images, but a beautiful thing, all fifties red lipstick and nubile glamour.

Without quite consciously creating her, he had created her nonetheless.

If he took the time, Spencer could just as easily deconstruct the magpie way in which his mind had collected snippets here and there from his everyday childhood life to generate James Oliver Duck and his young seductress. There had never been any delusion or confusion in Spencer's mind over the reality of it; it was simply a better story than real life, nothing more. A better fit. And after all these years of telling it, James Oliver Duck didn't seem so very distinguishable from Spencer's memories of the real people in his youth.

'The truth ... is less ... fulfilling ...'

Spencer lay a moment in silence, his cheek pressed against Guff's shirt. He focused on the faint warmth coming through the cloth.

'Fact is, I don't have a clue who my father is and that's probably a good thing,' he said quietly. 'Because my mother was raped. She never told me anything about it other than to say I ruined her life. She *was* a schoolgirl and her family *was* poor. Those parts are true enough. But they weren't the noble poor. And she ... well ... she was just an ordinary girl.

'Abortion wasn't an option in those days. It wasn't legal yet and my family weren't the kind who'd know how to go about getting things done that required a more sophisticated understanding of the world.

'If I'm honest ... I wish she'd had it. Had it and been able to put the rape behind her and get on with her life ... I really do, Guff ...

'I didn't live with her when I was young. She didn't want me ... or maybe she did. I don't know. Maybe she was just too young to be a mother. Whatever. Because what she really wanted was a life. Not a bastard. "If only I could have aborted you ..." It came up in every argument. It was the root of every problem she had – the drink, the dead-end job, the poverty – none of it would have happened, except for me.

'I lived with my grandparents for a while. I have these fleeting memories of their apartment. I was maybe two or three. Standing at a window, watching my mother get into a taxi. But they didn't want to start over, raising another child. My mother was the youngest. They'd already downsized. Their apartment was too small for a little boy. I remember my grandmother telling me that. Very lovingly. I was on her knee. She was caressing my shoulder and explaining how they couldn't keep me.

'I went to stay with my cousins after that. I don't remember anything about it. Just pictures in the photograph album. Otherwise, I wouldn't have even known it happened. My mother had started over in another town where people didn't know. She had a paying job by then, so I went to live with her awhile, except she couldn't manage. This friend of hers named Pam started to take care of me. I don't recall much about that either, except that once there was this big argument between Pam and my mother over something. I remember my mother snatching up my hand and storming out, and I was crying because she was pulling me along so hard it hurt. After that, I lived with Aunt Alma, except that she wasn't really my aunt. I don't know how I came to be there. She was old and her husband was crippled. She spent all her time caring for him. I remember helping her lift him into the bath ...

'Finally Duck came along. *Donald* Duck, would you believe? He married my mother the year I was nine, so I finally got to leave Aunt Alma. My mother enrolled me in school as Spencer Duck. I kid you not. Shit. I only *wish* that name had been made up. The kids were merciless. "Duck, Duck, Goose, Duck", "Fuck the Duck" and "Spencer Fuck" – and then they found out his first name was really Donald …

'But my mother loved him, and love changed everything. Certainly it changed my mother. When Lucy and Mike were born, she loved them so dearly. She couldn't get enough of them. Everything they did was like it was the first time any kid in the world had done those things.

'Not that she didn't love me. I'm sure she did in her way, but mostly I just sort of lived under the same roof as they did. They weren't bad to me. In a lot of ways they were good. Don, especially. He helped me pay for college and get a car. But truth is, only Mike and Lucy were their children.'

Spencer fell quiet for several moments.

'I want to say sorry to you, Guff. That's actually why I'm telling you all this. It's the best I can do for an apology, because the fact is, I laughed at you. Because of Ranger. "He belongs to a horse." I couldn't believe it. And I found it hysterical … so funny. I told everyone. I made such a big joke of it. Which is pretty ironic, I know, considering I've never belonged to anyone. Not even a horse.'

Silence again.

'Truth is, Guff, I wanted it to be me. I wanted to belong to Ranger the way you do. If I'm honest, I wanted to belong to you.

'But it hasn't happened. This isn't my world here. I so badly wanted to be part of all this, but I don't know how to do it, Guff. So, I'd like to say sorry. I laughed at you. But it wasn't funny.'

Chapter Thirty

The morning mist had only just left the clearing when Billy reappeared. Dixie ran out through the dewy grass to meet him.

'Golly, I was worried when you left like that,' she said. 'I was scared you weren't coming back.' She reached out for a hug.

'Of course I was coming back. You knew that.'

'Stand still long enough to give me a proper greeting. Kiss me, Billy. Jeez. You're roaring through like a locomotive.'

He hugged her briefly and the kiss was even less satisfying. Dixie eyed the bag Billy was carrying. 'I hope that's got food in it. It's starting to get hard to make a meal with what we got left.'

'Newspapers.'

'Newspapers?'

They had reached the cabin. Billy went on in ahead of her and put the bag on the table.

As Dixie lifted it up, she saw the logo. 'Pay'n Save? I hope you're recycling this and not been going in there, because that's taking real chances. Even Mama could have seen you in the Pay'n Save.'

'Your mama wasn't in there, so don't make a fuss.'

There was an unexpected pause, just a tiny sliver of time, but packed into it were all the questions Dixie wanted to ask, like why take even the slightest risk? Why was there a brand-new glue stick in the bag with the newspaper? What was going on? Instead, she said, 'If you were going in there anyway, I wish you'd have bothered to get us some food at the same time.'

Billy opened one of the newspapers. Pulling over a chair, he sat down. 'I'm going to send a note.'

'What do you mean?'

'It's been too long, Dix. I ain't heard a thing. *Nothing*. Zip. Zilch. It's like this kid never even existed.'

'*No*,' she said emphatically. 'We ain't getting into that kind of thing.'

'I don't see what else we can do, Dix,' he replied. 'Other than shoot him.'

'Don't talk like that, Billy. You ain't that kind of man.'

'Well, you better keep reminding me of it.'

'You ain't the kind of man who kidnaps little kids either and that's what it's going to be, if you send "a note", as you call it,' Dixie replied. 'You do understand that, don't you, Billy? It's not "a note". It's a ransom demand. And that turns all this into a kidnapping for certain.'

'Dixie, don't be stupid. It already is a kidnapping,' he said without even bothering to look up from the newspaper.

Somehow, Billy saying it out loud changed things. Up until that point, Dixie had still been able to see all of this as just one more of Billy's schemes. Stupid, yes, like so many of them had been. Seriously stupid, even, but never intentionally criminal. Never evil. Tears came to her eyes.

He looked up at her. It took him a moment to register her tears and when he did, he wasn't angry, as she'd expected. Instead, a warm smile crossed his face and he rose, pulling Dixie into an embrace. 'I won't ask for much. Not like it was a real kidnapping. Just enough to pay for taking care of him. Ten thousand. Just like you said the other day. That is enough. We can get by on that.'

'We're going to go to jail for this.'

'No, Dix, we're not. Don't get yourself in such a stew about everything. I got it all figured out. You want to hear? Sit down. Right on the chair, here. Sit down and I will explain it all out, because I have got it well figured and things will be just fine.'

Billy urged Dixie down into the backless wooden chair on the other side of the table. Then he sat down across from her, his hands reaching out to clasp hers. 'Here's what I plan to do: I make up a note and ask them to drop the money off by the Kipper Twee mine. It's dark as hell inside there, so no one's going to see me. I'll wait inside the mine and then when they're gone, I'll pick it up. But here's the smart part, what's going to fool them: instead of coming out – and that's what they'll be expecting – I'll take the money and go back down the mine. So even if they wait around, they're not going to see anyone coming to pick up the money and they're not going to see anyone leaving with the money and that'll make them think somehow they missed it. But when they go searching around Abundance, they're not going to find anyone, because he ain't there. If I stocked up some food and water in there first, I could stay quite a while down the mine. That'd fool them good.'

'Not if they decide to search the mine. And they will, Billy, because if no one comes out and no one goes in, but the money still disappears, the only place it could be is down the mine.'

'They can search all they want. They'll never find me. There's miles and miles of tunnels down there. Me and Roy have explored it lots of times.'

'You sure never told me anything about exploring around in that mine,' Dixie said dubiously.

'Yeah, well, I didn't want to worry you, because I know how you are. It was just me and Roy. We're pretty sure there's still some gold in there somewhere. So we been nosing around more than a few times, and, believe me, you could stay forever in those tunnels.'

'Yeah, along with the bones of all the other fools who've gone down there. What about cave-ins? Those tunnels are a hundred years old and nobody's kept them up. I wouldn't even dare breathe heavy in some of them, much less go deep down. That place is *dangerous*, Billy, and I'm sure as hell glad I never knew before that you and Roy were going in there.'

'Yeah, but here's the good part. Remember how Earl Ray was talking about how he thought there was another entrance? How when him and his brother were little, they used to ride their horses across the back of the mountain and once they near fell in it?'

'That's just a story,' Dixie said. 'You know how Earl Ray spins stories.'

'It's not just a story. Me and Roy, we've already figured out where it comes out. It's by the Indian Caves at the back of the mountain.'

'You've actually found this entrance? Because nobody's ever found anything connecting the Kipper Twee and the Indian Caves that I've heard of.'

'We haven't found it exactly, but it's got to be the Indian Caves. The mountain is hollow with them on that side. If I'm going to be down there three or four days, I'll have plenty of time to find it.'

'Billy, *no*. This is beyond a wild idea. The Kipper Twee was dug in 1879. If there is another entrance, it could be blocked up by now. It could be flooded. Half the Indian Caves are flooded. But most likely there isn't another entrance, because if there was, people would know about it by now. Do you hear me? It most likely *doesn't even exist*.'

He shrugged. 'In that case, I'll just have to wait them out down the mine, huh?'

Despair was building up behind Dixie's eyes the way a migraine does, the way it had that morning at the hospital when she was waiting for the surgeon to come in and tell her how the operation on Jamie Lee's heart had gone. Elbows on the table, she pressed her fingers against her forehead and closed her eyes.

There was something eerie about watching Billy sitting at the rotting table, cutting out words from the newspaper to make up a ransom note. It felt to Dixie as if she was trapped inside some kind of thriller movie, and it occurred to her that Spencer Scott wasn't the only one living a pretend life and mistaking it for real. But at least Spencer Scott made money from his.

Full of all his Indiana Jones plans about running around inside the Kipper Twee with loads of ransom money under his arm, discovering secret entrances and probably finding buried treasure along the way, Billy had pretty much forgotten about the boy. When Dixie asked him how the boy fitted into his plans, she could tell Billy hadn't thought about that part of it at all. He'd just drop the boy off where he had first picked him up on River Road, he said, his tone casual, as if he were some kind of taxi driver who had accidentally driven past his passenger's destination. Exasperated, Dixie pointed out the problems with this, not the least being that Spencer Scott might only hand over the money if the boy was there to be exchanged for it, which meant taking the boy with him. On the other hand, if he were intending to hand him over afterwards, Billy would have to be able to leave the mine first in order to get the boy.

Billy finally admitted he hadn't planned out this part of it. He was having such a good time planning the other part that Dixie pointing out this flaw didn't make him angry, but she didn't make much of an impact on his tactics either. In the end, he decided the best thing to say about the boy was 'AWAIT FURTHER INSTRUCTIONS'. This was how ransom notes were always written, he explained, as if he'd written a million of them before. That gave it a tone of authority, he said, as if maybe there might be another ransom demand and the police would need to go somewhere else or tap the phones or something.

While sticking the cut-out words from the newspaper on to the note, Billy stopped being Indiana Jones and turned into Al Pacino. Probably the police would think that the Mafia was involved, he said with undisguised enthusiasm. Or some other professional criminals, like a drug cartel or something. If it really was a drug cartel, they would want an airplane to fly them out. Maybe he should say that once they dropped the money off at the mine, they then needed to go to an airport to *await further instructions*. Billy's eyes lit up with excitement. Terrorists! That would be even better. Maybe he should say something about a bomb at the airport.

Dixie took two aspirin.

Once the note was finished, Billy packed up a few things to take with him down the mine. Most of their conversation was completely ordinary, things like: 'You want to take these blue socks?' and 'Do you need bug spray?' Dixie was always amazed by how the little stuff of life just kept carrying on, no matter how wrecked the big stuff got.

As she put a roll of toilet paper into Billy's rucksack, she asked, 'What have you told Roy so far about this?'

'Nothing.'

'Well, you better think of something. Otherwise he's going to wonder why you just disappeared.'

'It's women who wonder about things like that,' Billy replied. 'Roy won't.'

'Roy is the biggest gossip in town and you know it. So it's better Roy thinks you're doing something he'd expect you to do.' Dixie paused to consider. 'Tell him we're going down to the Tetons. Say how much I'm always asking to go camping there and now you're taking me. That's a good long distance away and Roy knows how much I like it there … and …'

'Yeah?'

'Call my mama too, would you? Tonight, when you get into town. She'll be starting to worry that I been gone so long without talking to her. Call her too and tell her that we've gone down to the Tetons.'

'I don't want to talk to your mama, Dix. I'll call Leola instead.'

'*No*. Don't call Leola. She'll hear from your voice something's up, Billy. Or she'll get out her cards or something. Don't you talk to Leola. Call Mama.'

'First thing your mama will ask is how come you're not calling her yourself,' Billy said. 'What shall I say to her? Maybe that you got a cold and lost your voice or something?'

'For Pete's sake, don't say that. If I got a cold, Mama'd want to know how come I'm gadding about camping instead of staying home, taking care of myself. Just tell her you dropped me off to get some groceries. Say we're in a hurry to get this camping done before you got to go on the round-up. That'll work with Mama. She'll get so mad thinking about you and your cowboying that she'll forget all about me.'

'You're good at this.' Billy grinned. 'You got a natural criminal mind.'

By three thirty Billy had everything together that he wanted. Dixie walked with him to the point where the path left the clearing and disappeared into the forest.

'Give me time to get all this done,' Billy said. 'I might need four or five days, especially if I can't find another way out of the Kipper Twee. So don't get yourself in a panic of worrying, OK? And even then, if I don't show up, remember I might just be waiting it out in the mine.'

'I'm worrying now, Billy. So don't expect me to stop.'

He drew her in for a kiss. 'You know what I mean.' He kissed her sweetly. Then he brought his hands up on either side of her face and kissed her again, deeply, passionately. He lingered over it, smiling as he slowly broke it off. 'Know what?' he said. 'You and me, we're going make us a baby when this is done. I decided that.' He patted her stomach. 'How'd you like that? That'd make you happy, wouldn't it?'

'Right now, what would make me happiest of all is you coming back safe,' Dixie replied.

'I will,' he said and turned. Hoisting the rucksack up properly on to his shoulders, he started off on the trail. Just as he was about to disappear into the trees he paused, turned back and waved. 'I love you!' he called cheerfully.

Dixie waved back and watched him disappear.

Dixie and the boy ate a skimpy dinner of bread and beans and afterwards they sat on the big log and played gin rummy until it was too dark to see. Finally the boy crawled off, curled up in his corner in the back room and went to sleep.

In the outer room Dixie remained sitting in the dark. Billy hadn't remembered to bring an extra gas cylinder for the lantern. The flashlight, never very reliable in the best of times, was growing dimmer with each use, so now she saved it for emergencies. This left only the dark. Dixie had become good at moving around without bumping into things. She laid out her sleeping bag, changed her clothes, found the water bucket, washed and got herself ready for night, all in the total blackness of the cabin.

This hadn't bothered her on other nights, but now, too jittery with apprehension to sleep, Dixie considered leaving the door of the cabin open, because then at least there would be starlight amidst the restless shadows of the aspens. In the end, however, she didn't.

Knees drawn up, arms around them, she just sat, staring into the gloom. What came over her was the darkness of long ago. The same sort of edgy anticipation had filled her then too, waiting, listening for Daddy's footsteps and the tinny sound of her bedroom door opening. All trailer doors were like that, making a lightweight, resonant sound when they opened, and she would keep herself utterly still, her muscles taut, willing the sound not to happen.

When Daddy had got in the bed with her, Dixie always pretended to be asleep. If she did that, it felt almost as if what he was doing was happening to some dream girl in bed with them and not to her. That made it not so bad. However, Dixie had never figured out a way to relieve the hideous feeling of anticipation that came over her as she waited in the dark for the door to open. Now, tonight, she felt just the same.

Chapter Thirty-One

Spencer woke early. A lacework of birdsong threaded through the trees. Above stretched a pale, peach-strewn blue sky. The sun had not yet fully crested the ridges of the mountains so the forest remained dim, and a heavy dew lay over all the grass.

Guff was still in Spencer's embrace, the old cowboy's back to his chest, and for a few moments exhaustion kept Spencer too groggy to move. Each sense seemed to come awake separately, first his hearing to the birds; then his eyes to the fading darkness; then he smelled the stink.

'What a champion fart, old boy,' he mumbled and sleepily reached to pat Guff on the cheek.

The information sent back by his fingers was momentarily incomprehensible. Then Spencer recoiled. Scrambling to his feet, he jerked back.

'No. *No*. No!' He moved forward again, bending down over Guff. He touched the old man's face tentatively at first; he then patted him. A harder pat. A gentle slap. 'Guff, *no*. Come on.'

Guff was dead.

Kneeling for a closer look, Spencer regarded the old cowboy. His eyes were closed. His jaw had gone slack, sagging to the left because he'd been lying on his left side. He'd wet himself. His bowels had opened too, which had caused the smell. Spencer had never seen a dead body before, not a human one, not a real one in its natural state. He hadn't expected the baseness of it, soiled and empty.

Reaching out, he touched Guff's cheek again. It was cold. Spencer realized that what he had mistaken for chilliness in the night had, in fact, been the approach of death. He had been clutching a corpse to him as he slept.

Spencer felt no disgust at this realization and this surprised him. He had expected revulsion and briefly through his mind went the realization that he was also expecting to make a story from this, a gruesome but blackly humorous tale of misadventure for his friends. Perhaps that still would happen, but at the moment it came as an alien thought, as if it was occurring in someone else's head and Spencer was just observing it. What he hadn't expected was that far from wanting to escape Guff, he longed to clutch the old man to him, to care for him and protect him in this last, greatest moment of vulnerability.

Spencer rocked back on his heels.

Once again, a longing for Sidonie flooded over him. A knee-jerk reaction to his distress, undoubtedly, since she was so good at keeping life the way Spencer liked it, but again it was as if he was simply observing his thoughts and not in them. There remained this strange distance that allowed him to see himself desperate to escape this responsibility but yet he experienced the longing differently. Even if Sidonie couldn't do anything about this situation, he simply wished she were there, even if she proved to be as helpless and lost as he was.

Was it weak to want someone to be with you like that? A dependency? Did he just want to use her like a drug to deaden the pain? His therapist had said to him once that he was using people in his relationships rather than relating to them. It hadn't made a lot of sense to Spencer at the time, because he really didn't know how to behave differently. Understanding what use people would be in a given situation had seemed a rational way to decide how he should relate to them. If life had taught him anything, it was that just wanting people to be there and care about you wasn't enough, whereas most people responded to being useful ...

... even if she weren't useful, he would have liked Sidonie with him just then. Would she have come under these conditions? Would Sidonie want to be here with him, even if *he* wasn't useful to *her*? If he didn't pay her? Would she stay ...?

He regarded Guff's body. He should clean Guff up before anyone found them. Guff wouldn't want the indignity of being seen like this.

Reaching down, Spencer gently tried to straighten the crooked jaw.

'What would happen if I asked Sidonie to marry me, Guff?

'What do you think? Would she laugh in my face?'

He smoothed Guff's shirt.

'How do I know what love is, Guff? Maybe what I'm feeling is just post traumatic stress syndrome or something. You think that might be it? Because otherwise I'm on new territory here. I never took her seriously before. It didn't even occur to me to. So why does she suddenly feel like the most important person in my life now?'

Positioning himself at Guff's feet, Spencer grabbed one of the weathered cowboy boots to remove it. 'OK, I'm going to tackle washing you up, because I know you wouldn't want anyone to find out you shit yourself.'

He tugged at the boot, fully expecting it to come off. Rigor mortis, however, had set in. While Spencer knew full well what rigor was, he had not realized quite how effective it was at locking the body into position. He tugged again hard, but the foot did not bend enough to get the boot off. 'Fuck,' he said in astonishment and tried again. The boot would not budge.

'Fuck!' He yanked ruthlessly, but all it did was pull the whole body forward.

Spencer let go. Disappointment washed over him and the intensity of it startled him, because why the fuck was he disappointed about not getting to wash the shit off some old guy's ass? Why the fuck *anything*?

Spencer dissolved into tears.

As the sun broke through the barrier of branches and the day warmed up, flies appeared. Would they eat the body? Lay eggs on it? How long before rigor mortis would pass? There was so much Spencer didn't know. He struggled to keep depression from settling over him. *Like a fly on just another piece of shit.*

The boy came unbidden into his mind at that moment. Helplessness, depression, a feeling of stupidity – they always summoned thoughts of the boy. That was always how it went. Think of the boy, feel helpless, feel hopeless, feel stupid. The same in reverse. Feel helpless, hopeless and stupid, and there was the boy.

For the first time Spencer became fully aware of just how very inextricably those two sets of thoughts were linked. On some level, he'd always known it but here, now, it came into his consciousness with a clarity he hadn't previously experienced. The 1, 2, 3 of it surprised him. He hadn't been thinking of Tennesee at all, but when the feelings of vulnerability overwhelmed him, up Tennesee popped, like a conjured spirit.

Spencer considered the connection, going back and forth between the thoughts, observing the tension in his muscles and the bleak emptiness of depression. Perhaps this was why he found it so hard to keep Tennesee in mind at times when he knew he should. Who wouldn't try to avoid feeling that particularly dispiriting kind of vulnerability?

It didn't take Sigmund Freud to understand how Tennesee and helplessness had become linked, but as Spencer contemplated it, for the first time he realized those feelings weren't actually about Tennesee. Tennesee hadn't violated Spencer. He hadn't manipulated Spencer's vulnerability to take from him what he had not consensually given. It wasn't by his doing that he was Phoebe's son.

Spencer tried to visualize the boy in a manner that was not coloured by his relationship with Phoebe. How would he have seen Tennesee, were, say, he simply one of the child extras on a movie set? Would Spencer have shown interest in him? Talked to him? Tossed a ball around with him, as he had occasionally done with kids on set?

Sitting on the grass beside Guff, Spencer was a spectator to his own thoughts as they moved quietly, fluidly, building up a detailed image of his son, almost as if a photograph were developing in front of him. *What of himself was in Tennesee?*

That was a thought too far. The moment of quiet objectivity dissolved and Spencer's mind went blank as completely as if a light had been switched off.

'Maybe think about that another time, huh, Guff? But for right now, look at these fucking flies. We need to get you cleaned up.'

Putting his arms under Guff's body, Spencer lifted him up and struggled through the trees towards the creek. The old man's muscles were still locked in rigor mortis, making the body unwieldy, but Spencer managed to reach the water. He knew he still wasn't going be able to get Guff's boots off, but after considerable effort, he managed to get the old man's jeans down far enough to wash away the filth.

Spencer had never cleaned the faeces off anything, much less a corpse. It wasn't that he had avoided dealing with the shit that accompanied babyhood when Thomas and Louisa were small. Growing up on the fringes of other people's families, he had never quite known what to do with one of his own and Kathryn was little help. She was so competent at everything that she left little room for someone who didn't know what he should be doing. Spencer had never found the words to explain how much like an outsider he still felt, when Kathryn was with the children. In the end, it was just easier to let it pass and shut himself away in his study to learn lines or read or whatever else it was he was doing.

Cleaning Guff didn't disgust him the way he would have imagined such a task would, if he were preparing to act it as a scene. If anything, Spencer found solace in the straightfor-wardness of what he needed to do and focused all his atten-tion on doing it well.

'I'll go find that horse afterwards,' he said as he worked, 'because I know what you'd be thinking, *Damn, there goes frigging Spencer, losing another one.* But I haven't, Guff. I'm sure she's still out there and not far away. I'll find her. Soon as I'm done with this.'

Everything, of course, was wet by the time Spencer finished, because he hadn't been able to remove any of Guff's clothes. However, the sun was well overhead by that point and the day was warming up. Things would dry quickly. It was just a matter of getting him back out on to the open grass.

There was no possible doubt that Guff was anything other than a dead body. The bluish-grey tone, the still slightly misaligned jaw, the sealed eyelids all spoke of lifelessness in such an organic way that it required no prior experience for recognition. Spencer reached over and touched Guff's cheek lightly. The most unexpected aspect of death to him was the waxy appearance of the skin. Like the exhibits in Madame Tussaud's, Guff looked both real and unreal at once.

Spencer struggled to carry the body out into the small clearing, moving carefully to avoid knocking it against the tree trunks or the larger rocks. Gently he lay Guff down in the long grass. Kneeling, he pulled the old man's shirt down and tucked it into his jeans before hooking closed the elabo-rate rodeo buckle. The stiffness held Guff's head slightly off the ground, which looked odd to Spencer. He located a flat stone and put it under Guff's head, but then that looked uncomfortable. Pulling moss from a nearby log, he padded the stone; sitting back, he regarded his handiwork. He smiled.

A helicopter came over the clearing in the late afternoon. Spencer had heard it approaching and pulled off his shirt to wave at it. The pilot must have been looking in a different direction or perhaps he just needed space to manoeuvre the helicopter, because initially he flew past the clearing, leaving Spencer frantically trying to out-yell the noise. Within moments, however, it was back, hovering over the trees.

There wasn't enough room to land, but the helicopter came very low. The passenger side door opened. A ranger leaned out, slowly lowering a rope. 'You OK to come up this way?' he shouted through the roar of the blades.

Spencer shouted that he was.

'Can you get the harness on yourself? You want me to come down and help you?'

'We need to take him,' Spencer yelled back, pointing to Guff.

'Dead?'

Spencer nodded.

A stretcher was lowered and the ranger came down the rope too. Between them, they fastened Guff's body in.

'There's a horse out there too,' Spencer said over the roar of the blades. 'I got her herded back in, but I couldn't catch her. She was just beyond the trees there.'

'Strap yourself into the harness,' the ranger said, helping Spencer with the fasteners.

'She'll have been spooked by the noise.'

'We'll get her,' the ranger replied and signalled to winch them up.

Spencer hesitated. 'Are you sure? I don't want to lose her.'

'The pilot will have the GPS coordinates now,' the ranger said. 'We'll find her.'

Reaching the helicopter, Spencer climbed into the seat behind the pilot and buckled his safety belt. The blades picked up speed and the machine slowly lifted up out of the trees to reveal the vast panorama of mountains slipping away to the valley, distant below.

'So,' Spencer said, 'tell me. What's the word on my son?'

Chapter Thirty-Two

Dixie and the boy were running low on food. Billy hadn't brought up new supplies and not now knowing when he would return again made it hard to estimate how much they could eat of what was left. Dixie decided in the end that she and the boy were going to have to make a more serious effort to live off the land.

'Hey, Joker, get up.'

He rolled over and pulled the bedding over his head.

'It's already light.' Dixie nudged him with her foot. 'Get up. We're going fishing this morning.'

'Fuck off.'

'This ain't a choice. We got hardly any food. Get up.'

'Leave me alone. I'm not going to go fishing. I don't eat fish.'

'You will if you're hungry enough. *Up.*' Dixie grabbed the edge of his blanket and pulled it.

The boy was in a contrary mood from that moment on. He didn't want to leave the back room. He didn't want to eat the cheese sandwich she'd made. He didn't want to help her assemble the fishing poles. He most certainly didn't want to catch grasshoppers in the clearing.

'I'll catch 'em. All you got to do is walk around in the grass to make them jump up. Yes? OK? Think you can manage that?' Dixie said, exasperated. 'You walk, I'll catch.'

The boy glowered at her.

She gave him a push. '*Walk*.'

There was more walking to do after that, because the creek that ran through the aspens at the back of the cabin was too small for fish. Dixie knew it would eventually have to empty into something bigger, so they needed to follow it into the forest. Before long, they were hacking through the underbrush, clambering over fallen trees and sliding down rocky outcroppings. She kept the boy ahead of her and carried the rods, the grasshoppers and the creel. He complained the whole way.

At last they came to a larger stream tumbling noisily down the mountainside. It was at too much of an incline to fish easily, so Dixie insisted that they follow it until it levelled out into less active water.

After fifteen minutes or so of scrambling downhill, they came to an area where the slope eased and the water rushed around a fall of boulders, forming several small pools. Dixie set down the equipment.

'So I'm taking it that you never fished before?' she asked, disentangling the two poles.

'No,' the boy said sullenly.

'What's the matter with you today? What you got to be so angry about?' Dixie asked.

'I don't want to do this.'

'So then what happens? Does your mom let you out of doing stuff if you pout enough?'

'I'm not pouting. I just fucking don't want to do this. And you can't make me. You can make me come, but you can't make me fish.'

'There ain't much to it. Leastways not the way I do fishing,' she said. 'Just get your bait, stick it on the hook and put it in the water. Then you wait. Some folks make all sorts of work out of fishing, casting all the time, worrying about how the fly's floating and all that. But truth is, you can catch a fair share of fish doing it the lazy way. So it ain't hard to do.'

'I didn't say it was hard,' the boy grumbled. 'I just said I fucking didn't want to do it.'

Dixie had placed the grasshoppers she'd caught into an empty Band-Aid box. 'These little boxes used to be made of metal,' she said, lifting the plastic top to take out the grasshoppers. 'When I was little, my daddy always kept his bait in a metal Band-Aid box that he put in his shirt pocket.'

The boy quirked up his lip in distaste.

'When I was a kid I loved catching grasshoppers. On real hot summer afternoons, me and Leola would go out back of where we lived and catch millions in this big field.'

'Yuck.'

'It wasn't yuck, Joker. It was fun. We kept them in a peanut butter jar. Would punch holes in the lid with a nail so they could breathe and then put some leaves in for them to eat and keep them in that.' Dixie smiled. 'One of the best feelings I remember from when I was a little girl was looking in the kitchen cupboard and seeing there was a whole bunch of empty peanut butter jars. I'd feel rich as a queen.'

'That's how stupid you are, getting excited about some fucking empty jars.'

Amiably Dixie shrugged. 'Yeah, but I didn't see empty jars. I saw all the fun I was going to have catching grasshoppers.'

'Yes, well, not only were you stupid, you were fucking cruel. Phoebe would never let me do anything like that. She's a vegetarian.'

Dixie laughed. 'You don't *eat* the grasshoppers, silly.'

'I *know* that,' the boy replied indignantly. 'But you're feeding them to the fish. Look what you're doing right now. You're sticking a fucking hook through them. Shit, how cruel is that?'

'You got to kill things.'

'No, you don't. That's how come Phoebe's a vegetarian. She doesn't eat anything with a face.'

'You're still killing. Even plants are alive. For us to stay alive, other things got to die. That's the way the world works,' Dixie said.

'Plants aren't the same as animals,' the boy replied. 'They don't feel things.'

'How do you know? Just because something don't look like you, that doesn't mean it's got no feelings. And just because it *does* look like you, that don't give it any more rights than something that's different. Besides, see here?' Dixie lifted her upper lip with one finger. 'These here are canine teeth. They're for eating meat. And we got a meat-eating stomach. If God meant us just to eat plants, he would have given us lots of extra insides like cows got so we could digest plants better, but He didn't. And the way I reckon, God don't make mistakes. So it's not about it being OK to kill plants but not animals. It's about appreciating something's got to die to keep you alive, and so you never take that for granted and get wasteful or thoughtless about it.

'So, here.' Dixie gently cast the line out and let the hook with its grasshopper sink into the water before handing the pole to the boy. 'Take this and I'm going to put my line in down there where those fallen logs have made another little pool.'

The boy wasn't any good at it. He cast like he was pitching a baseball and every time the line zoomed out of the reel too fast and went right over the creek and got tangled in the brush on the other bank.

'Let's put you up there,' Dixie said at last and pointed to an outcropping of rock, 'then you don't have to do any casting. The water will be deep below the rocks and you can just let the line down. Go right there, beside that boulder.'

The boy wasn't paying attention to what she was saying. Instead of feeding out his line alongside the boulder, he climbed right up on top of it and moved out to where it overhung the fast-moving water.

'Joker, get down from there. That's going to be slippery.'

'I'm OK.'

'Get *down*. It's got to be six feet high, that rock. It's dangerous.'

'Fuck off.'

'Joker.'

'Shut *up*, would you?' he shouted. 'You talk like you're the boss of me and you're not. I don't have to do what you say.'

Dixie glared at him. 'I'm just trying to keep you safe, you little nitwit. Now get back in off that.'

He was perched like a little spider, his fingers and toes splayed to grip the slimy green moss that covered the top of the boulder. 'I could run off, you know,' he said tauntingly. 'From right here. I could just take off and there's no way you could stop me, because you're so stupid you didn't even bring the gun.'

'Yeah, you could run off, if you wanted,' Dixie replied. 'You could also fall off that rock and crack your skull open. So get down from there.'

'You act like you think you're my mom, and you're not.'

'You're right about that one, Joker,' Dixie replied. 'I sure ain't your mom. 'Cause if I was your mom, I'd have washed your mouth out with soap so many times by now you'd be blowing bubbles out your ears. But she ain't here and I am, so it's my rules. Now get your little butt down off that rock this minute. It's too dangerous there.'

'And what if I don't?' the boy asked. 'Are you going to come beat me up like your fuck-ass boyfriend does?'

'The way you're acting, I sure have a mind to smack your bottom, yes,' Dixie said, ''cause, believe me, there's worse things in this world than a sore butt.'

'You just try, cunt,' the boy retorted.

In one smooth move, Dixie leaped up and had him by his ankle. He fell face forward on the mossy edge of the boulder as she jerked him back down on to the bank of the creek. Just as fluidly she brought him back up to his feet and slapped his bottom. Hard. The boy, dirtied by the fall but not defeated, writhed and struck out at her viciously.

Dixie was having none of it. 'I'm fed up to the back teeth with you and your mouth, Joker. The kind of words you use, they shouldn't be coming out of a hard-tack cowboy. So if you want me to let go and not smack your bottom again, you say you're sorry for calling me that.'

'Fuck off!'

'Jeez, you like that F word. I thought you were supposed to be so smart. So how come is it then that you got only one word you know how to say? Leola's Carrie Dee knows how to speak better than you when she gets cross and she's only two.'

'I *hate* you!'

'Yeah, well, I don't like you so hot right now either, but that's not the point. You say you're sorry for talking like that.'

'No! I'm *not* sorry. I'm never fucking going to *be* sorry to you. *Ever.* I hate you!' the boy screamed. Then he twisted sharply away and Dixie lost her grip. Sensing freedom, he sprinted up over the boulder again, fast as a lizard, and before Dixie could react, he was down the other side and off into the trees.

Dixie shot up over the boulder after him, but as she reached the apex of the rock, she halted. There was no boy anywhere. He had vanished. Only empty forest greeted her. For a long, frozen moment Dixie perched precariously on the slippery moss atop the huge stone and scanned the dense pines. There seemed no point to going further. There was no indication which way he'd gone. Instead, she lowered herself back down to the bank of the stream.

Her breath came as hard as if she'd been running. Her heart made so much noise thumping in her ears that for several moments she couldn't hear anything else at all, not even her own thoughts.

As she tried to still the frantic thudding, oddly it wasn't the boy who occupied Dixie's head. It was Leola. Dixie hadn't known Daddy was doing it to Leola too. Bad enough him coming into her room at night, but she had felt maybe somehow she deserved it. She'd always been the trouble-maker in the family. But never Leola. Leola had been placid and smiley from the moment she'd popped out. Even though she was younger, she was smarter than Dixie, and prettier too, and still so little. Daddy had no excuse for touching Leola. That's what Dixie told him too, that year she was fourteen, that day she found out what he was doing. As she lifted the .22 and took aim, that's exactly what she said.

As she'd pulled the trigger, an unspeakable relief had flooded through Dixie, knowing Daddy wouldn't ever be able to do those kinds of things again. But even as her mind was telling her that, her heart still knew how wrong it was to shoot him like vermin as he lay there defenceless in Leola's bed. It started beating so hard in her ears that Dixie thought maybe God was going to pull it right out of her. So it was now too, here in the forest. Dixie was overcome once again with that same terrible mix of doom and liberation.

Detail was the only thing that calmed her down. With intricate thoroughness, Dixie wound up the line on the two fishing poles, pulled them apart and fastened the reels care-fully. She put the Band-Aid box of grasshoppers, now mostly dead, into the creel. Then she started back along the path that she and the boy had made through the underbrush.

The sun was high when she came out into the flower-strewn meadow. Deep in the forest it was easy to think it was much later than it was. It felt that way in her head too, as if an aeon had passed since they'd left in the morning. Gazing up at the sun, Dixie realized it could only be just after midday.

She put away the fishing rods and took out the last can of Spam. The only food left was that, five eggs, half a loaf of bread and some Velveeta cheese. And a can of Mama's bacon grease. Mama saved bacon grease the way Midas saved gold, not only keeping what came from her own cooking, but giving out empty coffee cans to the neighbours so they could save theirs for her too. No need to waste money on all that fancy cooking oil when the good Lord put fat on pigs, she'd always say. No one could ever accuse Mama of being stingy either. Dixie was given a new can of bacon grease every time she stopped by home. It'd become a family joke, something she and Leola were always laughing about behind Mama's back. Now, however, as Dixie cradled the coffee can in her hand and felt the familiar ridges in the metal, the familiar weight, the familiar smell, she was comforted by Mama's generosity.

Putting the frying pan on the gas ring, Dixie opened the Spam and cut three generous pieces off the loaf and threw them into the melting grease. She cracked one of the eggs into the pan. To hell with eking the food out until Billy got back. She needed to feel full now.

As she cooked and then ate her meal, Dixie didn't think about the boy at all. She didn't think about Billy either. She was surprised when she realized it, because she had become so used to worrying about both of them that it felt natural to have her mind going around and around like a pinwheel. Now, however, it was perfectly still. Like a dead thing.

After eating, tiredness overwhelmed her, probably just because she'd had so little food at breakfast and had then done all the grasshopper catching and walking and hacking through the forest and clambering over rocks and stuff.

Probably also because she'd hardly had any sleep the night before. Dixie couldn't keep her eyes open. Rolling out her sleeping bag, she lay down and soon was fast asleep.

When Dixie woke, it was in a what? where? kind of way. She'd been dreaming about Jamie Lee, except he wasn't a baby anymore but a little boy of five or six, and he didn't have Down's. At least it seemed that way in the dream. They were in the Pay'n Save together and he'd gone off down one aisle and Dixie couldn't find him. He'd just disappeared, and Mama was there, saying, 'This is how things happen and it's always for the best.' Now suddenly here she was in the dilapidated cabin. Dixie looked around in confusion as long shafts of evening sunlight fell across the entrance.

Rubbing her face to disperse the sleep, she rose and went into the collapsed backroom of the cabin. It was empty. Just the rumple of dirty bedding and stained towels where boy had slept. Going to the door of the cabin, Dixie scanned the clearing. The blue wildflowers were going past their best. There was now a slightly fermenting smell to the clearing, especially late in the afternoon. Not a bad smell; you'd not really notice it unless you'd been there when the flowers were fresh. Standing in the doorway, she watched the shadows of the aspen lengthening over the dying flowers.

So, this was it. This was how it ended.

Chapter Thirty-Three

Dixie found it a very different matter being by herself in the cabin at night. This surprised her. Not only had she always thought of herself as being at home in the wilderness, but what good was the boy anyway? Whether it was a wolf or axe murderer who came along, he wouldn't have provided any protection. Indeed, he'd probably have been a liability. She was just as safe on her own until Billy came for her.

Billy. Oh gosh. What was going to happen now? How was Billy going to react to the boy getting loose? If it was going to happen, it should have been before he made up his stupid ransom note.

Maybe he'd be relieved. No boy to give back eliminated the dangerous business of how to return him without getting caught. Maybe they could take the money – supposing he had got any money – and then just go. Take off. Make a clean start. Calgary, maybe. The mountains were good there. Even bigger and more magnificent than those around Abundance, or at least that's what Dixie had heard. Billy could still do his cowboying in Calgary. Set up his guide business, if he wanted. They'd be safe across the border.

Even if he didn't get any money, they could still go. They could still get away and start over. Far from here. Far from the secrets that Crowheart would now hold.

Mama said everyone had secrets. When she'd come back from the hospital where the ambulance had taken Daddy, she'd taken Dixie and Leola into her bedroom and made them sit down on the edge of her bed. It was a dinky little room with only about a foot of space on either side of the double bed, so there the two of them were, squished together, side by side. What Dixie remembered most was that the bed had a bright pink chenille bedspread on it. It was the colour of cotton candy. That and the fact Dixie had had to sit next to the big bride doll Mama always set up against the pillows once she'd made the bed. It had been Mama's doll when she was a little girl, a special doll her uncle had brought her from Chicago, except that once her sister had used nail polish to try and give the doll eye shadow and it had never come off properly. So the bride had a red, cock-eyed look that had always scared Dixie a little.

Mama had closed the door, even though there wasn't anyone else in the trailer except the three of them, and then she'd explained how every family had some secret things that they could never, ever tell other people. She said sometimes a bad thing, like what Daddy had been doing, ended up spawning worse things, like what Dixie had done in shooting off his pecker, and if you didn't want it to just keep getting worse and worse, you had to make a family decision that that was going to be the end of it. Then you had to stick to that. And sticking to it was a kind of glue,

Mama explained, that kept families stuck together. That's exactly how she said it, making it clear that she saw secrets that were so terrible you couldn't speak of them as something that bound folks to each other instead of pulling them apart.

And so it was. Mama told the hospital people how Daddy had been getting ready to clean the gun, so he propped it up against the table in the kitchen, and then that damn cocker spaniel came charging through. It always had been an overactive dog, Mama said. She told the hospital people she'd thought of having it put to sleep for what it did to Daddy, but then the kiddies would be heartbroken. So Daddy was just going to have to live with the ignominy of being shot by a dog.

The sheriff came around later to have a look. He told Mama he had to have a look any time there was a shooting, even if it was the dog that had done it. Then he said that she and Daddy should consider moving into a house, because Daddy would find it too hard to use a wheelchair in the trailer. He told Mama his sister had a good house to rent down on Second Street and it wasn't too expensive. Would she like the phone number?

And that's how it ended. A story told and told again until it became what really happened. Except to the four of them, of course, who remained glued together by the truth.

Now there was a secret to glue her and Billy together too.

The morning dawned cold and overcast, and as so often happened at such high altitudes, wet snow fell instead of rain. The wind, blowing bitterly across the clearing, pasted it smoothly along the trunks of the aspen like royal icing.

Pulling her sweatshirt jacket tight around her, Dixie stood in the doorway of the cabin, watching the snow weigh down the fading flowers in the meadow, crushing them with beauty.

Once the sun returned, so would summer. The snow was already slush beneath the trees and hardly an inch deep in the clearing, but for the moment winter reigned. Dixie tugged her plastic poncho down over her clothes and picked up the water jug to go to the creek, as there wasn't enough left in it even to make a cup of tea.

Kneeling in the snowy grass, Dixie let the creek water flow slowly into the turquoise-and-white gallon container. That's when she heard the crying. Alert, she lifted her head and listened.

Dixie rose to her feet. Leaving the water jug beside the creek, she walked a little ways into the forest. 'Joker?'

'Where *are* you?' a panic-filled voice wailed.

'Over here, Joker. Where are you? I can't see you.'

She heard only wailing, so faint it might simply have been the wind.

'Can you follow my voice?' Dixie peered into the snowy undergrowth beyond the aspens. 'Joker? Joker, I'm here,' she called.

He came crashing through the brush several hundred yards higher up the slope. Bawling so hard he could hardly stagger on, he stumbled into her arms.

'You're freezing!'

'I couldn't *find* you,' he sobbed.

'Shh, shh, shh,' she soothed and pulled him in against her. 'Come on. Let's get you out of the weather.'

'I kept looking for you and I couldn't *find* you.'

'No. No, and I'm sorry about that.' Dixie kept his shivering body close against her. 'But it's all right now. Come on. I'll take care of you.'

Back in the cabin, Dixie boiled water to make him a hot drink. Then she fried up the leftover Spam and two slices of bread. 'Get this in you,' she said.

The boy was shaking uncontrollably, still weepy and unsteady.

'You got way too cold out there. Eat this.' She cut the food up into little pieces. That was how she'd done it for Jamie Lee, how she used to do it for Leola when she was tiny and didn't want to eat. Little pieces always tasted better.

The boy let her feed him. No fussing this time about Spam or bread cooked in bacon grease or mugs of plain hot water. Almost as soon as he had finished eating, he was asleep in the warmth of her sleeping bag.

Dixie sat beside him in the grey gloom of the unheated cabin and watched him as he slept. He was a mess. His long hair was matted with all manner of filth. His skin was scratched and dirty. He'd lost weight. Dixie hadn't really noticed it happening, but now, looking carefully, she could see the pudginess going from his cheeks and his jawline. Funny thing was that on one hand, he looked like a little cave boy to her because of all his dirt and mess. Just like one of those Neanderthal statues at the museum come to life. On the other hand, Dixie could, for the first time, see Spencer Scott in him – there, along his jaw – and it occurred to her that the boy had the possibility of turning into a handsome man.

*　　*　　*

The weather passed off in the early afternoon. The sun came out, a hot August sun that brought back with it all the birds and insects, and it was as if the snowstorm had never happened, except for the fact that now the blue flowers all lay prone in the clearing, like a fallen army.

When the boy awoke, he sat with the sleeping bag pulled close around him, as if he were still chilled. He said very little. Dixie worried that perhaps he was falling ill, so she offered him more Spam and bread. When he didn't want that, she offered some of the cheese. The boy shook his head. He wasn't hungry, he said.

Dixie regarded him. 'Know what I'm thinking, Joker?'

The boy looked up.

'I'm thinking we ought to sort out your hair. Let's give you a good cleaning up. You'd feel better.'

'I don't want to get in the water. I'm cold.'

'No, you don't have to. Let's just go outside and sit on the big log. Get ourselves in the sun. It's too damp in here now. Come sit outside with me and I'll cut your hair for you.'

'I don't want my hair cut.'

'You checked it out lately? Because one of these nights when you're asleep the wood rats are going to start building a nest in it.'

A concerned expression crossed his face and he lifted one hand to feel his hair.

'Your choice is to let me cut it or else let me try to take all those tangles out with my comb. Which do you want?'

The boy's face clouded over for a moment and then he dropped his shoulders. 'I can't cut it. Phoebe won't let me.'

'Phoebe ain't here.'

He let out a heavy sigh.

'You know what?' Dixie said, 'Every time you answer something, it's "Phoebe thinks this," or "Phoebe doesn't like that," or "My dad does this," or "He doesn't do that." Now I can understand that. They're your folks and it's a good thing for kids to pay attention to what their folks say. You're being a good boy telling me all the things Phoebe and your dad think. But the truth is, Joker, folks are just there to guide you, not to turn you into them. It's all right for you to be you. Even if no one else thinks so.'

The boy's eyes filled with tears.

'Hey,' Dixie said in surprise. 'I was just saying. I wasn't putting your folks down or anything. I didn't mean to make you cry.'

His mouth drew down in a sob.

'I'm sorry. Am I reminding you too much about home and missing your folks? Is that it?' Coming over, she opened her arms and drew the boy in against her. 'I'm really sorry. I didn't mean to make you feel sad.'

The boy wept in a way Dixie hadn't seen him do before. Long, hard, throat-catching sobs. She pressed him close, her hand cupping his head as gently to her as she had done with Jamie Lee.

'I was *so* scared,' he said at last in a tiny, ragged voice.

'You mean last night?'

He nodded. 'I was so, so scared. I thought I was going to die.'

Resting her cheek on his head, Dixie made soft, soothing, shushing sounds and rocked him in her arms. 'I bet you were. But you're safe now. You're OK.'

'I wanted to find you so bad.' And he sobbed again.

'I'm sorry it scared you so much, Joker.' She caressed his face, keeping him pressed close.

'Why didn't you come looking for me?'

'Because I was trusting you not to run away,' Dixie said softly.

'I was just mad.'

'Yes, I know you were.'

'But you let me go,' he wept. 'Why didn't you come after me? You said you would. That other time. Before we came up here.'

There was a long pause.

'It's because you don't want me back either, do you?' the boy said in a small voice. 'Just like my parents. Nobody wants me.'

'Joker, that isn't true. That isn't what was going on. The truth of the matter is that what we done to you isn't right. Billy shouldn't ought to have took you that night. I shouldn't ought to have been helping him. So when you wanted to leave so much, I thought maybe it was better just to let you go.'

'Up *here*?' he cried.

'There wasn't any choice about that. I can't go anywhere else right now either.'

'But I could have got eaten. You said that yourself. You said that it wasn't Disneyland up here and that mountain lions would eat me up if I ran away.'

Dixie kept her arms around the boy, kept him pulled in so close against her that she could feel his breath on her skin.

'You're no different than my dad. When I told him I was going to run away, he said go ahead. He said both him and me would be happier if I was gone.'

'Grown-ups get upset, Joker. They end up saying or doing things they don't mean, and we sometimes got to cut them slack for not being as strong as they should be.'

'My dad meant it. And Phoebe meant it when she told me she just wanted me to fuck off so she could be with her boyfriend. And you meant it when you said it wasn't Disney-land up here.'

'I'm sorry, Joker.'

'It's just I thought you were different. You've been so nice to me, so I thought you cared. But you don't. You're just like everyone else.'

'I'm sorry, Joker. I'm really, really, really sorry. I mean that. Because you're right. I shouldn't have just let you go. That was wrong of me. But you were wrong too, because you shouldn't have gone. I was treating you like someone I could trust and you broke my trust. You got to understand that when things go wrong, it's never just one person's fault.'

The boy wiped his eyes.

'Can you see that? Because it's important. Nothing happens all by itself. Everything's connected to everything else.'

He nodded.

'OK. Then let's just say sorry to each other and we'll both try hard not to do it again. All right?' Dixie asked. 'So, I'm sorry, Joker, that you got so cold and scared, and I'm sorry I didn't come after you.'

'I'm sorry I ran away,' the boy replied. 'I'm really sorry too.'

Chapter Thirty-Four

The next morning Dixie offered the boy the choice of staying behind in the clearing if he didn't want to go fishing, but she explained carefully that there was just no alternative to her going. They needed the food.

He came willingly. In fact, he even volunteered to help Dixie grub out worms and went about it in a businesslike way that soon filled the Band-Aid container.

They left the clearing the way they'd gone on the previous occasion, following the small creek. 'You pay attention this time,' Dixie said as they walked. 'Because it's possible to learn how to read these trees just like people learn to read books. Then you won't get lost. Are you a Boy Scout?'

'As if,' the boy answered dismissively.

'No, not "as if". Don't get snooty. You can learn lots of good stuff being a Scout.'

'Mostly it's stupid.'

'Mostly it's not, Joker. Folks are forgetting how to do survival things, like how to read the forest, and that's not good. Those things are the foundation for everything else.

It's all well and good learning how to do computer stuff or knowing what celebrities are doing what, but those things are like being up in the attic of a house. If you don't also know how to read the mountains or ride a horse or find food for yourself when you have to, then that stuff ain't going to do you any good, because you got nothing to connect you to the ground.'

'I'm not going to get lost again,' the boy replied, 'so don't worry.'

'No, I'm just telling you. Because everybody gets lost from time to time.'

Once they located the bigger creek, Dixie decided to follow it further downhill in search of good fishing. The downward slope grew abruptly steeper and the stream fell noisily down a series of waterfalls.

'Wow, look how pretty that is,' the boy said.

'Yeah, it is. Let's go down to the bottom of the falls. I can see where it flattens out some there and makes a pool. That'll be good fishing.'

'Wow. This is wicked. We're, like, explorers. I bet no one else has ever seen this,' he said as he scrambled down the rocks. 'This is so far up in the mountains and there's no roads around or anything. Maybe we're the first people to discover it. I want to name it Tennesee Falls.'

'Indians probably been here before,' Dixie said. 'These mountains were Crow land before the white people took it away from them. This was their home for a long, long time, so I expect they knew every inch of it.'

'Probably they wouldn't mind if I call it Tennesee Falls now.'

'Probably not.'

He eased himself down over the final rocks to the bank overlooking the pool. 'Maybe we should call it Crow Falls,' he said.

'That would be good too.'

'I don't like to think about what we did to the Native Americans. We learned about it at school and I think it's really sad. They were living their own kind of life but we thought European life was better, because we had more stuff. So we made them live our way and then took what they did have away from them.'

'Yeah,' Dixie said, 'it's sad the world works that way.'

The pool at the bottom of the waterfalls wasn't the Blue Lagoon. It was only about twenty feet across and crowded in on both sides by the forest. Everything was shady and damp from the spray of the waterfall.

'Shit, there's like a million bugs down here,' the boy said, swatting wildly around himself.

'Shush. We got to be quiet now, till we see if there are any fish. Noise'll scare 'em off.'

'They can hardly hear us through the sound of all that water.'

Standing on the bank, Dixie scanned the pool. 'Over there,' she said at last and pointed to a clutch of boulders at the far edge, just before the stream plummeted off on down the hillside again. 'Stand just on this side of it. That's where the fish will be.'

The boy grabbed his pole and clambered straight up over the stones until he reached the top one. He let his line out.

'You're too high. You won't be able to land a fish from up there, Joker. Move yourself lower down.'

He paused. There was a long moment when Dixie expected him to talk back, and by the look in his eye, she guessed he was considering it. Finally, however, he reeled in his line and slid back down the rocks.

The water went flat and fairly quiet just beneath the rocks, so Dixie showed the boy how to let his line out very gently to sink the bait into the water without disturbing it. Then she returned to her own pole and cast out into the middle of the pool.

Five, ten, twenty minutes passed. The whole time the boy was a menace. He kept reeling his line back up to check the bait, kept trying to cast like she did and kept ending up in a big tangle. He talked, shouted and lolled on the bank, peering into the water.

'Don't keep doing that. You're going to scare off whatever few fish you haven't scared off already.'

'I'm trying to see what I look like.' He patted along the top of his head to feel the stubble left from Dixie's haircutting efforts. 'I bet I look really stupid.'

'No, you don't. You look trendy. All your friends will want a cut like that when they see it,' Dixie replied.

He blew a raspberry.

'Anyway, get back from the edge. We won't catch anything at all with you messing around like you are. All the fish are probably in Wyoming by now. Come on. I mean it. Balance your pole on that rock there, and then put that other rock on top of the end of it to keep it in place. Then come back over here and sit beside me. You can tell from here if something bites your line.'

Reluctantly the boy did as he was told.

'How come your daddy's never taken you out fishing?' she asked. 'I know he fishes because he always gets his picture in the paper at the Trout Run.'

The boy shrugged.

'When I was your age, I loved going fishing with my daddy,' Dixie said. 'It was the funnest thing me and my sister did with him.'

'I don't see what the fun part is,' the boy said. 'Basically all we're doing is sitting and waiting.'

'Yeah, well, sitting and waiting's good sometimes. We don't often get an excuse just to sit around and talk to our friends or family without feeling we got to be rushing off somewhere to get something done. And we don't often get a chance just to sit in the countryside and notice how pretty the world really is. But fishing lets you do those things.'

The boy grimaced. 'Maybe that works for you, but to be truthful, I think this is totally boring.'

They caught one fish, a brook trout only about eight inches long, which Dixie hooked just as they were about to give up. In the normal course of things, she would have thrown it back, but hunger made her keep it.

The boy pronounced the whole business of killing and gutting the fish a 'gross out' and stayed well back up on the bank as Dixie did it. When they were back in the cabin, however, he willingly ate his half when it appeared piping hot on his plate. He even ate the skin, possibly only because Dixie reached out for it when he left it on the side of the plate. Seeing her move towards it, the boy popped it in his mouth in one bite.

His eyes widened with surprise. 'Fish skin looks so seriously pukey,' he said when he finished it, 'but actually it's really nice.'

'That's called hunger,' Dixie replied. 'It makes everything taste nice.'

'Dixie?' came the voice, small and tentative through the darkness. It was the first time the boy had called her by name.

'What you want, Joker?' she asked sleepily.

'I hear something outside.'

Sitting up, Dixie listened into the darkness. Beyond the walls of the cabin came a shuffling and snuffling. 'Bring yourself in here,' she said in a whisper. Reaching out, she picked up the flashlight and turned it on. The beam scarcely penetrated the utter blackness in the cabin.

The boy came stumbling into the front room of the cabin. 'What is it?' he asked. He sat down very close to Dixie.

'A bear, probably. But who knows? Could be just a curious moose or something. But I'm not about to go see.' She grinned at him, but the boy wasn't finding it funny.

'We're safe enough in here,' she said reassuringly. 'We don't got no open food and that's what a bear would be looking for. Aren't you glad you ate that fish skin right up and it's safe inside you?' She smiled again and poked his stomach.

'It wouldn't be a mountain lion, would it?' he asked in a tiny voice.

'Nah. If it was a mountain lion, you'd never know it was there. They're silent as snow.'

The boy's eyes filled with tears.

'Hey!' She pulled the boy tight against her. 'Don't get so scared. We're going to be just fine. Billy made that door strong again. A bear won't be able to come in here. And I've the rifle right here beside me, if somehow he managed it.'

He wrapped both his arms around her.

'Tell you what's the best thing to do. Sing. Because whatever it is, once it hears us making noise in here, it won't want to stay. It's always good to sing in the wilderness, because wild animals don't know what the sound means. They can't tell if we are being playful or getting angry, so it scares them and they run away. What songs do you know?'

The boy shrugged.

'Then let's sing "Jesus Loves Me". That'll help us remember Jesus is always taking care of us, so we're definitely all right.'

'I don't know it.'

'You don't *know* it? "Jesus Loves Me"? Gosh. Your mama and daddy, they didn't teach you nothing, did they?' Dixie hugged him closer. 'But that's OK, because it's a real easy song. My little niece Carrie Dee can sing it right through and she's only two. So here goes:

> *Jesus loves me, this I know.*
> *For the Bible tells me so.*
> *Little ones to him belong.*
> *They are weak but He is strong.*
> *Yes, Jesus loves me!*
> *Yes, Jesus loves me!*

'Come on. You sing too. In a nice loud voice. The bear will go away then.'

The boy joined in, hesitantly at first but then more bravely. He had a strong, clear voice. Dixie hadn't been expecting that. When he said he didn't know any songs, she'd assumed it was because he wasn't any good at singing. When she heard how lovely his voice was, she was transported briefly out of the gloomy chill of the cabin by thoughts that maybe when this was all over, Reverend Rogers could call around and see if the boy would like to be in the children's choir at church.

When this was all over.

Murky reality flooded back in, inundating the concern she had felt about whatever was outside the cabin with a deeper kind of darkness. She forced her focus back on to the song.

Huddled together, arms around each other, sitting on the cabin floor with the wan beam of the flashlight pointing upwards, they repeated the song over and over so many times Dixie lost count. When they finally stopped, all was soundless beyond the walls.

'There. See? He's gone.'

The boy loosened his grip on her arm and sat upright. For a long moment he listened to the silence. Then he expelled a long, slow lungful of air.

Unexpectedly, there came a loud, strangulated call just beyond the door. The boy screamed in alarm and grabbed hold of Dixie again.

'It's just an owl, Joker,' she said and laughed.

The boy's mouth drooped and tears spilled over his cheeks.

'I know. Just an owl, but you weren't expecting it, were you?' Dixie drew him close again, wiping the tears away with her thumb. 'You've had too many scares tonight, huh?'

'I just want this to be over *so bad*,' he wailed. 'I'm tired of being scared all the time. I'm tired of being hungry. I'm tired of being freezing cold. And dirty and full of bug bites and everything else. I just want to go *home*.'

'Yeah,' Dixie said in a soothing voice, as she rocked the boy. 'I want that too.'

He really had had too much. No matter how much Dixie cuddled him, the boy remained weepy and unwilling to settle back down to sleep.

'Tell you what,' she said at last and reached up to take the pack of playing cards off the table.

'I don't want to play gin rummy. I'm tired of gin rummy too.'

'No. No, you just sit here real close to me, and I'm going to do something different with the cards. I'm going to tell your fortune.'

The boy snuffled.

'My sister Leola's really good at this. She's got the gift. She can tell you exactly what's going to happen. In fact, you know what? She used her cards to tell me all this here was going to happen. No lie. She looked at her cards and told me about you, about us being stuck up here and everything.'

'Really?' the boy asked.

'Yes, really. That very morning of the day Billy took you, Leola read her cards and said everything to me that was going to happen. Not using exact words, of course, so I didn't know, like, your name or anything, but I recognized you were the joker straightaway.'

'Wow. That's cool.'

'And know what else? I got the gift too. Because me and her are sisters, after all. So that's what I'm going to do right now. Tell you your fortune.'

Dixie shuffled the cards and set the pack on the floor. 'Now. What's your favourite number between ten and twenty.'

'Twelve.'

'Good, you choose twelve cards. Any twelve you want.'

As the boy handed the cards to Dixie, she laid them out to form a circle. 'OK, let's start at the bottom of the circle with this card. A six of diamonds. Six is a travelling card. It means a journey, but a good journey, because diamonds are valuable. A journey that's going to bring you your heart's desire. And then this next one, a seven of spades. Spade is another name for a shovel. That means you can dig yourself out of a situation that's really difficult and seven is a very lucky number. It means you're going to get out of a situation you don't want to be in.'

'Is it saying this is going to end?' the boy said hopefully.

'Yes, that's exactly what it's saying. But here, this is a ten of hearts. Ten is a number that means patience. And the hearts, well, that means you need to be patient and have a strong heart. But see, right next to it, there's the king of hearts. That represents a man, a really important man ...'

'My dad?'

'I'm sure it is. See, the cards are saying that if you are patient and strong in your heart, you're going to get out of this situation. You're going to get to see him again.'

'Is that really what they're saying?'

Dixie kept her arm around the boy. No knowing what Leola would have seen in the cards. Leola's was a different kind of gift, but being able to create hope, that was a gift too. So Dixie nodded. 'Yeah, that's really what they say.'

Chapter Thirty-Five

The next morning while the boy still slept, Dixie gently eased herself from her sleeping bag and went out to the creek to wash. It was a clear, cool morning, the sky a cloudless, washed-out blue. As she sat in the sunlight and combed the tangles out of her wet hair, Dixie pondered when Billy might return. It was so easy to lose track of time when there were none of the usual things to separate one day from the next.

Billy had been writing his note on a Friday. The post office wouldn't get it until Saturday, even if Billy mailed it straightaway, so like as not Spencer Scott wouldn't receive it until Monday. Dixie lay down her comb and counted on her fingers. Billy had been gone three full days, so this had to be Tuesday. If Billy was intending to stay down the mine for a few days after the money was dropped off, this meant he wouldn't be likely to make it back up to them before the end of the week.

Dixie sighed. Everything about this was so outlandish that it was very hard to see it working out. What if the police caught Billy? What if the mine caved in? There were so many horrible possibilities and no way of finding out what was actually happening. She and the boy could very easily end up stranded in the wilderness with no food and no way out and no one knowing where to look for them.

For several minutes Dixie was absorbed in thoughts of how she'd cope, if that happened. They could try walking out. They wouldn't have to go the whole way. If they could get far enough down out of the mountains for a phone signal, then Dixie could call Leola. She had been very careful to make sure she'd turned her phone off as soon as they left Abundance, because nothing wore a battery down faster than the phone's constantly searching for a signal that wasn't there.

There was a chance they could manage that, if she and the boy stuck to always going downhill when they came across roads. She didn't quite know where on Crowheart they were, but it should eventually come out on the Abundance side of the mountains because the deep wilderness didn't have any roads that went in very far. Nonetheless, it would still take a couple of days, probably, and how would they manage that without more food?

Food was going to be the big issue. While they were at the cabin, fishing was as good a way to supplement their diet as any, but it wasn't practical for a long walk out because it took time and required them to stay near water. Better if she shot a deer or elk, but then how would they preserve the meat to take with them? How would she deal with a large carcass when she had nothing more than her pocket knife? And this was assuming she could bring a big animal down without wasting too many bullets. Dixie realized then that she'd better go back and count the bullets left for the rifle, because Billy probably still had most of the ammunition in the truck.

There was another possibility, of course. She could simply start a fire here in the clearing. This was the high-danger fire season, so rangers would be on the lookout for smoke and they should come pretty fast to investigate. The problem was how to keep control of a fire big enough to get attention in these tinder-dry conditions? Wouldn't do much good if they got the rangers' attention but then all the rangers found were crispy critters.

Hunger quickly turned the boy into a keen fisherman. When he awoke and came out to where Dixie was sitting, the first thing he said was how good that fish had been the night before. He cheerfully joined in catching grasshoppers, laughing at his clumsy efforts and talking about the elaborate traps he might construct for the purpose when they came back.

As they walked through the forest to the bigger stream, Dixie showed the boy 'Indian chewing gum' – the thick, resinous pitch seeping down the sides of the trees. The boy made a horrible face at the bitter flavour but kept chewing because it was 'almost like food'.

They went upstream this time, still looking for a place where the water wouldn't be rushing so fast it pulled their bait away before a fish could find it. The boy was getting better at spotting the kind of places fish might be.

The best moment, however, came when Dixie found a small number of wild strawberries growing where the forest thinned and moved away from the creek. Showing the boy how to identify the plants, she suggested he sink his fishing line into the water and secure the pole with a stone and she'd watch them while he went off to scour the forest floor for fruit. Eagerly he set off and returned half an hour or so later with a small handful. They shared them out between them. These were the best things he had ever tasted in his life, the boy said enthusiastically. From now on wild strawberries were going to be his favourite food.

Dixie had boiled the two remaining eggs to take with them for their lunch. As they sat on the bank of the stream with their fishing poles, she handed one to the boy. He was still savouring his strawberries, biting the tiniest little bits off the small fruit to make them last, so she lay the egg in his lap. Then she rapped her egg on a nearby rock to crack the shell and started to peel it.

'I've never actually eaten a boiled egg before,' the boy said as he watched her.

'I'll eat yours if you don't want it.'

'No, that's not what I'm saying,' he replied and tentatively tapped the shell. 'It's just they're kind of weird.' He touched the white of the egg gingerly.

'They'd be nicer with salt,' Dixie said and bit into hers, 'and they aren't the best eggs. They're stale by now, so boiling was about all I could do to make them edible.'

'Phoebe would have a spaz attack, because she thinks eggs are so bad for you.'

'Good thing she's not here then, huh, 'cause any kind of attack and you'd fall right in the water and drown.'

The boy laughed at Dixie's feeble joke.

'The only thing bad about these eggs is that they've been sitting around too long,' she said. 'And that they don't have lots of flavour to start with. That's because the hens who laid 'em are shut up in little tiny cages all day. What a hen likes is to run around and catch bugs and scratch in the dirt. Then you get a good-tasting egg.'

Pulling the white off the yolk, the boy cautiously tasted it.

'When I was little, our trailer was out on Eight Mile Road,' Dixie said. 'Mama used to keep hens then and I loved them so much. Hens get real friendly if you handle them enough. And they're smarter than you'd think. A rooster knows to tell his hens to hide under something, if he sees a hawk flying overhead, but if he sees a fox coming, he knows to tell them to get up high. And any time our chickens heard us clinking dishes, they'd come running, because they knew if we were clearing up after a meal, there'd be scraps.'

'Cool,' said the boy absently. Clearly he had decided the egg was OK, because he was eating it in tiny, tiny bites to make it last, all his attention given to relishing it.

'But we had to stop keeping them in the end, because the foxes would always kill them. Living that close to the forest, there were just too many, and nothing stops a fox who's trying to get what he wants. He'll claw his way into the hen house. Dig under the chicken wire. Even pull them through the fence, if that's the only way to do it. This one time a fox came right into our yard and it wasn't even dark yet. We looked out the window and there he was, just a-tossing chickens every which way. Eight chickens were dead already and four more we had to put down ourselves because they were hurt too bad.'

'I hate foxes. Foxes and coyotes and all those things that just kill to be killing. It's so awful they do that.'

'The thing you got to understand about them is that they're innocent of what they're doing. Foxes just love chickens. It's their favourite food. They got no idea they're destroying what they love most.'

'I still hate them.'

'Don't waste your feelings that way, Joker. There ain't no point to hating a fox for being a fox.'

That night Dixie woke with a start. She'd been dreaming about Leola and one of the tumbled-down 'ghost houses' in Abundance, but as she opened her eyes to the utter darkness of the cabin, the dream dissolved so quickly that only the impression of being with Leola in warm sunshine remained.

Beside her, the boy slept, his breathing deep and even. Dixie listened, trying to discern what had woken her. Beyond came the sound of fast-approaching movement. Her heartbeat quickened.

Billy burst in.

Relief washed over Dixie. Jumping up from the sleeping bag, she threw her arms around him. 'Gosh, I'm glad to see you!' She kissed him.

Billy broke her grasp roughly. 'Not now, Dix. We got to move. We got to get out of here. Kid, wake up.' He kicked the boy.

'What's going on?' she asked in alarm.

'Just get what you can and come on. We'll come back later for the other stuff.'

The boy stumbled to his feet. Shivery in the night chill, he pulled his blanket around him.

'Come on, Joker.' Dixie put an arm around his shoulders. 'We got to move.'

Urgency made Billy short-tempered. A confusing, panicky half-hour followed as he crammed as much stuff as he could into the rucksack and then marshalled them out of the cabin and into the night-time forest. Even with Billy's flashlight to guide them, it was difficult to hurry through the darkness after him. The boy had the good sense not to speak at all, but he kept a tight hold of Dixie's hand as they fled.

At last the trees parted and the pick-up was visible in the wan moonlight. Billy chucked the stuff he was carrying into the back and then turned to take Dixie's things. 'OK, kid,' he said, lifting the toolbox lid. 'Get in there and lie down.'

'No, Billy, don't make him do that. He can ride with us.'

'Kid, get *in* or I'll put you in.'

'Billy, let him ride in the cab with us. It's dangerous back there.'

Whap. Billy back-handed her. Dixie hadn't seen it coming at all and, not being braced for it, it knocked her right back on her butt. The boy went wide-eyed and jumped back.

'Kid, it's the last time I say it. Get in that toolbox and lie down. Or I'll do it for you.'

Wordlessly, the boy climbed up and settled down midst the clutter of things in the toolbox.

'Lie right down so I can shut it,' Billy said and brought his hand back as if to slap at the boy. 'Because I'll be going fast. If you sit up and lift that lid, the speed's going to make it fall right back down again and kill you. Got that? So I don't want to see you sit up till I say.'

The boy nodded. 'I got it.'

Chapter Thirty-Six

Something awful had happened, but Dixie didn't dare ask what. At each junction of the road, Billy jerked up on the clutch, throwing them forward, as if he didn't expect to have to stop. In between he drove too fast over the dirt road, flinging them back and forth in their seats like bobbles of dung on a calf's coat. Dixie feared for the boy in the back of the truck, knowing he'd be black and blue by the end of this, but Billy's tight-jawed silence kept her from saying anything.

Finally they were coming down out of the main part of Crowheart and into the foothills. Shading her eyes from the pale orange glow of the dashboard, Dixie peered out of the window. There was only a quarter-moon lighting the darkness. What she could make out of the countryside, she didn't recognize. This wasn't the road to Abundance.

Another forty-five minutes passed and then at last she saw the highway in the distance, a silver ribbon across the night landscape, and she knew where they were. There was a junction up ahead and, if you turned left, Abundance was about twenty miles west.

Billy came to a full stop at the junction and scanned the highway in both directions. There was nothing to disturb the deep, silent darkness. No headlights, no gleam from a ranch-house window, no yard light, nothing. Turning east on to the highway, he accelerated.

'Are they chasing us?' Dixie ventured softly.

'If they ain't chasing us now, they will be,' he replied.

Dixie's heart sank. She turned away from him to look out of the window again. The lights from the dashboard created a ghostly reflection on the glass to stare back at her.

The clock said 3.30 a.m. and the highway was empty. As far as Dixie could see, there was only the night. The air grew much warmer. Living so long at a high altitude, she'd forgotten how hot nights would still be. She rolled down the window to let in some air.

'I'd been down at the Horseshoe,' Billy said at long last. His voice was whisper soft. 'In the note I'd said they had to drop the money off at the Kipper Twee at ten p.m. So I thought I had plenty of time to get back up to the mine. Me and Roy had a couple of beers. Then ... I headed out by the new cemetery to take the Deer Creek road up to the mine. Then just as I went over the river ... there was the sheriff's Jeep parked on the roadside and all these other parked cars too. Must have been ten of them.' He sucked in a deep breath. 'And you know what I seen in the back of the Jeep?'

'What's that?'

'Dogs. Tracker dogs. A whole bunch of them. So, once I'd gone over the bridge, I just kept going so that I looked like normal traffic. Never even got close to the mine.'

'I thought you were planning to be in the mine a long time ahead and wait in there,' Dixie replied.

'Well, sure is a good thing I wasn't, huh? Would have stood no chance with them dogs.'

'Dogs were always a possibility, Billy.'

'Well, if you're so fucking smart, why didn't you say so?'

There was no point in getting him riled. 'You done the right thing, driving on by,' she said. 'They're not going to know it's you.'

'Yeah, except that I got food down there yesterday and a few other things to keep me going. Those dogs will take up the scent right away.'

Dixie rolled the window down all the way. Warm air rushed in around her, pushing her hair back. 'Dogs don't talk, Billy. No one's going to know you dropped off a few cans of food.'

'If they do DNA or whatever it is they do. Like you see on the TV all the time. They just got to have something you touched.'

'Yes, but there's no reason they got your DNA on file, is there? Or even your fingerprints. So they wouldn't have nothing to match it up with,' she replied calmly, so that he couldn't tell her blood was turning to ice.

Silence came again. The sun crested, causing the now-distant mountains to go briefly a golden pink. The sky showed the pale white of scorching August. Dazzled, Dixie shielded her eyes.

'Where we going?' she asked quietly.

'Away.'

'Wouldn't it have been better just to stay in the mountains?' she asked. 'There's so much wilderness.'

Anger flared in Billy's eyes as he glanced over. 'You want to run this show?'

Before Dixie had any forewarning of what was happening, tears filled her eyes and choked her throat.

'Oh shit,' Billy muttered.

'I'm not meaning to cry,' she said and tried to force the tears back. 'I'm just tired, that's all.'

'Well, we're all tired, Dixie, so don't think you're special. Stop your bawling.'

Leaning to the side, Dixie let the rush of air from the open window push the tears from her eyes. She did know why she was crying. Should have been for all the trouble they were in, but it wasn't. What was filling her head instead was a memory of being down on the old end of Second Street when she was maybe about eight. There was a bank there leftover from the glory days. It had been boarded up, the wood across the doors and windows grey with weathering even in Dixie's childhood, but there was still glass in some of the windows. If you wiped the dirt off enough to peek through, you could see the old bank counter with its huge, ornate grille that separated the customers from the tellers. The grille was probably brass or maybe even just wrought-iron painted gold, but when she was young, Dixie had believed the muted glint to be real gold and that if somehow she could break in and retrieve it, she would be rich beyond her wildest dreams.

She and Leola had spent hours and hours and hours thinking up ways of getting into the bank without getting caught. Even more than that, they had dreamed together of what they would buy once they had sold that grille – at the very least, a house for Mama and Daddy, a horse for each of them and all the candy at the Pay'n Save.

The bank was long gone now, torn down to build a gas station. That hadn't lasted either, and now the lot was full of broken-down farm machinery that Denny Paterson was trying to make a business out of repairing. Dixie and Leola had never managed to get inside the bank. They'd never touched the golden grille or stood behind the dark oak counter. She didn't even know what had happened to those, but the dream of that grille had never left her. She could still walk by Denny Paterson's smelly machinery yard and feel the spirit of the old bank, and always – for just a moment – it would magic her back to being an excited eight-year-old in a world full of promise.

Would she ever walk by that lot again? That's why she was crying, if she was honest. Would she ever see Abundance again? Or Leola? Or Mama? Or was it all, like the bank, disappearing into the past?

Gently Billy put a hand on her thigh. 'Look, I'm sorry I shouted.'

She snuffled inelegantly because there weren't any tissues and she didn't even have a sleeve to wipe her nose with.

'It's not going to be so bad, Dix,' he said. 'Don't worry. We'll manage.'

The sun had lifted clear of the far horizon but was still too low to be obscured by the visor. Putting her hand up, Dixie shaded her eyes.

'I borrowed some money off Roy,' Billy said. 'Got enough to keep us going. We've just got to stay clear for a while and see what happens.'

Snuffling again, Dixie turned away.

'You're too much of a worrier,' he said and reached over to touch her shoulder and then the back of her neck affectionately. 'Ain't nothing happened yet, has it? This is a great, big, wide state and we've already put plenty of miles between us and Abundance. I mean, really, if you look at it, what we got right now is pretty good. Money in our pockets, a truck that works, all this beautiful countryside and us able to go anywhere we want. I ain't going to wreck that any by worrying about what's happening a hundred miles back.'

'You're just like a dog, Billy. You forget the past in about ten minutes and got no sense of what's coming in the future. It's just here and now with you, and if you feel good, then you don't think of nothing else.'

Raising his eyebrows, he smiled. 'Can't say as I think that's a bad way to be.'

'Maybe not for you, but I doubt that boy in the back there thinks the same.'

It was still early when they passed through the first proper-sized town. There was a McDonald's just past the last stoplight. Billy agreed they could get food, but he decided to stay with the truck to watch over the boy while Dixie went in to order.

What a shock to see herself, when Dixie went into the restroom. In the unforgiving glare of the fluorescent lights, a filthy woman with careworn lines around her mouth stared back at her. Despite Dixie's best efforts to stay clean, her long hair was straggly, and she was covered with dirt. Hurriedly, she washed her face in the dinky sink below the mirror.

Probably just because he had money in his pocket, Billy wanted an enormous breakfast of pancakes, scrambled eggs, three hash browns and so much coffee it would jazz a football team. Ravenous as she was, Dixie knew that she shouldn't eat too much after so long on so little food, so she ordered the smallest Egg McMuffin and an orange juice for herself and pancakes for the boy.

Billy was ready to move again the moment she came out of the restaurant. She hardly had time to pass the food into the toolbox before Billy started to move the truck and yelled at her to get in.

'You should have let him go to the bathroom,' Dixie said as she slammed shut the door.

'Like, sure, I'm going to stop in front of McDonald's, open my toolbox and let some kid climb out to go in and use the bathroom. How much sense does that make?'

'He's wet himself.'

'Yeah, well, then he doesn't need to go into the bathroom, does he?'

'It's not right to do it that way, Billy. We should have him up here, normal-like. He's a good boy. He would have behaved. We shouldn't be treating him like this.'

'I thought you were the one telling me what a little fucker he was.'

'I'd be a little fucker too if folks did to me what we've done to him,' Dixie replied.

Billy took the interstate when they came to it, but he didn't stay on it long. Instead, he veered off on Highway 12. The Rockies began to give way to high plains with broader and broader stretches of flatland separating the mountain ranges. More of the land was cultivated, the valleys patterned with alternating wide strips of fallow land and wheat, heavy-headed and golden in the morning sun.

Dixie didn't know this part of Montana very well. For the most part, hers hadn't been a travelling family. Mama and Daddy had both been born and raised in Abundance. They went to Billings twice a year to shop at the big stores and they went to Yellowstone Park every summer, but otherwise the family had always stuck close to home. Mama always said how everything worthwhile could be found right there in Abundance.

Eventually the mountains faded away entirely to leave only arid, scraggy flatland broken by mesa-like hills and deep, rocky ravines. There was a monotony to the landscape that made Dixie wonder how people learned to find their way around without mountains to orient themselves by.

'Billy, we got to stop and let the boy out.'

'He'll be all right a while longer.'

'It's starting to get really hot out there. He shouldn't be closed in like that.'

Billy kept driving.

'He's not a bad kid, Billy. I been with him close these last days and I know he could ride in the cab all right. It'd look more natural. Folks would just think he was our boy.'

'I need to stop for gas and I don't want that kid showing at no gas station, because they got surveillance cameras.'

'All right,' Dixie replied. 'You stop for gas. Then soon as we're away, find somewhere to pull over so he can get out. All right? Then let him ride in the cab for a while and we'll see how we get on.'

There was no need to worry about anything so sophisticated as surveillance cameras at the place Billy stopped for gas. The town was nothing but a rundown general store with a couple of pumps out front, a handful of weathered trailers and two houses with front yards full of rusting farm machinery. There didn't look to be anyone around at all except for the tired-looking girl behind the counter in the store.

While Billy pumped gas, Dixie bought ice for the cooler, pop and a few canned goods. Taking the jugs around to the restroom, she filled them with water. When Billy came out from paying for the gas, he was carrying a small paper bag. He threw it on the seat between them.

They went about five miles further down the highway before Billy pulled off onto an unpaved road that took them down into a ravine full of cottonwoods. He parked and got out.

'OK, kid,' he said and unhooked the toolbox cover.

Blearily the boy sat up. The first thing Dixie noticed was that he had been sick on himself. He didn't look at all well. His skin had gone a yellow-grey and his eyes were glassy.

'Hey, what's happened?' she said in a tender voice and reached in to help him out of the toolbox. 'Here, drink this. It's cold.' She opened a can of Coke and held it to his lips. He revived at the taste of the liquid. Clasping it with both hands, he drank greedily.

Once he was on his feet and had the Coke in him, the boy seemed to come around. He was still a bit unsteady on his feet and the jarring ride had given him bruises, but otherwise he looked OK. Keeping a supporting arm around him, she helped him out of the flatbed and, once on the ground, she went with him down over the embankment so that he could pee.

'It got so *hot* back there,' the boy muttered, when he finally found his voice.

'Yeah, I know. I'm sorry about that.'

'I felt really, really awful.'

'Yeah, we need to get you cleaned up. Are you feeling better now?'

The boy nodded.

At that point, Billy appeared at the top of the embankment. 'What the fuck you doing down there, Dix? I been looking all over for you.'

'I just took him down to pee.'

Billy slid down the embankment to where they stood. 'He don't need no woman to help him pee.' Lifting his foot, Billy touched the toe of his boot to the crotch of the boy's pants. 'You keep your little prick to yourself, kid, if you know what's good for you.'

'*Billy.*'

'He ain't Jamie Lee, Dix. So don't go thinking he is.'

Billy rummaged in the bag he'd brought out from the gas station and pulled out two brand-new, bright green duckbilled caps with 'John Deere' emblazoned across the front in shiny gold lettering. Removing his well-worn cowboy hat, he popped one of the caps on his own head. Adjusting the other for size, he popped it on the boy's head. Billy smiled at the effect. 'OK, kid, from now on, you keep that cap on. Folks are going to think you're just a nice little sucker, wanting to look like his daddy. And here. Mama can wear this.' He set his cowboy hat on Dixie's head. Too large, it settled down on her ears. Billy chortled and then turned back to the boy. 'So, from now on, we're going to let you sit up in the cab with us, but there's two rules. Rule one: if I got my hat on, you better got your hat on. Understand that?'

The boy nodded.

'And rule two: if I see you doing anything stupid when you're sitting with us – and I mean *anything* – you're going be flung in the back again so fast your piss will come out your asshole. Got that?'

'Yes.'

'Yes, *sir*,' Billy corrected. 'Because any kid of mine talks to his daddy like he got manners. Understand?'

'Yes, sir.'

When they got back in the truck, Billy didn't return to the highway. Instead, he continued along the gravel road. The landscape grew rougher. Cultivated fields disappeared into what Mama always called 'cow country' – wide arid stretches devoid of anything but sagebrush. To the southwest, Dixie could see high mountains in the far distance and the white of their snow-capped peaks shimmered welcomingly in the heavy August heat. She longed for Billy to keep driving until they reached them.

Billy didn't go that way. Instead, he turned east on a smaller road, which he followed for about ten miles, then he turned on to a dirt road that threw up enormous clouds of dust. Driving slowly, he scanned the countryside. Satisfied that the road wasn't a ranch access, he finally turned around and backtracked a couple of miles.

'We'll stop there,' he said and took the truck off road and down a steep incline towards a few scraggy white willow trees beside a dry creek bed. There was just enough cover to get the truck out of the afternoon sun.

During spring run-off, the creek must have run wide because its bed of smooth, pale-coloured stones extended more than ten feet across, but now in late summer there wasn't even the smallest trickle.

'Think we ought to stop here?' Dixie asked. 'There's no water.'

'We got water along.'

'Not very much,' she said. 'When I filled up, I wasn't thinking in terms of needing to live off it.'

Ignoring her, Billy started pulling the creek stones together to form a campfire ring.

'Think we should be building a fire?' Dixie asked. 'A fire's going to show up a long ways out here and people will notice smoke at this time of year. They'll worry it's a prairie fire.'

'Yeah, well, it ain't and we haven't got a canister for the fucking gas ring, do we? Someone comes by, we'll just say we're picnicking.'

'Yes, but this will be private land, Billy.'

Billy threw down the sticks he'd been collecting. 'Shit, Dixie, would you lay off all your fucking complaints? You're always at me. Already damned near got me killed down that mine.'

'*Me?*'

'Yes, you. It's you that got me into all this, you and your harping about that funeral man. Then harping about taking the kid. Then harping about getting rid of the kid and making me write that note. You never fucking stop your harping.'

Tears sprang up. Dixie ducked her head so that Billy wouldn't see, but they came too fast.

'Oh, fuck it all, Dixie, don't cry.'

Tightly as she squeezed her eyes shut, the tears slipped out anyway, falling noiselessly onto the dust at her feet.

'What have you got to cry about?' he asked. 'I been the one doing all the fucking work.'

Dixie raised her head and glanced at the boy through a blur of tears. He was watching them. The passenger door of the truck was open, and he sat, his feet hanging out, his head resting wearily against the seat.

Billy spat in the dust. 'I'm sick to the back teeth of you,' he muttered. 'Sick of him too. I feel like shooting you both.'

Chapter Thirty-Seven

B illy carried on making a campfire pit. Dixie knew that it would have seemed too much like admitting she was right if he'd stopped right away, so he kept laying stones. He didn't, however, light a fire. Storm coming, he said, and nodded to the west where thunderclouds were building. No sense making a fire just to have it drowned out. So they sat together on the front bumper of the truck and ate a cold meal of beanie-weenies straight from the can.

In Abundance, there wasn't much sky. Three-quarters of the view was taken up by mountains, so you never really saw weather coming until it was right on top of you. Here, in this vast, open scrubland, the sky seemed too big for the ground under it. Watching the thunderclouds build in the west made Dixie anxious. In summer you always got these thunder-storm warnings coming over the TV, drowning out what-ever programme you were trying to watch with a deafening beeping sound to catch your attention. They were always for distant counties Dixie had never visited, so they gave her that same feeling as with horror movies, where being scared was kind of exciting. Standing out in the open, seeing one boil up like this, the cloud growing higher, wider and darker as it approached, the sky stretching itself into all sorts of odd shapes, brought up a much more primitive kind of fear. The tin plate balanced on her knee, Dixie sat on the bumper and stared, mesmerized.

With elegant slowness, like the vast starship at the beginning of *Star Wars*, the thundercloud moved over them. Lightning came first and then the wind, then a curtain of rain so intense that you couldn't see any of the landscape for several minutes. Billy rushed to get the cover over the flatbed of the truck before jumping into the cab with Dixie and the boy.

The thunderclaps were powerful enough to make the truck shudder. One bolt of lightning hit a barbed-wire fence not more than thirty yards away and Dixie watched the electricity spark from one barb to the next along the fence until it finally hit a post and ran into the ground. Then came the deafening clatter of hail. Not big stuff, fortunately. None of it was much more than the size of a grain of rice, but sitting in the cab of the truck was like being trapped inside a maraca.

'*Fuck*,' Billy said under his breath. 'Fuck almighty.'

The boy was sitting against the door with Dixie in the middle. They were already squished close together, because everyone was trying to keep from touching the metal parts of the cab, just in case, and so Dixie could feel the boy quivering. Putting an arm around his shoulder, she pulled him against her. 'Kind of scary, huh?' The boy didn't respond, but he slipped his hand in hers.

When the storm ended, the arguments began. Maybe it was just all that electricity in the air, but for whatever reason,

Billy and Dixie couldn't agree on anything. Worst came when they were trying to sort out the sleeping arrangements. Billy was convinced the boy was going to run off once they were asleep, so he needed to be restrained. Billy wanted to tie him up for the night and put him back in the toolbox again. Dixie tried to explain this was unnecessary because, one, they were dozens of miles from anywhere anyway, so where did Billy think he'd go? And two, the boy had been doing just fine, not being restrained, and she trusted him and didn't want to see him locked up again in the toolbox. Billy got angry with her for telling him what to do. In the end, he agreed to leave the boy untied but only on condition he slept in the flatbed of the truck and Billy would fasten the cover over. Dixie argued that that would be a hot, stuffy, uncomfortable place to sleep, but in the end she gave up trying for more.

Once the boy was under the cover, Billy grabbed hold of Dixie's arm and pulled her forward roughly. 'As for you, you need fucking. You're beginning to forget whose woman you are.'

'Stop it, Billy.'

'You been having his little pecker? Because I'm beginning to think that's it. Is that why you keep favouring him over me?'

'*No*, Billy. Of *course* not.'

'Yeah, well, time to put you straight.' He already had his jeans unbuttoned, so Dixie knew there wasn't much point fighting it.

*   *   *

The thunderstorm had not cleared away the built-up heat of day. Instead, the rain simply made it humid, leaving a stifling darkness. The air was hung heavy with the smells of the prairie – sagebrush predominantly, mixed with yellowed buffalo grass, aged cow dung and sandstone.

Dixie couldn't sleep. Mostly it was the arguing that had set her on edge, because she and Billy had bickered on and off for most of the evening, but it was also worry and home-sickness and just being fed up.

As the night drew on and she continued to lie quietly in the darkness, she became aware of another less easily articulated feeling, a sort of expectant desolation. The last time she'd felt it was in those weeks before Jamie Lee died, when Dixie would look at his little blue lips or listen to his faint, ribbony cry and admit in her heart that things weren't going to work out. Even though her mind hadn't quite got there yet, her heart knew the cause was lost. So it was again in the quietest hours of the night, her heart whispering what her head didn't want to hear.

The Milky Way spilled across the darkness as if God had knocked over a box of washing detergent. Dixie never had been any good at recognizing which stars were which, and, fact was, she seldom looked up to see them for themselves. Instead, they were the backdrop to the reassuring silhouettes of Crowheart, Lion Mountain and Lone Indian Peak and that was what was missing now. Yearning for the familiar view from the small gable-end bedroom window overtook Dixie and the starry sky blurred behind tears.

Everything tonight was reminding her of Jamie Lee. Thinking of the mountains made her remember how the whole family had been brought so close at the funeral. That brought the funeral back and made her realize she hadn't had a chance yet even to take flowers up to Jamie Lee's grave. Into her mind came the memory of how he'd looked that night at the mortuary, his small, lifeless body in the fibre-glass coffin. If only she could go to the cemetery. If only she could get down the box of Jamie Lee's clothes that she'd put in the attic. The desire to see his things again, to feel them, to smell his baby scent on them came with anguished intensity, catching in her throat and escaping as a sob before she could stop it. Dixie clamped a hand tightly over her mouth to keep from waking Billy.

Sitting up quietly, she groped for her sweatshirt jacket to find the tissue she knew was in the pocket. Beside her, curled on his side, his head nuzzled into the folds of his sleeping bag, Billy slept on. It was just amazing how he could always sleep so peacefully.

Dixie saw the keys to the truck lying on the ground on Billy's other side, along with his wallet. It'd be a simple matter to reach over him and pick them up. Billy probably wouldn't wake at all.

Dixie remained sitting. Her eyes were still on the keys but what she was seeing was Daddy. Daddy's big hand on her chest, holding her flat on the bed while he fumbled down there with his other hand. She could feel his breath, hot on her face and smelling slightly of beer. The first few times he'd done it, she thought he was wetting on her and she was horrified. She had cried out in disgust and tried to wiggle away, but he'd clamped his hand down tight over her mouth.

This is something you got to learn, he'd told her, something all little girls got to know about and it was best if their daddies taught them. Then he had come down very close to her face and said, 'But it's a *private* thing.'

She had wanted to say no so bad. Lying there in the darkness, night after night, she'd practised the word over in her head. No. No. *No.* Such a tiny little word. It should have been easy enough to say, but it never was.

That was Night Daddy, the one who came in and did those things. It was Night Daddy she wanted so much to say no to. The trouble was, she loved Day Daddy so much. Day Daddy took her and Leola to the park and bought them fudgesicles at the gas station on the way home, even when it was just before dinner and he'd have to fend off Raging Mama, as he called her when he did things she didn't approve of. Day Daddy took them to Sunday School and said the blessing at the table before meals. Day Daddy gave her fifty cents every time she brought home an A on her report card.

Day Daddy had a crucifix tattooed on his chest. When she was little, Dixie had thought it was the most wonderful thing she'd ever seen. She loved hearing how he'd got the tattoo done in San Francisco when he was in the army, and how every time the tattooist's needle went in, it made Daddy think of Jesus' suffering on the Cross. That always made Dixie feel so proud he was her daddy.

It was a big tattoo. The crossbar of the Cross was just below his collar bone and almost shoulder to shoulder. That way Jesus hung with His head right on Daddy's heart. Sometimes Daddy would wiggle his muscles just so and you could see Jesus sort of throbbing as He hung on the Cross, His head down, His crown of thorns dripping bright red blood. Dixie and Leola were always begging Daddy to take his shirt off and make Jesus move, because it felt just like having Jesus alive in their own house.

It was never light enough to see what was on Night Daddy's chest. Dixie didn't want to see anyway. In fact, she started sleeping in a sweatshirt so as never to risk feeling Jesus pressed against her skin.

Chapter Thirty-Eight

'Get up,' Billy hissed and prodded Dixie.

Groggily she rolled over in her sleeping bag. Dawn had come but the sun wasn't over the horizon yet.

Billy was on all fours, his muscles taut as a hunting dog's. 'Listen. I hear a vehicle.'

Adrenalin brought Dixie awake with jarring suddenness.

'Get in the truck. We're going,' Billy said.

'Billy, we should stay where we are. We'll look more suspicious if we run. It's an old pick-up. Can't you hear that? Probably just a local rancher.'

'Get in the truck!'

Whoever it was didn't care a bit they were down there, because he drove on by without so much as glance in their direction. Billy, however, was spooked. Soon as they had everything back in the truck, he drove back up to the road and sped off in the opposite direction.

From there on, Billy stuck to the back roads, taking this turn and that turn. By the position of the sun, Dixie could tell they were going north but otherwise she was totally lost.

The range of mountains she'd seen in the distance the day before had vanished completely, but long runs of flat-topped sandstone cliffs were now appearing. 'Rimrocks' were the local name for them and they would often run for ten or more miles at a stretch, calving massive yellow sandstone boulders on to the sagebrush beneath.

Dixie ached to talk to Billy about the boy. There needed to be a plan, if they were ever going to bring an end to all of this, but she was quite sure Billy didn't have one, even now. Or at least not one that would work. But how to bring it up in a way that wouldn't make him mad? And how to find a time when the boy, with his green John Deere cap dutifully clamped on his head, wasn't there squashed between them? Dixie sat in bleak silence and watched the scenery, made indistinct by the dust thrown up from the speeding pick-up.

Suddenly Billy whistled through his teeth. 'Wowie! Look at there.' He pointed across the steering wheel to the rimrocks on the right side of the road. At the base of one of the cliffs was a series of small caves. 'Now that looks good,' he said cheerfully. 'That's just the sort of place we need.'

As if. The last place in the world Dixie wanted to be was amidst the rock tumble at the bottom of the cliffs. It would be so snake-infested at this time of year that you'd think you were at a medicine dance for all the rattling going on, and that's assuming some twenty-ton boulder didn't calve off and squash you. 'I think you must have been a fox in your last life, you like going down in the earth so much,' Dixie muttered.

'Nah, this is good. Back behind us, did you see those cottonwoods? We can stop there,' Billy said. 'There'll be water and I can get the truck in the shade.'

There wasn't any water near the cottonwoods, just another dry creek bed, but Billy stopped anyway. Dixie knew he was itching to explore the caves. What mad idea he had Dixie didn't know and she didn't want to know. With Billy, it was always better to let him work off his energy first before you asked too many questions. That way he didn't have so much left over for getting mad.

Once he had headed up to the caves, Dixie suggested to the boy that they go for a walk along the creek bed to pass the time. 'Here, take this,' she said, handing him a length of fallen cottonwood branch. 'Rustle it ahead of you as you walk. Lots of rattlesnakes in a place like this. The stick gives them notice you're coming and they can get out of the way. Most snakes are peace-loving, if they don't get startled.'

Quirking his lip up in an expression of uncertainty, the boy said, 'I think I'd just as soon stay here.'

'Too hot. We might as well do something.'

He hung back.

'Want me to go first?'

He nodded and handed her back the stick.

The creek bed was wide and easy walking. As they came around the end of one ridge of rimrocks, Dixie paused and scanned the horizon. 'That cliff over there looks like it could have been a buffalo jump, the way it's shaped. See how the land comes up in a nice smooth slope behind it?'

'What's a buffalo jump?'

'In the days when the Indians lived here, sometimes they would drive herds of buffalo up the backside of cliffs like that. The buffalo would be running so hard to get away that when they came to the edge of the cliff, they wouldn't be able to stop. They'd just tumble over. Other Indians would be waiting down at the bottom of the cliff to shoot the injured ones with arrows.'

'Ew. Gross.'

'No, not really. It was a clever idea. They could get enough food for everyone in just one hunt and plenty of skins to make their tepees and clothes and things.' Dixie paused for the boy to catch up. 'What's fun is to look around the bottom of a buffalo jump, because oftentimes you can find Indian arrowheads and things.'

'Really?'

'Hasn't your daddy ever taken you out to the one out by Abundance? Out on Clark Creek?'

The boy shook his head. 'I've never even heard of buffalo jumps before now.'

'When I was little, we used to take picnics to that one all the time. My daddy made this screen thing so that he could shovel dirt into it, and then Leola and me would shake it like a sieve. That made the dirt fall out so that it was easier to find the arrowheads among the other rocks. We got loads from there over the years. Other things too, like scrapers that they used on the buffalo hides. Once Leola even found an obsidian spearhead, except that it was broken in half.'

They continued walking. Dixie had been wearing Billy's John Deere hat and she took it off to fan herself. A huge locust landed with a thump inside the hat as she was waving it. Quickly she caught it and held it out playfully at the boy. He squawked and jumped, but he laughed too. Dixie threw it high into the air and it spread its sandy-grey wings and flew off.

'You were so lucky,' the boy said at last.

'Lucky?' Dixie said in surprise.

'Yeah. I wish I'd been you.'

'How do you mean?'

'You had all these fun places to play. Like how you were telling me about ghost houses in Abundance, and you and your sister were going to break into that old bank. And you did all this fun stuff, like how your mom and dad always took you guys fishing and on picnics, and now you're saying you got to go looking for arrowheads. You were way luckier than me.'

'Not really. Everybody's life looks better when you're standing outside it, looking in, but that's never how it really is. We all got good things and bad things about our families. You do too.'

'No, I don't,' he said.

'Yes, you do. You get to go to Disneyland. I bet you've seen the ocean. I've never seen the ocean. Everybody's got different things, Joker. Good things and bad things. Nobody's got it perfect.'

He shrugged and kept walking.

'Whoa, it's hot,' Dixie said. 'Bet it's ninety-five degrees. You want to stop and rest under those trees?'

The boy threw himself down gratefully in the shade of a scraggy white willow. Dixie pulled out a crumpled-up tissue and mopped her forehead before unhooking the canteen from her belt. Unscrewing the top, she handed it over to the boy. He drank deeply and then passed it back. Dixie took a drink too.

The boy was watching her closely.

'What you staring at?' Dixie asked.

'How come you don't get your teeth fixed?'

'Nothing wrong with my teeth,' she said in surprise.

'They're really crooked on the bottom. And you got that one silver one there.' He pointed. 'I've never seen anybody with a whole silver tooth.'

'It's just a crown. I got it when I was eleven. Me and Leola were fighting and she pushed me off the bed and it broke my tooth off,' Dixie replied.

'Why isn't it white?'

"Cause it had to be strong because it's so close to the front or else I would have needed a bridge, and a bridge is too expensive.'

'It makes you look weird. You should get your teeth fixed. That's what Sidonie did. She had a gap right there,' he said, pointing to his top front teeth, 'and my dad kept saying how revolting it made her look. So she went to this dentist in LA and got everything capped. She did it for my dad's birthday last year. Every time it's his birthday, she gets something done to make her more beautiful. She had stuff pumped in her cheekbones this year.'

'That might be all right for movie stars,' Dixie replied.

'She's not a movie star. Sidonie's just tits and ass.'

'*Joker.* That's nasty to say.'

He lifted his shoulders in a gesture of innocence. 'I'm only repeating what my dad always says.'

'It's just as nasty if he says it.'

The boy shrugged. 'My dad says it's OK because she's using him too. Girls only go out with him because they think they'll get in the movies if they sleep with him. So he says you might as well make sure you only take the perfect ones. Besides, it doesn't matter because Sidonie's really stupid. Like, this one time she put the waffle maker in the dishwasher to get it clean. Even I know better than to do that. My dad says if she didn't have such good tits, he would have gotten rid of her long ago.'

'That's ugly, ugly talk, Joker. I don't want to hear it.'

'It isn't me saying it. I'm just telling you what *he* said.'

'Yeah, well, if your dad was here with me, I wouldn't want him to talk that way either.'

The boy giggled. 'You don't have to worry. My dad wouldn't ever be here. He wouldn't even notice you; you have hardly any tits at all.'

Dixie slapped him. Not a hard slap, but enough to be serious.

'*Yow!*' the boy shrieked and leaped up. 'What did you do *that* for?'

'Because you don't talk to me like that, young man.'

'You didn't have to *hit* me,' he wailed, cradling his cheek.

'Yeah, well, I'm sorry,' Dixie said. 'But I warned you you were being ugly. And I got my respect. No little boys talk to me like that.'

'I was just *saying*,' he replied in an injured tone. 'I was just telling you what my *dad* said.'

'Maybe they were your daddy's words, young man, but you were saying them, so you need to take responsibility for them.'

'But I wasn't *trying* to get you angry. I didn't think you were going to, like, *hit* me.'

'I'm sorry it upset you. It's just I don't like filthy talk and you keep doing it.'

'I'm *trying* not to. Jeez, I didn't even know I wasn't supposed to until you started hassling me. Phoebe never cares what I say. Nobody cares. They're just *words*.'

'They're hurting words, Joker. Good people try not to say hurting words to each other.'

Hunching his shoulders, the boy turned away from her.

Dixie lifted her head and scanned the nearby landscape. From where they were sitting, the cliff looked less like a buffalo jump. There didn't seem much point in going closer.

Finally he turned back. 'Do you still like me?'

'Of course I still like you. That's why I keep harping at you on this stuff. Because I know you're a good boy in your heart. I can see that.'

Faintly he nodded. 'Yeah, well, I still like you too.'

Chapter Thirty-Nine

Billy was in the flatbed of the truck, sorting through their gear, when Dixie and the boy returned from their walk. 'Oh, this is good,' he said, rubbing his hands together in anticipation. 'I checked those caves out good and I've got the whole thing planned now. You want to hear?'

As if there was a choice. Dixie opened a can of warm Coke and took a sip.

'OK, here's how I'm going to get the money. I'll take one of the fishing poles up with me to those caves. Get some good strong fishing line. Then I'm going run it along the ground from the bigger one of the caves down to this bunch of junipers I saw. Other than those, there's not much cover around. So I reckon if I tell them to take the money to the junipers and hook it on the fishing line, then leave, I'll be able to tell for sure that they do. But they're not going to be able to see me, because I'm going to be hiding in the other cave. There's no way they could put the sheriff on me, because I'll be able to see everything they do, but they won't know where I'm at without me getting warned.'

Dixie folded a piece of bread in half to make a bread-and-butter sandwich.

'We're pretty close to Billings, so I'll be able to get everything I need to do this. Big city like that, ain't no one going to being paying attention to what I'm buying, if I'm in one of them big discount stores. And I got a brilliant idea for writing the note. I'll make the kid do it. Prove to them we got him, because it'll be in his handwriting. So they'll know he's alive and OK, but we won't get no fingerprints on it that way. Good, huh? This is *so* good, Dix. It's finally coming together.'

No, it wasn't coming together. Unexpected, unwanted clarity dawned through the dream fabric of Billy's words. *This was not going to work. Nothing was going to work.* Not in the way Billy was intending. There was never going to be any guide business or paying off the funeral man or living happily ever after coming out of this.

Dixie didn't speak, because she knew Billy wouldn't hear what she was saying anyway. She didn't cry, because some things aren't healed by tears. Instead, she just kept standing there and chewed her bread-and-butter sandwich very slowly and thoroughly, forty chews on each bite, as they'd said to do in some magazine, if you wanted good digestion.

'I'll go into Billings tomorrow and get all the stuff,' Billy continued. 'The kid can do up the note tomorrow night and I'll mail it on Saturday. I'll say they got to drop the money off on Monday night, just to be on the safe side, because they got to drive quite a ways.' He grinned. 'This time next week, this will all be over.'

Rising, Dixie collected the dirty plates. There was no spare water to wash them, so she knelt beside the sagebrush and rubbed handfuls of dirt over the plates to clean away the food, then wiped them clean and stored them back in the cardboard box in the truck. Billy was following her around, still chattering.

'First thing I want to do when I'm in Billings is call Roy,' he said. 'I can still make the round-up out at the Baker ranch.'

'All this going on and, seriously, what you're worried about is making the round-up?'

'Dix, we talked this all through before. Remember? I said, when this was over, the best thing to do is just to go home and act real natural for a while. I'll go on the round-up. You ought to go back down to Mr Roberts and at least pretend you're looking for work.'

'Billy, stop a minute and listen to yourself. Listen to what you're saying.'

'It's real important I get on that round-up, Dix. Roy says he's pretty sure Ben Nicholson can get me at least five horses. Good, sound horses. I mean, now I'll have money to buy whatever I want, but I think it's a good idea to stick with Nicholson's horses for this season. Get me broke into the guiding business before I invest in really good horses.'

'Billy.'

'What?' he asked, and his expression was clueless.

'*Listen* to yourself,' Dixie said. Impatience crept into her tone. 'Listen to the fool things you're saying, Billy. *How* do you think we can go back to Abundance when this is over? Even you were saying the other day that we should take off to Canada. Now you think we can just turn around and go home?'

'You want to go to Canada instead?'

'*No*,' Dixie said. 'I just want you to listen to what's coming out of your mouth, Billy, because *it isn't going to happen that way*.'

Billy looked blank.

'You're talking *dreams*, Billy. All this buying horses and going on the round-up with Roy. You ain't never going to see Roy again, don't you get that? You ain't never going to see the Baker ranch or Abundance or anything we knew, because there's no way we can get ourselves from this moment we're in right now, sitting out here with this poor kid, back to our lives at home like we left them. You're talking like we will, and that's not even dreams at this point, Billy. It's just garbage.'

These things needed saying so badly, but even as she was speaking, Dixie knew she shouldn't have let her frustration get the better of her. 'Garbage' was too strong a word to use with Billy. When words were too strong, then the strength was all Billy tended to hear. The important, sensible stuff went right by him. All that stuck was that she thought his ideas were garbage.

Billy went from cheery to vicious in about twenty seconds. He got so mad he couldn't even form words. He just screamed at her, the vein in his forehead straining so hard against his skin that it looked like some alien worm trying to break free of its host.

When he was that angry, the only way Billy could express himself was physically, so he slapped Dixie. She slapped him back, because she was at the end of her tether. He punched her. She struggled to reach him. He grabbed her by the hair, twisted her head around and then kneed her. That brought her down. Keeping his grip on her hair, Billy dragged Dixie across the dirt and slammed her head into the side of the truck. It caused a dent, and this made him angrier yet. He threw her down over the bank of the dry creek and kicked a stone after her. Then he turned, opened the door of the truck, yanked the boy off the seat where he was sitting and threw him ferociously on to the ground. Slamming the door, Billy started up the truck and drove off.

Dixie lay in a heap. For several moments, she drifted in and out of consciousness. It was almost like drowsing except for the pain that inflated up like a snagged parachute each time awareness returned.

A gentle, tentative caress across her forehead made Dixie open her eyes again.

'Are you OK?' The boy was leaning down very close. He had a damp cloth and he reached out with it to wipe blood from her face.

'No, I'm not OK,' she said, 'but I'm still here.'

He was using his T-shirt to dab her face. He'd taken it off, folded it and dampened it with water from the canteen. With unexpected tenderness, he continued to wipe the blood away.

Everything hurt. There was a lot of blood, mostly from her nose. One eye was already swelling shut. Her upper left arm felt horrible, but she could lift it all right; so it wasn't broken. The most painful area was around her ribs where Billy had kneed her. She could hardly move for the ache.

The boy did the best he could. They didn't have a first-aid kit, because that had been in the truck, but at least they still had water. He was unexpectedly resourceful, tearing his T-shirt apart to make bandages before Dixie even realized what he was doing.

'Shouldn't ought to be doing that,' she murmured. 'You're going to get sunburned tomorrow.'

'I'll be OK,' the boy replied.

Summer twilight turned the sagebrush first to gold and then faintly pink before going a dark sludgy purple and drifting into night so slowly it wasn't obvious that the day had finally departed. Dixie had managed to get herself sitting up against one of the big stones on the bank of the dry creek bed. She accepted a cup of water from the boy to get the taste of blood from her mouth.

He sat down on a nearby rock. 'What are we going to do now?' he finally asked.

'Billy will be back. He storms off, but he always blows himself out,' Dixie said. 'Soon enough he'll be feeling real bad he done this and come back and apologize.'

'I don't want him to come back,' the boy said.

'Yeah, well,' Dixie said wearily.

Silence then, but just between her and him. The sagebrush basin was anything but silent as darkness seeped in. Like a raucous Greek chorus, crickets started up each time there was a pause in the conversation.

'Why do you stay with him?'

'How can I leave?' Dixie replied. 'We're out in the middle of nowhere and Billy's got control of everything.'

'I wasn't meaning right this minute,' he said.

Before Dixie could answer, the boy sat back on his heels and there came an abrupt silence, the kind that just turns up unexpectedly and slides into the heart of what's being talked about as sharply as an obsidian arrow into the heart of a bird.

'Would you do that?' he asked.

'Do what?'

'Leave right now, if you could?'

Even with her swollen face, Dixie managed a grin. 'How the heck you expect me to do that, Joker? I can't hardly even stand up.'

'No, I'm serious. I mean, if you could, would you just go now?'

In too much pain to think straight, Dixie closed her eyes a moment.

The boy's mouth began to quiver. 'You *would*, wouldn't you? I can tell by the way you're not answering.' Tears spilled over his cheeks. 'You'd just walk out of here. You'd leave me and go, if you could.'

'Hey, hey,' she said. 'I never said nothing about that, did I?'

'You don't have to. I can see it in your face,' he said. 'You want to get away too. Just be done with me, so you never have to see me again. Just like everyone else.'

'You can't see nothing in my face, Joker. It's that beat up my own mama wouldn't be able to see anything in it, so don't be silly.' Dixie reached an arm out. 'Come here. It's been a horrible night. It's starting to make you scared about things that aren't even real.'

He hesitated.

'Come *here*. I'm too sore to come to you.'

The boy crawled over. Dixie could just manage to get one arm around him. It hurt too much to hug him, but she brought him down to lay his head in her lap. She wiped his tears with her fingers.

'Joker, you're so far off the truth here,' she said. 'You ask me why I haven't left Billy. You're the whole reason I haven't. When I saw the stupid thing Billy had done in taking you, I felt like leaving him right that minute, because I knew this was wrong and I wanted no part of it. Except there was you. I didn't leave Billy then because of you. Because you're just little and I knew you needed someone to take care of you. You didn't deserve to have any of this happen, so I stayed to make sure you were going to be OK. And I sure wouldn't leave at this point without you. I'd never ever do that.' Tenderly she stroked his face.

He began to sob. His grubby fingers gripped the material of Dixie's jeans so tightly that the ends of his nails went as white as the little half-moons at their base. Noticing them, Dixie gently covered them with her hand.

'You're a good boy, Joker. I mean that. Your folks saying stuff about not wanting you around ... I don't know why that is, because I don't know anything about your mom and dad as people, but I can tell you this for certain: how they're behaving towards you and the things they've said – that's to do with what's going on inside them. It's not you. With my own eyes I've seen what a good boy you are. You're strong. You're brave. You're determined. If my little baby could have grown up, I'd have been proud if he'd turned out as good a boy as you are.'

Chapter Forty

The next morning, Dixie was so sore it took the boy's help just to get to her feet. The worst pain was where she'd been kneed. Billy must have cracked a rib, because every deep breath was an agony. The most annoying, however, was the swelling around her eyes. She couldn't see out of her left eye at all and the right one kept weeping.

Dixie hobbled into the shade of the cottonwoods and settled there, but just sitting left way too much time to think. Because what if Billy didn't come back? Or what if he was just really slow? Thank God both the water jugs had been taken out of the truck to keep them from getting too hot, because that meant they had enough water for the time being. And there was some bread and a couple of cans of food. It was pure luck they'd been eating just before the argument, because that meant the can opener hadn't been put away. It also meant Billy had had his army knife out and had left it lying in the food box. However, they had little else. Dixie hadn't unpacked much from the truck because she hadn't thought they'd be staying. All her personal things, including the cell phone, were still in the back of the truck. How would they get out of this situation if Billy left them too long?

The boy brought her water and cold ravioli from one of the cans he'd opened. Having used his T-shirt to bandage Dixie's injuries, he now had tied around his neck the brightly flowered picnic cloth they'd had their dinner on the night before. 'Look, I'm Superman,' he said and grinned, stretching the cloth out with his arm.

'Superman who got a makeover by gay guys from the looks of it,' Dixie replied. 'Flowers don't really suit you.'

The boy laughed. Sitting down in the shade beside her, he untied the cloth. 'It's better than getting a sunburn.' He showed her one arm. 'Have you noticed how tan I'm getting? Phoebe's going to freak when she sees this. She thinks, like, I'm going to die of cancer if I don't put a whole bottle of suntan stuff on each time I go out.'

'She's just trying to take care of you.'

He shrugged. 'I guess.'

There was a long pause. The boy was looking out across the sagebrush plain. 'I sure do miss my PlayStation.'

'Yeah, it sounds like you have fun with it.'

He looked over at Dixie, his expression hopeful. 'I don't suppose we've got the playing cards …?'

She shook her head. 'No, they're in my bag in the truck.'

'Too bad.'

They sat together in silence for several moments.

'There's still stuff we can play,' Dixie said. 'Let's play Imagine. That was me and my sister's favourite game when we were stuck someplace and didn't have anything else to do.'

'How do you play that?'

'Well, you think: what is the nicest thing I can imagine right now? Obvious stuff doesn't count. Like, for example, it's obvious the nicest thing right now would be to be out of here. That doesn't count. Instead, you think of little stuff that's nice and then you imagine up every single little detail about it to make it as real in your mind as possible and you tell the other person, and then it's their turn and they imagine up their nicest thing. If you do it right, it can feel almost like you're really experiencing it. I'll go first, so you can see how it's done,' she said.

'For example, what I think would be nicest right now would be a big, deep bath. But, see, to make it a proper game of Imagine then you got to add every little detail you can think of to make it just the most perfect bath ever. So, what I'm imagining is a really big bathtub, like one of those kind with the sloping back that is so big and roomy that I could slip right down in it up to my chin and everything that is sore or dirty can soak. It's in a pretty room that looks out on the mountains, and these got to be Abundance mountains. I got to see Crowheart right there in the middle and the scent of the pine trees must be drifting in through the window. The water's just warm enough not to get chilly, but cool enough to wash all this sweat off and leave me feeling fresh. It doesn't have any bubble bath, because even though bubbles are supposed to be fancy, I never feel clean with them. Instead I want nice clear water with some nice smelly oil. Honeysuckle smell. When I was little, I used to have this tiny, tiny doll and she came in a perfume bottle that was supposed to be honeysuckle scent and I loved that smell. I kept her special in this little treasure box I had that I could lock, and whenever I was feeling down, I used to take her out and smell her. I want my bath to smell like that.' Dixie looked over. 'So what do you imagine?'

'*Food*,' the boy said. 'I'm going to imagine a *big* hamburger. A double Whopper, with two patties of meat and mayonnaise and ketchup. But no salad stuff or onions. Definitely no pickles, because, yuck, I hate pickles.'

'That's your nicest thing?' Dixie asked. 'A hamburger from a fast-food joint? That ain't even a proper hamburger. You got to get your imaginator going, because what you're imagining is way too ordinary. See, now, if *I* was imagining a hamburger, I'd want an extra-thick, special one straight off the barbecue. My sister Leola does these wonderful hamburgers where she puts a tiny bit of ice in the middle before it goes on the barbecue and that keeps it really juicy, and it's got that scrumptious beefy taste and it's smoky and a bit crispy on the outside but nice and luscious on the inside, and you put it on a big old bun to catch the drippings and start adding your ketchup and whatever else you want.'

The boy's eyes went wide with desire. 'That sounds *really* good.'

'Yeah, you'd like our barbecues. We eat good then. That's the kind of food that's worth dreaming about. Leola makes her special hamburgers. Mama does her potato salad. I always make the ambrosia.'

'What's that?'

'It's got green grapes and mandarin oranges and pineapple and maraschino cherries and lots of little miniature marshmallows and it's all mixed up in whipped cream.'

'Mmmmm,' the boy said. 'Mmm-mmmm. That sounds *so* good.'

'Yeah, it is good.'

Silence came then. It started as just a pause while each of them lingered, savouring the imaginary food, but the conversation didn't resume.

The erratic drone of locusts slowly wore away the images to return Dixie to the parched heat and the pain of her injuries.

The boy looked over. For several moments, he studied her face. Dixie had her head turned slightly away from him, so she could only see him on the periphery of her vision and knew he probably didn't realize she was aware of him. Most likely he was looking at how gross the swollen eye made her look.

'Ain't polite to stare,' she said finally.

'What I was wondering was, do you think I'm ever going to see you again?' the boy asked quietly.

Shading her eyes with cupped hands, Dixie looked off across the bright landscape.

'Say yes, OK?' he asked.

'Joker, I'm thinking it's better we don't play Imagine with things that there's no imagining for.'

Billy returned late in the afternoon, the dust cloud of his approaching vehicle visible long before he was. He was in a roaring good mood when he climbed out of the cab and, by the smell of his breath, Dixie had no doubt what had put him in it.

Gleefully Billy grabbed her, ignoring her injuries, and wrapped her in an enthusiastic hug. 'I been to Billings, and, boy, have they ever got *stores*. Come see what I brought you.'

'Jeez, what have you done? Robbed a brewery?' she asked and winced in pain. 'Surprising you could even drive straight.'

Billy had bought a hopeless array of stuff. Four packages of lunch meat, cheese, milk, margarine, but no ice to put in the cooler. There were also four six-packs of beer and three half-gallon bottles of Coke but no water.

'And look at this!' He plopped a fresh, dripping, two-pound package of hamburger into her hands. 'We ain't had proper meat in us for too long. That's the real problem around here.'

Weariness overtook Dixie. Not having proper meat was so far from what the problem really was that she didn't know where to start. Billy hadn't commented on her black eyes or bruised body, nor had he said anything about being sorry. Dixie knew he was. That's what all the fancy food was meant to tell her. But what was she going to do with it? There was no way they could eat everything before it was spoiled by the heat. And what about the two pounds of raw hamburger that had been bouncing around in the back of Billy's truck since Billings? It was as if someone had slipped a hand around Dixie's throat, and then tightened it. Putting her fingers against her chin, she pulled at it to keep the grimace of tears at bay.

No worry about Billy noticing how close to crying she was, even if he could have seen any expression through all the bruises. He was hunkered down on a rock, trying to prise one of the beer cans out of the box. Dixie went over to the truck to get tissues out of her purse.

Feeling around for her purse, which had slid under the passenger side of the cab, she finally snagged the strap and pulled it out. With it came a rumpled, folded-over newspaper with the continuation of a front-page article showing. 'NEW LEAD IN HOLLYWOOD KIDNAP HUNT'.

Fear forked through her like lightning; her breath cut short so abruptly it caused the muscles of her chest to spasm. Dixie opened the paper up full. It was the local Abundance paper, several days old. At the bottom of the front page was a picture of the boy with curling, girlish locks, pudgy cheeks and a rather petulant expression, like a Michelangelo cherub.

Billy came up behind her. 'Here, have a beer. It'll do you good.'

'When were you planning to tell me about this?' she asked, turning.

'It ain't us they're looking for.'

'It sure the heck *is* us they're looking for, Billy. Of *course* it's us. Because we took him.'

'No, you read the article. Says that Spencer Scott was supposed to be playing poker in Las Vegas this week. Everybody knows the Mafia owns all those casinos there. I bet they think it's the Mafia. All those big movie stars are mixed up with the Mafia.'

'It says he was going to be playing poker for charity, Billy. A charity tournament. It doesn't say anything in here whatsoever about the Mafia,' Dixie replied. She threw the paper down on the seat and walked away to keep from shouting at him.

Billy came running after her. 'It doesn't say, because they don't want just anybody to know, do they? They got secret operations.'

'It doesn't say, Billy, because the Mafia has nothing to do with it. You're dreaming again. *You* think it's the Mafia.

They don't. Billy, *we* took the boy, so it's *us* they are looking for. And sooner or later they're going to find us.'

'Fuck, Dixie, don't cry. I'm so fed up with you bawling all the time. What the fucking good will that do?'

The tears came out as a strangulated gulp because the swelling around her eyes had blocked her nose. 'I'm sorry, but I can't help it. I just can't keep going on and on and on like this.'

'Yeah, well, how the fuck do you think it is for me?' Billy said. 'I keep trying to be nice to you, Dixie, and you're always being so fucking difficult. This has been no picnic for me either. Shit, I've had it. I don't want to be here any more than you do. You understand that?'

Dixie wept.

'So shall we end it right now?' he asked. 'Is that what you want?'

'Yes, it is what I want. It's what I've wanted all along, Billy, and you know it.'

There was a pointed pause. Then Billy shrugged flippantly. 'Yeah, OK, good. That's what you want, good. That's what we'll do then.'

Alarm caught in her throat.

'First, you go look that kid in the eye and tell him you got fed up. That he ain't going home because you didn't trust Billy to fix things.' He started to move away.

'Billy? Billy! What do you mean? What are you talking about?'

'You can do the digging. I reckon over there beyond those rocks would be good. Soil's loose. Shovel's in the back of the truck.'

'Billy, *no*!' Dixie screamed and threw herself at him.

Billy hadn't expected it or maybe he was more drunk than either of them realized. Whichever, when Dixie lunged at him, she took him right down. They fell heavily, crashing through the sagebrush to the pale, dusty ground. Sparks exploded in Dixie's head as she hit.

'Fuck you!' Billy cried, enraged. He groped for a good grip to give her a bashing. Dixie struggled frantically through the fog of pain to keep him away from her hair.

There was no way to get away from him. Billy pressed himself right down over Dixie, sagebrush becoming more a taste in her mouth than a smell. She felt his fingers curl through her loose hair.

'Stop!' came the shout.

Billy tightened his grip and pulled her head roughly back.

'I said *stop*! *Stop!*' Before the last 'stop' was fully out, there was a deafening crack and then the acrid scent of gunpowder overwhelmed everything. Dixie felt Billy's weight lift off her.

The boy stood perhaps ten feet away, Billy's hunting rifle in his hands, his finger on the trigger.

Billy had raised up on his hands. 'Hey, kid,' he said, alarm in his voice. 'Put that down. No. You don't want to do that.' Leaving Dixie lying in the dirt, he climbed to his feet.

'Stop there or I'll shoot you,' the boy said.

'Kid, put it down.'

'You come any closer and I'll fucking shoot you. I mean it.' The boy kept his finger closed around the trigger.

'Dixie, tell him to put it down.'

She slowly pulled herself to her feet.

Billy turned to look at her. 'Tell him to put it down, Dix,' he said again, but it was a request this time, not a demand.

With it an unexpected vulnerability filled his expression, a look Dixie had always loved in him because it told her how innocent Billy was. He wasn't an evil man. In spite of all the bad things he did, he wasn't evil, just someone who never really understood.

With effort, she hobbled towards the boy. 'Here, Joker, let me have the gun.'

The boy shook his head. 'I'm not letting him hurt you any more. I'll shoot him. I mean it.'

'Yeah, I know you mean it. You're a good boy, Joker, and I know you're just trying to take care of me, but you're too little to be responsible for this. We got things back to front here, 'cause it's the grown-ups who ought to be looking out for the little kid. So give it to me.'

There were tears on the boy's cheeks. 'I want him to go,' he said petulantly and kept hold of the gun.

'Yeah, he will. But you let me do it.'

The boy passed the gun to Dixie.

Billy's relief was audible. 'Shi-i-iiii-it!' he said and sighed.

'No, Billy. Don't start relaxing, because it ain't over for you yet.' She lifted the rifle to her shoulder and aimed at him.

'*Dixie?* What the *fuck* are you doing?'

'What I should have done right at the beginning, when you came home with this poor kid. Because maybe you thought what we were doing wasn't going to hurt anybody, but I knew all along it was wrong. So I never had an excuse.'

'Dixie.'

'Turn around, Billy. Go, get in that truck and start driving. Go to Canada or Idaho or Texas or wherever you want, as long as it's not Abundance. If you do that right now, if you drive off this minute and I never ever see you again, then far as I'm concerned, you ain't to blame for what happened. I won't never say you done this. But for that to happen, you got to go and not come back.'

For a moment Billy was so shocked that he looked like one of those fake statues people put in their gardens, all stiff and cement-coloured. As Dixie spoke, though, he began to get his wits back. He moved forward menacingly.

Dixie cocked the trigger. 'Don't try me, Billy. I've shot a man I loved before. I'll do it again, if I have to.'

He glared at her. She glared back over the barrel of the gun. One of those moments unfolded that tells you time isn't really anything except a trick of the mind, because it lasted forever and yet no time at all.

Finally Billy let out a deflated grunt. 'Fuck you,' he muttered. 'Fuck you. And you too, you little motherfucking shit.' He spat at them.

Dixie kept the gun up, the trigger cocked.

Billy spat a second time. Then he went over to the truck, got in, started it up and roared out, spraying them with grit and pebbles.

Chapter Forty-One

'What are we going to do now?' the boy asked.

'Go home.' Dixie rooted through her purse. Locating her cell phone, she pressed the button to switch it on.

How strange it felt to see the familiar little screen light up. It searched several moments for a signal, then found one. Not strong, but good enough. Dixie scrolled through the icons to the map application to figure out where they were.

The boy leaned into her, resting his head against her upper arm in such a casual way it felt affectionate. 'How come you never used that before?' he asked quietly.

'How come I ain't a different person than I am?' she replied.

Leola's voice went squeaky with surprise. 'Dixie! *Where* you been? What's been going on all this time?'

Leaning forward, her face coming down to touch her knees, Dixie began to weep at the relief of hearing her sister's voice. 'Billy and me have broke up,' she whimpered. 'But I'm a long ways from home, Leola, and I'm beat up. I hurt so much.'

'Yeah, well, that was my reckoning, that he'd took you off somewhere. That's exactly what I was telling Mama – that that fool Billy took her off. Wherever it is, Dix, it ain't too far for me. I'll come get you. Tell me where you are and I'll come bring you home.'

Tears overwhelmed Dixie and she couldn't speak.

Tenderly, the boy put his arms around her. Then he reached down and slipped the phone from her fingers. 'I'll tell you where we are,' he said.

'Who are *you*?' Leola asked in surprise.

'I'm Joker. You told Dixie about me when you read her cards,' he replied. 'And I have a map here on the phone, if you want me to say the directions to you.'

Only in Billy's imagination did a world exist where nothing had consequences. Dixie knew there was no going back to life as she'd left it in Abundance. Waiting for Leola in the dusty locust-embroidered shade of the cottonwoods, sadness overwhelmed her. How was it you never knew you had everything you needed for happiness until you lost it? How come no one ever told you that the most precious thing in the world was just an ordinary day?

The boy, in contrast, was jubilant. 'I'm gonna eat pizza!' he announced enthusiastically. That was the biggest thing on his mind: pizza with extra pepperoni and extra cheese. Before he did anything else, he was going to have a pizza and he was going to eat every single bite! He whooped up, punching the air like a champion. Dixie joked with him that before he did anything else, he'd better get a wash, because had he seen himself? He looked like a mangy coyote, she said. The boy laughed until he had tears in his eyes.

By Dixie's reckoning, it would take three or four hours for Leola to get there, what with needing time to see to her kids first and the task of locating them, plus just the sheer distance. The long wait and the still, dry heat of the afternoon slowly dimmed the boy's excitement. The shade shrank and they had to sit with their backs right against the largest of the cottonwood trees to stay out of the sun.

Both of them drowsed in the heat. When she finally felt the boy shift, his upper arm touching hers, Dixie opened her eyes. He was watching her.

'What you staring at?' she asked.

'I've been thinking about something …'

'Yeah? What?'

'Can I stay with you?'

Dixie straightened up. 'How you mean?'

'When this is over, when we get back, do you think I could stay at your house?'

'Aww,' she said and touched his cheek. 'How sweet of you to say that. I'd just love you to stay with me, Joker. But when we get back, we got to get you to your daddy. They're going to be sick with worry about you.'

'I don't want to go back to my dad. I don't want to go back to any of them. Not my mom or my dad. I want to stay with you.' He tipped his head. 'I've been sitting here thinking about it and, well … maybe if I kept my hair really short … you know, got it buzzed so that it looked OK. And I've lost a lot of weight. More than I lost at fat camp last summer, that's for sure. So maybe no one would know it was me …'

Dixie smiled gently and caressed his face again. 'I wish I could keep you. I really do, 'cause I'd be proud to have a nice boy like you. But the sad fact is, that ain't how things work. You already got a mama and daddy and you belong with them.'

'I *don't* belong to them. They don't want me. But you had a little boy that you really loved, but now he's gone. So let me belong to you.'

She put her arm around him and drew him close. 'Joker, that ain't true about your folks. You do belong to them. They're missing you something terrible. I found a newspaper in Billy's truck. There was a great big article in there about how your dad's worried and your mama's come up here and folks are looking everywhere to find you. They miss you. They really do and that's the truth. I read it.'

Tears trickled from the corners of his eyes.

'You're a good boy. I know sometimes your folks act like they don't want to be with you, but that's because of stuff going on in their lives, not because of you,' Dixie said.

'That doesn't mean I want to go back to them,' he muttered.

'No, maybe not, but they're still your people. And as I said before, nobody's got it perfect, Joker. My daddy done things to me too that are darned near unforgivable. But then I done things back to him that were bad too.'

Biting his lower lip, the boy hunched his shoulders and pulled away from her.

'All these things folks do to one another,' Dixie said, 'it's not because they're bad people. Not because my dad's a bad person or your dad's a bad person. Not because I'm a bad person or you're a bad person. These things happen just because life ain't a movie.'

'I know it isn't a movie, so you don't have to keep pointing that out,' the boy said sullenly.

'Yeah, but deep down in your heart, you're still be hoping it is. Everybody hopes that. That's why we like movies so much. Because for a little minute, they let us pretend the world is perfect. Bad stuff only happens to bad people in the movies and good people always get their happy ending. But that's just dreaming. The real world doesn't work that way. In the real world, we don't got that kind of control. Bad stuff happens to everyone, even good people, and there aren't any happy endings.'

The boy started to cry. 'Why are you telling me this?'

'Because it's important to know. Otherwise it's too easy to get sidetracked believing if you could just earn enough money or look beautiful enough or fall in love with the right person, then everything will turn out like in the movies, and you end up spending your whole life trying to get that little bit of control when it don't exixt. You miss out understanding happiness isn't about the world being perfect. It's about making peace with the fact it's not.'

'Holy Jesus,' Leola said, as she got out of the car. 'Look at the state of you.' Then she glanced over at the boy and did a double-take. 'Billy's stupider than I thought,' she said. 'Which I didn't think was possible.'

Once they were on the road, the only stop they made was for a pepperoni pizza and Cokes.

'This is going to stink up my whole car,' Leola muttered as she handed the pizza through the passenger side window to Dixie.

'Yes, but it's the best stink in the world,' the boy said from the back seat. He grinned.

'Yeah, well, you just don't get carsick on me, that's all I'm going to say.'

It took almost three and half hours of steady driving before Dixie saw the familiar outlines of Crowheart and Lion Mountain on the horizon. Leola slowed and turned off the freeway on to the minor highway that would take them to Abundance.

'So how's this going to happen?' she asked.

'When we get in town, take me to the police station,' Dixie replied.

'And then what? You just planning to walk in there with him?'

'I'm not going to get away with this, Lee, if that's what you're asking. However this shakes out, they'll want to know how I got involved. I'm not going to lie. I'm sick of living with one secret after another, and to be honest, by this point, I don't care what they do to me. I just want it to be over and done with.'

The boy leaned forward. 'When we get there, just let me out of the car by myself. Don't come in with me. Then they won't know it's you.'

Dixie put a hand back to touch his face. 'They'll still find out, sweetie. They're going to ask you a million questions and I don't want you lying either.'

'I won't lie. Because *you* didn't take me,' the boy said. 'If they think it's you, I'll say you got kidnapped too. And that you were trying to help me. Because that's true.'

'Well, we'll see.'

The landscape grew more and more familiar. Longing overtook Dixie so powerfully it thrummed in her ears the way memories do sometimes, as if some kind of internal music was playing.

The boy leaned forward between the seats again. 'Later ...' he started but didn't finish.

'Yeah?'

'Later ... like, maybe next week or whenever, but before I go back to Los Angeles ... could I come visit you?'

'That's probably not going to be possible, Joker.'

'Why not?'

She hesitated and looked out of the window. 'I just don't think it would work out.'

'What if, like, I happened to be walking down your street? If I just happened to be there and you just happened to be there at the same time? Like, maybe we bumped into each other. Would you, like, talk to me?'

Dixie smiled. 'Yeah, of course I'd talk to you.'

'So, like, will you write your street name down for me? I mean, just in case I'm walking down it?'

It was mid-evening when Leola finally reached the outskirts of Abundance. The first view a person got coming in on the north east highway was a jumble of derelict buildings. Most weren't intriguing ghost-town ruins but just the ordinary abandoned businesses of a fading community – vacant gas stations, boarded-up store fronts and an empty, old-fashioned 'cabin motel'. Above the buildings, the setting sun arced over the valley, illuminating the mountains so vividly that you could pick out individual trees.

Dixie was home.

Leola turned off Main Street on to Elm and drove the two blocks to the small police station. She pulled to a stop on the opposite side of the street. 'Here we are,' she said quietly.

For several moments, no one moved. Then Dixie unbuckled her seat belt and turned to look at the boy. His cheeks were awash with tears.

'You go in like that, they're going to think I hurt you,' she said. 'So you got to be strong now. You got to be my little man.' Pulling a tissue from the box in the footwell, she handed it back to him.

A few moments passed and then came the sound of the back door opening slowly. He got out, wiped his face again with his hands, and then closed the door.

'Can I kiss you goodbye?' he asked.

Dixie opened the car door, drew him in for a tight hug and kissed him. He kissed her back. Then he straightened up and gently closed the car door. 'Bye,' he said.

'Be careful crossing the street. I know it don't look busy, but cars can come awful fast, so look both ways first.'

'I will,' he said. 'Bye.'

'Bye-bye, Joker.'